The OXFORD INHERITANCE

𝓌𝓂

WILLIAM MORROW

An Imprint of HarperCollins*Publishers*

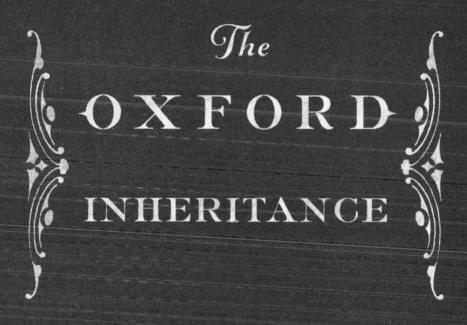

The OXFORD INHERITANCE

ANN A. McDONALD

This book is a work of fiction. The characters, incidents, and dialogue are drawn from the author's imagination and are not to be construed as real. Any resemblance to actual events or persons, living or dead, is entirely coincidental.

THE OXFORD INHERITANCE. Copyright © 2016 by 3 Arts Entertainment. All rights reserved. Printed in the United States of America. No part of this book may be used or reproduced in any manner whatsoever without written permission except in the case of brief quotations embodied in critical articles and reviews. For information address Harper-Collins Publishers, 195 Broadway, New York, NY 10007.

HarperCollins books may be purchased for educational, business, or sales promotional use. For information please e-mail the Special Markets Department at SPsales@ harpercollins.com.

FIRST EDITION

Designed by Janet M. Evans

Library of Congress Cataloging-in-Publication Data has been applied for.

ISBN 978-0-06-220367-0

16 17 18 19 20 OV/RRD 10 9 8 7 6 5 4 3 2 1

The devil is more laborious now than ever;
the long day of mankind drawing towards an evening,
and the world's tragedy and time near an end.

SIR WALTER RALEIGH

The
OXFORD
INHERITANCE

S he ran.

Through the tunnels, feet bare on the stone floor. Torches blazed along the main pathways so she veered deeper into the labyrinth, tripping down hidden stairs and along the dark, winding corridors until the air became heavy with decay and doors groaned their protest as she heaved them open. Still, she ran.

The chanting was getting closer, a dizzying hum that echoed off every wall, no matter how far she fled. It was all in her mind, she told herself. It had to be. A shadow suddenly reared up in the gloom and she stumbled in fear, falling hard in a bloody scrape of skin on sharp stone. But there was no time for pain, not with the knife gripped, slick in her hand, or the faint clatter of footsteps getting louder. Closer.

She hurled herself around another corner and up another flight of stairs, almost crying out with relief when she saw a familiar carved archway. Beyond, she knew was a side tunnel, and past that, freedom.

He stepped out of the shadows.

She faltered, coming to a stop just inside the anteroom. He didn't say a word, or even block her path, but the desperate adrenaline that had pushed her on through the darkness seemed to drain away in an instant, leaving nothing but a hollow ache

in her limbs and a sob of resignation welling, unbidden in her chest. Her fingers curled open. The knife fell to the ground.

Of course he'd found her.

The man strolled closer, reaching to brush the hair from her eyes in a gesture so familiar, it made her legs give way with grief. A sob escaped her, the cry raw in the heavy silence of the catacombs. He pressed his hand over her mouth, muffling the sound.

"Shhh," he murmured, breath soft against her cheek. "I've got you now."

He caught her as she fell, guiding her gently down until they were both folded on the dusty floor, her body cradled against him. Now that she knew the truth, she could feel the blackness seep out of him: drifting and curling in shadowed tendrils from the very tips of his fingers as he traced the outline of her jaw. But worse than the black touch—far worse still—was the unfurling she felt, deep in her breast. A wing-swept flutter as her own dark heart rose up to answer his call.

She struggled, but it was over. He knew it. "Shhh," he said, cradling her, gentler than any of the nights he'd held her before. The flutter was a beating now, drowning even her own heartbeat with its insistent thrum. She could feel the darkness rise, ready to take flight, ready to take her over completely.

"I've got you," he whispered again. His eyes were lit with triumph, a hungry anticipation of what was still to come. Her fingers searched desperately for the knife as he bent his lips to hers, and then she found it: cold steel on the dusty stone.

She surrendered to the kiss, sending up a silent prayer. Then there was nothing but red.

OXFORD IN SUMMERTIME WAS A CITY UNDER SIEGE. THEY CAME from across the oceans, from Norway and Brazil, India and Japan: civilizations old and new alike descending on the dreaming spires and neat, lush quads as a single invading army, sounding their battle cry in the chatters of foreign tongues, faces painted with warlike stripes of sunscreen zinc. Uniting to traipse the well-worn trail from the peaceful floral walkways of the Botanic Garden to the vast, soaring dining hall at Christ Church College, divisions of race and nationality blurred beneath the Union Jack baseball caps and souvenir sweatshirts. They clustered along the cobblestones of Cornmarket Street, consulting phrase books and foldout maps, and squeezed through iron gates for a better shot of statues and sweeping sandstone walls.

Shops along High Street carried a brisk trade in miniature flags, figurines, and long, looping scarves knitted in the muted rainbow of official college colors: mulberry and dark navy, mustard seed and hunter green. Cream teas were served in old-fashioned tearooms—dainty china clinking against gold-ringed saucers—and the river was gridlocked with punts: the long, low barges steered by students through the mossy waters as their passengers sipped Pimm's from cups floating with cucumber slices and nibbled sweet summer strawberries bought by the punnet from the fruit stands on the bridge.

From early May to the end of August, the ancient streets were clogged, dusty, and littered—or, more often, drenched with cold summer showers that sent the crowds scrambling into doorways and under shop awnings,

maps held aloft to shelter them from the sudden downpours. Then, as September dawned, the great quads were suddenly quiet again. The crowds departed, and the city exhaled a breath. The air took on a new, autumnal chill, and dewy mists hung over the Port Meadow fields each morning as the church bells rang out their baritone dawn chorus.

It was only a week or two, this gentle lull, for the shopgirls to slump idle behind their registers and the college groundsmen to set about pruning the rosebushes and mowing the neat strips of lawn.

Too soon, the next set of visitors arrived.

These weren't quite so temporary. They came bearing crisp new textbooks and fat induction packets, shined shoes and wide eyes, weighed down as much by their own hopeful expectations as the brand-new possessions they pulled behind them in overstuffed cases.

Summer was over, and it was time for a new generation of students to take their place in the hallowed roll call of Oxford's great academic legacy.

First, Cassandra Blackwell discovered, came matriculation.

She'd arrived late, her flight delayed by freak storms over the East Coast, so by the time she'd collected her baggage from Arrivals at Heathrow and made the two-hour ride up to Oxford by coach, the first official day of term at Oxford University was already well under way. She knew from reading the thick information packets what to expect, but still, it took her by surprise when she dragged her cases across the bumpy cobblestones and through the gates of Raleigh College to find a sea of students in strange black robes milling about the courtyard, shifting and spinning like newspaper twists in the English breeze.

Cassie paused in the middle of the bustle, drinking in the foreign scene. The students were assembling on a set of bleachers for an official photograph. But unlike the casual, jeans-clad freshmen she knew from college back home, these new students wore crisp white shirts and suits

under the robes; girls in blouses and black skirts, with dark ribbons looped at their necks and wide bands of black fabric trailing from their shoulders. It was an old-fashioned costume, the kind you'd expect to find immortalized in faded sepia photographs, yellowed with age. The only hint that this was the twenty-first century was the sea of cell phones students gripped as they lined up beneath the ancient honeyed sandstone walls to pose for their first photos.

The chimes of the chapel clock rang out noon across the courtyard. She was late.

Cassie looked hurriedly around. People were streaming in and out of the small guardhouse just inside the gates, so she made her way inside, ducking to avoid the low doorway carved into the stone. Inside, it was chaos: people lined three deep in front of the desk, clamoring for attention. She waited in line, unsure, before one of the staff—a weathered-looking man in a peaked cap and heavy cable-knit sweater—noticed her bags, and the information pack she was clutching to her chest.

"Are you a fresher?" he demanded.

"Yes." Cassie offered her papers. "Cassandra Blackwell. My flight was delayed; I only just got here."

The man's eyes widened. "You better leave your things and change before you miss the photograph."

"It's okay," Cassie tried to protest. "I just need to get settled into my room."

But the man wouldn't be dissuaded. "Here, pass me your case." He grabbed it from her before she could object. "Have you got your sub fusc?"

When Cassie stared blankly, he explained. "The robes and uniform. Never mind, you don't have time. Good thing you're wearing black." He rooted in a box and pulled out a robe like the ones she'd seen outside. "Get along with you; I'll find your room assignment. Cassie, was it?" She nodded. "I'm Rutledge. Come find me later, when you're done with

matric. Go on!" He shooed her away and was quickly lost in the bustle again.

Pulling on the robe, Cassie headed back outside, only to be swept up and directed to a place in line, near the back of the photo. The other students parted to let her through, barely giving her another glance as they chatted and joked, full of first-day nerves. They were too caught up in their own excitement to notice her.

Cassie felt her own excitement, but it wasn't the giddy eagerness written all over their faces. Hers was a curiosity at this new world, mingling with the sense of being an impostor, as if one of her new classmates would look too closely and see the truth of her intentions written all over her face. The true reason for her place among them, and all her secret plans for the year.

"Places! Everyone, please take your places."

She was barely in position when the photographer and his assistant began chasing stragglers to the edge of the crowd.

"Is this right?" The girl beside Cassie was fussing with her neck ribbon, tying and retying it into a looping bow. She had wide, birdlike eyes and a nervous tremble in her fingertips, her face lit up with a breathless glow.

Cassie glanced around, but the girl was talking to her. "Let me." She quickly fixed the ribbon in place.

"Thanks." The girl beamed. "Can you believe we're really here?" She didn't wait for a reply. "I've been dreaming about this my whole life," she babbled. "All that time, and I finally made it. Oxford University." She breathed the words gently, reverently—like a familiar prayer that had finally been answered. "Isn't it wonderful?"

Cassie glanced up at the crimson Raleigh flag, rippling on the far battlement. She'd seen it in photographs and glossy brochures, even in person, years ago, but now it seemed to loom larger, more vivid than ever before. The photographer's flash suddenly burst in front of her eyes, sending dark sparks dancing through her vision. She blinked,

dazed by the jet lag and travel, and the years of planning it had taken to finally make it inside the hallowed, exclusive gates of Raleigh College.

All her work had finally come to fruition: the scheming and lies, the sacrifice and risk.

"Wonderful," she echoed softly, as the bulb flashed again, blinding them all in the bright afternoon sun.

THE PORTRAITS TOOK AN HOUR, INTERRUPTED BY THE PLAYFUL roughhousing of a group of boys and sharp gusts of wind that sent papers skittering through the courtyard. Finally, they were finished, but before Cassie could collect her bags and go collapse, she was steered away from the gatehouse.

"You're due at the Master's Tea now," said a brisk-looking student as he consulted his clipboard.

"I've been traveling all day," Cassie explained, her exhaustion hitting hard. "I'll take a shower first, and go later."

He stared, surprised. "It's in the schedule. You only get a short slot. Attendance is mandatory."

Cassie opened her mouth to protest, then bit it back. She was supposed to be as eager as the rest of her group, already clustered ahead on the paved pathway. "Tea it is, then," she agreed.

"His lodgings are across campus. Neil will take your tour." He nodded to another helpful-looking student outfitted in the crimson Raleigh scarf.

Lodgings. It was just one of the foreign words that Cassie was learning. An American in England, there was already a language barrier, but in the few hours since she'd arrived, it had become clear that Oxford University was a world of its own. A federated system of colleges scattered across the city, it was a place with singular rules, culture, and even language. From eavesdropping on her new classmates, Cassie had already learned that Rutledge and the staff were known as porters; the gatehouse, the porters' lodge. But there was a cacophony of words that

were still a mystery to her, even as the students around her dropped the phrases so casually: junior common room, the buttery, pidges and tutes, Michaelmas and Trinity terms.

Cassie fell in behind her tour group, following the paved pathways that crisscrossed the lush quad.

"It wasn't just Sir Walter Raleigh who founded the college." Neil led them along, speaking loudly. "A circle of influential academics and thinkers of the era all contributed to Raleigh College's place at the forefront of Elizabethan public life. The famous astronomer Thomas Hariot, playwright Christopher Marlowe—they all gathered here to debate new ideas and share their visionary work."

Cassie knew the history. Raleigh wasn't the oldest of the Oxford schools, nor the richest, but it had an exclusive pedigree all the same. Founded by Sir Walter Raleigh in the late 1500s with the proceeds of his Spanish Armada plunder, the college sat on the outskirts of the city, a small kingdom of sandstone battlements and rolling lawns that stretched all the way to the moss-laden banks of the river Cherwell. The glossy prospectus she'd read boasted of the great halls and neat grassy quads, a hushed, wood-beamed library; richly appointed residence halls and open cloisters; and carved sandstone walls that kept the bustle and traffic of the city at bay. But here in person, it was enough to take her breath away, the history and beauty of the estate undeniable in its rich splendor.

"You have to remember," their enthusiastic tour guide continued, "that in a time when the church still had an iron grip on academic inquiry, the founding of the college was seen by some to be a revolutionary act. Many charged the group with plotting treasonous acts."

"Like that secret society?" One of the girls in the group spoke up.

There was laughter. Cassie looked around, wondering what the joke was. The tour guide noticed her confusion.

"Sir Walter Raleigh and his compatriots were the source of much speculation. Even Shakespeare jokingly referred to them as the School

of Night, due to the dark robes they supposedly wore during their meetings."

"Please," one of the boys beside her muttered. "If people are talking about your secret society, you're hardly secret anymore."

"Does this mean you won't be pledging Bullingdon?" his friend asked, smirking.

"Now, let's not be too hasty . . ." He laughed.

Cassie hung back, absorbing the battlements and buildings she felt she already knew by heart. They wound their way across campus, finally arriving at the master's residence: a stately building in more of the original sandstone, surrounded by rolling lawns and rose arbors, its Elizabethan architecture untouched by the ages. Inside, the space was equally as imposing: a grand staircase rose up from the corner of the foyer, walls were papered in thick hunter green paper, and there were deep carpets and antique side tables.

"And here we are," Neil announced. "Good luck, and remember, don't be nervous. We're all family here at Raleigh."

Family. The word lingered with Cassie as she stepped into the formal sitting room, where two dozen anxious undergraduates already milled around, chatting nervously as they clutched plates of cheese and crackers and tried not to spill wine on the brocade-upholstered couches. It was a mixer, of sorts, with professors and staff. The first chance for them to get to know the new students—and for her classmates to make a good impression.

The others made a beeline for the nearest professor. Cassie headed for the buffet table instead. She filled her plate with relief, her stomach growling after a long day with nothing but dry airline food and vending machine snacks. She found a seat on an empty couch and dug in.

"Chavez was from Argentina, right?" A young man sank heavily on the couch beside her. He was plump and sweating, dark patches already showing beneath the arms of his shirt.

"Venezuela," she replied.

He blinked. "I just spent ten minutes talking to Professor Kenmore about his nationalization of Argentinean industries." The horror of his mistake dawned. The boy paled. "Oh God." He lurched up again and fled toward the hall, knocking into another scholar as he passed. The woman stumbled, spilling her tea on the cream carpet in a dark stain.

The chatter paused for a moment, every single student giving silent thanks that they hadn't been the one to make such a clumsy mistake.

Cassie took in the tense postures and anxiously darting eyes, feeling a strange kinship with all these nervous strangers. She may have been older, and had already experienced a life they couldn't imagine, but today they shared the same need to blend in, to prove they belonged here. Their reasons may have been different, but the stakes were high for each and every one of them. Their futures were on the line.

Cassie finished her food and reluctantly began to mingle. She had stopped to examine a row of stern-faced portraits on the wall when a gravelly voice behind her announced, "Kit Marlowe."

Cassie turned to find the master of the college himself beside her. He was dressed in an old-fashioned navy pin-striped suit, with a shiny balding head and a face made stern by the heavy lines of age. "He was one of Raleigh's dearest friends, of course," he continued. "We have a first edition set of his plays in the library archive. You're welcome to look, but sadly, we had to preserve them against decay, so you won't be able to browse the pages as he intended." He held out his hand. "We've yet to be introduced. Sir Edmund Castle."

"Cassandra Blackwell."

The master's handshake was firm, his expression friendly. "I take from the accent you're one of our transfer students."

"Yes, I am. Junior year abroad," Cassie explained. "From Smith."

"Excellent college." Sir Edmund pumped her hand again. "Welcome, welcome. How are you finding it so far?"

"It's . . . kind of overwhelming," she replied, then added quickly. "The college has such beautiful grounds, and so much history."

"Finest in Oxford," he agreed. "But I may be a little biased. You know I was a student here myself, eons ago. And taught here, too."

Cassie nodded. She'd been fixated on Raleigh for years now, and there wasn't much she didn't have filed away in her notebooks and research file. Sir Edmund had distinguished himself as a mathematician and published several books before leaving academia for the rewards of the private sector. He'd made his fortune in hedge funds, then been knighted for services to the country's economy and finally had returned to Raleigh to serve out a genteel retirement padding the college endowment and playing host to visiting dignitaries. "I read your book on game theory," she told him, in an effort to make conversation. "I found your thesis fascinating."

"Did you now?" Sir Edmund looked at her afresh. "Are you a mathematician?"

"No," she answered quickly. "I was just reading for my own interest. I came across your work while I was researching the college."

"Very thorough." He assessed her with interest. "So what drew you to our fair shores, Miss Blackwell? It's a long way to come, and the slots for foreign students are mighty competitive."

Cassie took a breath. This was the question she'd prepared for and had been asked several times over during the application process and alumni interview back in Boston. "It's always been a dream of mine," Cassie said. "My parents traveled a little in England when they were young, so I grew up listening to stories about the city, and all the colleges. I think they had an Oxford calendar pinned above my bed before I learned how to read," she added, with a casual laugh.

Sir Edmund chuckled. "Well, they must be very proud of you."

"Oh, they are." Cassie smiled fondly, as if at a memory. "They're already planning their visit."

Sir Edmund looked away, catching sight of someone. He raised his voice. "Tremain! Come meet another of the Americans. Cassie, this is

Matthew Tremain. He's in charge of all you study-abroad folks, pastoral care, and the like."

They were joined by another man, this one in his forties, perhaps, and with none of Sir Edmund's polished style. He had a cautious, absentminded look about him, with two-day stubble and unkempt chestnut hair; his crumpled pin-striped shirt trailed from worn corduroy trousers.

"Pleased to meet you." Cassie reached to shake his hand, and, after a moment jostling his teacup and plate of biscuits, the professor managed to reciprocate.

"Blackwell, Blackwell . . ." Tremain's gaze darted over her, curious. "Oh, yes. Smith. PPE," he added, using the Oxford term for politics, philosophy, and economics, Cassie's chosen field of study. "You'll be taking philosophy with me this semester. I left a note in your pidge."

"Pidge?" she asked, hearing the strange word again.

"Pigeonhole," Sir Edmund clarified for her. "I forget how it all sounds to a foreigner. The wooden cubbies, in the porters' lodge. We use them for mail."

"Oh, right." Cassie added the term to her library of curious Oxford phrases.

"The professor here is a Raleigh institution," Sir Edmund explained. "He was a student of mine, back in the day. How long ago is it now . . . ?"

"Almost twenty-five years," Tremain supplied, and Cassie could swear she heard a note of resignation in his voice.

"Good student, too," Sir Edmund continued, "except he'd always leave things until the last minute. When was that time you pushed an essay under my door just ten minutes before your tute?" He warned Cassie, "You won't get away with that kind of thing."

Tremain's eyes met Cassie's for a moment with a faintly impatient expression. It was clear that these anecdotes had been told many times before. Nonetheless, Sir Edmund continued reminiscing. "Where does the time go?" He let out a dramatic sigh. "Feels like only last week I was

marking essays and telling you all off for making too much noise in the bar. We'll all be in the grave before long. What do you say, Tremain; they should dig out a corner of the meadow for us, ensure we never have to leave."

"Quite," Tremain replied.

"Were things very different here, when you were a student?" Cassie asked.

"Well, there was no Internet, for one thing," he said, scathing. "At least, not like there is now. If you wanted to plagiarize something, you had to copy it out of the book yourself, not just cut and paste from Wikipedia."

"No, I mean the student experience," Cassie pressed. "The culture."

Tremain smiled, a thin, almost rueful look. "Nothing ever really changes in Oxford. Especially here." He turned to Sir Edmund abruptly. "We should circulate. Miss Blackwell, perhaps we can set up that chat, go over some of the academic details?"

Sir Edmund shook her hand again. "A pleasure. I hope your time here is very productive. And be sure to take a look at the Marlowe manuscripts, but no touching!"

They moved off, Tremain quickly putting distance between them and striding to the other side of the salon while Sir Edmund landed on a new group of students and began shaking hands. Cassie lingered a moment longer, then, restless, slipped out of the room.

To her right was the main entrance foyer, echoing with stilted laughter, so she turned left instead and wandered deeper into the house, her footsteps light on the polished wooden floor. Away from the party, the hallway was still. She explored the rest of the rooms in turn, finding a cloakroom with an old porcelain sink, and a formal dining room—a table set for sixteen, with gleaming candlesticks and heavy leather place mats. It was like wandering a museum, but this was somebody's home: a place to live and work, surrounded by all these brocade-trimmed ghosts of time gone by. At the end of the hallway, she opened a heavy oak door

on a dim room presided over by a large mahogany desk and ceiling-high bookcases. This must be Sir Edmund's study.

Cassie wavered a moment on the threshold. This was surely out of bounds, and somebody would soon miss her absence from the main group, but curiosity won; she stepped inside, leaving the door slightly ajar to hear anyone approach in the hall.

It was a large room, paneled with wooden inserts on the walls, and set with somber oil paintings in heavy, gilt-edged frames. Cassie drifted to the desk. It was laid with papers and a row of matching fountain pens, the wood covered with a dark leather blotter. Old habits took over, and she rifled briefly through the papers, but they were basic administrative correspondence: memos on a pay dispute with the groundsmen, a survey on the structural integrity of the cloisters. Her fingertips traced the grained wood and thick papers; she smelled sandalwood, and something darker and acrid: the faint scent of tobacco smoke, lingering in the air.

It was another world. Even at Smith, with all its history, the older buildings had dated back only a hundred and fifty years, dwarfed by new lecture halls and dorms. Here, half a millennium at least echoed in the sandstone walls. Cassie moved to the bookshelves, lining the wall behind her. They were filled with clothbound volumes: first editions, weighty tomes. Shakespeare, Wordsworth, Wilde. And there, on the far wall, Cassie found the Raleigh College Records, a collection of yearbooks dating back as far as 1952, pristine as the day they were sent from the printers, their spines stiff and uncracked.

She ran her finger across the embossed leather until she found 1994 and pulled it down from the shelf, taking the large book closer to the window for a glimpse in the afternoon sun. She browsed reports from the chaplain, accounts of building projects and funding drives, interspersed with a roll call of student achievements and "in memorandum" tributes to deceased former members. Cassie turned each page impatiently, but even when she reached the list of first-year students admitted to the college, there was no sign of what she was looking for.

Footsteps came, heavy and unhurried in the hallway outside. Quickly, Cassie slammed the volume shut, replacing it on the shelf just as the door swung open and a strange man appeared in the doorway.

Cassie froze. He was older, in his seventies or eighties perhaps, dressed in an immaculate dark suit. He had a shock of white hair and a deeply lined face, but it was his eyes that chilled her to the very bone: their blackness seemed to pierce right through her.

"What are you doing here?" the man demanded. "This is private."

"I know, I'm sorry. I was looking for the bathroom," Cassie covered quickly.

He didn't move, his gaze shifting slowly from Cassie to the desk and back again.

"I got distracted by the building," Cassie added, stepping away from the bookcase. "The original design. . . . It's all so beautiful."

The man's gaze raked over her, and Cassie felt a rush of thanks that she was still dressed up in her robes, like any other new freshman, just one of the crowd. "Your classmates are leaving now, for the ceremony," he said icily.

"Thanks." Cassie took several quick steps toward the door. "I'm sure I'll catch another; you guys probably break out the Latin every week."

She was aiming for a joke, something to break the tension, but the look on the man's face was anything but amused.

"You think it's funny?" He said sharply. "That we're all just parading around in our robes for no good reason? Our history is everything." He glared at her with a harsh, flinty stare. "Tradition is what makes us who we are, and if you think you're above it, then perhaps you're in the wrong place."

Cassie bit her tongue. The parades and photographs and formal teas? This wasn't history, this was a costume play. They were all pretending in dress-up, while the modern world outside the sandstone walls kept spinning, unconcerned by their robes and rituals.

But instead of retorting, Cassie forced herself to look contrite. "I'm

sorry. I understand, about tradition. It means the world to me, too. I didn't mean to offend you."

The man's lips pressed together in a thin line.

"It's why I'm here," Cassie offered. "Family tradition. History. I guess I'm still a little jet-lagged," she gave a weak smile. "I'm sorry if you misunderstood me."

For a moment, he didn't move. Cassie's skin prickled, her heart beating fast. Then, finally, he gave a curt nod. "Your group is leaving now, you better catch up."

She felt his eyes on her, trailing every step down the long hallway. Luckily, her group was being ushered out and replaced with a new crop of students, so Cassie fell in line, her pulse still racing from her near miss as they emerged back into the cool afternoon sun.

The group veered right, skirting the lawn, but Cassie ducked away in the other direction instead, into the cloisters and down a side passageway, emerging in the shadow of a grove of willow trees set back by the college walls. The small garden was bordered by a low stone wall spilling over with pansies and late-flowering chrysanthemums: an oasis away from the main college bustle and completely private.

Cassie paused there in the silence, breathing in the fresh scent of cut grass and blossoms. It had been a mistake sneaking into Sir Edmund's office like that; she'd risked everything, and for what? Her first day, and already she'd drawn attention to herself—threatened to expose her secrets, the secrets that she'd come all this way to untangle for good.

Because for all Cassie's easy chat about her family back in America— her childhood gazing up at the dream of Oxford and its many academic splendors, her parents' enthusiasm and support—her life was nothing like the happy picture she'd painted for the college.

She hadn't been raised with stories of academic greatness. Her path to Raleigh hadn't been a smooth and foregone conclusion.

Everything she'd told them was a lie.

DAWN MISTS HUNG OVER THE COLLEGE THE NEXT MORNING AS Cassie zipped her hooded sweatshirt and turned off the pathway away from her new dorm. After the tea, she'd been too tired to do anything but drag her bags up to her room and crash, sleeping through the rest of the afternoon and night. She'd woken early, her limbs screaming with new energy only an early run would satisfy.

It looked like she was the only one. As she walked briskly along the neat pathways, the Raleigh campus was still and silent in the dawn light. Cassie stretched, then skirted the back wall until she found a path down to the river. She broke into a jog, her sneakers pounding the dirt as she headed deeper into the lush green of the college grounds.

As she settled into her usual stride, Cassie felt her tension ease for the first time since boarding the plane back in Boston. She loved this time of day. It gave her a moment to think, a space that was all her own. A certain hush fell over a city in the early morning, and she could see now that Oxford was no different; it was a swath of calm broken only by gentle birdsong and the low rumble of traffic out beyond the college walls. October had just begun. The mists hung low over dewdrop lawns, and her only company was a flock of swans gliding gracefully along the dark waters of the river.

Cassie turned out from the back gates and ran along the scenic walk that wound out from Raleigh's manicured lawns, her strides lengthening as she followed the path of the river out past the gardens and into the wilderness of the woodland beyond. With every footstep she felt the

years fall away, stripping back the winding journey that had brought her here, halfway across the world—years when home had meant the contents of her duffel bag, and success simply enough cash to pay the rent that month. When Oxford was just a distant city, as arbitrary a destination as a pin pushed randomly into a creased old map.

Until the day the package came.

Cassie had found it propped outside her door one icy morning three years ago. The foreign stamps were peeling, and the original Oxford postmark was smudged and faded, the labels pasted in turn, redirecting the box through old apartments and past crimes all the way back to the original recipient.

Her mother.

Cassie had turned the battered manila envelope over in her hands, wondering how the package had found its way to her at all. She was in Providence, Rhode Island, that month, renting a room above a Polish restaurant, the air smoky with the scent of paprika. She paid cash to a wizened old woman in baggy knit cardigans, who would pluck the skin on her bony wrists in disapproval and leave Tupperware containers of dumplings and broth outside the door. But aside from this well-intentioned *babula*, Cassie remained invisible. She didn't appear on any electoral rolls, had no credit or store cards, and kept any cash locked in a heavy tin fishing box slipped into the ventilation shaft above her bed. Deleting herself from the record of everyday life had been a conscious, careful decision. As far as Cassie was concerned, in the eyes of the world, she didn't exist.

She'd been wrong.

You can't hide the truth forever. Please come back and end this for good.

The note was simple, written in small, blocked letters and tucked inside the package along with a collection of mysterious items.

Cassie had sat down with a thump on the top step of the staircase and reached for her pendant, the only thing of her mother's she had been

able to keep. Joanna had been gone for nearly ten years now, and the rose quartz cameo was chipped with age, the strange, twisted design of the gold setting faded and peeling. Still, Cassie couldn't bring herself to throw it away. It was the only anchor she had to her past, and a warning of everything she could become, if she wasn't careful.

Her fingertips traced the familiar cracked pendant as she wondered what the note could mean. Her mother had stayed friendless, drifting; Cassie had never even seen her write a letter, let alone speak of anyone she stayed in contact with. And surely, any friend she'd had would know by now of her passing.

Ten years was a long time.

What did the note mean? And, after everything, should Cassie even care? It had taken her years to sand her life down to its current friction-less state. Did she really want to dig up painful memories and disturb the ghosts that had barely been laid to rest?

The answer seemed obvious.

No.

Cassie had crumpled the letter back into the package and pushed it deep into the back of her closet, ignoring the questions dancing in her mind for the rest of the week. She sidestepped the creeping whispers of curiosity, filled her every waking moment with screens and pages and a constant stream of noise from her headphones, but still, the question wouldn't go away. Soon, she was waking at three A.M. in a cold sweat, shaking from dark, desperate dreams that saw her trapped in her child-hood house, searching, racing through the shadows trying to find some-thing that always stayed just out of reach. She took to running, pounding the empty downtown streets in the early morning darkness, but her mother's poetry began whispering in the fog-breathed air, stanzas and whole sonnets Cassie hadn't even known she'd learned by heart. She tried to medicate the curiosity away with pills and weed and glinty-eyed strangers in dive bars, but nothing helped.

After ten straight sleepless nights, the gray winter weather finally broke. Trees unfurled with cherry blossoms on the hills above town, and Cassie retrieved the package from its dark hiding place and began her quest for answers.

*A noise broke Cassie from her memories. Another runner was approach-*ing from the opposite direction on the path in the Raleigh woodlands. He was in his late twenties, with fair hair peeking out from under a knit cap, and dressed in dark sweats with earbuds snaking up from under his shirt.

Cassie moved to the far side of the dirt track to let him pass, but instead the man slowed and pulled out one of his earphones. "Careful up ahead," he told her, with a friendly smile. "There's still ice on the path."

She nodded her thanks, but then waited until he'd disappeared behind the next bend before slowing to a stop. She caught her breath, feeling her heart beat fast. In the distance, church bells began to ring out across the meadows: five, six, seven. Cassie looked ahead to the inviting curve of the path; she would happily run for another hour, out, away from the confines of the libraries and first tutorials that awaited her, but she had work to do.

The mysterious package had sent her here for a reason, and there was no time to waste.

HER NEW ROOMS WERE IN CARLTON HALL, A STATELY BUILDING at the back of the college more like a country mansion than a student dorm. Cassie let herself in and climbed a flight of wide, creaking stairs to the second floor. The rest of the world was waking up now, and the building clattered with distant chatter as her fellow students set about their days. The noise filtered under doorways and down the hallway as she passed. It would be an adjustment, sharing space, and a bathroom, with other people; she had been on her own a long time.

She reached the second floor and turned down the hallway, then stopped dead. Her door was ajar, and her suitcase was tossed haphazardly in the hallway outside with a couple of boxes; her books and winter coat were draped carelessly to the side.

Cassie quickly stepped inside the room. It was three times the size of her old studio apartment back in Providence: a sitting room and a separate bedroom with bare floorboards and pale blue walls edged with white corniced trim—and a neat stack of matching luggage in the middle of the polished floors where only an hour ago Cassie's own case had been. A butter-soft leather jacket hung over the back of a desk chair, and in the bedroom, a pile of linens sat waiting to replace the bedding the college had provided. Cassie ran her fingers over the soft cotton, smooth and soft. Expensive.

There was a noise from the hallway, and moments later, a young woman backed into the room, her arms laden with bags. "Careful with that box, Hugo," she was calling. "Those are antique lamps in there." She turned and stopped, seeing Cassie beside the bed.

"Excuse me." She arched an eyebrow, sweeping Cassie with an icy stare. "Who are you?"

Cassie tensed. She'd met her share of wealthy people; life in Cambridge, and New Haven, and Providence made sure of that. There were a dozen breeds—oblivious old money, brash immigrant fortunes, younger, disheveled kids who thought they could mask the family name with thrift-store denim and clove cigarettes. But what gave them away every time was the confident tone to every syllable, an innate superiority that was born and nurtured through prep schools and summer trips, an entire life spent cocooned in a marvelous certainty that they belonged, that this—grades, or jobs, or lovers, whatever it was that took their liking—was theirs by rights.

This girl was one of them. Beautiful in an angular, aristocratic way, she had piercing blue eyes and a sweep of glossy blond hair. She wore tight black jeans and an aged suede jacket, and had smudged eyeliner, but there were pearl studs at her ears and the bags looped over each arm were crafted leather and clearly designer.

Cassie knew she was sweaty and disheveled in her sweatshirt and leggings, but she held her ground. "I think you've got the wrong room. This is mine."

The girl glanced at the heavy wooden door, marked with dull bronze numbers. "Five eighty. Sorry, you're the one who's mistaken." She dropped her bags to the floor. "We'll need the rugs," she called outside the door. "And tell Parker to bring up that cabinet, the one . . ." She stopped impatiently. "Hugo? Hugo!"

There was no reply, and the girl gave an exasperated sigh. "I can help get the rest of your things together," she offered Cassie. "The office will sort out a new room."

"No thanks," Cassie replied stubbornly. "I'm good here." She sauntered over to the window seat and sat down, lounging back in the narrow seat. Beside her, the view stretched all the way to the riverbanks, grassy and bright in the afternoon sun.

She shouldn't be causing a scene, but Cassie couldn't help it. She had learned the importance of territory in her first group home, where the kids had squabbled over a few feet of bedroom space. She certainly wasn't about to give up her claim to this vast spread of gleaming honeyed floorboards and smooth, cool walls.

The girl looked at Cassie again, as if sensing her steely determination. Her frown smoothed into a wide smile, and suddenly, her face was transformed to something warm, even friendly. "I'm so sorry," she exclaimed. "Where are my manners? I've been lugging boxes all day for the move. I didn't even ask your name."

Cassie introduced herself, cautious.

"Lovely to meet you." The girl smiled. "I'm Olivia, Olivia Mandeville. I'm sorry to cause you all this bother."

"Like you said, it's probably a mix-up." Cassie stood her ground. "I'm sure the office will be able to sort you out another room."

Olivia laughed, a musical sound. "You're a transfer?" she asked.

Cassie frowned. "What does that matter?"

"It matters because these are the finalist rooms. Third years." Olivia gave an apologetic shrug. "We drew a ballot last year for rooms; my friends and I all picked Carlton. Foreign students are over with the freshers in Hartwell, round the back, by the kitchens." She turned away to bellow out of the door. "Hugo!" Her voice rang, strong and arch, and then she was gone, back out into the maze of creaking hallways and dusty stairs, the air above her baggage drifting with golden particles of dust, as if even the ripples she left in her wake were gleaming with some certain touch of wealth.

Cassie's territorial instincts proved to be no match for Raleigh's official dorm policy; back in the porters' lodge, Rutledge confirmed that Olivia was right: Carlton Hall was for upperclassmen only. "Let's see what's left . . ." He hummed, clicking through his records on the old computer.

"I could put you with the rest of the freshers if you want, but they can get rowdy. First time they've been away from home," he added, with a weary look on his well-lined face.

Cassie grimaced at the thought of all-night dorm parties and freshmen running wild. "Is there anything else?"

"I've got it." Rutledge turned behind him and plucked a new key down from the board. "Up in the attics. You'll be sharing, but it's a cozy little flat. The other girl's a grad student, seems a sweet girl."

"I'll take it," Cassie said gratefully, eager to just be done with the whole mix-up.

"I can help you with your bags, if you want—" Rutledge offered, but Cassie cut him off.

"I'm fine, thanks." She was almost out the door again when she paused, turning back. "If I wanted to do some research about Raleigh, where should I start?"

Rutledge paused. "What kind of research?"

"Just general stuff." Cassie shrugged casually. "College history, old students, that kind of thing."

Rutledge narrowed his eyes at her for a moment, and Cassie felt a flutter of unease. Then his expression cleared. "Well, there's the library, that's a good place to start. But if you want the real stuff, you'd be best off trying the vaults."

"The vaults?" Cassie repeated.

"Down below the cloisters." Rutledge nodded. "Everything gets filed away down there sooner or later. They keep talking about getting an archivist, sorting out a proper filing system, but for now, if it happened here in the last hundred years, it's in there somewhere."

"Thanks." Cassie smiled. "I'll check it out."

Her new—and she hoped, final—room was over in the East Wing, a corner of the college filled with wood-paneled study rooms and more of

those wide, creaking stairs. There were no other residence rooms in the building, and the place was silent and still as Cassie dragged her case up two flights. In the top corridor she found a square-set, iron-barred door.

"Hello?" Cassie unlocked the door cautiously, peeking her head around to peer in. "Anyone here?"

According to Rutledge, Cassie would be sharing with another older girl named Genevieve DuLongpre, a grad student. There was no sign of life, so Cassie pulled her things inside and let her load fall on the table with a sigh of relief before she took a proper look around.

It was nowhere near as grand as Carlton Hall, that much was clear. Cassie was standing in a large, hexagonal-shaped living room, furnished with a long dining room table and mismatched chairs. Two musty, worn couches sat on the other end of the room in front of a bare-brick fireplace; threadbare rugs lay on the wooden floor. A short, narrow hallway led off to a galley kitchen in one direction and a bathroom in the other, both tiled in old-fashioned shades of mustard and green. The ceilings were low, slanted into the attic eaves, and although one side of the living area was lined with deep windows cut into the stone walls, the effect was hemmed in, almost claustrophobic, some might think.

Cozy, Cassie decided.

The door was open to one of the bedrooms, showing it strewn with a carpet of loose notes and discarded sweaters, so Cassie took her things into the other room. Again it was small, with the slanted ceilings and wooden built-in shelves lining one wall, the other set with her bed and desk. She went to the window and opened it wide to air out the room, glimpsing afternoon light filtering through spaces between the carved stone gargoyles that perched atop the edge of the walls. The faint sound of laughter and passing traffic hummed in the street below, but here Cassie was high above the city, and completely alone.

She quickly unpacked and retrieved a thick file from the bottom of her suitcase. She brewed herself a cup of tea, found a pack of stale biscuits in the cupboard, and finally settled at the wide dining table in a

pool of midday sun. Opening the folder, she laid out the familiar contents in front of her like a fortune-teller setting out the tarot.

First, the note. *You can't hide the truth forever. Please come back and end this for good.*

Then the rest of the contents of that mysterious package.

A ticket stub. Plymouth to New York, by boat, in the spring of 1995.

A rose quartz pendant, just like the one she always wore.

And a photo. Her mother, looking impossibly young. Dressed in a white blouse and long black skirt, a black ribbon tied at her neck. She was smiling, her teenage face alive with laughter, sandwiched with another girl between two boys in matching formal costume, the three-quarter-length robes around their shoulders trailing wide bands of material in the breeze.

Cassie had spent the previous afternoon in an identical outfit, surrounded by such boys. She would know the setting for the photo even without the unfamiliar scrawl on the back.

Raleigh College. 1994.

She stared at the evidence, as she had a hundred times over since opening that package. Taken separately, they were fragments, a mystery. But together . . . ?

Cassie had tried, and failed, to make these new facts somehow fit the story of her life. Her mother, Joanna, who had never talked of college, not once even mentioned leaving America, had come to England to study, had been a student here at Raleigh, one of the most prestigious and elite schools in the world. She had walked these same stone pathways, perhaps even clambered the stairs in this very building, and she had not uttered a single word to Cassie about it.

Cassie remembered every cruel, furious taunt, and every sobbing entreaty. She'd been on the receiving end of her mother's wrath for fourteen years, blamed for every missed opportunity and sacrificed dream. If her mother had even once hinted at this previous life of hers, Cassie would have known. It had been a secret Joanna took to her grave.

◆ ◆ ◆

Special, they had called her mother. Fragile. As if Joanna was a rare butterfly or exquisite vase. But for Cassie there had been nothing fragile about the fits of rage that blazed through her childhood, leaving her mother weeping on the kitchen floor in a pool of exhausted tears. Cassie had been born when Joanna was only twenty, and there had been no family around; her mother never spoke of Cassie's father except to say he had gone, that *we were better off without him,* so Cassie was left tiptoeing alone through her childhood in a constant state of alert, doing her best to keep the peace.

But there was always something that slipped past her watch. Sour milk turning in the fridge, a button fraying on Cassie's grade-school blouse—her mother would ignite at the smallest tinder, a wildfire of inexplicable anguish that would sweep through the house, raging for hours about the sacrifices she'd made, the great poet she could have been without the drudge and toil of domesticity dragging her down. Cassie soon learned to hide from her wrath, racing for the one lockable room in the house at the first sign of temper, crouching, hidden, behind the bathroom door in a tight ball of fear as she counted under her breath. Five hundred. Six hundred. Sometimes she would clear a thousand before the house would fall silent. Eventually, often hours later, Cassie would emerge with an aching head and empty stomach, to find nobody there—or, worse, a plate of grilled cheese waiting on the kitchen counter and that terrible look of shame and guilt in her mother's eyes.

Still, for all the ragged-nail anxiety of the fever dreams, Cassie preferred them to what came after: long months of lethargy, when her mother seemed to forget she was a person at all, and all Cassie could do was bring her slices of dry white toast, cover her with blankets where she lay unmoving on the couch. They moved around so much that nobody noticed her permission slips were signed with a vague scrawl, and that her mother's attendance at parent-teacher events was only at best sporadic.

Eventually, a mix of medication and maturity evened out her mother's more extreme attacks, until Joanna's dark days—as she called them with a nervous laugh—only came once or twice a year. They moved for the fifth and final time, settling on a tree-lined street in a city in the middle of Indiana. Her mother kept her poetry volumes packed away, found a job, and even married. Cassie had almost begun to believe things would be normal again when the fever dreams returned, and her mother opened her wrists one afternoon in the cracked enamel bathtub, bleeding to death with a half-empty bottle of pills beside her to underscore her final act.

Cassie's brief glimpse of stability was gone for good. The husband lasted another few months before dying, drunk, with the house burning to ash around him. Social services took Cassie into care, but after bouncing around the foster system until she turned sixteen, she took herself off the grid. After that came years of cheap motels and diner coffee as Cassie drifted, skittish, from one town to the next: dealing fake IDs and prescription pills to get by, and circling ever closer to her mother's fate until she found a currency more lucrative than most.

Knowledge.

It was simple, far easier than any of her other crimes. Her mind had always been voracious, devouring new ideas and systems the way her grade-school classmates had absorbed Sunday morning cartoons. A few hours of work on her computer cloning a student ID card, and she was free: slipping into the stream of undergrads passing through the campus gates, working at the back table of the local coffeehouse, camped out in the fifth row of a lecture auditorium, listening to the professor ramble on about esoteric theories in astronomy, physics, mathematics. She sold term papers to the lazy, privileged college kids who were content to outsource their hundred-thousand-dollar education to someone with an actual passion for learning, sometimes even sitting tests in their place if the security was lax enough. All the benefits of college without the rules, the grades, the arbitrary authority. Cassie was just another face, anonymous, in a crowd of thousands.

Until she opened that package and found that the few, painful truths she'd built her life upon weren't really true at all, but a fiction dreamed up by a woman who, it turned out, she'd never really known at all.

Now, Cassie stared at the pieces of the puzzle, as if this time they would rearrange themselves into a clear picture.

Oxford. A boat trip. Then, five months later, Cassie was born.

She'd looked at the photo a thousand times, but even now, it felt like the first. The Joanna in the photograph appeared light, youthful, innocent. Cassie's mother had been none of those things. By the time Cassie was old enough to register the expression in her mother's eyes, that joy had been drained away, leaving only flashes of bitterness and ill-concealed resentment in its place; frustration where there had once been promise, defeat where hope had once shone.

Cassie stared, lost in her mother's unfamiliar smile, until the sound of a key in the door broke her from her reverie. She quickly swept her papers back into the file as the door swung open, revealing a slim sprite of a woman with blond hair twisted into a crown of braids and a vivid print scarf wound loosely around her pale throat. She was weighed down under a shoulder bag, books, and a take-out container. Cassie leaped up to help.

"Hi," the woman said breathlessly, her eyes bright. "You must be my new roommate! Rutledge said there'd been a mix-up. Welcome to the garret. I'm Genevieve; call me Evie."

"Cassie," she replied, helping unload Evie's bags.

"First week back, I swear we should all be walking around with back braces," Evie said, setting down her mountains of books. She kicked her heels off into a heap in the corner. "Part of me is tempted to get one of those old lady shopping trolleys and just wheel it along behind me to the library and back!" She collapsed into a seat at the table and opened the take-out container with a contented sigh. Steam rose from a pile of limp fries smothered with cheese and some kind of curry-scented

sauce. "Ahmed's," Evie explained, using a plastic fork to spear a clump. "I shouldn't, but then every night I'm back in line, waiting for my fix."

"Ahmed's?" Cassie repeated.

Evie's eyes widened. "You haven't been? Oh, you must, he's practically an institution here at Raleigh. It's a kebab van," she added. "Although you should never touch the kebabs. We don't know what he puts in them, but only the strongest of stomachs survive." She took a bite, her face melting in contentment, then pushed the box toward her. "Go on, try."

Cassie cautiously speared a fry and tried it, soggy yet pungent. "Good, right?" Evie asked. "One time Ahmed got into an argument with Rutledge down in the lodge about the noise, and he up and parked on the other side of the city for a month. There was an uproar. Letters were written; the JCR, the Junior Common Room, passed a motion in defense. In the end I think the master had to go beg him to come back before we all rioted."

Cassie slowly chewed, warming to her new roommate. There was something effortlessly sweet about Evie's tumble of gossip, the vivid spark in her blue eyes.

"So what's your story?" Evie looked her over with interest. "I would have thought you were too old to be an undergraduate. Did you switch degree specializations?"

Cassie paused. "Not exactly. I started late. I . . . left education, out of high school. It took time to find my way back around."

Time, and resources. When she'd first opened the package, she'd bolted straight for Oxford: taken her meager savings, hopped a flight, and found a cheap motel on the edge of the city to stay in while she hunted down her mother's past life.

She'd found nothing.

She hadn't even known where to begin, or what she was looking for. The closest she'd gotten to Raleigh was an official tour: ushered along the public pathways with a group of tourists, kept away from any dorms or student areas, anything of use. She was an outsider.

So she'd bided her time. First, back in the States, a place at Smith, a college that had both a program for nontraditional adult students and strong study-abroad ties with Oxford. She'd studiously amassed recommendations and glowing transcripts until finally, her junior year arrived, and the Raleigh program accepted her application.

"You came back to academia after all that time? That's great," Evie chatted, still munching on her food. "And brave, putting up with all these kids again. I couldn't do it."

Cassie remembered the pages of notes she'd seen strewn around Evie's room. "What is it you're studying? You're a grad student, aren't you?"

Evie brightened. "History, Elizabethan literature, a real mishmash. I'm doing my thesis on Sir Walter Raleigh and the intellectual renaissance here at the college."

Cassie tried to remember her tour from yesterday. "You mean that secret society everyone was talking about?"

Evie laughed. "It sounds strange, but the conspiracy theories aren't actually that far-fetched. The ideas being bandied about at the time were heresy and treason, so they did stay pretty secretive. But no dark rituals and murder. They just sat around discussing philosophy."

"Wild," Cassie noted dryly.

"I was worried when I applied that the subject would have been done a million times," Evie confided. "But it turns out only a couple of people ever researched it. Most of the papers and documents haven't been touched for years, so I'm practically living in the vaults these days."

"Are they part of the library?" Cassie inquired casually.

Evie nodded. "You don't need to worry about them yet, most of the catalog is aboveground. It's only us grad students who get banished down into the cellars." She yawned as her cell phone buzzed loudly on the table with a text. Evie checked it, then bounced to her feet."Shit, I'm late. Some friends are having a get-together at Carlton Hall. You should come."

Cassie shook her head. "Thanks, but I'm beat."

"Okay, sleep well. And if you have any questions or anything, just ask," Evie told her, pulling her jacket back on. "I know this place can be rather overwhelming. I was wandering round in a daze my first few weeks."

"Thanks." Cassie watched Evie slick on a fresh coat of lipstick and bound out the door, just as the bells outside began to chime midnight.

Alone again, she drifted back to the windows. On this side of the walls, Raleigh lay dark and still. The heavy gates were shut, and old spotlit lamps glowed along the side of the buildings, casting shadows that seemed to flicker and dance. She caught a glimpse of movement from the cloisters as someone emerged, striding across the courtyard, a smudge of black against the dark cobblestones. A dedicated student, heading to the library, perhaps, or a professor back from a late drink. Then the shadow was gone, and all was still again.

Cassie retrieved the photo of her mother again. She didn't have time for mixers and college parties; she'd come here for a reason. It had been almost twenty-five years since that sun-dappled day in the photograph, and although Cassie wasn't naive enough to think her mother's classmates would still be here, she knew places like Oxford never liked to let you go. There would be alumni associations, old boys' club meetings, mailing lists, and donor events. She was no great hacker, but she could track a man using nothing but his supposedly anonymous online username; these people, who weren't even trying to hide, would be far easier for her to find.

All Cassie needed was one of them, just one, to tell her who her father was.

CASSIE HAD SPENT MOST OF HER LIFE BOUNCING RESTLESSLY between apartments and cities, until she found it easy to make a home wherever she found herself. She quickly settled into the attic apartment and turned her attention to the start of classes. She'd hoped that the pomp and ceremony of the first day of term would be quickly replaced with a more regular blue-jeans version of the college experience, but she was mistaken. Her formal matriculation ceremony led to a welcome dinner in the grand hall, complete with soaring wood-paneled ceilings and long rows of dining tables silently waited on by staff. And still the invitations continued, materializing in her pigeonhole every day, a confetti of colored paper and stiff cards all beckoning her to some new social function.

Departmental drinks, JCR games night, pleas from sports teams and student organizations to join their festivities—the avalanche of social engagements gathered pace over the course of the week. Even her new roommate left nightly invitations to join her out on the town, but Cassie stood firm, watching from her corner of the couch as Evie dashed out in a flutter of silk cocktail dresses, her high heels clattering on the cobblestones beneath the window late into the night.

Luckily, thanks to the tutorial system of learning at Oxford, Cassie would be given free rein to pursue her extracurricular mission. Instead of being graded on attendance, and issued pop quizzes and final exams, students at Raleigh were left largely to their own devices; they were taught in small groups of two or three, meeting weekly with a professor

to discuss the research essays they had prepared from a set reading list. There would be no classes, and only the occasional seminar; even lectures were entirely optional.

Cassie was certain she could breeze through the work required for her tutorials and have plenty of time left over to track down her mother's past. For the fall semester, she would be studying economics under Professor Kenmore and philosophy with Professor Tremain, the disheveled man she'd met at the mixer on her first day. He had already sent out a summons demanding her presence at an induction session; "Mandatory" had been written in bold, so at six P.M. on Friday she reluctantly put her mother's files aside and headed out across the campus.

Professor Tremain's office was located on the north side of a set of open stone cloisters that, even now in early October, whistled and hummed with a wind that slipped beneath her bulky parka and sent shivers along her skin. Cassie climbed the staircase to the first floor and pushed open the door to find a dim, wood-paneled study already filled with a group of students crammed on the threadbare couches and old antique chairs. They all turned to look at her, and Cassie flushed as she stepped inside the room.

"Come on in," Professor Tremain called from behind his desk. He was wearing an identical outfit to the first time she'd met him at the introductory tea: a tweed jacket with worn leather elbow patches and a pair of faded corduroy pants. He gave her an encouraging nod and then continued: "I was just explaining about research resources. You should be familiar with the libraries by now," he added, turning back to the group. "Raleigh is well stocked, and there's also the Ashmolean, for older texts. Being unable to locate the right reading material is never an excuse for substandard work."

As the professor moved on to proper footnote citations, Cassie looked around the room. Her classmates already seemed at home. They squeezed together on the couches, passing printed sheets around and loaning each other pens as if they'd known one another forever.

But of course, they had. She was the interloper here; they'd all been studying together for a year, at least. Sophomores now, nineteen or twenty years old, they all looked impossibly young to her, but completely at ease with Tremain's stern warnings about source materials.

One girl, hair neatly styled in a French twist, raised her hand. "Are there specific lectures you recommend?"

Tremain gave her an approving smile. "We'll be starting this term with Descartes and his meditations, but you need to prepare for later in the year. Each tutor will send out a list, but I can tell you now you should be looking at Ethics, perhaps the series on Kant and Rousseau. By now, you'll all be familiar with Warnock, Soteriou . . ."

The students scribbled on as he listed a dozen different recommendations, and Cassie felt a flicker of unease. She struggled to copy down the roll call of unfamiliar texts; maybe she'd been too quick to dismiss the amount of work it would take to stay afloat.

Professor Tremain paused his list of reading recommendations and looked around the small, dim room. "Essays should, of course, be around three thousand words. If it's less than two thousand, you haven't explored the material in enough depth. Footnotes don't count. What we expect from you is a reasoned, persuasive argument that assesses the major concepts of the reading, while also drawing original conclusions." He gave them a wry smile. "Be warned, you may think just because you survived the first year it's smooth sailing from here on out. I'm afraid to say there'll be some choppy waters as you come to grips with the more advanced materials. But don't worry—I'm here to help, however I can. If you have questions about the reading lists, just ask. It's not a test, we're all here to learn."

Cassie let out a small breath of relief. Tremain produced another sheaf of photocopied pages and began passing them around. "These are your first week reading lists. I've listed your tutorial group and schedule on the back. That's it for now. I'll see you all for your first tutorials next week."

Cassie glanced at her study materials as the rest of the class gathered their things and spilled back down the stairs. According to Tremain's list, she was grouped with students named Sebastian and Julia, set for eight A.M. Friday morning to present their essays on Descartes and his meditations about body and mind. That seemed simple enough. She'd already picked up a grasp of basic philosophy from her patchwork education, so she should be able to rattle off a paper in no time. Her new economics professor had e-mailed her other essay questions already, and they were just as basic—a breakdown of simple macro- and micro-economic concepts that anyone with access to an Internet search engine could answer.

She crumpled the reading list in the bottom of her bag as she reached her classmates, gathered in the cloisters.

"Time for a pint," a tall, reedy boy with carrot-red hair groaned.

There was laughter. "How are you not still hungover from last night?" the girl with the braid demanded as the group began sauntering toward the college bar. "You puked all over the roses."

"Fertilizer, my dear. I was doing them a favor."

Cassie turned away and headed in the opposite direction, across the courtyard toward the looming spires of the college library, a tall and ornate building with iron-paned windows and a stained-glass frieze. At the entrance, she heaved open the heavy wooden door and waited a moment on the threshold, her eyes adjusting to the gloom. The library was set on three levels, with the main room housing the circulation desk and a bank of gleaming new computers. Stairs led off to the side up to the reading room above, which was bordered on every wall by more stacks—these old and wooden, bearing clothbound volumes, stiff with age. Above that level was a mezzanine, the balcony running the full circumference of the room, with books stretching even higher, up to the lofted ceilings crossed with thick beams.

Consulting a map on the wall, Cassie saw the entrance to the vaults was in the back of the main floor. When she got there, she found a heavy

wooden door propped ajar, with a dim stone staircase spiraling downward, leading to another door. This one was shut, armed with a surprisingly modern card swipe.

Cassie's heart fell. Of course it wouldn't be so easy, she scolded herself: library archives would be restricted to authorized personnel who had a legitimate reason to be rooting through the old college files. And her reasons were anything but. She studied the access panel carefully, wondering if it could be hacked. Most of these security systems, for all their bells and whistles, could be bypassed with a magnetic strip and some electronic store equipment. She snapped a quick photo with her cell phone, then climbed back up to the main library level.

Navigating her way into the depths of the stacks, she found the next best thing to the archives: a case of college yearbooks like the ones she'd seen in Sir Edmund's offices. Cassie heaved down several books, covering the time period her mother must have attended the college, and found herself a study carrel in a dark corner.

The years fell away, each page a snapshot from a different era. She worked systematically through the yearbooks, checking the student lists for the freshman class of 1992. The undergraduate intake at Raleigh was always small, and that year the college had admitted only eighty-five new students, but as she'd seen in the study, there was no Joanna Blackwell listed on the page—nor for 1990, 1991, 1993, 1994, or 1995. Cassie stared at the books, her disappointment blossoming into curiosity as she examined the pages again, lit by the dim glow of an iron-cast lamp in the corner.

Why wasn't her mother's name listed? Even if she'd been a foreign transfer student like Cassie, her name should still be on the rolls with the other study-abroad programs. Cassie expanded her search to other college records and rolls, working through the evening until darkness fell outside the windows, but still, she found no trace of her mother among the dusty faded pages. Joanna Blackwell was a ghost, a figment.

Cassie stretched. Her eyes were dry and tired from hours poring over the tiny type, but she felt more frustrated than anything. She'd thought that once she was here in person to access the records, the answers she'd been searching for would fall into her lap.

She returned the yearbooks to their shelf, then stopped by the front desk. An older woman with a gray-blond perm and a drab cardigan was stacking returns. "How would I get access to the college archives in the vault?" Cassie asked.

The librarian looked up. "I'm afraid the vaults are restricted. Too many delicate manuscripts to have people trampling through all day," she explained. "You need to have a faculty member apply for a pass-card for you."

"Oh." Cassie's face must have fallen, because the librarian paused.

"You can also request materials and we'll bring them up. What is it you're looking for?"

"Nothing in particular," Cassie said hurriedly. "I was just wondering, that's all."

Luckily, the librarian was prevented from quizzing her further by the blare of the alarm from the door sensors, where a wide-eyed boy froze, guilty.

"Did you demagnetize?" the librarian called, impatient. Cassie quickly slipped away.

Outside, it was dark and chilly, and the campus pathways were busy with students on their way to the dining hall, or heading out to dinner. Cassie zipped up her parka and headed back toward the attic, deep in thought. The information had to be there somewhere. She just wasn't looking in the right place. Maybe her mother had attended a different Oxford college, and only stopped by Raleigh to celebrate with friends, or perhaps there was a simple explanation why her name was missing from the rolls. An administration mistake or a printing error. She would just have to dig deeper—and that meant gaining access to those locked archives.

"MORNING."

Cassie did a double take when she emerged from her room early the next morning. Not only was Evie awake, but she was bright-eyed and waiting in the living area, lacing up a pair of running shoes. "I thought I could come out with you, if you don't mind," Evie asked. "I haven't done any exercise in so long I swear my muscles have atrophied."

"Sure," Cassie replied slowly. She preferred the time alone to think, but she'd been rebuffing Evie's invites all week. "I mean, of course you're welcome to. It's not very interesting," she added, zipping up her sports jacket. "Just out to the meadows and back."

"Believe me, I need it." Evie laughed. "See if I can't sweat some of these cocktails out of my system."

"You were out again last night, weren't you?" Cassie asked.

Evie groaned. "Too late, and I shouldn't have gone. But someone was having a party, and then we needed food, and before I knew it, we were propping up the bar until closing, like always!" They headed downstairs, walking out toward the back entrance. "Have you been past the Botanic Garden?" Evie suggested. Cassie shook her head. "It's not far, out beyond Magdalen College. We could loop around by the river, it's nice and peaceful."

"Lead the way."

They started jogging, and soon fell into a slow, steady pace as they headed down the street and across the bridge to where the river wound away from Raleigh in the opposite direction of the route Cassie had been

taking. This wasn't as secluded as her usual path: they passed museums and parkland, but still the early morning silence was draped over the city, muffling distant traffic with birdsong and the gentle lap of the river on its banks.

Evie chatted easily as they jogged, about her upbringing in the leafy north Hampstead suburbs, her private schooling, her dramatic French mother. She had studied for her undergraduate degree in history and literature at Cambridge and made the move to Oxford to work on her thesis at the site of Raleigh's activities. Her parents were retired now, idling near a vineyard in the South of France, while Evie happily pursued her master's digging through dusty Elizabethan research and drinking dry gimlets in the elegant city bars.

It was a world away from Cassie's own upbringing, but she found herself enjoying the gentle chatter and glamorous stories all the same, like an anthropologist hearing reports from a foreign tribe. Unlike some of the other students she'd encountered, who boasted loudly about their foreign houses and extravagant vacations, Evie was simply being friendly, and she peppered her own stories with questions about Cassie's life. Cassie evaded as much as possible and repeated her cover story about a lifelong fascination with Oxford.

"Is it everything you imagined?" Evie asked, when they took a break to rest by the Botanic Garden. The glass hothouses sat neatly by the river-banks, manicured lawns winding with trimmed pathways. Cassie could see the lush green and vibrant colors of the exotic plants housed within.

"Oxford?" Cassie paused a moment, catching her breath. "I don't know yet. I built it up so much in my mind, I'm not sure anything could have equaled the vision I had."

This was true. She'd imagined Oxford to be a mythic place, full of answers, where she'd finally come to know the truth about her mother, but instead . . . It was just a city: beautiful and old, yes, but still a real place, the same as any other, full of darkness and mystery but also the buzz of traffic, wet autumn rains, tourists clustering the streets.

"It never quite matches what we had in our minds, does it?" Evie replied softly.

Cassie looked over, surprised by the disappointed note in Evie's voice.

"My degree." Evie gave a bashful shrug. "I thought it would be . . . not easy, but clear. That I'd know exactly what to do, the way I always do. Things make sense to me, they always have, but now . . . I just can't find the answers I'm looking for."

Cassie gave her a sympathetic smile. "You just need a plan," she said. "Be methodical, and you'll figure it out. Step by step."

Evie nodded. "Hey, thanks. For listening; I know I can babble on."

"No problem." Cassie smiled. "I'm sure you'll figure it out."

They turned back to the college. As they jogged slowly along the river, a familiar figure drew closer—the young man Cassie had seen out running before. His brown hair was ruffled by the wind, ears tipped red from the chill. As he approached them, he gave Cassie a wide smile. "You again," he called. "What are you, stalking me now?"

Cassie didn't reply. She waited for him to pass them by, but instead he slowed, then jogged backward as they kept moving toward him. "I'm Charlie," he told her, brown eyes alive with amusement. "I figured it was time I introduced myself."

"I'm Evie," Evie volunteered. "And this is Cassie."

"You students?" Charlie asked, still jogging backward.

"Postgrad," Evie replied. "At Raleigh."

"Fancy," he teased. "You know, I'm always looking for a running buddy," he added, attention still fixed on Cassie. "If you're worried about keeping up, I promise I'll go slow." He grinned, broad and cocky.

But Cassie wasn't looking for whatever this man had on his mind. Romance, dating—they were foreign concepts to her, and she had bigger things on her mind. She gave him a withering stare and lengthened her pace, speeding up to leave him there by the bridge. Evie caught up with her a moment later. "What's wrong?" she asked, panting. "He was cute."

"I'm not interested," Cassie said, feeling a flush of embarrassment.

"Sorry," Evie said quickly. "I figured you guys had, I don't know, a friendly runners' thing. He seemed to like you," she added.

"Trust me," Cassie said. "Men are the last thing on my mind right now."

"Then I'll say no more." Evie mimed locking her lips shut. "God, this is why I don't exercise; I'm burning up inside. Want to stop by Harvey's for a breakfast bap on the way back in?"

"Sure." Cassie tried to relax, checking the path behind them to see if Charlie was gone. "Sounds good to me."

Her information pack listed a couple of libraries outside the college that could be used for her classwork, so after showering and changing, Cassie struck out across the city to see if one of them might hold any clues about her mother. There was an official university archive housed in the Radcliffe Camera, an eighteenth-century domed building set off Brasenose Lane. A flow of tourists posed for photographs out front. Inside, Cassie used her Raleigh ID to register for a reader's card and filled in the request slip for the records she needed.

"The official record for *every* college?" The clerk looked over his fashionable black glasses frames at her. He was in his twenties, his hair slicked back, his fingertips paint-stained. He frowned at Cassie's cursive script. "For nineteen ninety-two—"

"And ninety-three, and ninety-four," she finished. "Is that a problem?"

"No," he said, but he sighed with a mournful air. "Wait here. I'll have the first batch sent up in a minute."

Cassie spent the day tucked away in the upper reading room, systematically working her way through the books that the clerk called up for her in batches, each time greeting her request slip with the same weary sigh. Here, the crowd was older than at Raleigh: grad students, the occasional professor with his half-moon glasses and worn leather elbow patches. They built forts with their research materials, blocking off cor-

ners of their desks to keep out prying eyes, and it was easy for Cassie to blend in: just another reader, researching some old, faded records in the pools of afternoon sun.

She broke only for lunch, which she bought from a café in an old converted church across the square, and ate in the shade of its leafy courtyard, among tourists and their cream teas, and clusters of blue-rinsed pensioners gossiping over fragrant lemon cake. It was a sea of strange faces, save one: Professor Tremain, deep in conversation across the courtyard. He saw her from across the courtyard and gave a wave, almost knocking his tea to the ground.

He was a curious man, Cassie thought, waving back. A relic, an oddity in his tweed and absentminded concentration, he seemed as if he could have been transplanted from fifty or a hundred years ago. But then again, that was Oxford: its cobbled streets unchanged, the lamp-posts still old-fashioned wrought iron even if the bulbs inside were new.

This was an odd, timeless place, a city out of step with the rest of the world, where walking down an empty backstreet along the snaking line of an ancient college's walls, Cassie could almost forget which century she was in—until a cluster of noisy undergrads spilled out of some back-alley pub, with their modern fashions and noisy buzz of cell phones breaking the spell.

It was still strange for Cassie to think of her mother here. She would have loved it, Cassie knew: the bustle of the city center, with its collision of old worlds and new: the old Tudor row houses and college walls, the modern office buildings and traffic that snaked through the winding streets, the horizon of turrets and curving spires. To have seen her there, immersed in such literature and tradition . . . It was a fantasy, impossible, Cassie knew, but as she searched through the old college records, expecting to see Joanna's name on every next page, she could almost glimpse it. That laughing smile, that glow of possibility.

What had happened to her, to strip away all that great potential and leave her so broken, so full of rage and sorrow? Or had it been inevita-

ble, the time bomb in her delicate DNA: the threads of instability woven deep, and only surfacing later, when it was already too late?

The DNA they both shared. Cassie shivered and turned back to her books, but the thought lingered. For years, she'd known that she'd inherited too much from her mother; not her blond hair or blue eyes or perfect singing pitch, but the darkness lingering beneath the surface. A poison of sorts, running in her veins. Her mother's sickness had been the manic episodes, the heightened emotions, the dizzying, knife-edge depths.

For Cassie, it took a different form.

She'd been a kid still when they started. Tantrums, disapproving teachers would call them, but to Cassie, they were anything but a choice. The anger would take her over in a heartbeat, a pounding, furious storm that she was powerless to control. People used the term *blind rage* so casually, but Cassie knew from the inside exactly what it meant. She would lose track of herself, overcome with a red-hot fury that demanded release, until finally something broke through the fever or it ebbed away, leaving nothing but wreckage behind.

It terrified her, losing control. She feared that she was becoming her mother, only worse. Sharper, more dangerous. Her mother only screamed and cried in the grip of her episodes, but Cassie . . . Cassie wanted to burn the whole world down.

Her mother knew the signs. She held fast against doctors and medication until there was no ignoring the damage. But instead of submitting Cassie to the drugs that she swore numbed her to the world, Joanna taught Cassie her own coping mechanisms, making out like it was just a game. Hold on to the magic pendant, and count; imagine they were lying on the trampoline in the summer sun. Safe thoughts. Careful numbers. Keep the furious hunger at bay.

Cassie knew the pendant was nothing more than chipped stone, and the simple meditation techniques designed for stress, but it was all she had. She focused that wild fury, boxed it up in walls of whispered chanting until she was safe, until it was contained.

It didn't always work. There was an incident with bullies when she was eight years old, the time on the school bus when she was twelve. Broken bones, black eyes, a trip to the ER, and little Cassie in the middle of it all, unharmed and unremorseful. They took her out of school in the end—it was just safer that way—and away from the daily battle of other kids, taunting and not understanding, she found it easier to keep control. A calm life, a simple one; that had been all Joanna wanted for them both.

But it hadn't worked out that way in the end.

By the end of the afternoon, Cassie had found nothing, so she packed up her things and left the hushed confines of the library. After so many hours sitting cooped up in a study carrel, her muscles screamed for activity, so instead of heading back to Raleigh she struck out in the other direction, exploring the city center as the crowds of shoppers and after-work commuters filled the darkening streets with bustle and movement. Everyone at Raleigh might act like the college was the center of the Oxford universe, but it turned out there was a whole world waiting beyond the sandstone walls. Cassie discovered a covered marketplace, filled with tourist stalls and produce vendors, where you could buy cheap key chains alongside cuts of meat from the local butcher stand. Farther down St. Giles, in the Jericho district of town, she found an art-house cinema that screened foreign movies on its small, velvet-fringed screen, and a tiny ice cream shop where students clustered despite the cold weather.

She was walking back toward Raleigh, worn out from her roaming, when the skies opened, drenching the cobbled streets. Cassie ducked inside a nearby storefront to take shelter, gasping against the icy water, but it was only as she shook off her coat and looked around that she realized she shared a name with the cramped, old-fashioned bookstore: Blackwell's.

"Are you in or out?" a grumpy-looking man demanded, trying to open his umbrella as he passed.

Cassie stepped deeper into the store. It was a world away from the cavernous chain stores back in America: set in a row of crooked buildings, the wood-beamed walls housed thousands of texts. Remembering her essays, still yet to be written, Cassie collected an armful of economics textbooks and settled in the corner of the café upstairs, watching the rain fall through the iron-paned windows as she sipped a coffee and watched the bustle of students and tourists ebb and flow through the cozy rooms.

She was deep in theories of microeconomic preference when there was movement at the table beside her; it was the clerk from the Rad Cam library, Cassie recognized: dark hair slicked back in a retro, fashionable style, black-rimmed glasses faintly fogged from the cold. He pulled off his thick winter coat and draped it over the back of one chair, strewing a scatter of sketchpads and pencils across the table to stake his claim before heading for the café counter across the room. Cassie thought for a moment of the irony: leaving his day job among the library stacks to come here, surrounded by yet more books. But that was Oxford, she supposed: home to bibliophiles. Several times in the Rad Cam she'd seen browsers bend their heads to the pages of an old book and inhale deeply, almost as in prayer. Not for them, the sterile touch of a smooth screen, or the sacrilege of electronic books that could be bought at the click of a button, and just as easily deleted.

Cassie turned back to her textbook, making brief notes for her tutorial the next morning, but she was interrupted by a sudden jolt: the table shuddering as the clerk tripped against it, his coffee spilling over Cassie's book. She cursed, leaping up.

"Oh, shitface!" The clerk abandoned his drink and grabbed a clutch of paper napkins. Cassie dabbed quickly, and eventually the liquid disappeared, leaving only the faintest stain.

"Thank God," Cassie exhaled with relief.

"Sorry," he said, sounding wholly unapologetic, "but you shouldn't have left your bag out like that."

"This is my fault?" Cassie bridled. "You nearly cost me . . . fifty-six pounds?" She checked the price on the back cover and gaped.

"Welcome to the rip-off that is the educational textbook market," the clerk replied in a sardonic voice. He folded himself into the seat beside her and looked mournfully at his half-empty cup. "Fuck, I really needed that. Someone had me chasing college records all over the place." He unwound his scarf and relaxed back into the seat, giving her a meaningful look. "You know, every old book you call up, I have to go hunt down from the vaults? Sixty-seven steps, there and back."

Cassie opened her mouth to object, but then stopped; there was a sarcastic glint in his eye. She pushed over her plate, with the remainder of her cookie. "Bygones?"

"I'd say my forgiveness can't be bought so cheaply, but I'd be lying." He broke off a corner of the chocolate pastry and offered his other hand. "Elliot."

"Cassie," she replied.

Another crowd of undergraduates crammed in at the next table, armed with textbooks and glossy carrier bags spilling new college scarves and sweatshirts. Elliot sighed extravagantly and edged his seat closer in Cassie's direction. "So what in God's name are you looking for down there? If you don't mind me asking."

"Nothing much." Cassie shrugged. "I'm just interested in the history of this place, that's all."

"Fine, be mysterious." Elliot rolled his eyes. "At least you're not having me fetch up every edition of Mills and Boon romance novels."

Cassie laughed. "People do that?"

"Oh yes." Elliot sent his eyes briefly to the ceiling. "We're a copyright library, so we have every book published down there somewhere. There's a grad student who swears it's for research, but she just sits in the Lawler room all afternoon, reading and chewing on her hair. At least, I hope that's all she's doing."

Cassie relaxed. "Are you a student here?" she asked.

"I was." Elliot didn't look thrilled at the thought. "Fine art, which as you can so plainly see, perfectly equipped me for the modern job market. I graduated a few years ago but haven't quite got around to leaving yet."

"It's a beautiful city," Cassie commented, nodding.

"It has its appeal . . ." Elliot's gaze drifted over to a boy in the corner; he was blush-cheeked with a freshman glow, wrapped in a scarf of black and white: Magdalen colors. The boy met Elliot's eyes and looked away quickly, flushing hard. Elliot turned back to Cassie with an amused smirk. "Give him another term, and he'll be dancing on the tables down at the old Firehouse." He took in her blank expression and explained, "It's a gay club, over near Park End. You really are new." Pausing, he eyed her again. "Let me guess, Wadham. No, St. Hilda's. Some dreadfully dull thesis on feminist theory or some such."

"Raleigh," Cassie corrected.

"Really?" Elliot dragged out the syllables. "Well, forgive me for not doffing my cap, m'lady." He mimicked the gesture, bowing as low as the narrow seat would allow.

Cassie laughed. "So it's not just me?" she asked. "I figured everyone here was, you know . . ."

"Posh as a pheasant?" Elliot finished. "No, we all are, but Raleigh students are blue through and through. Blue-blooded," he added. "Tell me, is it true they serve caviar for formal hall every night, and fire the waitstaff if they dare to look you in the eye?"

"I wouldn't know. I don't really go to those things." She caught Elliot's disappointed expression, so she mustered what shred of gossip she could recall. "But they were serving sauterne like it was lemonade at the president's tea. I counted at least a dozen bottles out for pouring."

Elliot clucked in delight. "Bastards," he said fondly. "I'm only jeal-

ous because I couldn't get in. It was a blessing, I suppose. God knows I'm not so high and mighty as that lot."

"Oh really?" Cassie teased.

Elliot laughed, a bright snort of mirth. "I stand corrected: some of you aren't so high and mighty at all."

Cassie stayed another hour in the warm café, enjoying Elliot's insider's guide to the city. Each of the colleges, she learned, had its own character and reputation: from Christ Church's wealthy exclusivity to the serious scholars of Merton and the private-school socialists at Wadham. Then there was Raleigh, aristocratic to the last. From the mix of awestruck envy in Elliot's tone, Cassie deduced that it was the most revered—and despised—of all. Famously cliquey, Raleigh's students rarely ventured out to socialize in the clubs and bars of Oxford, instead taking the train or private cars down to London to enjoy the members-only clubs where they could mingle with their circles, away from regular student life.

Cassie finally checked her watch. "I should really get back," she said. "But I'll see you tomorrow in the library."

"My poor calves can't wait," Elliot shot back. "You know, you should tell me what it is you're looking for in those archives," he added. "I'm not just a pretty face, I know my way around a card index. I could be of some help."

"We'll see." Cassie laughed, avoiding the question. "Have a good night."

She headed back to Raleigh, feeling torn. It would make life much easier to simply tell Elliot who she was looking for, but she couldn't help but remember the secrecy that shrouded this mysterious period in her mother's life—and the ominous tone of the note she'd been sent.

You can't hide the truth forever.

There was a reason her mother had never uttered the name Raleigh. The fewer people who knew what she was searching for, the easier she'd sleep at night.

When she arrived back at the garret, as Evie liked to call it, the attic was empty, her roommate's papers and books strewn about the living room. Cassie yawned, moving to clear them from the coffee table. She had more work to prepare for her first tutorial on Friday, notes and articles that she should have read already. For all her hours in the libraries, she had barely put a dent in her real college work, and she anticipated a long night of study ahead.

Then her eyes landed on Evie's book bag, spilling folders and lip balm on to the floor.

And her student pass-card to the Raleigh library vaults.

CASSIE CAUGHT HER BREATH. SHE CHECKED EVIE'S ROOM, JUST to be sure, but she wasn't home. The apartment was silent.

Her heart beat fast as she scooped up the card, weighing the slim plastic in her hand.

This was her chance.

Cassie swiftly pulled her boots and coat back on, gathered her notebook, and quietly let herself out of the apartment, closing the door behind her with a click.

She hurried down the stairs. It was late, past ten P.M., and the dark campus was quiet as she skirted back around the courtyard to the library. She hugged the walls carefully, keeping to the shadows, and was relieved not to see another soul as she made her way back to the main library.

Inside, the library was hushed and empty, too early in the semester for any all-night cramming sessions. Cassie slipped unseen through the stacks, back to the entrance to the vaults. She heaved the first door open, flinching at the groan of the hinges, then descended the stone steps to the second door. She pulled out the pass-card, holding her breath as she swiped it through.

The security point beeped. The light turned green. The door clicked open.

Cassie let out a shivering breath of relief, stepping through the door into a long corridor lined with stone and lit by flickering neon strip lights overhead: a curious mix of old architecture and new. She must be under the courtyard, she realized, heading back in the direction of the

cloisters. A maze of tunnels and vaults below the surface of the college, out of sight, secret from the world.

Her footsteps echoed fast on the stone until she reached the end of the hallway and stepped through a doorway into the main room: a long, low-ceilinged space filled with old bookshelves and filing cabinets.

She was in.

Cassie flipped on the lights, illuminating storage boxes and archive shelves stacked neatly against every wall, the vast collection extending deep underground in the distance. The floor had a slight slope downward, and Cassie could imagine it continuing for forever into the shadows, a vast archive the size of a football field at least, buried under the main college grounds.

Pulling out her notebook, Cassie began to make her way down one of the aisles, looking for some kind of system to the storage. She found a reference desk midway down the aisle, with a diagram showing the filing system: the years she wanted were buried in the middle of a set of library stacks, in boxes marked with the date and color coding.

Cassie settled cross-legged on the floor in the aisle between the shelves and got to work, checking each box in turn and sifting through their contents. Rutledge had been right: everything related to college life was stored down here, with little thought to consequence or order. In one box she found a stack of menus from the dining hall bundled beside chaplain's reports and handwritten minutes from a meeting of the bursars; in another, a collection of snapshots from a lively college dance and a haphazard stack of student essays.

She was thorough and methodical, hunting carefully through the night for any mention of Joanna Blackwell, but still Cassie found nothing. She saw the same student names appear over and over, until she felt intimately acquainted with the class of '95, but the one name she longed to see more than anything still eluded her.

Finally Cassie lifted her head from the files and yawned. She checked her phone. There was no reception here underground, but her clock told

her it was after 1 A.M. She deliberated how much longer she could keep searching. She shouldn't stay out too long; Evie's hours were erratic, and there was no telling when her roommate might come home, or go looking through her purse for something and find the pass-card gone.

Cassie assessed the boxes around her. Just another couple of hours, that should be long enough to find something. If there was anything here to find at all. She stretched her aching muscles and bent her head again to check the next box, reaching for a file marked "Yearbook." Inside lay a stack of loose photos, remnants from that year, she supposed. Now-familiar faces flashed past as she flipped through the scenes: students in the bar, sporting teams, formal dinners. The fashions were grungy and draped, and Cassie noted with amusement that she'd seen several groups of students around town that afternoon outfitted in a similar way, the cycle of fashion turning full circle.

Then she froze, her blood turning to ice in her veins.

Joanna.

Her mother had been snapped in a candid photo wearing the crimson-and-black Raleigh sports uniform, a hockey stick slung over her shoulder. She was turned away from the camera, only her head glancing back, as if someone had caught her attention at the last moment.

She was real. It was true. Cassie's heart pounded as she flipped the photograph over.

Margaret Madison. Raleigh Hockey X11.

Margaret? Cassie blinked. But before she could check the box again, she heard the sound of a door closing, loud in the thick silence of the vaults. She froze, looking wildly around. Heavy footsteps were approaching down the stone corridor, getting closer to the library.

There was no time to get the lights, or clear the mess of boxes and papers she'd pulled down. Cassie tucked the photograph into her sweat-shirt pocket and shrank back against the library stacks, scuttling quickly down the aisle to take cover behind a long shelf of hardbound books, out of sight of the front entrance.

The heavy footsteps came to a stop just inside the vaults. Cassie silently moved a book aside and peered through the gap in the shelves.

It was one of the porters, a man she'd never seen before: in his forties, perhaps, with a pinched face and a potbelly bulging under his coat. He looked around the room with deep-set eyes. "Hello?" he called out. "Anybody here?"

Cassie shrank back out of sight and held her breath. The man's footsteps sounded again, and she peered back through the stacks, hoping he was leaving. But instead he continued down the aisle and came to a stop by her corner of research. He took in the mess of files. "This is a restricted area." The man's voice rang out sternly. "You'd do well to come out now, and we'll sort this out."

Cassie backed away from her vantage point, panic rising. She wondered if she could fake it: saunter out of the stacks and play the overworked student, try and hurry past him before he had a chance to question her closely. But he could demand to see her pass-card. He might know Evie personally from around college, and then she'd be caught for trespassing, and stealing her roommate's access card in the bargain.

No. She would just have to stay hidden until he left. Cassie pulled her hood up over her head and melted into an alcove, waiting for the porter to tire of this mystery and return to the lodge for a cup of coffee and the racing post. But instead he began a methodical search of the space, pacing in turn up and down each aisle.

Cassie squeezed her eyes shut for a moment, desperately trying to think of an escape. The layout of the room was all wrong: she had no way of dashing for the main entrance without revealing herself, and back behind her there was only darkness and endless rows of library stacks receding down the gentle slope into the black.

The footsteps sounded louder, closer.

A familiar heat began to rise in Cassie's chest. The squeezing choke, cornered and desperate. Cassie clutched at her pendant and tried to think clearly. There had to be another way out. She hitched her bag and

quickly tiptoed down the aisle, deeper into the vaults, doing her best to tread silently on the dusty concrete floors.

The deeper she plunged into the unknown, the thicker the air seemed, dense and untouched. Then she felt a whisper of fresh air dance across her face.

She stopped. The draft was coming from the wall beside her. As she moved closer she could see this section was hung with a dense tapestry, and when Cassie lifted it aside, she found a narrow passage and a spiral staircase cut into the stone, twisting upward.

"Hey!" The shout came from behind her. Cassie spun around to find a flashlight beam, bright and dazzling from the end of the aisle. The porter started toward her. "Stop!" he called.

Cassie bolted into the passageway and raced up the stairs. She could hear the porter chasing loudly after her, his labored breathing echoing in the narrow space. Higher she climbed, heart pounding, praying fervently that she'd find an escape at the end of it, but when the ground finally leveled out, Cassie found herself in a long, narrow passage.

She raced on. The porter was still lagging on the stairs; she'd put some distance between them, but for all she knew she was racing headlong into a dead end. And then there it was, at the end of the corridor: a window set high into the far wall. She could have cried out with relief, but instead she reached up to get the catch. The hinges were rusted and stiff, but Cassie finally flung the window open and pulled herself up to the ledge.

The night air was cold and sharp after the stifling air of the vault, but she barely had time to glance down and register she was on the first floor, high above a cobblestone passageway, before the noise of the porter came again down the hall. Cassie swung her legs over the ledge and gripped hold of the rough stone ledge, lowering herself until her legs were dangling, fifteen feet above the darkness.

Cassie said a quick prayer, and let go.

She hit the ground with a shuddering jolt, rolling quickly to her side to absorb the force of the fall. But not quickly enough. Pain shot up

through her ankle, so fierce she had to bite down on her lip hard to stop the cry of agony. She struggled to her feet, feeling the sting of her grazed palms against the stones.

"Hey, you!" the porter's angry yell rang out in the dark courtyard.

Cassie turned to see him leaning out of the window above her. She quickly bent her head away from him and limped through the narrow pathway. She was toward the back of the college, by the service entrances to the kitchens; boxes were piled in heaps by the doors, and the trash bins waited in neat rows. Every step sent a fresh shard of pain ricocheting up her ankle, but she didn't have time to slow. He would be coming after her, she knew, doubling back through the vaults or taking some other route out of there.

She slipped through an archway, and through a series of small courtyards, trying to get her bearings as her heartbeat thundered loudly in her ears. This was a part of the college she'd yet to explore, away from the main study rooms and student haunts, and she lost precious time ducking down a walkway only to meet a dead end by the walls.

Cassie retraced her steps, shivering. It was still dark out, but a lamp was shining from the top of the tower, and she used it as a navigation beacon, making her way through the rabbit warren of passageways until finally she emerged into the main courtyard.

"Watch out!" The voice came as Cassie hurtled into a tall, solid mass that caught her by the arms before she could stumble. Cassie braced herself, expecting to find the porter and all his rage. Instead, she looked up to find a stranger staring back at her.

Cassie felt her breath still. He was tall and blond, in his twenties, perhaps, with his suit cut precisely over a taut, lean torso. Backlit by the glow from a nearby lamp, she would almost have said he looked angelic. Then he moved into the light, and that simple description fell away: his features were too bold, too deeply etched for such a soft, sweet description. No, this was a fallen angel: all angles and razor-cut cheekbones, his eyes unnervingly dark against the pale gold of the rest of his coloring.

His eyes met Cassie's, and she felt a chill in her chest. A flash of recognition.

"Where are you going in such a hurry?" he asked, arching an eyebrow with amusement.

Cassie stepped back fast. "I . . . the library," she managed to lie. "My computer just crashed, and I have an essay due."

His lips curled into a smile. "A fresher," he said, lingering over the words. His low drawl sent a shiver down Cassie's back. "Don't worry," he told her, smirking. "The tutors all like to scare you, but they won't bite."

"I should really . . ." Cassie gestured vaguely. She glanced behind them anxiously, expecting the porter to appear, but the courtyard was silent and still.

The man's face changed. "You're bleeding," he said quietly.

Cassie looked down at her hand. "It's nothing," she said quickly. "A scrape."

Before she could move away, the man took hold of her hand, prying the fingers open to reveal the cut.

"I'm fine," she protested again, thrown by his touch, but the man didn't let go. He ran his thumb lightly over the wound, his eyes not leaving hers. Cassie stared back, trapped. For a moment, she felt the old anger rise up in her, a surge of fierce heat. Then he pressed down, hard against her wound, and pain shot through her hand.

Cassie yanked away. "Ow!" She clasped her fist closed over the bloody wound. "What the fuck?"

"My apologies," he said smoothly, but Cassie was already backing away. She didn't have time for this, not with the porter so hot on her heels. "The library is that way," the man added, pointing in a different direction from the one in which Cassie had been heading.

"Thanks," she replied shortly and limped away without another word. She didn't look back, not until she'd found her way across campus to her rooms and up the stairs, locking the attic door tight behind her, finally safe and out of sight again.

MARGARET JOANNA MADISON.

That was her mother's real name. All the time Cassie had been fruit-lessly searching for Joanna Blackwell, she'd been looking for a lie. It was no wonder she hadn't found a mention of her online, in the student rec-ords or yellowed old newspaper clippings: the woman she knew as her mother had appeared from nowhere one day in April, when she booked the ticket for America, and left her old life behind in England for good.

Now that she knew her mother's true identity, avenues of research opened up to her again—all those dusty yearbooks she'd scanned were suddenly full of potential once more. Yet Cassie found herself hesitat-ing, reluctant to delve into the tangle of lies her mother had worked so hard to keep hidden. Arriving in Oxford, Cassie's purpose had been so clear: to find out more about her mother's time here, to discover the truth about her father's identity. She had presumed the pregnancy was what sent her mother fleeing back to America, a simple case of a college freshman making a bad decision and putting an ocean between her and the source of that mistake. But now . . .

Now Cassie remembered the ominous note. Dropping out of college and leaving the country was one thing. But Joanna hadn't stopped there. She'd changed her name, casting off her former life so as to leave no trace behind. Cassie couldn't help but feel a shiver of unease.

What had her mother been running from?

◆ ◆ ◆

As the first week passed and Michaelmas term began apace, Cassie watched Raleigh settle into its industrious term-time routine. The eager freshmen who had spilled through the college gates at all hours of the night—their drunk and raucous cries echoing up to her attic rooms— could now be found quiet in the college library, contemplating their stacks of reading material with a panicked resignation. Upperclassmen who had sauntered around campus with an easy confidence now hurried along the pathways heads down, the reality of exams and dissertations looming large. Clubs and societies settled into their sports, and soon Cassie's early morning runs were no longer so solitary as she shared her riverside route with crew teams hunched over their oars on the icy waters. Fall took hold of the grounds, turning lush green foliage to a blazing canopy of rust; blustery downpours blurred the edges of the pristine quad muddy and wet, while the winds that whipped through the courtyard and cloisters sent students and staff alike scrambling for warm down coats and ski jackets, and lamb's-wool-lined leather gloves. Cassie learned never to leave her room without a sturdy umbrella.

After the close call in the vaults, Cassie focused on her lectures and first tutorials, which thankfully passed without event—Cassie staying mostly silent as her fellow classmates argued over their essays and dominated the professors' time. She crept around the grounds with her heart in her throat, keeping one anxious eye out for the porter who'd chased her that night. She'd been wearing nondescript dark clothing, with her hood pulled low over her face—she knew it was unlikely he'd even caught a glimpse of her face, let alone be able to recognize her in the crowd—but still she couldn't help but feel her pulse race every time she hurried past the gatehouse lodge, head down, eyes fixed on the stone ground.

Then came the test. She'd been in the mail room, sorting through the usual handful of flyers and committee invitations, when he'd stepped

through the narrow doorway with a fresh batch of mail to deliver. "Sorry," she stuttered, heart in her throat. She quickly stepped aside for him to reach a mailbox near her, bracing herself for his eyes to widen with recognition, an outraged scowl to descend over his face.

But nothing of the sort had come. "No worries," he smiled at her, his eyes drifting over her face. "Blackwell?" He checked the label on her box. "I think I've got something . . . Yes, here it is." He passed her a letter and then set about distributing the rest of his stack.

It wasn't until he'd exited that she sank back against the shelf and exhaled the breath she'd been holding for days now. Reckless, that's what she'd been, stealing Evie's card and hurtling off to break into the vault without planning, without preparation. Cassie felt the ache in her ankle, fading now, and the sting of her grazed palms and knew she deserved them: punishment for risking everything she'd worked for. It had taken her years to gain entry to Raleigh's battlements, and now that she was here, she could have thrown it all away in one night.

But it had been worth it. She was closer than she'd ever been to the truth about her mother, and despite her unease, Cassie's curiosity burned too bright to be ignored. When the week had passed without incident, she gathered up her file and her newfound knowledge of Margaret Madison, and she returned to the Radcliffe Camera library in the city center.

"You're back." Elliot was pacing at the bottom of the steps of the library, one hand jammed in the pocket of his overcoat while the other, clad in fingerless gloves, clutched a cigarette. "Going to send me running up and down to the basement another hundred times?"

"If it's any consolation, you'll have the best thighs in the city," Cassie pointed out.

He laughed. "Small mercies." Stubbing out his cigarette, he held the door ajar for her. "So what are we looking for tonight?"

"Same as before," she said, passing him the request slips she'd already filled out. He looked at them and frowned.

"But you've already seen these."

"I need to look again. Sorry."

Elliot sighed. "I hate this job," he said, and disappeared into the back.

Cassie made her way into the main reading room, heading for the study carrel she'd adopted in the British history room. A figure emerged from the stacks as she entered, almost knocking into her. "I'm sorry," she apologized quickly and looked up to find her professor, Tremain, with his arms full of books.

"My fault entirely," he said automatically, then looked closer. "Ah, Miss Blackwell. A little out of your way, aren't you? Philosophy texts are on the second floor."

"I prefer it down here," she explained. "Quieter."

"Great minds think alike." He nodded, his gaze drifting around the room absentmindedly before landing back on her again. "How are you getting on with the reading list? Any problems?"

"Only finding the books," Cassie confessed. "They've all been checked out of the Raleigh library."

"Ah yes." Tremain grimaced. "It's a bad habit among some of the other students. They check them out en masse the minute I post the reading lists. You can usually find them here, though, or at the newer Social Science library. It's just a little more of a trek."

"Thanks," Cassie replied. "I'll remember that."

"Have you made it to any of the mixer events yet?" Tremain continued, juggling the books in his arms. "We have a thriving international community at Raleigh, lots of other transfer and study-abroad students."

"Maybe one day," Cassie lied.

"You should drop by. Some excellent discussions."

Cassie nodded and smiled, until Tremain glanced past her. "Well, I better get these back to the front desk before that stern fellow gives me another dressing-down." Tremain shot a look toward Elliot, then nodded at Cassie. "See you on Friday."

<p style="text-align:center">◆ ◆ ◆</p>

When Cassie returned to collect the first set of yearbooks from Elliot, she found him mournfully gazing at his cell phone.

"What's wrong?"

"I have a date tomorrow with a delightful boy from Balliol."

"And that's bad because . . . ?"

"The other clerk just quit on us yesterday and I have nobody to cover for me."

Cassie paused, spying an opportunity. "I could do it," she offered.

"Really?" Elliot narrowed his eyes suspiciously. "What's in it for you?"

She paused. The thought of scanning through five years of records all over again was a daunting prospect. Working in the library, she'd get access to all their records and vaults—plus Elliot's help. And besides, she was probably being paranoid with her secrecy. It had been almost twenty-five years since her mother was a student. Whatever had sent her running was probably long gone.

She made a calculated risk. "Maybe you could help me with something. Or rather, someone. I'm trying to find out about an old student here, Margaret Madison."

Elliot quirked an eyebrow. "This is what you've had me running around for? Who is she, anyway?"

"She's a . . . family friend," Cassie lied. "She died a few years back. I'd love to find out more about her time here, maybe talk to some of her old classmates."

There was a noise; Tremain was by the doors, fumbling with an umbrella. Cassie watched him finally force it open and head out, slamming the door behind him.

She turned back. "Do you think you could help?"

"Cover for me tomorrow, and the information is yours."

"Done!" Cassie felt her spirits lift. "Do you have time to look for anything now?" she asked hopefully.

Elliot snorted. "Easy, girl. I have five thousand returns to process before closing. I'll get to this as soon as I can," he added, tucking the slip in his pocket. "Thursday or Friday at the latest."

Cassie bit back her disappointment. "Thanks," she managed. She'd waited years to get the answers she needed; she could wait another few days. "I really appreciate it."

With nothing to distract her any longer, Cassie spent the rest of the afternoon working on her essay for Tremain's class. His tips about the reading lists paid off, and Cassie was able to gather most of the resources before settling in back at the attic, deep in theories of corporeal existence and proof of their own existence.

In a way, Cassie could relate to Descartes, and his philosophical kin. They were men in search of certainty and truth, desperate for a system by which to view the world and make sense of all its contradictions and falsehoods. They were enemies of assumption, soldiers for fact, willing to dismantle brick by brick everything they had once believed about themselves—and the world around them—in order to rebuild a more solid foundation. Descartes was asking not just what made him himself, but what, if any, of the external world could really be proven to exist.

Cassie knew his frustration. The story of her life, her mother's life, had always been a fixed point on a shifting horizon—the basic frame of reference for everything she thought she knew about herself. If it was all a lie, then who was her mother? Who was Margaret Madison?

And more important, who then did that make Cassie?

"What are you working on, your first essay?" Evie's voice interrupted Cassie's thoughts. She looked up to find her roommate digging through the laundry hamper, wearing a long, floating black dress with tangles of gold chain necklaces falling from her throat.

"Yup." Cassie sighed. "My first philosophy tute is tomorrow. I think I'm done, but I don't know . . ."

"Don't worry about it," Evie reassured her. "They always make a big deal about the essays, but the truth is as long as you show up ready to discuss the reading material you'll be fine."

"I hope so." Cassie thought of Professor Tremain. He'd seemed encouraging, but that was only because she'd barely said a word so far in class.

"You need a break!" Evie decided. "You've been hiding away for weeks now. Come out and have a drink with me."

"That's kind, but I'm not really in the mood for a night out."

"It's not 'out,' not really," Evie argued. "The Senior Common Room is having a mixer. It's barely across campus."

"Would I have to put on pants?" Cassie countered.

Evie grinned. "C'mon. I'm not taking no for an answer, not this time. One drink," she proposed. "All this work isn't healthy. You need to pace yourself, otherwise you'll crack before we get to Christmas break."

Cassie smiled. "Fine," she reluctantly agreed. It might not be a bad idea to go out with Evie, to take a break from her mother's ghost and all the studying she still had left to do. "One drink."

They arrived to find the room already hot, full of people talking loudly over music, clutching wineglasses and small china plates of crackers and cheese. Cassie looked around, curious. As an undergraduate, she was officially a member of the Junior Common Room. Undergrads had their rooms on the other side of cloisters: a large TV room filled with old couches, and a general room with a pool table and vending machines. Cassie had peeked her head around the door once to find a riot of noise and activity, the teenagers gathering to play loud music on the entertainment system and watch Australian soaps all evening.

The SCR was smaller, but more lavishly appointed, with views over the back lawns, leather seating, and a small bar area with polished countertops and rows of liquor bottles that glittered in the evening lights.

"Let me see who's here . . ." Evie scanned the room as her cell phone let out a buzz. She glanced down, her expression dropping. "Oh shit,

Paige got dumped. Listen, will you be okay if I run out for a sec? I promise I won't be long!"

Cassie opened her mouth to object, but Evie was already gone, her handset pressed to her ear. "The bastard!" Cassie heard her say. "I'm on my way."

Cassie was tempted to turn right back around again, but she'd changed into real clothes at Evie's urging, and even run a brush through her hair. Her roommate had said she wouldn't be gone long. Cassie could wait fifteen minutes, at least.

The room was packed, so she took a glass of red wine from the full table by the bar and slipped through the crowd, listening to snatches of conversation about European tax policy and South Pacific biological research. For the first time since arriving at Raleigh, she was mixing with people her own age, but now a new tremor of insecurity rose in her chest. These were the real Oxford students: brilliant scholars from all over the world. She couldn't help but feel like an impostor next to their sincere dedication to their studies.

Cassie found a seat on the wide, cushioned ledge of an open window and sipped her wine, watching the crowd and waiting for Evie to return. Observing the scene, she noticed the lack of diversity in the room. In fact, Oxford in general had shocked her on this point: from the sea of pale first-year faces in the Raleigh matriculation photo to the overwhelming whiteness on the streets of the city. Just like the Ivy League, this was clearly still the home of the old elites, for all the self-satisfied talk of diversity and inclusion she'd skimmed through in the college brochures.

"Welcome to Raleigh." A voice behind her made Cassie turn. A blond man in his late twenties smiled at her, earnest in a pin-striped shirt and corduroy pants. "I'm Miles. Whereabouts are you from?" he asked, before taking a large bite of cracker. Tiny crumbs cascaded down his shirt, and he swiped at them, flushing.

"Smith," she replied.

He brightened. "Ah, Massachusetts. I spent a semester at Harvard as

a research fellow, under Professor MacIntyre. Don't suppose you know him?"

She shook her head. "No, sorry."

"Ah well." He took another bite. Another torrent of crumbs scattered to the carpet. "What brings you over here? I'm doing my postdoc in international law."

"Junior year abroad," Cassie explained. "I got the Raleigh Scholarship."

His eyes widened. "Impressive!" Miles caught a woman as she passed, tugging her into our circle. "Devi, this is the one you were talking about, the girl who snatched the scholarship this year?"

The woman, who was Southeast Asian, raised an eyebrow, assessing Cassie. She had her dark hair pulled back in a loose braid and wore a severe navy shift dress. "Congratulations," she said in a cool tone. "My cousin made it through to the final interviews. He already received his bachelor's degree in biochemistry from Harvard and was named a young musician of the year for his piano concertos." She offered a wan smile. "You must have a very impressive résumé to have won the prize."

Cassie cleared her throat, feeling even more inadequate. "And lucky, I guess."

Devi twitched an eyebrow again.

"Tell us about your summer," Miles urged her, before turning to Cassie. "Devi was working with the refugee camps in Somalia," he explained. "She's studying displacement and rape as a weapon of—" He broke off, catching sight of someone across the room. "Hugo!" he cried, taking off through the crowd without a backward glance, his voice carrying. "What are you doing back, you old rotter? I thought they were finally giving you the heave-ho!"

Devi launched into a description of her time on the Ethiopian border, but Cassie's gaze stayed with Miles, following him to a group of people holding court in the corner of the room. They were dressed for dinner, in formal suits and starched shirts, and the studied way they held their

wineglasses and tilted back their heads in laughter made Cassie think of a scene from an Oscar Wilde play, or some foreign painter's frieze. As she watched, their bodies shifted, revealing the young man in the center of the group, the focus of Miles's adoring enthusiasm.

She froze.

It was the man from that night, the one who'd caught her in the courtyard. Now, even out of the darkness, he was as striking as before: dressed in another expensive suit, draped languidly over his frame, the crisp white shirt open at his throat, revealing skin a pale gold in the lamplight.

He looked up, catching Cassie's gaze from across the room with his dark, piercing stare. She flinched back as if burned and quickly looked away.

" . . . security, you wonder what we're paying for." Devi was still talking, but Cassie could barely hear a word. Her heart was suddenly racing, a shiver of something new in her veins: panic, mixed with curiosity and fear. The potent cocktail sent adrenaline spinning through her bloodstream, and she felt too restless to stay still a moment longer.

She slipped down from the windowsill, bumping against Devi as the crowd shifted again. "I'm sorry," she apologized quickly, glancing back across the room. The blond man had been swallowed out of sight, but Cassie's unease remained, a hot surge prickling her skin.

"I said, did you hear about the break-in?" Devi repeated. "Apparently someone was rifling through the old archives the other night."

Cassie snapped her head back around. "Hmm? Oh, no, I didn't." She cleared her throat quickly and made an effort to speak normally. "Did they steal anything of value?"

"Nothing was taken," a petite woman with cropped hair said, joining them with a gossiping expression on her round face. "And Harris didn't get a good look at him."

"I wonder if it was a rival academic," Devi mused. "The Raleigh libraries are first-rate."

"Why not just sign up for a reading pass?" the other woman argued. "I think they were looking for rare first editions. You know the college has a whole stash of Raleigh's manuscripts locked away somewhere."

Cassie tried to focus on the conversation, but she felt a burning on the back of her skin again, a shiver of awareness. She glanced back across the room, already knowing she would find him watching her.

He was leaning against the bar, a wineglass tilted in one hand, his dark eyes fixed on her. She knew she should look away but was unable to drag her gaze away from the elegance of his face. The moment stretched between them, shimmering in the hot, packed room.

Then he raised his glass to her in a toast, his expression still unreadable. Cassie felt his curiosity even through the crowd. Curiosity, and something more, that same recognition that she'd felt when they met in the courtyard that night. His gaze trailed across her body, and Cassie felt as if she was naked.

Hunger. That was it: the sharp glint in his eyes. The realization broke Cassie from her trance. She reeled back. He was approaching now, weaving through the crowd toward her. Cassie grabbed for her coat. She needed to get away, and fast. She'd felt the urge to escape before, on dark streets, and in empty, echoing buildings. It had saved her too many times, and now it was beating so loudly she couldn't ignore it if she tried.

She turned her back on Devi and the other woman without even a mumbled explanation, hurrying through the crowd back toward the exit. But as she approached the door, she found her escape blocked.

"Cassie!" Evie caught her in a hug. "Thanks for waiting; God, the drama never ends. Come meet everyone, I was just telling them about you—"

"I'm sorry." Cassie tore away from the friendly embrace. "I have to go. I'll see you later!"

If Evie replied, her voice was lost in the crowd. Cassie took the stairs two at a time. She stumbled down to the cloisters and fled into the dark of the college, until the noise of music and laughter faded into the night.

DESPITE SETTING HER ALARM, CASSIE WOKE LATE, AND SHE HAD to scramble to arrive at her philosophy tutorial in time. She'd wanted to be poised and prepared, but instead she found herself hurrying across the Raleigh campus with her shirt hanging loose and an empty growl in her stomach. As the chimes of the college clock boomed out nine strokes, she turned the corner to the cloisters.

Cassie heard laughter as she rushed up the stairs, and when she opened Tremain's door she found the professor handing out cups of coffee to the two other students. "Sorry," she apologized, as the chimes faded away outside the window.

"Miss Blackwell," he said coolly. "Good of you to join us. I'd ask how you take your coffee, but I'm afraid refreshments are only served to those who make it promptly to class."

Cassie took a seat, confused. Tremain had never seemed like a stickler for punctuality; last week, he'd been the one to show up ten minutes late, with jam staining his shirt collar.

The other girl, Julia, gave her a sympathetic smile. She was slight and dark, her hair pinned neatly up behind her head, her blouse starched beneath a mint green cashmere V-necked sweater. Across from them sat Sebastian, a large, athletic-looking boy slouching on the leather wing-back chair with one leg propped over the other and a smug expression on his face.

"Who wants to start?" Tremain folded himself into his rickety chair and looked around. "Miss Blackwell, perhaps."

Cassie felt a tremor of nerves, followed with sharp relief when Sebastian spoke over her. "I'll go first."

"Works for me," Cassie breathed quickly. Julia said nothing at all, simply waited with her pen held, poised for action.

"Very well." Tremain nodded, rifling through his papers before pulling out what Cassie assumed to be the boy's essay: a thick stack of papers, printed with dense black type. "Whenever you're ready."

Sebastian cleared his throat. "Does Descartes show that he is not a body?" he began. "How does Descartes think mind and body are related?" He launched into a discussion of empirical thought that left Cassie struggling to keep up. The essay question had seemed straightforward enough to her in the dim light of her midnight attic, but now Sebastian was dissecting theories of authors she had never read, devoting whole paragraphs to different interpretations of a single phrase.

"Good work." Tremain rewarded Sebastian with the briefest of nods. "Now, about distinctness and separation," he continued. "Did Descartes think that the mind and body were potentially or actually separate?"

Julia took in a breath. "Actually?"

Tremain turned. "Is that a statement or a question?"

Julia checked back through her notes. "A statement," she responded, her voice becoming surer. "Descartes thought that if two things could be separated, they were distinct, whether or not they were apart."

Tremain doled out another approving nod. "As Margaret Wilson noted in her critiques."

"But that whole argument rests on an assumption of the existence of a God to separate them," Sebastian argued, and soon they were engaged in fierce debate, with barely a thought for Cassie, silent on the end of the couch. Not for the first time, Cassie was glad to be left unnoticed, watching the clock on the mantelpiece count down to her escape.

"Miss Blackwell."

She snapped her head up to find Professor Tremain arching an eyebrow at her. "What do you think about Descartes's thesis that he is solely a thinking thing?"

"I . . ." Cassie glanced down at her notebook, as if the crosshatch of aimless lines would hold some answer. In other rooms—other lives—she would have relished the chance to bluff and argue, but all her usual confidence had fled, and even she recognized that she was out of her depth. Just as her silence was becoming unbearably awkward, the bells began to chime ten o'clock. Tremain gave a nod.

"That's enough." He closed his leather-bound file. "We can explore the meditations more next week. Perhaps an essay on error and the will; check Williams again, maybe some Carriero too."

The others collected their things and exited, but Cassie was stopped by a sharp summons. "Miss Blackwell?"

Cassie turned, bracing herself. Professor Tremain held her essay paper aloft, gripped between his thumb and forefinger as if dangling something particularly distasteful. She approached him and took it, expecting a river of red ink, but to her surprise, there was not a single notation on the pages. No comments, or angry strikeouts. Cassie looked back at him in confusion.

"I think we both know it would be futile to bother with that." Tremain's eyes bored into her, coal black with derision. "I'd rather you turned in nothing at all than something so amateurish."

Cassie felt her cheeks flush. "I'm sorry," she said. "I thought I was getting the hang of it, but I guess I'm still finding my feet here. I'll do better next week."

"That's what I thought last time. I let your lackluster effort slide then, but two weeks at this level is unacceptable."

Cassie felt the sting of criticism. "I'm sorry," she murmured again, feeling like a failure. She bundled the offending pages in her bag and turned to make her escape.

"I read your file," Tremain added, stopping her short. "I sit on the Raleigh scholarship committee. I had my concerns then about awarding you the place. Raleigh is an exacting academic environment. Filling it with substandard candidates does the rest of us a disservice. Your classmates, for example, should have enjoyed another perspective in their debate, instead of . . . what was it you brought to mind? An addled spectator at Wimbledon."

"I can do better," Cassie protested. "Now I've seen the way you expect—"

Tremain cut her off. "Some things can't come with practice. Either you have a grasp of the fundamentals, an intuition for argument, or you don't. To pretend otherwise is a foolish error. Let's not forget your place here is dependent on your grades. If we don't see progress, and fast, we may have to terminate your scholarship."

Cassie took a breath, opening her mouth to respond, but Tremain was already looking away, flipping through a stack of papers on his desk. She was clearly dismissed.

As she made her way back through the cloisters, Cassie burned with anger. What gave him the right to speak to her like that? She'd dealt with her share of high-minded professors at Smith—the patronizing, the world-weary, the men too wrapped up in their own quest for academic glories to bother with something so lowly as teaching mere undergraduates—but she'd never in all her years of education come across one as dismissive as Professor Tremain. Weren't tutors supposed to teach, to nurture and encourage? Her mind was to be molded, her potential realized, but Tremain had only looked at a single essay—no, before that, her application file!—to decide Cassie wasn't worthy of his time and expertise.

But as quickly as the anger swept through her, it receded, leaving Cassie with a new fear. She hadn't realized her study-abroad place could be rescinded. She could be sent back to America empty-handed. Locked

out of the hunt for her mother's past for good—and just when she was beginning to find answers.

She couldn't let that happen.

Cassie felt worn-out by the time she arrived back at the attic. She found Evie yawning, wearing a crumpled nightshirt, a phone trapped between her bare shoulder and ear. "Want to grab breakfast?" she whispered, dark shadows under her eyes. "I'll be ready in ten minutes."

"I'll jump in the shower," Cassie agreed, glad for the chance to recover from her tutorial ordeal. She ran the water as hot as she could bear, and stood, head bent, under the torrent. The bathroom was old-fashioned, equipped with a claw-foot bath and mustard tiling that had survived decades, if not longer, but the shower was blissfully modern and soon filled the small room with a haze of steam. Cassie let the water beat into her tired muscles, trying to send her tension and unease away. One bad tutorial, that's all it had been. Professor Tremain was simply trying to scare some diligence into her. She would have to put her research into Margaret aside, give herself more time with the next assignment.

She lost track of time under the fierce heat of the water. When she remembered Evie and their breakfast date, Cassie wrenched off the faucet and wrapped a towel around her body, piling her wet hair on top of her head. "Sorry," she called, emerging from the bathroom. "Just let me grab some clothes, and I'll be ready."

"Don't feel the need to dress on my account." The voice was male and edged with wry amusement. Cassie froze, two steps into the living room, and found herself staring into piercing dark eyes.

It was *him*.

Blond hair, angled cheekbones. He lounged on the couch, relaxed and totally self-assured. Cassie's heartbeat quickened as she took him in, remembering their strange encounter in the midnight courtyard, and his predatory stare at the mixer.

He rose from the sofa and approached. "Hugo Mandeville," he introduced himself, those dark eyes trailing over Cassie's naked shoulders, still dripping wet. She paused a moment, clutching her towel. Her mind raced. Had he tracked her down somehow?

"You must be the roommate we've been hearing so much about." He smiled. "Evie is . . . Well, I don't know where she went, but the door was open, so she can't be far."

Evie. They were friends then, that was the reason he was here, Cassie realized, not to accuse her over the break-in at the vaults.

Cassie breathed in relief as Hugo extended a hand and reached slowly to shake hers. His fingers were cool and long, like a concert pianist's, but his skin seemed to burn against hers. Cassie snatched her hand away almost immediately, bringing it back to clasp her towel tight around her chest. She was painfully aware of her body, naked under the thin towel.

"How's your hand?"

Cassie blinked. "What?"

"You hurt your hand, that night." Hugo looked at her curiously. "I didn't recognize you for a moment, without the . . ." He gestured to his eyes, to indicate the layers of eyeliner and mascara Cassie usually wore. "You should leave it off more often," he added, his lips curving in a smile. "You're prettier this way."

She stared, thrown by the comment. Up close, Hugo's eyes were lined with thick lashes, flecked with a gold that gave a strange halo to those fathomless dark irises.

"Did you want something?" Finally, Cassie found her voice. "I can tell Evie you stopped by."

A flicker of amusement crossed Hugo's face, as if he could tell how unsettled she was. "I'll wait." As he spoke, he sat back down on the sofa, completely at ease. "Aren't you going to offer me tea—or a coffee, perhaps; that's more American, isn't it?"

Before Cassie could reply, Evie piled through the door, laughing. "He didn't!"

"I swear it, right on the floor at Annabelle's." Another voice trailed her in, followed a second later by its owner, the girl who had so unceremoniously ejected Cassie from her first dorm room. Olivia.

"Hugo!" Evie lit up. She had pulled a men's black cashmere sweater over her nightshirt and applied a slash of bright pink lipstick. "Perfect timing. This is my new roommate; she just had a tute, poor thing. Remember those days?"

"Remember?" Olivia hugged Evie from behind, kissing her cheek affectionately. She was wearing black jeans and an elegant white T-shirt slouched off one shoulder, a tangle of gold chains Cassie recognized as belonging to Evie twisted around her neck. "I have finals this year; I have nothing but bloody sleepless nights ahead."

Hugo. Cassie looked back at him and realized Olivia had been calling to him in the stairs at Carlton Hall when she'd evicted Cassie from her room. They must be related; there was a definite resemblance in the honeyed tone of their hair, and the sharp angles of their profile—not enough to be siblings, perhaps, but bound by blood in some way.

"Please," Evie giggled, rolling her eyes expressively. "Until you have thesis advisers on your back all day, you don't get to complain."

Hugo laughed. "I hate to pull rank, but I've been pulling all-nighters and thesis meltdowns for seven years now, so none of you know my pain." He sauntered over to Evie and dropped a casual kiss on her lips. "Ready to go?"

"Cassie?" Evie turned, expectant. "Coming?"

Cassie faltered. She'd been looking forward to breakfast with Evie, but the prospect of a group trip—with this effortlessly elegant clique, and Hugo's smirk of watchful amusement—was different. "I don't know . . ." she demurred. "I still need to get dressed—"

Olivia tugged on Evie's arm, brandishing her cell phone. "Evie, come look!"

Evie crowded around to see. "No!"

"Ladies!" Hugo sighed. "Can we perhaps move this somewhere with

coffee, before I grow old and weary and have another five years in this place pass me by?"

"It's your own fault, cuz." Olivia thumped his arm good-naturedly as she passed. "Daddy says if you'd just finish the damn thesis and graduate . . ."

"Ah, but why would I do that, when there are so many delicious distractions around?" Hugo swept Evie into a hug, burying his face in her neck. She squealed, protesting, but it was clear from her smile that she was delighted. Hugo's eyes met Cassie's for a moment over Evie's head. He gave her an arched, teasing smile, a small, private expression that, to Cassie, felt dangerously intimate. She turned away.

At last, with Hugo's urging, the group hustled out into the stairway. Evie turned back almost as an afterthought. "Cassie, do you want to come? We can wait down in the lodge, if you want. I need to check my mail."

"No, it's fine." Cassie forced a smile. She was already backing away in the direction of her room, anxious to put a locked door between her and Hugo. "I'm too tired. I'm just going to crash."

"Okay, then come out with us tonight," Evie insisted, still flushed and bright-eyed. "We're getting drinks at Freud's; you must come."

"No." Her reply was sharp, but Cassie quickly softened her tone. "I have an appointment. Some other time."

"Oh! I forgot to ask." Evie blinked at her. "How was the essay?"

"Fine," Cassie answered quietly. "It went fine."

"Okay, sleep tight!" Evie blew a kiss, and then was gone, her laughter echoing in the stairwell and up through the open windows as the group emerged in the courtyard below. Cassie moved to the windows and watched them go, Olivia and Evie with their arms linked, still bent over Olivia's cell phone, while Hugo matched their pace. The sunlight caught in their hair, glowing and vibrant; their voices rang with happiness.

For the first time in a long while, Cassie felt a pang of loneliness.

SHE ONLY MEANT TO REST BRIEFLY, BUT WHEN CASSIE WOKE, THE light was fading outside her windows. She slowly swung her feet to the floor. She'd dreamed of Indiana again, playing in the orchard while her mother shelled peas for dinner and sang along to the radio. Now, in a cold, empty room, her loss was something real and solid in her chest, a longing for the past Cassie had relentlessly kept at bay all these years, folding it into a smaller and smaller space in her heart, out of the way of her everyday life.

Disoriented, she shook off the cobwebs of slumber. She was due at the Radcliffe Camera to cover for Elliot.

When Cassie reached the library, she found Elliot pacing impatiently by the front desk. "You're here, great, okay. Let me give you the tour."

He led her back through an arched passageway into the hidden depths of the building. Behind the scenes, Cassie discovered that the library facilities were far less grand than the front rooms; what funds they had were clearly spent on the upkeep of the elegant reading room furniture and the plush carpets of the curving stairs, not the warren-like maze of maintenance and storage rooms kept out of sight of the library guests. Elliot quickly showed her around the endless twisting stone corridors and perilous spiral staircases to the echoing vaults beneath the ground level. It was like the Raleigh vaults, only on a much grander scale: stadium-sized warehouse rooms filled with hundreds of thousands of books, the packed shelving stretching deep into the distance.

"Take the request slips, check the system log here, then go fetch," Elliot explained, checking his watch. "A trained monkey could do it, no offense."

"None taken," Cassie replied. There was a hush in the library, a warm glow from the lamps on the walls. It was cozy and felt like a safe retreat, far from Raleigh and Hugo's piercing gaze. "I'll be fine. You should get going for your hot date."

"Okay." Elliot looked around. "That's everything, I think. I'll be back to close at midnight. Oh, and I forgot, I looked into that friend of yours, Margaret."

"You did?" Cassie caught her breath, her heart suddenly racing. "Did you find anything?"

"Just call me King of the Vaults," Elliot preened. He pulled a slim file from under the circulation desk. "Some of my best work, if I do say so myself, considering the time limits."

Cassie snatched the folder, eager. "Thank you," she said. "I really appreciate it."

"Let's just hope my date is worth it," Elliot replied. "Try not to burn the building down while I'm gone." He left her with a salute.

Cassie took a seat behind the desk. The evening library was still and silent, even the dedicated academics of Oxford having a better way to spend their Friday nights than locked among the dusty stacks. She was alone with the past.

True to his word, Elliot had done a thorough job. He'd started with the most readily available source: the same Raleigh yearbooks Cassie had fruitlessly searched. Now, with Margaret Madison as the subject, Elliot had found more: her mother's face, sandwiched in the back of a group matriculation photo—lined up beneath the Raleigh tower just as Cassie had stood on that first day of term. Margaret's name, listed as part of the girls' hockey team; news of an award for English composition, and a poem, published in the dense record, to accompany photographs of the college grounds in winter. There were richer details too, which

Elliot had dug from sources Cassie didn't even know existed: copies of the Raleigh student rolls, broken down by subject group, and dormitory listings showing Margaret had occupied rooms above the West Quad. Tutor names, sporting activities. Newspaper clippings mentioning her team achievements, and a photo of her in a group of girls wearing matching fancy dress outfits, breathless from some charity run.

Cassie drank it all in. Here, at last, was a real window into her mother's life, so vivid she could almost see her: laughing on the quad between classes, hanging out in the Raleigh bar with her teammates, late at night. She felt a pang of grief well up. The woman Cassie had known was an anxious loner, uncomfortable in crowds, never one to form close friendships no matter what town they moved to or which whirl of her manic phase was under way. But here she was, looking normal and cheery, just a regular college freshman brimming over with excitement and possibilities.

Cassie had never known this side of her mother, and now she never would.

The night passed uneventfully, with a few requests from researchers. Cassie was left to contemplate the file until Elliot returned after midnight to close up, his cheeks flushed and his sweater askew.

"Good date?" Cassie asked, teasing.

"A gentleman doesn't kiss and tell," Elliot replied with a wink. He looked at the file spread out on the desk. "Was the info any help? Like I said, I'm just getting started. I thought I'd make a list of her old classmates next. The intake was small that year, only ten other students in her English class, so it shouldn't be too hard to find someone who knew her."

Cassie paused. She'd been secretive about her search to date, but curiosity was winning out. "That might be a good idea." Cassie nodded. "Either way, this was just what I needed."

"I'll let you know when I dig up something more." Elliot glanced around. "No problems tonight?"

"Nothing to report." Cassie pulled on her coat. "Some kids were making out in the Egyptian room, but I left them to it. And I know you said to leave the returns for you to deal with, but I didn't have anything else to do, so I checked them back in and reshelved them downstairs."

Elliot gave her a look. "Well, aren't we industrious? You know, if you enjoy slaving away for a pittance, we're looking to replace the clerk who just quit on me, said something about a hostile work environment . . ." He rolled his eyes. "The job's yours if you want it."

"I do," Cassie replied immediately. Her savings and stipend wouldn't last for long, and although Raleigh's official policies frowned on students holding jobs during term time, they surely couldn't find fault with the respected library. She would be able to access the archives any time she liked.

"I'll tell the boss and have you come in for a proper interview." Elliot yawned. "Now, be gone before I rope you into tidying up."

"Good night." Cassie turned to leave but Elliot called after her

"Be careful. They found a girl by the river the other week, strangled to death."

Cassie stopped. "Was she a student?"

He shrugged. "I don't know. Local girl, I think. But it's a big bad city, so be sure to watch your back."

"Don't worry," Cassie reassured him. "I can take care of myself."

She was almost home when she remembered that she'd meant to go grocery shopping that afternoon; there was no food up in the attics. She hitched her bag and kept walking, striking out north across Magdalen Bridge and up Cowley Road, which snaked through the outskirts of the city. Here, the streets were wide, cracked concrete, rumbling with local traffic and public buses, and lined with a grimy patchwork of twenty-four-hour Indian take-out stores, discount supermarkets, and church thrift stores advertising cut-price electric goods and community luncheons.

Cassie walked briskly, remembering Elliot's warnings. This part of Oxford was a far cry from the elegant city spires, but tonight the change of scenery was a relief. Away from the distractions of the library, her mind circled back to a face she'd rather forget. Hugo. The memory of him in her living room rattled in her mind. She could see him now, that dark, piercing stare, those casual, elusive smiles, as if he knew a secret and wouldn't tell.

She shook the thoughts away, arriving at the large, neon-lit supermarket she'd found on a past exploration. It was half empty at this hour, with only a few lone shoppers pushing their carts up and down the wide, stacked aisles. Cassie picked up a basket and began to wander, picking out cheap food, pasta, tinned sauces, end-of-day cuts of meat she could freeze or make into a nourishing stew. Eventually, she made her way back to the checkout aisles and unloaded her basket onto the conveyor belt. The shop assistant was a bored-looking teenager, a girl with bleached hair and a yawning expression. She began to ring up the sales, as Cassie kept a watchful eye on the register total.

"And here we are again." The voice came from behind her. Cassie turned to find the jogger she kept encountering moving into line behind her. He grinned, setting his basket down on the conveyor. "Charlie, remember?" he told her. "And you're Cassie."

Cassie looked him over. He was dressed casually tonight, in jeans and a faded T-shirt that stretched over muscular, tanned arms. Under his open parka she made out the faded logo of the Rolling Stones emblazoned on the front, and recent scabs healing on the knuckles of his right hand. His smiling gaze scanned the contents of her basket and he whistled. "Anyone ever tell you to eat a vegetable? You'll get scurvy at this rate."

"Anyone ever tell you to mind your own business?"

He laughed, undeterred. "Some fruit would help with those mood swings too. Happy chemicals, and all."

Cassie looked down at his shopping: two six-packs of beer and a

bag of potato chips. "Because you're really the guy to lecture me about proper nutrition."

Charlie clutched his chest. "A direct hit! She wounds me."

Cassie tried not to smile.

"Twenty-two seventy." The checkout girl yawned. Cassie turned back to her, and carefully counted out the foreign banknotes, loading her groceries into her backpack.

"You need help with that?" Charlie offered, trailing her forward in the aisle.

"I've got it," Cassie replied, hoisting the bag onto her back.

"Suit yourself." Charlie gave the checkout girl a wink. "Modern women, they can do everything themselves. Won't need us for anything soon."

Outside, the midnight streets were dark and quiet, lit by the flickering neon of the streetlights overhead and the occasional headlights beaming from a passing car. Cassie pulled her jacket tighter against the late chill and set off back toward college, but she was only halfway down the street when she heard her name called from behind her.

She turned. Charlie was walking briskly toward her, a plastic bag swinging from his hand. "Which way are you heading?"

"Home." Cassie hoped he'd finally take a hint, but when she turned away and started walking again, he fell into pace, his long strides easily matching hers.

"Me too. Ain't that a coincidence." He pulled a crumpled packet of cigarettes from his jacket pocket and offered it to her.

"I don't smoke."

Charlie shrugged. "Me neither," he agreed, pulling one out and producing a lighter. He lit it, and took a long drag. "I quit six months ago. Nasty things. They'll kill you one day."

Cassie continued briskly down the street, but Charlie stayed beside her. When she turned across the road and he followed, Cassie stopped abruptly on the corner. "What are you doing?"

"Walking you home," Charlie announced matter-of-factly. "It's not safe out here, late at night."

"No."

"No what?" Charlie grinned again.

"No to everything," Cassie snapped. She knew how this went. He would walk her back, then hover expectantly outside the door, suggest a coffee, perhaps, or ask to see her place. She was supposed to feel indebted, obliged to him, swayed by the charming anecdotes he'd tell, and the persistence of his attention. She was supposed to give him whatever he wanted. "This isn't going to end in my bedroom, okay?"

A look of amusement flitted across his face. "Don't get the wrong idea. I'm just keeping an eye out. You never know what kind of big, bad beasts are out there, lurking in the shadows."

Cassie gave a bitter laugh. "It's not those beasts I'm worried about. You're the one who won't leave me alone."

Charlie looked wounded. "Hey now, that was uncalled for."

"Was it?" Cassie sighed. It was late, and she was too tired for this. "I don't know you. I don't know anything about you. You're just some guy who keeps showing up, and now you're following me home. For all I know, you're going to leave my body in the river."

"Hey," he protested. "It's not like that. I have the full backing of the Oxfordshire County Police Department, see?" He pulled a badge from his pocket and opened it for her. "Police Constable Charles Day."

Cassie looked at the badge, peering in the dim light at his identification photo and the official stamp. She snorted. "Just because you're a cop doesn't make you safe. In my experience, you guys are the ones I have to worry about."

Charlie's smile faded. "You don't have to be such a bitch about it."

"Why not?" Cassie shot back. "I didn't ask you to keep talking to me, or come after me now. I can take care of myself."

"Clearly." Charlie gave a sullen shrug, hands back in his pockets. The light was gone from his expression, and he looked almost hurt enough for Cassie to take it back. "I was just trying to be nice."

"Don't," Cassie said firmly. She walked away, fast on the empty street, her footsteps a sharp rhythm of anger on the dark sidewalk. This time, Charlie didn't follow. She crossed another intersection alone and was turning up toward the bridge when the sound of footsteps came again. She turned, ready to yell at Charlie again, but nobody was there, just a stray cat scuffling in the gutter for scraps.

Cassie shivered. She pulled her jacket tighter around her and hurried back toward the lights of the city.

⭢ 1 1 ⭠

CASSIE WOKE TO SCREAMS.

She lifted her head, groggy. She was at the table again, arms splayed over her philosophy reading, with a sheet of her notes stuck to her cheek, ink smudged with drool. She peeled the page off, yawning, reality and her dream world still tangled and opaque.

There was another scream.

Cassie lurched to her feet. The noise was coming from Evie's room, and it increased as Cassie approached: a babble of screams and unintelligible softer whimpers.

Cassie tapped on the door. "Evie? Are you okay?"

There was no response, only another cry, cut off halfway. Cassie flung upon the door, expecting to find a struggle, but Evie was alone. She was still sleeping, illuminated in the pool of neon light falling through her open bedroom window. Her oversized nightshirt was twisted, the covers thrown off the bed as she writhed, clawing at some unknown assailant.

Cassie crossed quickly to her bedside. "Evie, sweetie, it's okay." She shook the girl's shoulder gently, not wanting to pull her too sharply from her dreams. "Evie, wake up now."

Evie recoiled from her touch, retreating to the far side of the bed and curling, knees pressed tightly to her chest. She was sobbing, muttering a strange babble of words that Cassie couldn't make out.

"Evie!" Cassie shook Evie harder, raising her voice to a shout. "Wake up!"

Evie awoke with a gasp. She blinked, her whole body trembling, eyes darting in the dark room.

"It's okay," Cassie told her, quickly flipping on the bedside lamp. The room filled with a warm glow, the shadows suddenly receding. "It's me. You had a nightmare, but it's all right now."

Evie caught her breath. She gripped Cassie's hand as slowly her eyes adjusted to the light. "A nightmare?" she said, her voice still uncertain.

"Just a dream." Cassie gently rubbed her shoulder. "You okay?"

Evie nodded slowly. "Yes. Yes, I think so . . ."

Cassie pulled back. She hadn't realized, but she'd been holding her breath too. "Look at you, you're like ice," she said, rising to her feet. The room was freezing, sending the hairs on her arms rising. She crossed to pull the window shut, latching it firmly. "You shouldn't leave the window open like that, you'll catch a chill."

Outside, the first streaks of dawn were crossing the Oxford skyline. Cassie tied the curtains firmly back and turned. Evie was still sitting huddled on the bed, blinking and lost. Cassie pulled the thick terry-cloth robe from the back of Evie's door and draped it around her shoulders. "How about I make us a cup of tea? Tea, and some of those fancy Choco Leibniz cookies. I'll go put the kettle on."

Cassie settled Evie on the living room couch, wrapped in her robe and an ancient woolen blanket from the cupboard. She turned on every light, filling the attic with a bright, warm glow that seemed to seep into Evie, bringing her color back as Cassie fussed around the small kitchen. "The cure for all ailments, right?" she said, bringing over the tray.

Evie smiled—stronger this time—and reached for her cup. "But only real builder's tea," she agreed. "None of that Assam and rose petal stuff."

There was silence for a moment as they both sipped their drinks. Cassie took a chocolate-covered biscuit and slowly dipped it in the tea, a custom she'd learned from watching the other patrons in the bookshop café. The trick was to leave the biscuit in the hot liquid long enough to start to melt the chocolate, but not so long that the biscuit broke off. Fo-

cusing on the simple task, she felt herself slowly relax. The sound of the screaming had sent Cassie back to the nights her mother would sob and babble, rushing half asleep to pluck Cassie from her bed. It was the medication, she'd been told many times, but that was little comfort when her mother's cries cut through the thin walls.

"Do you get nightmares often?" she asked Evie.

Evie shook her head. "I didn't used to, but now . . ." She sighed, clutching her mug of tea between two small, slight hands. "It's probably stress. My thesis adviser keeps on me to settle on a specific research angle, and I have outlines due, and teaching . . ." She trailed off, looking overwhelmed. Cassie could only imagine. She was worried enough about her own studies, but that was nothing compared to Evie's load, preparing for a thesis with all the research and teaching hours too.

"Maybe it's time to cut back on the partying," Cassie suggested carefully. Evie was still maintaining a whirlwind social calendar with Olivia, Hugo, and their fashionable crowd: out every day for lunches, afternoons spent in the exclusive Oxford Union buildings across town. Cassie had expected the early partying to fade, or at very least be relegated to weekends, but Evie was still coming home late almost every day of the week. Up close, without her makeup, Cassie could see it was taking its toll; the shadows under Evie's eyes were smudged and translucent, her skin dull.

Evie gave a rueful grin. "Probably. I don't know how those guys manage it. Practice, I guess. You know Hugo's been working on his thesis here for five years now?"

Cassie flinched at the mention. "What's holding him back?"

"I don't know. He doesn't like to talk about it." Evie smiled, her affection clear. "You should come out and have a drink with us sometime. He's always telling me to invite you along."

"I've got enough on my plate," Cassie hedged. "It's my turn to read my essay this week and I can't give Tremain another chance to tear me apart."

"He won't," Evie reassured her. "I've seen how much work you've been doing; he won't have the chance."

"I hope so." Cassie managed a smile. "You want to join me and make a study day of it? It's supposed to rain all afternoon. I'm going out for a run, but after that I'll be working straight through."

"I don't know." Evie bit her lip. "I'm supposed to meet the girls for brunch, and then shop for gowns for the Christmas balls. . . . But you're right," she decided finally. "If I finish a proposal, it'll get my adviser off my case, and I'll have more time for fun over the weekend."

"There you go," Cassie said, relieved Evie would be getting some rest. "I'll grab some food on the way back for us. It'll be fun."

Cassie sprinted hard, her breath fogging the early morning air as her feet pounded the riverbank path, now frozen and tough beneath her stride. She let her mind empty, focusing only on the flow of breath into her body and the satisfying ache in her limbs. By the time she looped back past the meadows to the side gates, her face was numb from the cold and her muscles screaming their protest. She bent double to recover, panting for air, as the college bells chimed seven. Gradually, her pulse began to slow.

"How's it looking out there?" the elderly porter, Rutledge, asked, when she ducked into the lodge to check her mail.

"Same as usual." Cassie nodded her greeting. "Colder, though."

He chuckled. "You just wait until January," he warned her, busily sorting a stack of parcels. "They'll be out cutting ice to let the rowers through." He took a gulp of coffee from his Raleigh mug and nodded at the clutter of junk mail in her hand. "Anything from home?" he asked.

Cassie gave a hollow laugh. "No. It's just me."

"Sorry to hear it," Rutledge replied, just as Cassie realized her mistake. According to the cover story she'd spun for Raleigh, she had a pair of devoted, adoring parents waiting for her back in America. It was only a small slip, but she couldn't be too careful.

"I mean, they're busy," she quickly covered. "We talk more on the phone."

"Technology." Rutledge shook his head with a bemused expression. "I remember when letters took three weeks. Now I Skype with my niece all the time, over in France." He took another drink of his coffee. "Whereabouts is it you're from, anyway? Boston?"

She shook her head. "Indiana, way out in the middle. But we moved around a lot."

"And what brought you all this way?"

She gave him a smile as she turned to leave. "Why does anyone come to Raleigh? History."

She made her way through the gatehouse and out onto the main street outside. Half a block away stood Harvey's—a deli/sandwich shop that was apparently as much a daytime staple to the Raleigh students as Ahmed's kebab van was come nightfall. Ever since Evie had introduced her to it, Cassie had found it the perfect place for an inexpensive—if not entirely nutritious—meal, and she often detoured there after her runs to wait in line in the small, fog-steamed storefront to claim a hearty breakfast bap of sausage, egg, and lashings of tomato ketchup.

That day, the line was only a few people deep. Cassie took her place in the queue, turning her attention to the day of study ahead. Her next philosophy tutorial with Tremain was the next morning, and she hoped to have her essay written and submitted by the end of the day, leaving plenty of time for a long night's rest so that she would be alert and prepared to defend it.

This time, Cassie was determined to prove Tremain wrong. He thought she was a waste of the place, that she wasn't up to the standard of her classmates, but Cassie knew he was wrong. She might not have attended the best schools like them, enjoyed private tutors and costly after-school activities, but she could hold her own.

She had to. With the threat of expulsion hanging over her head, there was too much at stake to fail over poor grades. She wouldn't be

intimidated by Tremain's sneering; she would find a way to change his mind.

The line inched forward, until Cassie drew level with the glass-fronted cabinet filled with containers of wafer-sliced salami, crumbling chicken, and salad, dripping with oil. The grill behind the counter hissed, staff moving in a practiced ballet around one another to expertly crack eggs onto the blackened hot plate, flipping and sliding orders along as the demands kept coming. They had her order filled and packaged in barely a couple of minutes.

"What about the Merton ball?"

A pair of girls was walking in front of Cassie, effortlessly fashionable, even bundled in their autumn wear, the ubiquitous Raleigh college scarves looped around their necks.

"Not this year." Their voices drifted back to Cassie. "It's been a bore over there ever since Freddie and the gang graduated."

"What about your dear professor?"

"Oh, right. Whoops!" The girls laughed, and Cassie realized one of them was Olivia Mandeville, with a dark-haired girl Cassie hadn't seen before. They paused at the traffic lights, and Olivia turned, noticing Cassie three paces behind them.

"Oh, hi!" She bobbed forward, kissing Cassie on both cheeks before she had time to react. Olivia's blue eyes shone; her cheeks were pink with the cold. "You found Harvey's then?" she said, noticing Cassie's brown paper packages steaming in the cold air. "You have to try the bacon and brie, it's divine." She turned back to the other girl. "Paige, this is Cassie, Evie's roommate."

"Oh, of course." Paige scanned Cassie from head to toe with a curious stare. "Lovely to meet you."

The lights changed, and Cassie fell into step with them, crossing toward Raleigh's imposing front gates.

"How are you liking it so far?" Olivia asked in a friendly voice, a world away from her calculated smiles the first time they'd met. "Evie says you're doing PPE."

"It's . . . an experience," Cassie replied evenly.

Olivia laughed. "You'll have to come out with us sometime; there's a whole city you never see stuck in here. Where is Eves, anyway? She was supposed to meet us for breakfast."

"She's feeling under the weather," Cassie told them as they entered the courtyard. Students were bustling across campus, and a group of early tourists was milling about under Rutledge's watchful gaze, waiting for a guided tour to start.

"What a shame. Shall we come by with a care package, cheer her up?"

"Maybe later," Cassie said. "I think she's just resting today."

"It's this bloody flu." Olivia sighed. "Everyone's dropping like flies. Send our best, will you?"

The girls took off toward the cloisters, drawing attention from the group of tourists as they passed. Cassie watched them go. There was something glamorous about Olivia, paired with easy confidence; she was always relaxed and secure like a gleaming gemstone against the gray weather and scruffy students.

Girls like Olivia had always fascinated her, the way the world parted so easily to let them through. Here in Oxford, it was magnified: the circles of old private-school friends and boarding-school chums strolling about the city like they owned it. And perhaps they did, sharing a comfort and security the rest of them never knew. Vacations and first drunken nights sneaking champagne from their parents' wine cellars; a sprawling web of friends, and cousins, and old classmates that stretched so wide they need never be faced with a room of unfriendly strangers. Cassie envied their security, their certainty of their place in the world. They would never have to face the judgmental stares of strangers or wonder for a second about the correct protocol for a formal dinner or event.

They would never be told that they weren't good enough, that they didn't belong.

*She made it to the attic just as the sky broke, and the few splatters of driz-*zle were replaced with a torrential downpour. Cassie opened the door to her rooms to find Evie looking more like her usual self. Dressed in a capricious cashmere sweater and flowing woolly skirt, she was flitting between her bedroom and the living room, unloading great armfuls of files and paperwork in crooked stacks on the large, low coffee table.

Cassie shrugged off her damp sweatshirt, hanging it on the radiator to dry.

"I need to look at the big picture," Evie announced, slamming down another stack of loose-leaf notes. The pages shivered at the impact and slipped out of order, drifting to the floor. "I'm spending too much time caught up in the small details; I have to see how it all fits together. What Raleigh and the group were trying to achieve, their manifesto, instead of all the historical minutiae. If I figure out their purpose, it should give me mine: a broad thesis of intellectual ambition, and how it related to the Crown and church. They were on the forefront of everything: Science, arts, literature . . . right here in Oxford. I need to find the link that bound them together, and how it shaped the evolution of the fields." Evie stopped. "Sorry, listen to me. I guess I just need a sounding board."

"Sound away." Cassie smiled, glad to see Evie's cheeks flushed with determination and the haunted look in her eyes replaced with something livelier. Although the skies outside were cloudy and wet, the attic was bright with lamplight, and with such a bustle of life and activity now filling the small apartment, the dark terrors of night seemed like a distant dream.

Leaving the food packages on the table, Cassie drifted closer to the table, seeing photocopies of old documents and curled, typewritten pages. "I found some papers by an undergrad from years ago," Evie explained. "She was looking at the myths and conspiracy theories surrounding the School of Night, but she led me to a whole new cache of

documents. Well, new old. They've been sitting down in the vaults for decades, can you believe it? If it wasn't for that break-in the other week, nobody would have remembered they were even down there."

"I'm glad you found something useful." Cassie hid her smile.

"Not yet, but I will." Evie exhaled, looking around at her piles of notes. "Eventually." She shook her head swiftly, as if to snap out of the contemplative mood, and wandered over to the kitchen. "Ooh, you got food. Thanks so much!"

"No problem." Cassie joined her, pulling down plates from the drying rack and unpacking the wedge of paper napkins. Her breakfast sandwich was still warm, oozing ketchup and the vinegary brown sauce Cassie had become so attached to since arriving in England. "I ran into Olivia," she remembered. "And this other girl too, Paige."

"You did?" Immediately, Evie brightened. "Aren't they the best?"

Cassie nodded slowly. "They said they hoped you felt better."

"They're just great. I can't believe we only just met this term; we have a ton of people in common."

Cassie was surprised. "You seem so close, I assumed you guys went way back."

"I know, right?" Evie took another bite. "That's how it is sometimes, I suppose—you run into someone here and find out they spent their summers in the next villa along, and their sister dated your best friend from riding camp."

Not for everyone. Cassie thought back to her friends and neighbors in Indiana. She wasn't likely to meet any of them here, so far away.

After their lunch, Evie bent her head over a thick stack of essays, and Cassie returned to her philosophy essay, cozy in the attic as the rain slashed against their windows. But only a couple of hours had passed when Evie's phone sounded with a chirp. She glanced at the screen, and then snatched it up. "Hi you," she breathed, voice low and intimate.

Cassie tried to focus on her books. It was Hugo—she could tell from the delight in Evie's voice and the coy giggle she sounded in response to whatever he said. "I can't," she murmured, wavering. "I have to work . . . No, you know I can't . . . I have that outline due, remember?" As Cassie watched, Evie blushed, biting her lip in indecision. "Hugo, I can't. No . . . Without me? You wouldn't . . ." Finally she laughed. "Okay, all right. I'll be down in ten." She snapped the phone shut and leaped up. "They're going down to London," she explained. "It's Miles's birthday."

"What about the outline?" Cassie asked. "Another late night, after what happened . . . ? You need your rest."

"I feel fine," Evie insisted, already heading for her room. "Hugo says we won't be out too late. One or two at the most. And he really wants me there . . ." Her face slipped into the secret smile again, and Cassie knew there would be no stopping her.

"Have fun," Cassie told her, accepting defeat. "Think of me, working the night away, while you're off sipping champagne."

Evie laughed, and soon she was out the door, leaving Cassie alone for the evening. The rain continued its soothing drum against the attic windows, and she read on.

" . . . SO DESCARTES'S ATTEMPTS TO RECONCILE A BENEVOLENT God with errors in human judgment are fundamentally flawed, and his reliance on faulty interaction between understanding and will cannot support his larger argument."

Cassie lowered her paper and took a deep breath, trying to calm her fluttering nerves. She was back in Tremain's study, and all the attention was on her. She'd gone overboard preparing: proofreading her essay three times and submitting it well before the six P.M. deadline. This morning she'd arrived, alert and neatly dressed, long before the nine o'clock bells began to chime, carrying a freshly printed copy to read aloud. She'd even declined the begrudging offer of a cup of espresso, for fear of knocking it to the floor and doing irreparable damage to the antique rug. Now she waited, looking to Tremain for some indication of approval, any reaction at all.

The professor scribbled a note in his leather-bound file and gave the slightest of nods. "Mr. Rhodes?"

Sebastian raised his head from the Moleskine notebook that, from her angle, Cassie could see was hollowed to contain a slim phone. Julia sat across from them, but as usual remained silent. Sebastian had barely glanced over as Cassie read, instead absorbed by whatever he was surreptitiously reading on-screen. "Well, clearly he didn't have a leg to stand on."

There was a pause. "Would you care to expand on that?" Tremain prompted.

Sebastian shrugged. "They were all pretty much stuck, weren't they? I mean, as long as you try and bring God into the equation, everything else falls apart. There's an irony to it, really: all these men going on about certain knowledge and fact, and then wiping it all away with their ancient ideas about God."

"You find the two incompatible?" Tremain raised an eyebrow.

"Not just me, all of the analysis." Sebastian lifted his lip in a superior sneer. "For supposedly smart men, they were all rather stupid. Why bother wading through all that history if it all relies on a faulty premise?"

Cassie happened to be looking at Professor Tremain as Sebastian spoke and saw the change in his expression, an almost-imperceptible stiffening of his jaw. "Is that how you feel about our curriculum?" Tremain asked, his voice quiet. "A waste of your precious time?"

Sebastian seemed to realize his mistake. "I . . . no, I was just saying, I mean . . ." He blustered, finally lost for words.

Tremain regarded him coolly. "Perhaps your classmates agree? Miss Jessops? Miss Blackwell?"

Julia slouched lower in her seat, shaking her head, eyes wide.

"I don't," Cassie said, her voice clear in the small room. "Even if their arguments were flawed, they're a reflection of the era. We're looking at the evolution of the debate here," she added, with a look to Sebastian. "You can't just take what we know now and cast off everything that came before. That doesn't tell you anything about how we got here, how the arguments developed. It's all nothing without context." Cassie kept her tone controlled, but there was a special fervor to her voice. "Nobody— not ideas, or people, or things—exist as their pure current state; everyone and everything is the product of their past. Acting like that doesn't matter is willfully naive at best."

Sebastian's face darkened, but Tremain let out a chuckle. "Well said, Miss Blackwell," he said, and Cassie felt a wave of relief. "Now, Mr. Rhodes, you're excused."

Sebastian startled, and even Julia looked up from her notes in shock. "What?"

"From the tutorial." Tremain let his gaze slide across to him. "Since discussing flawed reasoning holds no interest for you, I think it's best you leave. Perhaps you can study Miss Blackwell's essay and return next week more willing to participate."

Sebastian flushed, an angry mottled color. He opened his mouth as if to protest, and then closed it again. Shooting Cassie a look of pure venom, he grabbed his coat and strode to the door. His footsteps echoed angrily down the staircase.

Professor Tremain waited until the sound had faded, then lifted his copy of Cassie's essay, stone-faced again. "Miss Blackwell, let's discuss your points about limitless will. I have some issues with your theories on dual faculty reasoning . . ."

Cassie made it through the tutorial with her nerves—and scholarship— intact. Although Tremain tried to trip her up with questions, she was able to keep it together and defend her essay until at last the college bells rang out, signaling the end of the session.

"Your structure is still sloppy," Tremain added as a final word, passing her back the essay that was now covered in red marks. "We don't have time to play catch-up with you every week."

Cassie gritted her teeth and held back her retorts until she was safely out of the room.

"He's not always like this," Julia offered, as they made their way downstairs. "He's the nice one. At least, he used to be. I don't know what's happened this year."

Cassie watched as Julia scurried away. Just her luck. Cassie sighed, crossing the courtyard and ducking into the mail room, brushing past a girl who came bolting out of the room at full speed. "Hey," Cassie protested, but the girl was already gone, the brim of her winter cap pulled low over her eyes.

Cassie found her pidge and sorted though the mail, still thinking about Tremain and his inscrutable glare. Flyers, society leaflets—and a photograph.

She stopped, her breath freezing in her chest.

It was her mother, Joanna. *No,* Cassie corrected herself, *Margaret;* she was wearing a formal gown, arms linked with another girl, flanked by two boys in tuxedos. They were posing at a dinner table set with silver and polished goblets, in a room somewhere with portraits on the wall.

Cassie turned the photo over, her heart racing.

Black is the badge of hell, the hue of dungeons, and the school of night.

She felt a shiver of fear. Then it hit her: there was no envelope, no address on the photo. Somebody had delivered it in person. Somebody who knew the truth about who she was—and what she was looking for.

Her secret was out.

Cassie rushed straight to the Radcliffe library. She found Elliot in the back room cataloging returns. "Did you send this to me?" she demanded, putting the photo on the desk in front of him.

Elliot barely glanced at it. "Nope," he replied, distracted. "Say, are you free for a shift this afternoon? I know we haven't done the paperwork yet, but I'm snowed under."

"Are you sure it wasn't you?" Cassie asked again. "Elliot, look. Does this look familiar at all?"

The panicked note in her voice made him look up properly this time. "I've never seen that. But it's Margaret, right?" Elliot studied her, curious. "What's going on? Where did you find it?"

Cassie quickly caught her breath, trying to sound calm. "Someone put it in my mail. It must have been one of my other friends, that's all."

Elliot gave her a look, as if he was unconvinced, but didn't press. He flipped the photo over and read the back. Then he sounded a laugh. "Somebody's big on intrigue."

"What?" Cassie asked. "Where's that from? I don't know what it means."

Elliot slid his wheeled desk chair across the floor. "Here . . ." He clicked through on the computer, loading a search site. A moment later, the same quote appeared on-screen. "It's from *Love's Labour's Lost*. Meant to refer to Sir Walter Raleigh and his cabal of dastardly atheists."

"You mean the founders of the college?" Cassie asked, recognizing the names listed on-screen. "My roommate is doing her research into them. She says they were at the forefront of all the big advances of the time. An intellectual group."

"Or, as many think, a corrupt secret society who ruled the country through scurrilous means," Elliot said, smirking.

"You don't sound convinced."

"Do I think a group of intellectuals hung out in the sixteen hundreds, chatting about God and literature? Yes." Elliot gave her a look over the rims of his black square-framed spectacles. "Do I think they were an all-powerful secret society whose influence still runs the country today? Not so much."

Cassie perched on a bench nearby. "People think the School of Night is still around?"

"Rumors and legend." Elliot shrugged dismissively, turning back to his card catalog. "If Oxford held even half the secret societies people say it does, you and I and every person in the city would have to be a member. Don't get me wrong, there are groups around," he added. "Drinking societies, so-called secret groups. But they're just excuses for overprivileged children to dress up and prance around with secret code words. The real power you need to worry about is out in full sight." He nodded toward the bulletin board of flyers on the wall behind her, covered with political campaign ads for the upcoming Oxford Union elections.

"But the photo." Cassie tried to focus his attention back on the most important thing. "Do you think Margaret had something to do with one of these societies? This School of Night?" She stared closely at the

photo, trying to distinguish some new clue from the frozen scene. The students were wearing their formal robes, but she didn't recognize the paintings behind them, so they weren't in the Raleigh dining hall.

Elliot plucked the photo out of her hands. "That's stretching a little. Odds are, they were just palling around with some rich bastards."

"But those are the people who would be part of a secret society, aren't they?" Cassie's mind ticked on, pulling apart the puzzle. "Groups like that wouldn't advertise if they were really powerful. It's supposed to be a secret."

"And therein lies the conundrum." Elliot laughed. "How do you know which drunken idiots are just pissing away the family fortunes, and which are secretly running the world?"

He kept working, scanning bar codes for returned books, but Cassie thought carefully. "Well, groups like this are always hereditary, right? Legacy students, passed down from generation to generation. They don't just invite anyone, they keep things private, to their own kind."

"I guess." Elliot shrugged, not taking it seriously. "Welcome to the joys of the British class system."

Cassie drummed her fingertips on the pockmarked old desk. "So how do I find out more about this School of Night?"

Elliot sighed. "You really want to track them down? Find a group of the most obnoxious rich bastards in this whole place. Odds are it'll be them."

"Elliot," Cassie protested. "I'm serious."

"I know you are, but this is just someone messing with you," Elliot insisted. "If you want to know more about your Margaret, just call up her old classmates and ask. You don't need to go chasing after conspiracy theories. Now, do you want to help with these returns? I was supposed to be done already, but *someone's* been distracting me."

*Cassie stayed until evening, helping Elliot and working on her own stud-*ies. She decided to take his advice and use the class rolls to try and

track down Margaret's old classmates. It was a risk, especially now that somebody knew she was looking for Margaret, but Cassie told herself she was being paranoid. She needed the information, and there was no harm in seeing if anyone remembered anything. They'd scattered by now, some as far afield as China and Australia, but a few were still living in London and even Oxford itself. She sent a short e-mail, explaining she was a friend of the family looking to talk about Margaret's time in college; hopefully at least a few of the former students would reply.

By the time she arrived back at Raleigh, it was almost dinnertime, and students were making their way in the direction of the grand dining hall, decked out in their flowing black formal robes. Twice a week Raleigh hosted a "formal hall"—a lavish three-course meal complete with wait service and wines, for which ceremonial robes and RSVP payment was required. Cassie had never attended, but she knew it was popular with the other students, who enjoyed inviting visiting family or friends from neighboring colleges and dressing up in their fancier clothing. They would gather in some of the event rooms for cocktails beforehand, and often afterward too, tipsy laughter echoing late into the night.

When Cassie walked in the door, Evie was getting ready to leave, fixing on a pair of sparkling diamond earrings and shimmying her feet into a pair of heels. "There you are!" she exclaimed. "I've been waiting for you. When will you get a cell phone, like everyone else?"

"Sorry," Cassie apologized, setting down her bag. "What's up?"

"Formal hall at Merton," Evie announced, naming a college nearby. "We've got a spare ticket, want to come? It'll be fun, I promise."

"I don't know . . ." Cassie was already shaking her head.

"You're always promising to come out with me, and you never do," Evie told her, mocking a pout. "Olivia was asking after you."

Cassie paused. "Olivia will be there?"

"The whole gang." Evie nodded, slipping a lipstick into her jeweled clutch. "What do you say?"

Cassie thought fast. She wanted to talk to Evie about her research into Raleigh and the rest of the School of Night. Despite Elliot's denials, she wasn't so sure that this society was just a rumor; somebody had slipped the photo into her mailbox for a reason, and if the group still existed . . . If her mother had been involved with one of Oxford's most elite secret societies . . .

There were too many questions whirling around her mind, shadows and possibilities, but Cassie knew she wasn't going to discover the truth holed up alone in her garret or cloistered in the library. She needed access to the most exclusive social circles in the city for her answers. And there were none more exclusive than the Mandevilles and their clique.

"Okay," Cassie agreed.

Evie gasped in surprise. "Really?"

"Really." Cassie laughed at her shocked expression. "I'm in."

MERTON COLLEGE WAS HIDDEN DOWN A COBBLED BACKSTREET lined with old-fashioned streetlamps. The traffic and city noise from High Street faded as Cassie followed Evie up to the main gates, their footsteps clattering on the uneven paving stones.

Cassie looked around, intrigued to go behind the walls of another college. When they ducked through the wooden gatehouse, they emerged into a small courtyard. While there was a chapel, and wings of sandy brick three stories high, manicured quads and squares radiating out from the long pathways, it was nothing compared to the scale and grandeur of Raleigh's great spread of buildings. Instead, the college was thick with history, age showing in the thin slit windows carved deep into the buildings they passed, the faint curve of the buckling supports, and the scarred cobblestones underfoot.

"It was built back in the thirteenth century," Evie explained.

"Before Raleigh?"

Evie nodded. "There was a big rivalry when Sir Walter Raleigh moved in. He got the lands as part of his reward for his naval victories, and he swore he'd built the grandest college in the city. It wasn't as prestigious as it is now," she added. "People were suspicious of academics. With the church and Crown in such upheaval, it was dangerous just to be associated with the colleges."

"I guess that's why so many groups gathered in secret, right?" Cassie said.

Evie nodded, leading them across the courtyard. "All it took was one wrong lecture, and you could be brought up on charges of heresy or treason. It's why it's been so hard for me to find original source materials. I thought the college would have plenty among Raleigh's archives, but they were all pretty cagey with their correspondence. Nobody talked about their meetings at all, even though I know from secondhand sources that they all met regularly, every month here at the college, sometimes more."

Cassie was just about to ask more about these group meetings when the bells chimed through the courtyard for dinner. They joined the crowd heading up the stone staircase to the grand dining hall. She tugged awkwardly on her hem. Evie had insisted on lending her a dress for the occasion, and although Cassie had rejected all the wispier chiffon outfits, she had finally submitted and accepted the loan of a simple dress in deepest black silk. The bodice hugged her torso, but she was several inches taller than Evie, so the hemline skimmed several inches above her knees. Even swathed in her usual thick down coat, with her formal robe layered over the top, Cassie felt exposed, vulnerable to the brisk winds that played around her. Still, as she glanced around at the other students and diners slowly filing into the building, she was glad of the outfit, and Evie's simple gold bangle on her wrist.

Inside, the dining hall was wood-paneled and imposing. After weeks at Raleigh, Cassie was used to the style: high arched ceilings and long tables running the length of the room, adorned with heavy silver place settings and vases brimming with white roses and lilies.

"Evie!" The call came from across the room, and Evie quickly led them through the crowd. The Mandeville group was clustered at a table near the head of the room: Paige, Olivia, and Hugo with a few others, all of them dapper in formal suits and glittering cocktail dresses.

"You made it." Hugo rose to kiss Evie on the cheek. "You didn't say you were bringing company." His eyes drifted over to Cassie. "Good to see you again, Cassie."

Cassie tried not to react to his dark stare. "You too," she murmured, busying herself by taking off her coat and carefully folding her scarf into a small, neat square as the others exchanged their usual round of air-kiss greetings. She was so focused on ignoring Hugo that she was startled to hear someone greet her by name.

"Cassie, good to see you again." It was Miles, Cassie recognized, the blond man from the drinks mixer. He was wearing a suit with a small red bow tie, and he reached to shake her hand enthusiastically. "How are you settling in? Any three A.M. breakdowns yet?"

"Not yet." Cassie smiled. "But it's early days."

"Don't say that," Evie scolded. "She's doing great. I can't imagine it, getting plunged into everything without any time to adjust. We all at least were freshers first."

"Are you crazy?" Miles asked, eyes wide with drama. "First year was the worst. I nearly dropped out half a dozen times. I was going to go set up a surf shop in Brazil," he told Cassie, pulling out a chair for her to take her seat.

"Why didn't you?" Evie asked, moving to a free place beside them.

"No, Evie, you're here with me," Olivia interrupted, patting the free space beside her. Evie obediently circled the table as Hugo spoke up, answering for Miles.

"Because he hates the water and can hardly swim." Hugo slid into a seat directly across from Cassie. He met her gaze with a small knowing smile. "Don't listen to a word of it. Last month he was convinced he should go live in an ashram for a year."

"I should," Miles protested, shaking out his cloth napkin with a dramatic gesture. "Inner calm would serve me a whole lot better in life than this bloody doctorate."

They all laughed, and Cassie felt herself relax, just a little. She'd been wary, bracing herself for the same chilly indifference she experienced from her classmates in her tutorials at Raleigh, but instead, the group seemed welcoming and warm.

"That's a cute purse," Olivia remarked from Cassie's other side, as the waitstaff began to circulate with wine and water.

Cassie glanced down at the only part of the outfit that was her own, a small box clutch with gold detailing. "Oh, thanks."

"Vintage?"

"Uh, yes." Cassie had found it for a pound in a thrift store on Cowley Road.

"The best things are." Olivia sipped her wine and glanced around the room, eyes drifting over the crowd. "Lewis," she called out. Cassie watched her flutter a wave to an older man. In his thirties, he wore the traditional professor's tweed jacket and a boyish, eager grin that stretched across his face as he hurried over to their table, jostling a waiter on his way.

"Sorry, so sorry," he stammered in apology, arriving at Olivia's side with flushed cheeks. "Liv, if I'd known you were coming . . ."

"Last-minute thing." Olivia shrugged, leaning up to kiss him lightly on both cheeks. "Come sit by me."

Lewis looked conflicted. "I have guests."

"They can take care of themselves." Olivia's mouth curved downward into a pout. "You know how these things bore me."

"I . . . of course! I'll be right back." Lewis all but sprinted across the room.

Olivia turned back to the table and caught Cassie's observant stare. She gave a tiny shrug, her lips curving in a smile. "Sweet man. I had him for tutes last term."

"He's a professor?" Cassie was surprised. Olivia must have been twenty at the most, and from his clear adoration, she would never have guessed the man was her teacher.

"Oh yes, an expert in Renaissance art history," Olivia replied.

"That's not all he's an expert in," Paige added with a wicked grin.

Cassie dropped her voice, turning to Miles. "I didn't realize staff could date students."

"Not officially," he replied, smirking. "It's frowned upon. But no one pays attention to the rules. Especially Olivia." He gave her a meaningful look. "Playing with fire, that one. If the tabloids found out . . ."

"Why would journalists care?" Cassie asked.

"Her father, of course." Miles took in her blank look. "You don't know? Mandeville Senior is head of the opposition in Parliament. Striking distance from the prime minister's office come May, if the polling's to be believed."

"Oh." Cassie looked back across the table, where Olivia was whispering in Evie's ear, the pair of them flushed and giggling. "I didn't realize."

"Everybody here is someone," Miles continued, pointing around the table. "Paige is really Lady Pembroke, heiress to half of Gloucestershire. Harry's parents run an aeronautics company that supplies the armed forces, and Sasha's family runs one of the largest shipping companies in Europe."

"What about you?" Cassie asked.

"Me? I'm practically a peasant," Miles joked. "Aristocracy fallen on hard times, as my mother likes to say. We're up to our eyeballs in debt, will probably go into foreclosure on the estate before the year is out."

Cassie took in the crowd, wondering if they were likely suspects for the School of Night. They seemed more concerned with cocktails than any shadowy rituals, but they certainly fit the bill when it came to exclusive backgrounds.

Soon, the diners were all seated, and an elderly man seated at the dais table rose to his feet. A hush fell over the hall.

"Welcome. Professors, students, honored guests. Welcome to Merton." He paused, and everyone bent their heads. "*Oculi omnium in te respiciunt, Domine. Tu das escam illis tempore opportuno. . . .*" As he murmured what were clearly familiar words, Cassie looked around from under her eyelashes. She was struck with the sense of history, of continuity to these solemn words, how they had been performed week

after week for hundreds of years, the faces the only thing that changed in the great hall. How many times had this incantation been made—the silver candlesticks lit, the words echoing through the cavernous space as if passing back through history itself?

Cassie's eyes met Hugo's across the table. All heads around them were bent, cast low for the grace, but his gaze was steady on hers. Again, Cassie felt that instinctive shiver, a strange sense of recognition passing between them. She snapped her eyes down as the incantation drew to a close, determined to ignore him. He belonged to Evie. He shouldn't be looking at her like that.

"*Per Jesum Christum dominum nostrum, Amen.*"

"Amen," the crowd murmured, and then noise and chatter swept through the hall. Waitstaff came out, dressed in formal black outfits, expertly balancing heavy silver trays carrying the first course, and at every table, diners greeted their seatmates and refilled their glasses of wine.

"Red? White? What's your poison?" Miles asked, holding a bottle in each hand.

"Red, thanks," Cassie answered. "But only a little."

"'There's no such thing." He grinned, continuing to pour, until her glass was almost full. "To Oxford." Miles raised his glass in a toast, and around the table the others followed suit. "Long may we enjoy its bountiful fruits."

"Some, longer than others," Olivia murmured with a pointed look at her cousin.

Hugo laughed. "To Oxford."

AFTER DINNER, THE GROUP HEADED FOR THE OXFORD UNION buildings across town, piling into black cabs along with their coterie of friends and hangers-on. Dinner had been a parade of delicious, elegant food, a far cry from Cassie's usual snatched takeout. They'd started with pheasant and persimmon salad —"Bird shot on the college lands," Lewis informed them proudly—followed by filet of beef, rich and bloody. By the time the waitstaff cleared their dessert plates, which had contained tiny meringue cages filled with cream and fruit, Cassie was sitting easy in her chair, laughing along to Miles's eccentric future plans, and Paige's account of walking the runway at Paris fashion week the previous fall.

She'd accepted the invite out of curiosity, wanting to learn more about the group and maybe even the mysterious School of Night, but to her surprise she found herself enjoying the evening, lulled by the wine and friendly chatter that enveloped the group. Cassie's usual sense of being other, somehow, adrift from her fellow students and their cut-glass accents, melted away under the twinkling chandeliers, until she felt the warmth of being included, on the inside at last. She sat sandwiched between Miles and Evie in the cab after dinner, the city slowly passing outside the windows in a blur of shadows and neon streetlights, until they were ejected, stretching, on a familiar patch of cobbled street, close to Blackwell's and the other shops of the high street that now sat empty and still.

Cassie was confused when the cab stopped on the street close to Blackwell's and Miles directed them down a backstreet to a Victorian-

style redbrick building. "This is the students' union?" she asked. "I thought that was across town, in the big concrete block."

"They're both called the union." Hugo looked amused as they approached the entrance, lined with crumbling pillars and an elaborate stone portcullis. "There's a general union organization, but this is a private, members'-only club."

"They're famous for the debates," Evie added. "They've had all kinds speak here: prime ministers, presidents, even Madonna."

Cassie looked around with interest as they filed inside. The decor was more of the English hunting style she'd become so used to since arriving in Oxford, wood beams overhead and dark leather wingback chairs arranged around low antique coffee tables. Groups of students and older adults clustered in corners, enjoying their evening drinks.

Cassie paused, recognizing the thickset outline of Sebastian's shoulders among them. The scene at their tutorial felt like weeks ago, though it had only occurred that morning; now he was at the bar with a couple of other athletic-looking boys. He glanced across the room, eyes widening as he saw her there. Cassie couldn't resist fluttering a wave in his direction. Sebastian's expression darkened.

"Cassie?"

She turned. Evie was waiting for her, gesturing to a staircase beyond the bar. Cassie caught up with them, leaving Sebastian and his friends behind.

Cassie followed the group upstairs to a private lounge. "The personal domain of the Union president," Miles told her grandly. Cassie looked around curiously, drinking in the scene. Here, the party was already well under way: music playing loudly, people clustered on couches and lounge chairs, passing around wineglasses and cut-glass tumblers.

She followed Hugo and Olivia as they cut through the crowd, greeted by cheers, backslapping, and air-kisses. It wasn't just Raleigh they ruled, she noted, but here too: people stepped aside to make room

and the couch was vacated for them. Soon, Cassie too was seated in the center of it all with a tumbler of fine whiskey in her hand.

"Glad you came?" Evie smiled, curled on the sofa beside Hugo.

Cassie nodded. "Thanks for dragging me out."

"My pleasure."

"How about a little bump?" Miles took a slim sachet of white powder from his breast pocket, then cut the lines of cocaine on the glass-topped coffee table. He took a first snort, then offered his rolled banknote in their direction. "Evie?"

Evie blushed and shook her head so fast her hair shimmered in the lamplight.

Olivia laughed. "Not Miss Genevieve," she drawled. "She's a good girl, aren't you?"

Evie flushed again, cheeks pink. "I have an early meeting with my supervisor!" she protested as Olivia bent her head and inhaled, tracing the neat line along the glass.

"She's kidding; we envy your virtue." Hugo dropped a casual kiss on Evie's forehead before his gaze slid over to Cassie. "What about you?" He arched an eyebrow, looking smug, as if he expected her to decline too.

Cassie felt an itch of rebellion. She usually steered clear of chemicals. Alcohol, drugs, they were all too dangerous to her hard-won self-control. But tonight, she was already off her guard. What harm would it do?

"Sure." Cassie held her hand out.

Hugo's lips curled with surprise. "Well, well, well."

Cassie ignored him, bending her head to feel the first fierce spark of the drug hitting her bloodstream. She only did half a line, but it was enough to bring the memories rushing back: the sharp itch of adrenaline, the restless burn beneath her skin. Her heart raced as she lifted her head again, finding Hugo's gaze still fixed on hers.

Her skin prickled. Cassie looked away and turned back to the group.

"Hartwell will get treasurer," a short, stout man was saying. He already had the look of middle age about him, even though Evie murmured that he was still a finalist at Christ Church. "And King president, I'd bet the house on it."

Miles must have caught Cassie's confusion, because he leaned in to translate. Apparently, Union politics was a hotbed of bribery and corruption, with students using whatever means they could to win a seat on the various steering committees and organizing associations. "Bloody hacks, running for office. Can't see the point myself."

"That's because you don't do anything that involves getting out of bed before noon," Olivia replied, getting up. She picked her way over the coffee table on bare feet and collapsed with a laugh on the other side of Evie, snuggling in close.

"I don't know why it's such a big deal," Evie remarked. "I can't imagine wanting to be treasurer or first secretary, or whatever it is. Nothing but boring meetings and budgets, on top of regular college work."

She laughed, but Olivia's expression turned stony. "It's experience, for later in life. And the status, too. Being president of the Union really means something."

"To whom?" Hugo countered. "The head of recruiting at Deloitte? Your future boss at Barclays?" His voice was scornful. "Forgive me for not wanting to join the herds on a fast track to their investment banking fortunes."

Olivia flickered her eyes skyward. "We're just saying if you're going to hang around here for God knows how long, you should at least do something constructive."

"It's called a doctorate," Hugo drawled, but Cassie could see the faint tension in his jaw. Although his body was draped casually on the sofa, one arm propped on the brocade-covered arm, there was a certain air of power about him, an intensity that was winding tighter by the moment.

"I don't see why you're so against it," Olivia snapped back. "You're too old to be rebelling just for the sake of it. You have to grow up some time."

"That, my dear cousin, is entirely up for debate." Hugo downed the last of his scotch and unfolded his limbs from the seat. "Now, I'm off to get another round, unless that's not constructive enough for you?"

He headed for the bar. Evie leaned forward for a moment, as if she wanted to go after him, but then sat back, watching him with an anxious expression. "You shouldn't push him like that," she told Olivia. "You know how it winds him up when you talk about politics."

Olivia looked impatient. "Then he shouldn't be so sensitive. He's next in line to a fucking dynasty. He's meant to be a member of Parliament already or at the very least some local government hack."

There was something bitter in Olivia's tone. "What about you?" Cassie asked. "Why don't you run for office?"

Olivia face snapped closed. "Don't be ridiculous." She laughed, but her eyes were like steel. "It's like Evie says, why would I want to spend my time on all that boring stuff when I could be out having fun?"

The conversation moved on, but Cassie watched Olivia. She'd recognized something new in her, a flash of frustration. Ambition thwarted, perhaps, or even jealousy.

Had anyone ever considered her next in line to the dynasty, or was that fate for Hugo alone? He and Olivia seemed so different, but they were more alike than they probably knew. Cassie had watched them all evening, and now she had new insight into their world. Each of them struggled against invisible restraints; Olivia, overlooked when it came to the political legacy; Hugo, bitter under that same weight. Cassie wondered what it would be like, to move through life with such high expectations. A name to live up to. A duty to fulfill. People had only ever thought the worst of her, a badge she learned to wear with grim pride.

"All this election stuff," Cassie said deliberately, spying an opening. "Isn't it all decided in back rooms anyway? I heard that the results were fixed by those secret societies."

There was silence. Cassie suddenly realized all eyes were on her.

"Which societies?" Miles asked.

"I don't know." She tried to laugh it off. "Some guy in my tutorial was just going on about how it was rigged, how everything was run by those groups."

"God, I wish," Miles snorted. "It would save us all the torment of this bloody campaign season."

"Or they could do it the old-fashioned way," another guy piped up. "Pistols at dawn on the commons, winner takes all."

The conversation moved on, and Cassie let out a private sigh of relief. She'd been clumsy, saying something outright like that. She had to be more careful; she didn't know what she was dealing with yet.

She waited until attention was elsewhere then excused herself, slipping away in search of the bathrooms. The bartender pointed her down a long passageway that, like most hallways in Oxford, was lined with old photos and portraits, reminders of the generations who built and crafted the legacy current members enjoyed. Cassie thought of Olivia and Hugo, and the Mandeville legacy they were both so sensitive about. She'd never had a family to navigate like them.

But perhaps she did.

Cassie paused, realizing for the first time that if—when—she found her father, there would be a family to go along with him. She'd never even known her grandparents, but she could have a whole sprawling network of strangers linked to her by blood: cousins, aunts, uncles. A history, a legacy of her own.

"Enjoying our illustrious forbearers?" Hugo's voice behind her made Cassie jump.

"You scared me!" She stepped back. He was too close in the narrow hallway, his eyes dark on hers. "Why are you always sneaking up on me like that?"

"Me?" Hugo looked amused. "You seem to be the one making a habit of wandering where you're not supposed to be."

Cassie remembered the night she broke into the vaults. She looked away. "I didn't realize this was a private area," she said quickly, covering.

"You're fine," Hugo replied. "If anyone asks, you're with me."

"And the Mandeville name opens doors around here?"

He shrugged. "It has its blessings. And its burdens," he added, with a dark look. "Just ask Father." Hugo nodded to one of the portraits. A blue-eyed student stared back, stiffly holding a ceremonial gavel.

"Union president, nineteen ninety-four," Cassie read the inscription.

"Grandfather's up here too, somewhere back there." Hugo pointed down the hallway. "A couple of uncles. My aunt Beatrice. Cousin James."

"But not you." Cassie recognized something in his voice, almost wistful.

"Not I." Hugo gave her a twisted smile. "I never even ran."

"Why not? It sounds like you'd have it sewn up. The great Mandeville legacy," she added lightly.

Hugo shrugged. "Legacy is a curious thing. When people have expectations . . ." He stared at the picture, deep in thought. "I wonder sometimes if I'm fighting destiny even trying to go my own way. Or if it's better just to give in and accept that my fate was set before I was even born."

Cassie felt a chill. She'd wondered the same thing, many times. If her mother's curse would be her own; the madness and instability already encoded, deep within her DNA. She could run forever and still not escape that terrible day, the stain of blood on cracked porcelain. "I don't know," she answered softly. "Maybe all you can do is try."

Hugo turned back to her, his expression thoughtful. "Why are you here?"

Cassie froze. "What do you mean?"

"Here, tonight. Partying like . . . like you're one of us. You're not."

Cassie tensed. "I'm here because I was invited," she replied, icy. "Why? Am I not important enough to enter your hallowed halls? I'm sorry that my ancestors don't merit a place on your walls, but—"

"That wasn't what I was saying," Hugo tried to interrupt.

Cassie shook her head. "I know exactly what you meant." She gave him a scornful look. "You know, for someone who is so ambivalent about

his own legacy, you're pretty quick to judge everyone else's." She turned to stride away.

"Wait," Hugo said. She didn't stop, but then he was in front of her again, blocking her path. "Really, I didn't mean it like that. I just meant you're different, that's all."

"Fine." Cassie shrugged, still tense, her heart racing.

"Listen, do you want to get dinner sometime?" Hugo asked.

She paused with a shock, certain she'd heard him wrong, but Hugo seemed sincere, hesitant even as he continued, "Or a movie maybe. I've seen you out by the art-house theater in Jericho; we could see a film, this week perhaps."

Cassie stared at him, her mind racing, trying to decipher this latest game. "You're with Evie," she said finally.

Hugo looked confused. "We're just seeing each other. It's not serious."

"Tell that to her!" Cassie exclaimed. She couldn't believe this, the ease with which Hugo could forget the girl who only moments before had been sitting across his lap.

"It's not like that—" he tried to say, but Cassie cut him off.

"No," she said sharply. "I'm not interested in whatever game it is you're playing. Just stay away from me, okay?"

She left him there in the hallway, but as she made her way back through the lounge she was stopped by a hand, heavy on her arm. Her temper flared. "What part of 'not interested' don't you understand—" Cassie whirled around, the words dying on her lips when she realized it wasn't Hugo this time, but a young blond man, his cheeks flushed with alcohol, his collar crumpled. "What do you want?" Cassie bit out.

"Another round here," he told her. "An' some of that scotch."

She shook him off. "I don't work here."

"Don't worry, James." A smug drawl came from her other side, and then Sebastian was beside her. He slowly lifted a tumbler to his lips and looked Cassie up and down with a sneer. "It's an easy mistake. Some people just look like staff, don't they? You know, I think

they're hiring. You could pick up some useful skills for when you graduate."

"You mean how to deal with childish assholes?" Cassie replied loudly. "That's okay, I get enough experience with that putting up with you."

His friend snorted with laughter, and Sebastian's smile dropped.

"See you in tute next week," Cassie said, victorious. "Try to come prepared," she added. "As Tremain said, it brings the whole quality of discussion down when you don't."

She walked away before Sebastian could reply. Back upstairs the party was louder now, and wilder. Empty bottles littered the tables, and the men had discarded their formal dinner jackets and loosened their ties; the girls were draped over the couches, hair tumbling, eye makeup smudged. Evie was lying with her limbs splayed across Olivia, half asleep on the couch. Hugo was nowhere to be seen.

Cassie made her way through the revelry to Evie. "I'm going to head out now. Are you ready to go?"

"But the party's not over," Evie protested. She cradled a wineglass, almost spilling it on her dress.

"Stay." Olivia lazily tugged on Cassie's arm. "We're just going back to Miles's place."

"Not me." Cassie managed a smile, though she was still tense. "But thanks for inviting me. This was fun. I'll see you back at college."

"Let us call you a cab," Evie said.

"No, it's fine. I feel like a walk, and college is only ten minutes away." Cassie said her good-byes and quickly hurried downstairs to the exit, wanting to escape the party before she found herself involved in another scene.

She emerged from the Union buildings onto the dark street. It was past two A.M., and the night air was cold on her bare legs. Cassie pulled her coat more tightly around her as she set off in the direction of Raleigh, passing the darkened storefronts and looming college gates along Holywell Street.

As she walked, she couldn't help but think of Hugo. She didn't understand him, how he could flirt with her so easily with Evie just upstairs. She hated to admit he affected her, those dark eyes that seemed to cut through her defenses, the shadows behind his sly and knowing smile. She could write it off as the wine and drugs, still jittery in her system, but Cassie knew the charge between them was something more. Something dangerous, something she needed to avoid at all costs.

The city was empty at this hour, not another soul in sight. Gold-tinted light pooled on the cobblestones, cast from old-fashioned wrought-iron lampposts along the street, and each college Cassie passed was lit up by the front gates, illuminating sandstone, red brick, and stone statues keeping watch from the quads. Cassie veered to take a shortcut down a winding, residential street banked with old town houses. It was darker here, empty and still, and in the quiet of the deserted street she heard the faint sound of footsteps behind her.

Cassie quickened her pace. She crossed to the other side of the street, glad she was almost back at college, and then quickly turned onto the back road that wove along the edge of Raleigh lands.

The footsteps remained, steady behind her. Cassie knew she should head straight for home, but she couldn't stop herself from pausing on the corner and turning to check behind her.

Nothing. There was no sign of life besides shadows in the street behind.

She hurried on. The gatehouse lodge closed at midnight, she knew; instead, students used the late gate, a small wooden door cut into the wall toward the rear of the college. Cassie followed the college walls along the street, already reaching for her keys, still listening for the footsteps that trailed behind the staccato tapping of her own heels.

They were there, closer now, louder.

Cassie's pulse kicked with fear, and she found herself wishing she'd taken Evie's offer of a taxi, regardless of the expense. She couldn't run in those heels, not far, and her legs were pale and bare below the black

silk of her dress. Exposed. She broke into a run as she reached the back door, hurrying to unlock it. Her hand shook, her keys scratching metal against metal until finally she fit the key in the small lock and turned. The door swung open, and she stepped quickly inside, stooping through the small opening and slamming the door shut behind her, letting out a small sigh of relief as the lock clicked back in place.

Cassie caught her breath, heart still pounding. She'd been imagining things.

The latch turned behind her.

Cassie swung around, nerves on edge, and found herself face-to-face with Sebastian again. "You . . ." she exhaled, suddenly angry. "You shouldn't follow someone like that, it's not funny."

Sebastian stared at her a second as the gate slammed shut behind him. His eyes were out of focus, faintly bloodshot in the light above the gate. "What, did you think I was some big bad beast out to get you?" His hand shot out, gripping Cassie's elbow. She flinched.

"Go sleep it off," she told him, trying to pull away.

Sebastian didn't let go.

"I mean it," Cassie told him. Sebastian glared at her, eyes narrowed in anger, and she was suddenly aware that although they were inside the Raleigh walls, they were all alone. The late gate was far from the lodge, or any of the dorms; they were in the shadow of the new auditorium building. The palatial spread of Raleigh's grounds, which had always seemed to Cassie so peaceful, now lay silent and dark. Deserted.

"Sebastian." Cassie's voice was sharp. She backed away, finding only the rough sting of the stone wall behind her. "Go sleep it off," she said again, trying to hide her panic. "You'll feel better in the morning."

"Don't tell me what to do." Sebastian's voice was slurred. Cassie's panic flared. She tried to wrench free, but Sebastian caught her wrist, trapping and scraping it against the wall.

"Sebastian, let me go. I'm warning you . . ." Cassie tried to struggle, but he was too large, too close. Her shoes offered no support, and

she stumbled back, pressed by his weight with no room to maneuver or break free.

"What?" Sebastian may have been drinking for hours, but the expression in his eyes had a frightening clarity, a hatred that burned fierce enough to send another surge of panicked adrenaline through her body. "What are you going to do?" he taunted.

Cassie swallowed. He was stronger than her, larger: his body bulky and broad. "What do you want?" she asked quietly. "Think about this," she added, trying not to let her fear show. "You don't want to do anything stupid."

It was the wrong thing to say. At the word, Sebastian's face twisted. "Stupid?" He shook her, hard. Cassie's back slammed painfully against the wall. "You're the one who made me look stupid. Did you feel good, watching him tear me down? Did it make you feel special?" He slammed her back again, this time sending her head against the stone with a crack.

Cassie felt pain burst across her skull. "Stop it!" she cried, loud, a scream in the empty night. "Stop!"

Sebastian's hand went to her throat, cutting the words short. Cassie struggled for air, flailing against him, but his weight was too heavy against her small body. "You don't ever do that to me," Sebastian growled at her, lifting her up the wall until she was dangling, scratching on her tiptoes for footing, dizzy and trapped. "You don't ever think for one minute you're better than me."

Cassie closed her eyes against the rage in his expression. The alcove was too far for anyone to hear her scream, the hour too late for any fortunate passerby. She was alone, and entirely at his mercy.

Sebastian reached for her thigh. "Do you like that?" he murmured cruelly. Cassie felt his fingers dig into her bare skin, pushing the flimsy fabric of her dress up as his breath hissed hot against her face. "You do, don't you? Fucking whore." His other hand moved to her breast, grabbing at her painfully.

Cassie opened her eyes. Sebastian paused, waiting for some reaction, but she didn't give it to him. If that was all she could do, then she wouldn't

flinch, not for a moment. With desperate concentration, she tried to separate from herself, fixing her gaze on the smudge of shadow on the auditorium wall ahead and willing herself out of her body, one more time.

She'd been here before: folding herself into a small corner of her mind and waiting for it to be done. Waiting for it all to be over. She'd thought that she was different now, that she would never let something like this happen to her again, but sometimes there wasn't a choice.

There was never a fucking choice.

"You like that?" Sebastian was still murmuring, a fervent rhythm to his words as he groped and clawed at her, fumbling with his belt.

Cassie felt bile rise in her throat. She thought she'd blocked out these memories, but her body remembered, imprinted with other hands clawing at her, someone else's breath on her cheek. She knew how this would go. There was the scratch of his zipper sounding, there was the quick catch in his breath as he reached between them, there was his hand, hard, shoving her thighs apart. And all along, his eyes were black with victory. "This is my world," he hissed. "Don't you ever forget it."

His words snapped her from her daze. The anger erupted, red and dark.

Cassie let out a cry, wrenching away from him as she dropped into a crouch and hurled herself at him with all her force. Sebastian stumbled back, losing his balance, and fell, pulling Cassie to the ground with him. She managed to twist away before they hit the ground, landing heavily on her side. He grabbed her ankle and hauled her back, flipping her so his body pressed her into the gravel, smothering her. She tried to scream, to make any sound at all, but his hand was hard on her mouth, arm against her throat, still pressing at her, still reaching between them with furious determination.

Cassie gasped for air, her blood pounding as she clawed wildly at his face with her nails. Her thumb found his eye socket; she thrust in hard.

Sebastian let out an animal cry. His hold loosened, just for a moment, but that was all she needed to bring her knees up and push out, rolling

from under him. Her shoes were lost, kicked aside in the chaos, and she struggled to find her footing on the sharp stones of the gravel. She lurched away. Sebastian was still moaning on the ground behind her, clutching his face.

Cassie's breath was coming fast, body bruised and aching. She stumbled forward another step. Their corner was still dark, totally silent, save for Sebastian's whimpers and her own labored breathing. Nobody was coming, no one had heard.

"Bitch!" Sebastian was writhing in pain on the ground. "You're going to pay for this, you hear me? I'll kill you! I'll fucking kill you!"

Cassie stopped, rage still humming like a bass line in her every limb. She felt it blossom, deep and rich like the wine she'd been drinking earlier that night. Her terror was easing, the panic receding like a tide that left nothing but her anger on the shore: steelier and more certain than anything she'd ever known. It welled up, it washed through her, hot and fast and deep until it felt like her rage was something living, breathing.

Demanding.

He'd done this to her because he could. Because he thought her body was his to abuse as he liked. She was nothing to him, not a voice, or a mind, just a body. A thing.

But she was more than that. She could make him hurt too.

CASSIE WOKE WITH A HEADACHE SCREAMING THROUGH HER skull, and every limb stiff and aching. She flinched back from the light flooding through her open drapes, her throat dry.

She was back in her room, collapsed on her bed, still dressed in last night's clothes.

She struggled to sit up, shocked at the pain ricocheting through her body. She felt used up, a crumpled shell of herself, and it took all her energy to creep slowly from her bedroom, hand by hand along the wall to keep her balance. "Evie?" she called out, the words catching in her pained throat. But there was no reply; the attic rooms lay empty.

As Cassie stumbled toward the bathroom, she caught sight of her reflection in the bureau mirror. She stopped. Bruises were laced across her throat, dark violent smudges on her pale skin, and there was another mark blooming on her right cheekbone. She stared in horror, tracing the tender flesh as she tried in vain to remember what had happened. Sebastian . . . the late gate. She remembered him grabbing her, and then—

Then there was nothing but black.

She locked herself in the bathroom and let the shower beat against her tired bones, as hot as she could bear, until her headache was thundering, red and raw. In the kitchen, wrapped in her bathrobe, she swallowed three aspirin with a gulp of cold coffee. Then she sank slowly to the kitchen floor, her back against the cabinet, and waited for the painkillers to work their soothing magic. She stared at the bruises on her wrists—ugly, shadowed blotches—and tried to remember, but the

night only came in fragments: the tap of her heels on cobblestones, the glitter of the chandeliers at dinner, the hum of conversation in the Union lounge.

The crack of bone against concrete.

Slowly, Cassie's unease blossomed into fear. This darkness, this gap in her memories, she'd known it before—right down to the familiar taste in her mouth: bitter and metallic. Panic gripped her. Those other times, she'd surfaced from the blackouts to find a terrible wreckage in her wake. Broken bodies, buildings burned to ash. But she'd been a child then. Not to blame. Now, here in Oxford, where her secrecy mattered more than anything . . .

What had she done?

Cassie wasn't sure how long she sat there shivering, or even what time it was when she finally registered a knocking on the main door. She startled, tensing. "Wait a second," she called, the words painful in her bruised throat. She pulled herself up to her feet, paranoia sending her to the bedroom to make sure her research files were hidden out of sight behind a loose panel in the wardrobe.

She yanked the bathrobe tightly around her body and crossed to the door. She cracked it, cautiously, and peered out.

"Miss Blackwell?" Rutledge was standing there, wearing his usual heavy cable-knit sweater. His eyes widened at the sight of her, and she heard his sharp intake of breath.

"What's going on?"

He cleared his throat, looking apologetic, and that's when Cassie opened the door wider, revealing another man standing farther back at the top of the staircase, wearing a battered jacket and corduroy trousers.

"We, uh, need you to come to the master's lodgings and answer some questions." Rutledge met her gaze, clearly uneasy. Cassie looked back at the other man. He was in his forties, perhaps: a weary, balding man with an impatient air about him, who seemed to be looking everywhere except at the bruises on her face.

"This is Detective Inspector Bradshaw," Rutledge added. "They, uh, need you now. I'm sorry." His voice dropped, and she could see the sympathy in his eyes. "I said I could bring you, but they insisted on the escort . . ." He trailed off.

Cassie nodded. "It's okay," she told him, her mind racing. "I'll be right out."

"You can put some clothes on," Bradshaw said curtly, from his position down the hall. "We'll wait."

Dressed, but feeling no closer to human, Cassie followed the men across campus. It was late in the afternoon, gray skied, and the pathways were empty, a weekend lull as students busied themselves with sports or coffee dates or catching up on their sleep. Cassie was glad of the empty quad. The group was drawing looks from the few people they passed.

The last time she had visited Sir Edmund's lodgings the trees had stood full and green, but now the sandstone was fringed with bare branches, stripped and wet, the grass muddied and wilting underfoot. Inside, Rutledge led them directly to Sir Edmund's study, but Cassie registered the ominous sense of hush that had fallen over the office as she trailed across the plush crimson carpets. It confirmed her very worst fears.

They were afraid of her.

Rutledge held the door open for her. Cassie braced herself and stepped inside. Sir Edmund was behind his desk, looking stern and tired, with Professor Tremain seated on one of the wing chairs. There was another man by the windows, and as he turned, Cassie inhaled sharply in recognition. It was Charlie, except now he was in full police uniform. She opened her mouth to speak, but Charlie quickly shook his head.

"Miss Blackwell." Sir Edmund gestured to the chair. Detective Bradshaw was behind her, blocking the exit. Cassie sat.

"We need to talk to you about the incident last night."

Cassie swallowed, her heart pounding. Had someone witnessed the attack, reported it to college authorities? But if that had been the case,

surely she would be sitting with some sympathetic female officer by now, not surrounded by an array of accusing, male faces.

Again, the question taunted her. What had she done?

"Sebastian Rhodes," Detective Bradshaw announced gravely. He flipped a notebook open, pen raised to take notes. "You saw him last night?"

Cassie paused, wary. "Yes," she admitted at last. "I ran into him at the Oxford Union."

"And then you left together?"

She looked up sharply. "No. I barely spoke to him. I walked back to college alone. He followed, and . . . attacked me." She didn't remember everything, but she knew that much was true. The image of his face was branded in her memory: sneering, furious, delighting in her pain.

Detective Bradshaw exchanged a look with Sir Edmund, who leaned forward onto his elbows, fixing her with a stern glare. "You need to be truthful with us, Miss Blackwell."

Cassie tried to stay calm. "I am," she said, biting back her anger. "Or do you think I choked myself, for the fun of it?" She yanked down the neck of her sweater, revealing the bruises on her throat. "He tried to rape me."

There was a pause, the word hanging dirty in the air between them. She could sense the discomfort, the way Sir Edmund and Tremain looked to the side and cleared their throats.

"Mr. Rhodes was admitted to hospital last night," Sir Edmund said at last. "He was severely beaten. He sustained several broken ribs, a fractured jaw, and internal bleeding."

The words slowly sank in. He was alive.

Her relief must have shown, because Sir Edmund glared. "This is a serious matter, Miss Blackwell. What do you have to say for yourself?"

"What do I . . . ?" Cassie echoed, her momentary relief turning to disbelief. "Didn't you hear what I said? He tried to rape me." She

looked to Bradshaw, stoic and worn, and Charlie, still standing by the windows. Charlie looked down.

Then she knew. They weren't there to take her account of events, or check if she was all right, to press charges on her behalf. They were there for him.

Cassie let out a short breath. She should have known. The furnishings might be elegant, these men, educated and refined, but it was the same here as everywhere else. She didn't matter to them, and she never would.

"What do you want from me?" Cassie asked, icy. "Since you're clearly not here to check on my well-being."

The men exchanged more looks. Detective Bradshaw flipped his notebook shut. "His family wants to press charges, for grievous bodily harm."

"Then I have some charges too," Cassie spat back. "Assault, battery, attempted rape."

"Sebastian was very badly injured." Sir Edmund sounded aghast.

Cassie felt the fight leave her. "He attacked me." she told them, worn-out. "He followed me back and grabbed me. He wouldn't stop, even when . . ." She shook her head. "You're worried about *his* injuries?"

They were interrupted by a noise from the hallway outside. "Please, Mr. Rhodes, if you'd just wait—" the secretary was saying, her voice rising.

"Get out of my way," a loud male voice demanded. The door swung open and a man in his fifties, well fed and graying at the temples, burst into the room. He was wearing an immaculate charcoal suit and thick red tie, and his eyes blazed with anger. "I won't stand for this," he barked. "I want to know what's being done."

"Mr. Rhodes—" Professor Tremain rose from his seat. "If you could just wait outside."

"No, I won't wait, not after what she did . . ." Mr. Rhodes's gaze landed on Cassie. "You!" he yelled, stabbing a finger in her direction.

"What did you do to my boy?" His face was mottled pink with fury, a vein bulging against his forehead.

"What he deserved," Cassie snapped. "Since you clearly never taught him that no means no."

"How dare you?" Rhodes quivered with rage. "My son would never—" He stopped. "That you would—" Another breath. "You almost blinded him. He may never recover vision in his right eye!"

"He's lucky I didn't kill him." Cassie's reply was matter-of-fact, but they would never know how true the words were. She could see Sebastian in his father now, see the mirror of entitled rage. The short fuse, the reckless fury. She barely had a moment to process it before he lunged toward her. Tremain and Bradshaw scattered out of range, while Cassie scrambled back.

Only Charlie moved to restrain Rhodes, casually blocking with his hands as if he was just another drunken lout on a Friday night. "Easy now. Calm down."

"Did you hear her? What she said?" Rhodes struggled for a moment, then deflated, breathing heavily.

"Jeffery, please," Sir Edmund added, looking concerned for the first time. "We can handle this. Detective, perhaps you could escort Mr. Rhodes back to his car? If you don't have any more questions."

Cassie caught a look between Charlie and Detective Bradshaw, but it was Bradshaw who spoke. "No more questions." He tucked his notebook away. "Thank you for your time."

The police officers ushered Sebastian's father out, and Sir Edmund followed them into the hallway. Cassie could hear his voice through the door, the soothing tones reassuring Rhodes that everything would be settled.

When Sir Edmund rejoined them, he regarded Cassie with a look of weary resignation. "As you can see, the family is very distressed, and for good reason. Sebastian underwent emergency surgeries. He lost a lot of blood."

Cassie didn't reply. The mood had shifted now, without the police present, and just Sir Edmund and Tremain left with her in the room. She looked between them, wondering what their next move would be.

"I think I could be able to dissuade him from pressing charges," Sir Edmund continued slowly, "and allow us to handle this internally. That would be in everyone's best interests, don't you think?"

"As long as I don't press charges either, you mean," Cassie said, realizing what he was really saying.

"If you do, then I'm afraid Mr. Rhodes will also file. And that won't help anyone. You see, criminal proceedings will revoke your visa," Sir Edmund explained in a helpful tone. "And of course you would be asked to leave Raleigh."

"Which you still may be." Tremain spoke up for the first time, his face a mask. "We'll hold a formal disciplinary investigation, and if we find evidence of violence or—"

"I don't think so." Cassie cut him off, furious. "If there was evidence, the police would be the ones investigating, but they don't seem interested."

"Raleigh has an ongoing relationship with the local police force," Sir Edmund replied. "They trust us to handle this internally, rather than waste their time."

Cassie thought fast. They didn't want a scandal, news reports muddying the good Raleigh name. "Then it looks like we're done here. After all," she added bitterly, "if you can't believe me when I say he tried to rape me, you can't very well believe his claims that I was the one who beat him." She got to her feet.

"Miss Blackwell—" Tremain objected, but Sir Edmund waved him silent.

"I'll discuss this with the disciplinary board and let you know our findings." He rose too and ushered her toward the door before pausing. "We do demand confidentiality when investigating accusations like this. You mustn't talk to anyone, especially the press." His eyes bore into her, flint gray. "The college has a reputation to protect."

"Of course it does." Cassie let her gaze drift over them: Sir Edmund, so concerned with the good Raleigh name, and Tremain, his obedient lapdog. She would have felt anger, if she hadn't been so drained. Instead, she was left with nothing but contempt. "The college comes first."

Back outside, Cassie wandered blindly. She was burning with rage, with helplessness—and relief. She'd been let down by the system for so long—an endless rotation of ineffectual bureaucrats and spineless social workers—that she'd thought her faith in the rules of authority was long since stamped out. But now, Sir Edmund's soothing voice still echoing in her mind, Cassie realized she'd had some last shred of faith left to be destroyed.

It made a cruel kind of sense. Sebastian was one of them. They would never punish him, not against her word.

And perhaps she did deserve punishment, after all.

Cassie pushed the thought away. Whatever she'd done to Sebastian, he'd deserved it. She was a survivor, she always had been. And if she'd lost control, gone too far . . . Well, there was no changing it now.

She was turning to cross the main courtyard when she saw Charlie and Detective Bradshaw talking by the porters' lodge. Cassie dropped back a moment, watching as Charlie reached to answer his phone, then gestured for Bradshaw to go on ahead. The detective exited through the main gates and was soon out of sight on the street beyond.

Cassie strode quickly toward Charlie, arriving just as he ended his call. "What was that?" she demanded fiercely. "What the hell happened in there?"

"Shh," Charlie hushed her, glancing around. Before she could object, he pulled Cassie to the edge of the courtyard, out of sight down a back alley.

"What's the problem?" she demanded, pulling away. "Don't want to be seen with the dangerous crazy chick?"

"Cassie—" Charlie tried to calm her.

"Is that what you were talking about when you said I had nothing to worry about from you?" she spat angrily. "That it was your job to protect and serve?"

"I tried!" Charlie hissed, looking again to see if they were being watched. "You think I don't know what they did back there? It was a sham." He spat the word like a curse. "This whole thing was a fucking sham, from the start."

"What do you mean?" Cassie asked, her anger fading. She'd expected weak excuses and denial, but instead, Charlie looked bitter.

"When I got to the hospital, old man Rhodes was already there," he explained. "The family solicitor too. When I found out it was about you, I tried to get them away, question the kid properly, but they wouldn't leave him, not for a minute. Sebastian barely even spoke, just let his dad do all the talking. And then Bradshaw comes in and tells them we'll sort it out with the college, doesn't even ask for a statement. I tried to press it, but Bradshaw gave me a bollocking for even suggesting we investigate. I can't risk it again." Charlie looked torn. "I'm on probation as it is."

"Why?" Cassie asked, curious. "What did you do?"

Charlie sighed. "There was a brawl on Cornmarket a couple of weeks ago. I made the mistake of booking the guy who threw the first punch. Turns out daddy's on some government committee, so he gets off and they move me to college liaison duty. Now I'm stuck logging stolen laptops." He shook his head as if brushing the distraction away. "Don't you see? I can't dig into this. Even if I did, it wouldn't make a difference—these colleges are like fucking embassies: what goes on inside stays there."

"And the police turn a blind eye," Cassie finished.

Charlie nodded. "Bradshaw's been running this beat for years. I didn't know before, but he makes it all disappear. It's way out of my hands, and above my pay grade."

Cassie slumped back against the wall. "So Sebastian just gets away with it?"

"He's got three broken ribs and a cracked jaw," Charlie pointed out. "That's hardly nothing." He gave her a crooked smile. "Guess I should have believed you when you said you could take care of yourself."

Cassie couldn't smile. "I did what I had to," she said, as much to convince herself as him. "It wasn't like I enjoyed it."

Charlie's face changed. "Are you okay?" he asked, moving closer. "Did he . . . ?"

"What, get what he was after?" Cassie flinched back. "Don't worry, I didn't let him get that far."

"That's not what I meant." Charlie looked hurt.

Cassie looked away. "I'm fine."

He nodded slowly, then reached into his pocket. "Here, take my card." He pulled a business card and a cheap ballpoint pen from his jacket pocket and scribbled a number on the back. "This is my cell too. Call me if you have any trouble with Sebastian, or anyone else."

Cassie took the card and slipped it into her back pocket without looking at it.

"I mean it," Charlie added, his tone so intent Cassie looked closer. "Rhodes was demanding all kinds of stuff," he warned her. "Charges, deportation . . . Most of it was probably bullshit, but you can't get mixed up in something like this again, not if you want to stay out of trouble."

"I didn't—"

"I know," Charlie cut off her angry protest. "It's not you. But that won't make a difference. You're the outsider, and the system is fucking rigged. You're the one who's going to get hurt. Understand?"

Cassie gave a short nod. She did understand, better than he would ever know.

"I've got to get back. The attack, where did it happen?"

"The late gate," Cassie replied. "He followed me back from the Union, down Holywell, and got me just inside the walls. By the auditorium."

Charlie nodded. "I'll see if I can dig up anything."

"You already said it's too late. It won't matter."

"Maybe." Charlie exhaled. "But it would give you something, leverage maybe, if they tried to kick you out."

Cassie felt a chill. If there was surveillance showing Sebastian attacking her, it would show what happened after too. "Don't risk it," she told him. "I can handle it."

Charlie looked as if he wanted to disagree, but Cassie's determined expression must have been deterrent enough. "Take care of yourself," he offered softly, before walking away.

Cassie watched him go, brown head ducking out of the main gates, black police jacket dark against a tide of returning college students wrapped in Raleigh colors. He was as much an interloper as she, and for a moment Cassie envied his ability to simply walk through those heavy wooden gates and slip back into the real world that lay beyond.

She could leave anytime she wanted, she told herself. Get on a plane, disappear back to her old life, leave the mysteries here rotting into dust. She could just walk away.

But Cassie knew that was just an idle fantasy. She couldn't stop now, not with so many questions still unanswered. The photograph. Her mother's secret life. And all the reasons that haunted Cassie late at night, the secrets her mother took to the grave.

Cassie turned back toward the spires of Raleigh, and let the gates fall closed.

SIR EDMUND HAD CAUTIONED HER ABOUT THE IMPORTANCE OF secrecy, but almost immediately Cassie sensed the stares and hushed whispers that followed her across the Raleigh campus, girls turning away to murmur to their companions, young men sending steely glares as they passed. Cassie told herself that she didn't care. Let them gossip; they would never know the truth, and she didn't need them to believe her side of the story.

But she did consider confiding in one person: Evie. Cassie returned to the attic after her meeting with Sir Edmund and the police already forming the sentences in her head, prepared to spill everything. She'd always held back her personal life, but now she needed to find an ally, someone who would reassure her that everything would be okay.

But Evie didn't come home that day, or the next one either. When she finally did return, and Cassie found her sipping tea at their kitchen table, she looked distracted and absent.

"Where have you been?" Cassie asked, pausing in the doorway. Evie looked frailer than usual, dark shadows smudged under her eyes.

"We spent the weekend at Hugo's place in the country," Evie replied. "Sorry, did you worry?"

"No, I figured . . ." Cassie looked closer, noticing Evie's taut expression. "Are you okay? Did something happen?"

Evie paused. "I . . . We're taking a break." Her voice twisted. "Me and Hugo. We broke up."

Cassie immediately went to sit beside her. "What happened?" she asked.

Evie's eyes began to water. "He . . ." She swallowed, correcting herself. "*We* decided to pause things for a while. You know, have a breather . . ." She tried to muster a smile, but her expression was pained.

"I'm so sorry," Cassie offered.

Evie's lower lip trembled, her eyes filling with tears. "I just don't understand." She let out a plaintive sob. "All weekend he ignored me. He acted like I wasn't even there, and then, then . . . He said I was getting too serious, that I thought this was something it's not. I don't understand!"

Cassie patted her shoulder gently. "Maybe it's for the best," she suggested, her voice artificially bright. "You'll have a chance to focus on your thesis. You've only been seeing him a few weeks now."

Evie nodded blankly. "I just, I thought this was real. That he cared. And now . . ." She swallowed back another surge of tears. "Now it's all over." She offered Cassie a pale smile. "Thanks for listening. I think I'm going to go take a nap." She slowly rose from the table and padded softly down the hall.

Cassie watched her go, feeling a shard of guilt. She'd known Hugo wasn't taking their relationship seriously—the way he'd flirted with her, invited her out behind Evie's back. She wondered now if she should have said something sooner. Would Evie have listened, or turned against her too?

Regardless, it was too late to tell her about the attack now. The moment had passed.

As the week wore on, Cassie noticed a worrying change in Evie's usually exuberant mood. Instead of bounding around the flat, a whirlwind of activity, she now stared for hours at her notes, or pored over books, curled under a blanket on the couch. Hugo wasn't the only one who had broken things off; Olivia and her friends stopped calling too, and Evie's glittering social life faded into memories, replaced with days she barely

moved from the sofa. She deflected Cassie's concern, saying she was just buckling down for her thesis deadline, but Cassie feared the looming due date wasn't the only reason for the change. The only spark of life Cassie saw was when Evie's phone buzzed, late in the dark afternoons; Evie would snatch it up to check whatever text or call came through, then deflate, throwing the phone aside and retreating to her bed again to mourn the passing of her brief relationship.

Cassie watched the quicksand shifts in mood with a growing sense of fear. She'd seen them before, spent her childhood tiptoeing through sudden tempests, and now, watching Evie swoop between such extremes, she couldn't help but be reminded of her mother's manic phases. She warned herself not to overreact, but concern danced on the tip of her tongue every time she saw Evie reach hopefully for her phone, or found her yawning, dead-eyed, over breakfast the next morning. After her first few gentle nudges were met with stony silence, she learned to swallow her concern. This was just a breakup. Evie was a grown woman, making her own choices. She would be fine.

At the end of the week, Cassie set out for her morning run, lengthening her strides on the hard winter ground as the Raleigh campus receded from view. It had taken her body a few days to recover from Sebastian's attack, but now she was back in condition, completing her long loop around the river walk and far meadow in ever-shorter times. She would need to strike out farther soon, Cassie decided, as she slowed to a walk and began her cooldown, her breath fogging the chilled morning air. Down past the fields on the outskirts of the city, or across the high street perhaps. There were long trails that wound out past Christ Church College to the wide spread of the river proper where the crew teams would race come summer, the riverbanks lined with genteel boathouses and flag-waving supporters.

Back at Raleigh, she was detouring to the lodge to check her mail when she noticed a familiar figure heading back across the courtyard.

"Olivia?" she called. The blond girl was just inside the gates, clearly just returning from another night out.

"Cassie, hi." Olivia swooped in for an air-kiss. She was swathed in a white coat with fur trim, her cheeks flushed from the cold, and her hair peeking out from under a looped scarf. "How are you? How's Evie doing? Is she holding up okay?"

Cassie paused, not wanting to seem disloyal. "She's fine. It was a little bumpy at first, but she's doing much better."

"I'm so glad." Olivia sighed. "It was just awful. Such a scene." She shook her head. "I could have warned her," she added ruefully. "Hugo doesn't do relationships. Everything's fun and games until someone starts caring for real."

"You should drop by to visit," Cassie suggested. "I know Evie would love to see you. Or go for cocktails or something with the gang."

"I wish I could." Olivia made a regretful face. "But I promised Hugo I wouldn't get in the middle of things. It would be so awkward, don't you think? He's a wretch but he's family, you know?" She gave a helpless shrug. "But you should come out with us sometime," she offered. "It's Miles's birthday, we're all going out tonight. You must come!"

Cassie was taken aback at the invitation. She assumed from the dirty looks she'd been receiving around campus that news of Sebastian's attack—at least, his version of it—was general gossip now, but Olivia was acting as if nothing was wrong. "I couldn't," Cassie said firmly. It wouldn't feel right to take Evie's place while she sat weeping at home—even if Cassie still had questions to ask about the secret societies in town.

"Well, you change your mind, just say so." Olivia glanced over Cassie's shoulder and grimaced. "Don't look, but Tremain is giving you the evil eye."

Cassie turned. The professor was approaching from the cloisters, his trench coat whipping around him in the wind.

"Ignore him, he's always prowling around college looking grim,"

Olivia advised. "Anyway, I have to dash. Call me if you ever feel like lunch!" She quickly skittered away, leaving Cassie just as Tremain reached her.

"Miss Blackwell." Tremain scowled after Olivia. "I was just going to leave a note for you. I was hoping we could have a chat."

"About?" Cassie tensed, remembering his silence during the meeting with the police, how he didn't speak up for her, even for a moment.

Tremain looked uncomfortable. "Perhaps we could find time to meet in my office—"

"I'm busy," she told him shortly. "I have essays due." She turned to walk away, but Tremain trailed her across the courtyard.

"Miss Blackwell." His voice was sharp. She reluctantly turned. "I talked with Sir Edmund," he said in a low voice. "There won't be any disciplinary actions against you."

Cassie bit back another sarcastic retort. "Anything else?" she asked coolly. "I really do need to get to the library."

Tremain looked pained. "College policy dictates that anyone involved in a . . . traumatic event must spend time with a counselor. I've taken the liberty of scheduling you an appointment, for this afternoon."

"You're kidding me." Cassie blinked in disbelief. "You're actually pretending like you give a damn how I feel?"

"Please." Tremain looked away. "I think it would be for the best. Somebody to talk to, help you process things."

"In case you're forgetting, the official line is that nothing happened," Cassie replied icily.

Tremain sighed. "It's procedure," he repeated, pulling a printed sheet from his satchel. He held it out to her. "Just one session. Then we can all move on and draw a line through the episode."

"And if I don't?"

"I'm trying to help here." The professor looked at her. For a moment, his expression seemed almost regretful, but Cassie didn't care. She snatched the page away from him.

"Then thank you for your concern," she said, scathing, turning to walk away.

"If you don't like it, you can always leave."

She froze and turned back. "What did you say?"

Tremain met her gaze, cooler now. "Raleigh isn't suited to everyone," he continued. "After everything you've been through, perhaps it would be better if you cut your study-abroad program short."

"Better for whom?" Cassie retorted. "The college? Sebastian? You?"

Tremain's gaze didn't waver. "There's no shame in admitting you're unhappy here."

Cassie kept her jaw clenched. He thought she wasn't cut out for her studies. That she wasn't Raleigh material. "I'll see the counselor," she bit out. "But if you want me gone, expel me. I earned my place here, just like everyone else. I'm staying."

The address Tremain had given Cassie was a stark series of buildings on the edge of town: The Center for Psychology and Neural Research. Cassie entered through spotless sliding glass doors and looked curiously at the steel and chrome decor, a world away from the musty libraries of the rest of the university.

"Cassie?" A woman breezed toward her, hand outstretched. "Thessaly Mortimer. You have perfect timing, I was just getting a coffee. Want one?"

"Uh, no. Thanks." Cassie quickly looked her over. Thessaly was in her late thirties, with a mane of glossy auburn hair and perfect makeup. She was wearing a silk blouse and a dark pencil skirt; a lab coat was folded over her arm and her stilettos tapped on the polished floor as she led Cassie down the hall to a coffee machine.

"Terrible habit." Thessaly sighed, filling a cup. "I should know better, especially in my profession. Everyone knows you feed rats caffeine and their brains just light up, they go crazy."

"So why don't you quit?" Cassie asked. She was still studying the woman, trying to get a read on her.

Thessaly took a sip and gave Cassie a rueful smile. "The eternal mystery of human behavior: we know something is bad for us, but we do it anyway." She glanced at her watch, a thin gold band on her wrist. "We better get moving. My day is packed, and I'm sure you don't want to hang around here a moment longer than necessary."

"Well, no," Cassie answered, taken aback, but Thessaly was already striding off. She led Cassie back through a maze of offices and labs to a room that was as stark as the rest of the building: a leather couch and chairs, a glass-topped desk, framed sketches of the human brain on the far wall.

"So let me tell you a little about myself," Thessaly began as Cassie drifted around the room, examining the framed diplomas. Master's in neurological, Ph.D. in psychology. "As you can see, I'm not a traditional counselor, but I like to offer my services to the university and give support to students dealing with emotional stress." Thessaly gestured for Cassie to sit on the couch. When Cassie hesitated, she laughed. "Don't worry, it's not like psychiatry. I won't ask you to lie back and talk about your parents." She paused. "Unless you want to, of course. We can chat about anything."

Cassie took a seat on the very edge of the couch. "I thought you were supposed to talk to me about the attack," she said.

"Only if you feel like it." Thessaly settled opposite her in one of the chairs and gave a reassuring smile, but Cassie didn't relax. "It's okay," Thessaly added, as if reading Cassie's reticence. "This is all private now, patient confidentiality. I'm not going to report back to Raleigh, or anything like that."

Cassie shrugged. "There isn't anything to report. I'm fine. I don't know why I need to be here."

"Probably because Raleigh doesn't want to get sued for student welfare failings."

Cassie looked up, surprised at the other woman's candor. Thessaly studied her a moment, then relaxed back in her seat. "Look, I understand. Something traumatic happened to you, and you'd rather not talk to a stranger about it. And that's fine too, as long as you have your own

way of processing it." She paused. "Have you talked to anyone yet: a friend, roommate?"

Cassie slowly shook her head. "I . . . was going to," she replied. "But my roommate's going through her own stuff right now. It's not something you can just lay on a person, and she's got her own problems."

"Oh?"

"She just broke up with her boyfriend," Cassie explained, "And I'm . . . worried about her."

"But not yourself?" Thessaly commented.

Cassie paused. "No, I'm fine. I can handle it. But Evie's . . . she's fragile."

"It's common to focus on other people after a traumatic incident, to distract oneself from your own problems," Thessaly noted.

"It's not like that," Cassie protested, but then she reconsidered. She *had* been focusing on Evie, on her mother, on anything to keep her from reliving that night over again. "Maybe," she admitted.

Thessaly gave a small smile. "So, if not Evie, is there anyone else you have to talk to? Friends back home? Your parents, perhaps."

"No." Cassie shook her head. "That's not . . . I mean, I'm fine." She pressed her lips together determinedly. "It happened. It's happened before. But I'm fine, I don't need to talk about it."

"All right then." Thessaly stood. Cassie blinked up at her in surprise. She'd been expecting more questions, an hour of well-intentioned interference, but instead, Thessaly was walking back to her desk and scrolling through her phone. She looked up, catching Cassie's expression. "I'm not going to keep you here." She smiled gently. "It sounds like you have a handle on things. Just know you can call and arrange to see me anytime."

"Oh. Thanks." Cassie grabbed her bag and headed for the door.

"And tell your roommate to come see me if she needs to," Thessaly added. "Mental health is important, especially in these pressured environments. We don't want anyone slipping through the cracks."

CASSIE WORKED LATE AT THE LIBRARY THAT NIGHT, THEN HAD AN early-morning lecture and economics tutorial the next day. She turned her key in the lock around noon, hoping for a quiet afternoon by the fire, but when she stepped into the apartment, Evie was in the living room on her hands and knees, anxiously hunting through papers and files that were scattered and sprawled across the room.

"Hey." Cassie began the unwrapping of her coat, scarf, and extra sweater. "How are you feeling?"

Evie didn't look up. "It's not here." She flipped back and forth through folders and research books, her expression becoming more agitated. "It's not here," she said again, eyes darting across the debris, "Nineteen fifty, fifty-one . . . The Marlowe files, or maybe Hariot? No, Marlowe, Marlowe . . ."

Cassie felt a tremor of unease. She drifted closer. "What is it you're looking for?"

There was no reply. Evie pulled another box closer and tore through the contents, carelessly discarding papers to the floor that Cassie could see were delicate and yellowed with age. "Easy there," she told Evie, scooping up the papers and placing them gently on the coffee table. "Tell me what you're after. Maybe I can help."

"But I saw it!" Evie exclaimed. "Right here; it was here. She had it all figured out!" She spun around and began to dismantle another stack of papers.

"Evie," Cassie soothed her. "Evie, stop!" But the other woman didn't seem to hear her, of if she did, Cassie's voice didn't break through whatever panic she was swept up in, not until Cassie reached out and touched her gently on the arm.

Evie sprang back in shock. "Hey, it's okay," Cassie soothed her quickly. "Just take a beat, and we'll figure this out." Evie's breath was coming in fast, shallow pants. Her cheeks were flushed, but instead of being relieved that there was color back in her face after so many pale, translucent days, Cassie could only see the fevered spark in Evie's eyes. "How about you take a break," she suggested again, trying to steer Evie away from the mess. "I'll put the kettle on and we can break open those fancy biscuits you got."

But her roommate stood firm. "I have to find it!" Her voice was edged with a raw panic.

"And we will." Cassie was careful not to make any sudden movements as she guided Evie across to the kitchen area. "You just need a moment to clear your head. Maybe you should get out, take a walk. I find fresh air always help get me focused again."

Evie glanced up. "Wait, what time is it?"

Cassie checked her watch. "Twenty after noon."

Evie let out a gasp. "I was going out! I was supposed to meet Olivia across town."

"Did she call?" Cassie asked. "That's great."

Evie shook her head violently. "I kept getting her voice mail, but I said I'd be there. Now they'll all think I've let them down." She grabbed her purse from the sofa and rifled through it until she pulled out her cell phone, quickly scrolling through her messages. Cassie watched her face fall and knew the truth even before Evie exhaled. "She didn't call."

"Well, then it's all okay," Cassie tried to argue. "You can see her later. And what about your other friends? You had some before you met Olivia and the gang, right? If you want to get out and about, why don't you arrange to see them instead?"

"You don't understand," Evie cried. "It's not about party plans! Olivia can help, she can explain things to Hugo. I need to fix everything." Cassie watched as Evie turned away, murmuring into her cell phone. "Hi, Livvy, it's me. Sorry I bailed today, work got away from me. Let's do lunch later this week. Or drinks. Or . . ." Her fake enthusiasm faded, and the desperation in her tone came loud and clear. "Whatever you want, just call me, okay? I miss you!" She hung up and stood frozen in the middle of the room.

"It's probably a good thing you stayed in today," Cassie tried to console her. "I bet you've got tons of work done, and if you get a good night's sleep too—"

"Don't." Evie cut her off sharply. "Don't talk to me like I'm some kind of fucking child."

Cassie took a step back. "I'm sorry," she said, carefully. "I'm just trying to help."

"Well, I don't need your help." Evie's voice rose. "I can handle this for myself. Everyone always acts like I don't see what's happening, but I do." She waved an accusing finger at Cassie, eyes bright. "I see it, okay; I got too close, but you can all stop pretending now!"

Cassie held her hands out, palms to Evie, trying to calm her. It was automatic, a gesture of submission that brought back memories of her mother and the nights she'd raged over nothing. "Everything's okay," she said quietly.

"It's not okay," Evie cried, backing away. "Just look at it!" She gestured wildly to the mess littering the room and the notes pinned to a board by the mantelpiece. "My proposal is due and nothing is adding up! I thought I could see it, the reason they were all bound together, it was so clear, but she's the only one who found it, and I can't . . ." Evie trailed off, grabbing at another stack of papers.

"Who found what?" Cassie asked, but Evie was too far gone.

"I don't know what happened, it was here and now it's gone and now nothing makes sense anymore."

"We'll find it." Cassie felt helpless. She didn't know what to do—she didn't even know how this storm had started, only that it was raging now, fierce and broken, reminding her of those awful days hiding in the bathroom, waiting for her mother's panic and mayhem to subside. But she couldn't hide from Evie that way, couldn't close her eyes tight and count as high as she could to block out reality. She had to do something. "Listen to me," she said, louder, as Evie began to sob. "I can help."

"I don't want your help," Evie cried. Tears were streaming down her cheeks, her torso shuddering with violent sobs. "I don't want anything. I just need you to leave me alone! Why can't you all just leave me alone?" With a final cry, she grabbed her files from the table and sent them crashing to the floor. Cassie jumped back as the pages scattered on the carpet. Evie released another sob and then turned and fled for her room, the door slamming behind her.

Cassie sank down on the edge of the armchair, catching her breath. The attic was still now, distant traffic noise audible through the far open window. She hoped that Evie would sleep and then wake up refreshed and calm, just as her mother had done after her more treacherous episodes.

But they weren't the same, Cassie reassured herself, as she bent to the ground and began gathering up the mess of notes and paper. Her mother had been ill, unbalanced by chemicals that sent her reeling off a fragile tightrope, doomed from birth to ricochet to the extremes. Evie was simply tired, overworked, stressed from her studies and too many sleepless nights. Her roommate would be all right, Cassie told herself, sorting the scattered papers into neat piles. Christmas vacation was coming soon, just a few weeks away. Once she'd had time back with her family, away from the lure of Olivia and Hugo, she would be fine again, back to the old Evie, so effervescent and bright.

Soon the room was returned to some semblance of order: cushions arranged back on the sofa, blanket straightened over the back of a chair. Cassie paused over Evie's notes, scanning through the dense hand-

writing as she tried to pick out any familiar names or references to the School of Night.

Evie's research was more academic than narrative: she was tracing the evolution of ideas during Raleigh's life, the conditions that allowed a hub of creative, revolutionary thought to flourish despite the suppression of the Crown and church. Astronomers, playwrights, mathematicians, and intellectuals all found a kinship in one another, and a pursuit of some higher purpose and knowledge in a society rife with religious persecution.

So how did this group of intellectuals become the secretive society they were today? If such a group even existed in modern-day Oxford. It was still a shadow she was chasing, and part of Cassie couldn't believe she was worrying about centuries-old rumors. They were superstitions, and Cassie was the last person to buy into those kind of fanatical conspiracies, but she couldn't shake the fact of that photograph, with its ominous scribbled caption.

Black is the badge of hell, the hue of dungeons, and the school of night.

She was still no closer to discovering who had slipped it in her mailbox, who at Raleigh knew the truth of her identity, and the reason behind her quest.

Cassie shivered, looking at Evie's spread of chaotic notes. Maybe the answers were there, or maybe she was chasing after nothing, distracted from the real purpose of her trip.

Her father's identity.

The college bells rang out, shattering her thoughts, and Cassie realized with a start that she was late; she was set to work the afternoon shift at the library. She sent an anxious look toward Evie's bedroom. She didn't want to leave her, but she couldn't stay and babysit a locked door all afternoon. Scribbling a quick note to Evie, she grabbed her coat and let herself out, heading down to the main gates and along the busy streets toward the library. She hated to admit it, but since the attack she'd changed how she moved across the city, keeping to the main roads,

staying away from the winding backstreets. She resented the new anxiety she felt, pulling her coat tight around her and walking fast, alert and ready, but she couldn't help it. Sebastian had shown her that Oxford wasn't the safe idyll it pretended to be.

Elliot had left a note for her tucked in the circulations desk, telling her to meet him at Blackwell's after her shift.

I have news, his cryptic scrawl promised, and Cassie spent the afternoon on edge, wondering what he'd found. She'd had only a smattering of responses to her e-mails to Margaret's old classmates, and all of them apologized for having nothing to share. They barely remembered her; she'd left before their first year was done; it was all so many years ago. Cassie tried not to feel frustrated, but coming up against another dead end was a frustrating blow. She'd thought discovering her mother's real name would be all it took to unlock the secrets of her past, but now she saw that although Margaret had been the most important person in her life, to the others she'd mingled with in college she'd been just one in a crowd of hundreds. She'd barely left a shadow of memory behind.

At last her shift was over and Cassie walked the short blocks over to Blackwell's, finding the crammed aisles busy with browsers, just one free seat to be had in the bustling café. Elliot was wedged into a seat in the corner, trying to protect the other chair from a determined-looking woman. "See, she's here," Cassie heard him say meanly as she wove through the pack. "Finally," he exclaimed, greeting her. "I thought she was going to shank me."

"Over a free seat?" Cassie laughed, unwinding her scarf.

"People have died here for less," Elliot retorted. "Now, how about some cake?"

Cassie obediently went to get them coffees and refreshments, parting with most of her afternoon wages before she shuffled carefully back to

the table. "What you have better be worth it," she said lightly, only half joking. "They're charging an arm and a leg for the chocolate torte."

"Worth every penny, I promise." Elliot made room on the table, pushing his newspapers aside. "How have you been getting on with the search, anyway?" He looked at her over his trendy spectacles. "Any new developments since last we spoke?"

Cassie shook her head, taking a sip of hot, strong coffee. "Nothing from me. I wanted to talk more to my roommate about the group, but . . . she's been busy."

"Well, I did a little more digging into your mysterious Margaret," Elliot began, rummaging in his leather satchel and pulling out a dog-eared spiral notebook. "I know we tracked down her classmates, but I thought I'd widen the net. This one name kept coming up, Rose Smith. Ring any bells?"

"No," Cassie replied, but she felt a shiver. Rose was her middle name.

"Rose and Margaret seemed pretty tight," Elliot said, looking down at his notes. "They were roommates that first year, and both played on the hockey team. I found a team photo, and look." He slid a printed page across to Cassie, pointing to one face.

Cassie peered at it. "It's the other girl from the photo!"

"Exactly."

Cassie pulled out her own folder and the photograph from the formal dinner. She placed them side by side, but it was unmistakable: Rose was the girl sitting next to her mother in the shadow of the great portraits, wearing a matching smile.

"Maybe this Rose was involved with the society too," Elliot added.

Cassie looked up, surprised. "So you believe it then?" she asked eagerly. "That the School of Night society could still exist?"

Elliot rolled his eyes theatrically. "I don't know. Stranger things have happened. And like you said, if there was ever a good place to form your supersecret ruling elite, Oxford would be it. Anyway, I didn't have time

to check what Rose is up to now. I bet if you found her, she'd have more to share. They seemed pretty tight."

A new lead. Cassie felt her excitement rise, staring at the photos of her mother and Rose together. "Thank you." She slipped them into her purse. "This is a real help."

"Now business is out of the way," Elliot announced with barely constrained delight, "what else is new with you? Any debauchery? One of us at least should be enjoying themselves."

"What about that classics scholar you had a date with?" Cassie asked, relaxing back into the seat.

Elliot made a face. "He left me high and dry. Turns out he's 'not sure' about his 'identity.'" He made air quotes, but Cassie could tell he was wounded.

"Give him time," she said. "And besides, he was way too young for you."

Elliot chuckled. "The good ones always are."

They sat chatting in the cluttered café for another hour, as darkness took hold outside the steamed windows and students lingered hopefully on the edge of the room, waiting for a seat to become vacated. At last Elliot yawned, pressing his fingertips to the plate to capture the last crumbs of cake. "Well, at least we're over the hump now."

"What's that?"

"Halfway point," Elliot explained. "Only three weeks until Christmas holiday."

"I forget the semesters are so short here." Cassie felt a curl of unease in her stomach. She was almost a third of the way through her year in Oxford, with nothing but mysteries to show for it.

"Are you jetting off home?" Elliot asked.

She shook her head. There was nothing to go home for. "No, I'll be here."

"Good, you can cover my shifts at the library. We stay open all of break." He grimaced. "Cater to all the poor souls who have no place else to go."

Like her. "Sure, I'll take the shifts," Cassie said. "Do you have family nearby?"

"A whole rabble, down in Sussex." Elliot sighed. "My mother insists on a happy family Christmas, every year. Walks on the downs, board games, drunken Uncle Andy ranting about women's lib."

"Sounds nice," Cassie replied, wistful.

"Sure, it's all fun and games until someone mentions the war."

"Which one?"

"Any of them."

Cassie laughed, looking around the room. Then her gaze landed on a familiar face, and her laughter died in her throat. Hugo was sitting in a corner seat, lounged back, watching her.

"Jesus, what happened?" Elliot turned. "Oh," he murmured, turning back with a grin. "Well, hello."

Cassie looked away quickly, back to Elliot. "It's not like that. He's just . . . a guy I know."

"You don't have to explain yourself to me." Elliot launched into an anecdote about a man he'd been accidentally stalking all year, and although Cassie tried to stay focused on him, she couldn't help but feel Hugo's gaze burning into her skin from across the room.

After a few more minutes, Cassie couldn't take the discomfort any longer. "I should really be getting back," she said, cutting Elliot off and reaching for her coat. "I have another essay due."

"Oh, the petty travails of the undergrad," Elliot said, not unsympathetically. "Well, see you Thursday. It's reshelving day; see if you can contain your joy."

"I'll do my best." Cassie forced a laugh as she rose to her feet. She shot a quick glance across the room to check on Hugo, but he was gone, the seat now occupied by a dour-looking man with his crossword.

Cassie exhaled in relief. She was imagining things, thinking he'd been watching her. She tripped lightly down the stairs and outside, wondering if she should pick up some groceries and cook Evie dinner.

After her roommate's outburst earlier, it would be nice to have a relaxing evening in together.

"Cassie."

Cassie whirled around. Hugo was leaning against the wall outside the bookstore, his hands in his pockets. "Who's your friend?" he asked, casual.

"None of your business," Cassie replied shortly, trying to recover from the shock. Her pulse was racing, alert to danger.

Hugo arched an eyebrow. "Heading back to college? I'll walk with you."

"No thank you." Cassie began walking away, toward the main street, but Hugo fell into step beside her. She turned to glare at him.

"I can't help it if I'm walking in the same direction," he protested with a smile. "Would you prefer I trail you, five paces behind?"

Cassie stayed silent, walking quickly. Hugo's long strides easily kept pace.

"So how have you been?" he asked easily.

She looked over. Surely he must have heard the gossip about what happened with Sebastian? But Hugo's expression wasn't glib; instead, he had a look of quiet concern on his face. She felt a flush of discomfort. "I'm fine," she said quickly. For the first time since the attack she felt embarrassed that details of her personal life were in wide circulation. She didn't care about the other Raleigh students glaring in her direction, but Hugo . . .

"If you ever need . . ." Hugo paused. "If you ever need anything, just ask."

Cassie was taken aback by the sincerity in his voice. "What I need is for my roommate to stop weeping all over our apartment," she said sharply, to remind herself as much as him of Evie's distraught state. "I don't know if you were just stringing her along or if this is all a game to you, but it was real to her, okay? And now she's lost all of you, and I'm the one left dealing with the fallout."

Hugo blinked. "Cassie—" he began, but she didn't want to hear any more of his charming excuses.

"Look, I need to go." She hoisted her bag higher on her shoulder and stepped out into the street, leaving Hugo behind as she ducked through traffic and put a safe distance between them.

She closed the final distance to college, wondering how she let him get under her skin. From the first moment they met, out in the courtyard that night, there'd been something about him that set her on edge. And now, with the breakup with Evie, she had even more reason to stay away.

Except somehow, there was something drawing her in too. Brief glimpses of connection, the tempting depths of those dark eyes.

Back home, Cassie shook her head, turning in through the college gates and toward her building. She should be relieved. Without Hugo hanging around Evie, her home was safe from intrusion again: no way-ward guests, no risk of late-night visits. It was her domain once more. Safe and sound.

She climbed the stairs to the attic, fumbling with her key before real-izing the door was already unlocked. Evie must have forgotten the latch again. She pushed it open, taking three steps into the room before she glanced up, and everything changed.

A scream froze in her throat. The world fell away.

Evie was hanging dead from the rafters.

CASSIE HAD BURIED HER MOTHER IN THE GRAVEYARD OF THEIR small-town Indiana chapel among the weeds and crumbling head-stones, neglected under the leaves of fall. Her stepfather was the only other mourner. He stood beside her, swaying, still drunk, as Cassie dug her nails into her palms and counted silently in her head to keep from weeping as the priest said the words, the coffin was lowered, and the only person Cassie had ever loved in the world disappeared into the hard, unforgiving soil.

Evie's memorial service filled the great Raleigh chapel. There were embossed programs printed on heavy cream card stock, and the an-tique pews were packed with family and classmates. Evie's parents wept together at the front of the procession, sunlight bursting through the stained-glass windows while the choir sang "Pie Jesu." Evie's father, younger brother, and uncles served as pallbearers, dressed up in black suits, their faces pale with grief. The wood of the coffin gleamed, smooth as silk, wound with wreaths of calla lilies and white roses, Evie's favor-ite. She'd been embalmed in a pink silk party dress Cassie had helped her mother pick from the wardrobe, her cold lips painted red, a favor-ite scarf wound gently around her neck to hide the bruises her clumsy clothing-line noose had left behind.

Cassie still couldn't believe she was gone. By the time she'd screamed, rushed forward to uselessly lift and heave at Evie's dangling body, it was already too late. She'd been dead for an hour, the coroner report said.

The porters had to cut her down with garden shears in the end, the only thing they could find sharp enough to sever the line.

They filed out of the chapel after the service, a sea of somber black. Cassie didn't say a word, and nobody tried to speak to her. But she could feel the eyes on her, hear the hushed whispers.

"She's the one who found her."

"And after that thing with Sebastian too."

"Why didn't she say anything?"

"Cassie?"

She didn't hear the voice for a moment, too wrapped up in her numb haze. Then she blinked awake and found Evie's parents in front of her, their faces still crumpled with grief. "We're heading back to London for the burial," her father said, his voice hoarse. "But we wanted to thank you. If there's anything we can do . . ."

Cassie shook her head. "No, you shouldn't even have to offer," she said. "Have a safe trip back."

Evie's mother gave her a trembling smile. "I hate to ask, but Evie's things . . ."

"Don't worry about them," Cassie said immediately. "I'll pack everything up and have the porters send it on. That is," she paused, "If you want . . . ?"

They exchanged a look. "Yes," Evie's mother nodded, clutching a tissue. "Whatever you think . . . I mean, whatever mattered to her. And if you want to keep anything, some of her jewelry maybe, or clothing . . ."

Cassie inwardly recoiled from the idea. "Thank you, I'll see," she lied.

"I'm sorry," Evie's father said, ashen. "For everything we've put you through. I'm so, so sorry."

"No," Cassie objected, "You shouldn't be—"

"Take care." He spoke over her.

"And look after yourself." Evie's mother threw her arms around Cassie. Cassie stood helpless in the grief-stricken embrace. She should be the one apologizing, not them. She was the one who'd seen the signs. The warning fragments, the mood swings; it had been the same with her mother. She should have known. But she'd been so wrapped up in her own problems that she'd ignored it all.

This was her fault, not theirs.

At last Evie's mother pulled away. Her husband wrapped an arm around her and steered her away, toward where Sir Edmund was waiting with a somber expression to take them to the hearse. The burial would be a private, family affair back in London. Cassie had been invited, but she'd politely declined. One day of this hell was enough.

Cassie looked blankly around the courtyard and caught sight of Olivia and Paige with the rest of their group clustered by the chapel entrance, wearing their best mourning suits, looking somehow too glamorous for such a grim affair. There was no sign of Hugo with them. Cassie had been watching for him out of the corner of her eye, but it seemed he'd stayed away from the service, as if he knew the quiet rage that danced in her bloodstream, the blame that waited on her lips.

Olivia caught her eye and made her way over. "Cassie." She gave a weak smile, reaching to squeeze Cassie's arm. "How are you holding up? It's just awful."

"I'm fine," Cassie said quietly, looking away.

"We were just going back to Carlton. I thought I should offer everyone someplace to go have a drink, after the service. Will you come?"

"You're having a party?" Cassie's voice rose with disbelief.

Olivia's eyes widened. "No," she said quickly. "Not like that. A wake, I guess you could call it. A moment to share our memories. Everyone's so shaken up."

"Oh." Cassie took a breath. "Thank you, but, no."

"Please." Olivia kept hold of her arm. Her blue eyes were full of ur-

gency. "I know it's not your thing, but . . . We all lost her. I think it would be good for you to just be with other people. You shouldn't be alone."

Cassie paused. She remembered after her mother's service, how her stepfather had gone straight to the local bar to drink himself into oblivion, and she'd sat home, alone. The house had never been so empty.

She found herself nodding. "I'll see you there."

She could have walked over with the rest of the crowd, but Cassie didn't want to stay another moment in her funeral dress. She'd bought it cheap from a store on the high street, a plain black shift she knew she'd never want to wear again. She stripped it off and left it in her trash, changing into a pair of jeans and a sweater. She pulled on her coat again and headed for the front door, but she couldn't help stopping just inside the living room.

Her eyes went to the beam. She saw Evie there, all over again. Cassie felt her chest constrict. It had been wrong, all wrong, to find her like that, with everything else around her so ordinary. Evie's notes, arranged neatly on the table, a half-drunk mug of tea, crumbs from the biscuit plate. She wondered for a hundredth time when the terrible decision had been made. Had Evie sipped her tea and planned it? Put down her mug, walked to the supply closet, paused to organize her notes in a neat pile before she looped the makeshift noose across the beam?

Cassie forcibly stopped the black thoughts crashing through her mind. She turned her gaze away from the scene of the crime and hurried out of the flat, her footsteps thundering on the staircase as she tried to leave the terrible image behind.

By the time she pushed the door to Olivia's suite ajar, two dozen students were milling in the room, arranged on the couches and sipping wine with hushed voices. She barely recognized the room from the blank canvas it had been when she'd thought it her own; now there were

framed abstract, colorful paintings on the walls, an exotic rug covering the hardwood floor, a tufted settee in pale blue velvet set back by the windows beside a vintage bar cart, fully stocked. The door to the bedroom was cracked open, a careless tangle of clothing strewn on the bed, high-heeled shoes scattered on the floor.

Paige came and swept Cassie into a hug. "If you need anything," she said, joining the long chorus of people who'd promised just the same thing. Cassie nodded and let Paige steer her over to a seat. Miles and a few of the other clique were all there, Olivia's professor Lewis too. There was a heavy silence in the air as they murmured small talk, nobody sure what to say.

"Did her parents get off okay?" Paige asked quietly.

Cassie shrugged. "As well as can be expected."

Paige fell silent. Miles tugged at the collar on his dress shirt. "She'd hate this," he said. "All of us sitting around, so fucking morbid."

"Miles!" Paige hushed him, but he didn't stop.

"I'm serious. Evie was fun, she was joyful, she was the life of the party. Remember how we almost missed the bus back from London, and couldn't find a taxi, and she started singing right there in the middle of Regent's Park?"

Paige gave a faint smile. "And you and Eddie joined in and Hugo took her waltzing around the bicycle racks."

The group around Cassie relaxed, nostalgia drifting across their faces.

"I thought we were going to get arrested," Miles added. "But then she asked the policeman to dance, and he couldn't make up his mind whether to read her the riot act or accept!"

Paige laughed. The other people in the room drifted closer, crowding round to hear.

"She was in my library group," someone else spoke up. "She always forgot her password, she never could keep it straight."

"It was 'Persephone,'" two classmates said at once, and then laughed.

"I suppose she thought if everyone knew, someone could always remind her," one added with a fond smile.

They began sharing stories in turn, anecdotes about Evie and all her misadventures. Somebody turned the music up, and soon the room was full of lively conversation, laughter, and warmth. Cassie sat in the middle of it all, feeling more of a stranger than ever. She hadn't known the Evie they were all talking about, not really. They'd shared afternoons together, yes, curled up in the attic with their books and tea, a few morning runs, that night Evie invited her to the formal dinner at Merton. But listening to Paige and Miles, and the rest of them, talk about Evie's favorite food, and taste for gin cocktails, and habit of discarding her high heels before the end of the night and demanding a piggyback ride from the nearest tall man, Cassie realized that she'd never really known Evie at all.

But these people had. They'd partied with her, shared drinks and dinner dates, and had stories enough to fill the room with laughter. And they'd turned their back on Evie when she needed them most. Nobody was sharing the story of avoiding her calls, dropping her like an unwanted nuisance the moment Hugo moved on.

Cassie felt a spark of resentment. It was like all the sympathy baskets and cards she'd received after her mother died. Meaningless words from people who hadn't cared enough to notice while she was alive. A waste of paper, a waste of space. She shot to her feet, her chest too tight to breathe. She caught a concerned look from Paige, but nobody moved to go after her as she left the room. They were too caught up in their happy memories of Evie, all their pretty lies.

In the hallway, Cassie gasped for air. A whirlwind of guilt and sorrow and unexplained rage was storming in her chest, drowning everything out, demanding release. She stumbled down the corridor, blind to everything, feeling the dark clutches of the past threaten to take hold of her and never let go. *No,* she told herself. *Not now, not here.* She'd held those demons at bay too long to fall apart now.

Then she heard it, through the thunder of her heartbeat. The sound of a piano. Bach. One of her mother's favorite symphonies, playing melancholily through an open doorway farther down the hall. The delicate notes washed over her, bittersweet, bringing with them the faded memories of a sun-drenched room, tulips in a vase on the mantel. Her mother's sweater, soft against her skin.

Slowly, Cassie's heartbeat slowed.

The darkness fell back, just enough for her to breathe again. The world steadied on its axis.

She took a few more steps down the hallway and pushed the door open.

Cassie stopped. Hugo was sitting in the dark room, his head bent away from her over the piano, fingers moving slowly over the keys. He missed a note, discordant, and hit it again, letting out a twisted laugh as he reached for the whiskey bottle balanced on top of the piano.

She pushed the door wider; the hinge squeaked. He turned. "Cassandra, Cassandra . . ." he drawled, sloppy. "Don't you look lovely tonight?"

Cassie's anger returned, sharp in her gut. He was hiding away back here, too cowardly to face them at the funeral. "You skipped the service," she said, icy.

"Miss me?" Hugo slammed the piano lid closed and spun around on the stool.

"You should have paid your respects. Her parents were there."

"You think they'd want to see me?" He met her gaze, lifting the bottle in a bitter toast. His face was pale and gaunt in the dim light, but she could see the shadows under his eyes. "Figured I'd cut the bullshit, give her an Irish wake."

Cassie shook her head in disgust. "How can you just sit here like this?" Her fury grew. "Just laze around feeling sorry for yourself, when, when—"

"When it's all my fault," Hugo finished for her. "That's what you're

saying, isn't it?" he demanded, rising. "That's what they're all saying. Trust me, there's nothing you can throw at me I haven't already told myself." He closed the distance between them until she could see the tension trembling in his jaw, feel the energy radiating from his body. "You think I don't lie awake at nights, going over it time and time again?" His voice rose. "You think I don't ask myself what I could have done differently? If I'd only seen what was happening, if I'd known . . . I should have seen it. I should have known how far gone she was. I could have stopped her, I could have made it different." His eyes were full of misery, guilt turning his dark irises black. Cassie recognized it better than anything: her own emotions, mirrored right back at her. The ache of regret, of wishing it could be any other way. The shame of knowing it was all her fault.

She exhaled in a rush. Her anger slipped away, leaving her empty again. Cassie took the bottle from Hugo's hand and stepped around him, walking over to the dark windows, looking out across the gardens illuminated by the floodlit lamps. She took a long drink of the whiskey, feeling the burn snake down her throat, warming her whole body. "We failed her," she whispered, staring out at the dark.

She felt a movement beside her, and then Hugo was there, one hand resting lightly on her shoulder. "You didn't do anything wrong."

"I did," she admitted softly, pressing her fingertips to the cold glass. "I saw what was happening to her. She was depressed, erratic." She swallowed back a sob. "I knew the signs, I just didn't want to believe it."

"You're wrong," Hugo said firmly. "You couldn't have known."

"And you could?" Cassie turned. "I was her roommate, I was right there. I was the only one, not you or Olivia or anyone else."

Hugo's jaw clenched. "What about Olivia? What did she say to you?"

"Nothing." Cassie shook her head. "That's what I'm trying to say. You guys, you weren't to know. She pretended everything was fine, but I was the only one who saw the truth about how bad she was. I should have told someone." She felt a sob well in her throat. "I could have stopped it this time."

She realized too late the mistake she'd let slip. She tried to turn away, but Hugo lifted his hand to her cheek, stopping her. "What do you mean, this time?" he asked quietly, his eyes searching hers.

Cassie looked away. She'd forgotten the happy family of her cover story, the lies she was tripping over.

"Cassie?" Hugo whispered softly. The sound slipped over her, and Cassie felt the fight ebb from her limbs.

"My mother slashed her wrists in the bathtub when I was fourteen years old," she said quietly. "I didn't see it coming," she added, her voice cracking. "But this time . . . I know what to look for. I can't believe I didn't . . ."

Her words were swallowed up as Hugo pulled her against his body, enveloping her in a sudden embrace. Cassie flinched from the contact, but he held her tight, and after a moment, she surrendered, relaxing into his warmth. She could hear the beat of his heart through his chest, could smell whiskey on his breath. A curious sensation overwhelmed her: a sense of comfort, but edged with something more, an awareness of him and his body, unwelcome but impossible to ignore.

A moment of weakness, Cassie told herself, resting her forehead against his shoulder. That's all it was. All she was allowed.

Hugo didn't move or speak, and neither did she. They just stood there, holding each other in the silence and the dark, until there was a sound in the doorway.

They broke apart.

"There you are." Olivia stared, taking them in. Then her face changed. "Jesus, Hugo, look at you." She strode toward them, reaching to pull Hugo away. "I'm so sorry for my cousin," she apologized. "He's been like this all day. I told him to pull himself together, but . . ."

"It's okay," Cassie said quickly, but Olivia turned back to Hugo, her lips set in a thin line.

"You stink of booze," she hissed, "and everyone's asking for you. I can't believe you'd do this, today of all days—"

"I'm sorry I'm missing your perfect little party." Hugo scowled, the bitter look back on his face. "I guess I'm not so good at pretending everything's fucking fine!"

"I can't talk to you like this," Olivia said grimly. "Go sober up and pull yourself together." She turned back to Cassie, forcing a taut smile. "Come on." She linked her arm through Cassie's and steered her from the room. Cassie glanced back at Hugo, but he was slumped, raising the bottle to his lips, so she let Olivia lead her away, back out into the hallway. "I really am sorry," Olivia apologized again. "He didn't make a nuisance of himself, did he? Evie's death really hit him hard. I mean, it shocked all of us, but he's been a total mess since it happened. It was all we could do to get him out of bed."

"I . . ." Cassie was still recovering from the strange embrace. "No, it's fine."

"Good. Will you come have a drink? I'm so glad you came." Olivia squeezed her hand warmly, but Cassie couldn't imagine returning to the wake, not now.

"I should be getting back," she excused herself instead. "I have to pack up Evie's things, for her parents . . ."

"Oh God." Olivia's blue eyes widened. "How awful. Do you need any help?"

"No, I'll be okay. But, thank you," she added. Olivia had been one of the only people to speak to her after the service. To acknowledge Cassie's grief as part of all the group's loss, instead of acting as if she was an alien, stranded alone with her feelings.

"Where are you staying now?" Olivia asked, accompanying Cassie to the staircase.

"What do you mean?" Cassie replied. "I'm still in the attic."

Olivia stopped. "You mean, they're keeping you there?" She gasped. "You have to go there every day, to where . . ." She trailed off, her words fading. Then she recovered. "It's ridiculous. You'll stay here, with me. I've plenty of room, and the couch pulls out—"

"It's okay," Cassie cut her off. "There's no need, I'm fine where I am."

Olivia shook her head. "I'll speak to someone, they can't possibly expect you to—"

"Don't." Cassie stopped her. "I appreciate the offer. But I really need to get going. This was a nice idea," she added softly. "Evie would have liked it."

She left Olivia and hurried down the stairs, hearing the echo of her own footsteps fill the hall. Outside, rain was spitting, cold against her face, but Cassie couldn't face returning straight to the attic. Despite everything she'd sworn to Olivia, the room was too full of shadows and dark ghosts for her to take, not with her nerves still weak from the service.

Instead, Cassie looped back toward the chapel and peeked inside. It was empty now, the echoing space deserted, candles flickering in a golden line along the altar, flowers still lining the walls. She took a breath, then stepped inside, the heavy door swinging shut behind her. There, in the hush of the stained glass and candlelight, she felt some semblance of her self return. Churches always helped center her. It was strange, for she had no time for organized religion, the rituals and rules of services with their mandated prayers and response. But the buildings, great and powerful things, built as safe havens, shelter—those always felt like a relief, filled as they were with the hopeful prayers of believers who knew the security of a faith she could only envy.

Cassie wandered the aisles, drawing closer to the altar. The memorial display still adorned the platform: Evie's photograph blown up on a poster board, surrounded with flowers and candles. She looked happy. She looked free.

A sound came from behind the altar, startling her. "Hello?" Cassie called out. A moment later a workman emerged, dressed in overalls. "Sorry," she apologized. "I didn't know anyone was here."

"Just finishing up with the engraving," he replied, lifting a box of tools. She must have looked puzzled, because he nodded in the direc-

tion that he'd come. "The *in memorandum* wall. They keep a tribute to all the students who died during their time here. I'm sorry for your loss," he added, awkward, before tipping his cap and exiting.

Cassie pushed aside the heavy velvet drapes to reveal the space at the back of the vestibule, a bronze plate set in the wall, neat lettering engraved in a list.

William Randall Jefferson. 1840–1862. Scholar and friend.

Jeremiah Saracen Hargreaves. 1880–1901. Deeply missed.

And so it went on. Cassie reached out and traced the names, imagining what fates might have taken them so young. There was a cluster around 1918, and through the 1940s. War had touched even the ivory towers of Oxford. But aside from the tragic roll call during those dark years, the names were infrequent.

Juliet Annabeth Hopkins. 1963–1980. Beloved daughter RIP.

Rose Caitlin Smith. 1976–1995. In heaven we will be reunited.

Cassie stopped, her fingertips pressing against the shallow etching. Her mind raced as she read it again. Rose. Her mother's roommate, Margaret's best friend.

Feeling a sudden chill, Cassie backed away from the wall. Rose had died in 1995, the same year Margaret had fled Oxford across the ocean, changing her name and casting off all hints of her former life—except one final tribute to her former friend.

Cassandra Rose Blackwell.

She'd been searching for the reason her mother left. Now, Cassie knew in her bones that she'd found it. The key was right there in front of her, etched in brass on the chapel wall.

Rose's death was the beginning of everything.

"IT DOESN'T SAY HOW SHE DIED."

Cassie squinted at the screen with tired eyes. It was Sunday afternoon, and she and Elliot were the only people left in the archives room downstairs at the Radcliffe library. He was shelving returned books with a weary sigh while she painstakingly spooled through the microfiche of local newspaper stories from the month of Rose's death.

"'Police have called off the search for missing Raleigh undergraduate Rose Smith, following a three-day search by divers in the river Cherwell. Miss Smith's coat and belongings were discovered by the bridge early Sunday morning, prompting the search.'" Cassie read aloud from the faded newsprint on the slide. "'A spokesman said she was now presumed dead, and that nobody was being sought in connection with the death. It is not thought to be suspicious.'" She looked up. "What does that mean? She accidentally drowned?"

Elliot got down from the stepladder and joined her, his gaze scanning over the print. "No, she killed herself."

Cassie shivered. "How do you know that?"

"It's press policy not to report suicides," Elliot said, going back to his task. "They think it'll trigger copycats, or something, so it's all coded and discreet. If it was an accidental death, they would have said so. In the absence of suspects, it can only mean one thing. She topped herself." He caught himself, looking back at Cassie with panicked eyes. "Shit, I'm sorry," he said quickly. "I forgot. I mean, I didn't think—"

"It's okay," she told him, feeling a dull ache in her chest. "You didn't

mean it." She swallowed the pain down, turning back to the screen. It had been days now since Evie's funeral, a week that Cassie had survived only by throwing herself into this new task of digging up every last scrap of information on Rose Smith that she could find. She'd wanted distraction from her feelings of helpless guilt and shame, the low wooden beam she passed every morning in the living room, and the hushed whispers around college, but nothing she discovered had done anything to ease the nervous twist in her stomach and the terrible feeling she had that something was terribly, seriously wrong.

Rose had been the girl in the photograph with her mother, raising a chalice in a smiling toast. They were roommates, friends, teammates on the field-hockey squad, scattered through yearbooks and listings—but only until May of 1995.

That was the month Rose died. One week later, Cassie's mother had left Oxford, packed up her things and fled: changed her name and never uttered one word about what she'd left behind.

Margaret. Rose. Evie. Another dead girl, another wretched suicide. Another life cut short, with no rhyme nor reason to the tragedy. It was too close to home for Cassie, with Evie's things still sitting boxed around the attic, waiting to be delivered back home. And instead of giving her clarity and purpose, this newspaper report only raised another dozen questions.

"This is interesting."

Cassie glanced over. Elliot was perched at a terminal now, scrolling through the internal library records. "Your Rose is listed as an author on one of the books in the catalog."

"But she was an undergraduate." Cassie frowned. "She barely had two semesters here before . . . before she died."

"I know, it's rather strange, except . . ." Elliot typed briefly, then clicked the mouse. "Ah. That explains it. The Raleigh anniversary collection." He looked over. "Every college does it. They hit a big centennial, or whatever, and have students submit things for a big display.

You know, florid first-year poetry about the snow glinting off the deer park." He rolled his eyes. "Or a dozen photographs of the clock tower at sunset. Raleigh had its four-hundredth-year celebration, and Rose must have done something for that."

"Can you find out what?" Cassie asked.

"Sure." Elliot shrugged. "I'll pull the record. But . . ." He paused, a wary look flitting across his face. "How much further down the rabbit hole do you want to fall?"

"What are you talking about?" Cassie snapped her notebook shut and got up, stretching her aching limbs.

"I mean . . ." Elliot hesitated. "We started with Margaret. Just an old family friend, you said. Now we're chasing after this Rose girl too, and don't tell me it's just curiosity. What's really going on?"

Cassie paused. For a moment, she thought about telling him the truth about her search. But then she remembered the ominous print on the back of that photograph, the unanswered questions that haunted her in the night. *Black is the badge of hell* . . . "It's nothing," she finally replied, meeting Elliot's gaze with what she hoped was a blank smile. "I mean, I guess I'm just looking for something to make sense. After . . ." Deliberately, she allowed her words to trail off. "It helps," she added truthfully. "To have something to focus on outside of college and work and all that. Maybe I have been getting a little obsessive. But Christmas vacation is coming soon, and I just want to wrap all this up before the break."

Elliot gave her another look but seemed to be satisfied by her explanation. "I get it. It's easy to get carried away digging around in these files; it's like a puzzle. And they said Wikipedia holes were addictive."

Cassie managed a laugh. "Right. It's the challenge."

"Okay." Elliot got to his feet. "I'll look this one up for you tomorrow, see what I can dig up about the mysterious Rose Smith." He waggled his eyebrows dramatically.

"Thank you." Cassie reached out and squeezed his arm as he passed.

"Not just for this but everything. The job, getting me off campus . . . I really needed it."

Elliot looked uncomfortable. "My pleasure. Now can we please go take a break aboveground before I go cross-eyed and make like one of your American postal workers?"

After snatching a quick coffee with Elliot, Cassie made her way to Thessaly's office across town. She'd told the counselor she wouldn't need another appointment—but that had been before Evie's death. Now she'd received another letter summoning her to therapy—Tremain's work, she guessed—and with so many questions and guilt gnawing at her, Cassie didn't have the heart to resist. She had nobody else to talk with.

"I just don't understand it." She picked at a hangnail, worrying the broken skin until blood pooled. Thessaly sat behind the desk, making notes, as elegantly put-together as the last time they spoke. It was after hours on a Sunday, but still she was dressed immaculately. "She was stressed, sure, but suicidal? It's not right. It doesn't make any sense."

Thessaly nodded. "It can seem that way, from the outside."

"No," Cassie insisted. "You don't see. Evie was . . . happy. She was bright and vivacious, full of energy. I know she'd been a little up and down with her moods, but if you're having problems at school, you take some time out, you talk to your tutors or friends, you don't just end it all."

Again, she saw the body hanging, lifeless and broken.

"It's only natural to want answers," Thessaly soothed her. "But the sad fact is, sometimes there are none. The human mind . . . It's a complex thing. Even I haven't begun to understand it, and it's been my life's work, studying the thing."

Cassie inhaled deeply, then blew out her breath in a huff of frustration. "It happened so fast," she protested. "One minute, she's on the top of the world, out partying every night. And then . . . Something's wrong, I know it is."

Thessaly frowned. "Are you saying . . . ?" She paused. "The police were clear. There was no sign of an intruder, or struggle. Evie even called her parents and left a voice mail saying good-bye."

"I know, I just . . ." Cassie stopped, helpless. She couldn't explain it, how it didn't add up. She'd been there with Evie, she'd seen her. Even in the midst of her rage and upset, Cassie had never seriously thought Evie would take her own life. Depression wasn't the same as suicidal; stress didn't mean somebody would go to such extremes.

"I understand you feel guilty." Thessaly's voice broke through her thoughts. "I'm not saying you should," the counselor added. "But you were her roommate, you saw her more than anyone. And you say, you saw her mental state slipping—"

"Not this far." Cassie vowed. "It was too soon. Two weeks, that's it, from when he broke up with her and everything started to slide. You can't fall apart that quickly."

Thessaly gave her a gentle smile. "It sounds like your friend's troubles went much deeper than a breakup. Do you know anything about her history, her mental health?"

Cassie paused. "I . . . No. Why?"

"From what it sounds like, I'm guessing she may have had issues with bipolar disorder," Thessaly explained. "The wild highs, the sudden crash. It's typical of people with long-running problems."

Cassie shook her head. "Evie wasn't like that, she was fine."

"Was she?" Thessaly countered. "Did you ask her parents? Do you know if she was on medication?" When Cassie slowly shook her head again, she continued, "Like you said, you only knew each other a short amount of time. You can't hold yourself responsible for a problem that probably started long before you ever met her. It's tragic that she couldn't see a way through it, but sadly, it's all too typical for girls like her. Especially here."

Cassie shivered, remembering the names etched on the chapel wall, the news report about Rose's death. "Do you see a lot of suicides at Oxford?"

Thessaly nodded. "The same characteristics that make brilliant students also can lead to mental health issues. The pressured environment, the sense of isolation many feel. . . . It's a sad fact, we lose several students every year. It's part of my work here, to try and work with the colleges to implement better support systems. Some respond more readily than others," she added, with a thin-lipped look.

Cassie sat quietly. She didn't know if she'd been expecting answers or explanations, but she still felt anxious and lost.

"I know this may sound trite to you," Thessaly said. "But the best thing you can do is accept that you may never know what was going on in Evie's mind. Her choices were just that, hers, and if you try and search for meaning, I'm afraid you might never heal. What's done is done," she added. "Sometimes, the only thing we can do is lay the past to rest and move on."

As Cassie left Thessaly's office, she wished what the older woman had said was true. That the past could be put aside so easily, her quest for the truth simply left to gather dust. But she had nothing else but this search for her parents: no job, no life waiting for her back in America, nothing to set this fool's errand to rest.

Cassie had always thought it a virtue that her life was so seamless. Friends, relationships—she'd learned hard and early that people would only let her down in the end. Abuse her trust, betray her. Leave. But now she looked around at the students passing by on the street, clustered in groups and pairs, on their way back from bars and cafés. They filled the evening with laughter and chat, cloistered safely in a world that was much simpler than hers. They went to lectures, met for coffee and dates, planned their glittering futures. For the first time, Cassie felt an ache of longing. All this time, she'd told herself they had no idea what the world was really like, as if her own hardship was a badge of honor, a sign she knew so much more than they did. Now, she wished she could be like them, still innocent and naive. Even Elliot didn't understand the

forces driving Cassie: the hunger that clawed in her heart, the bitter determination fueling every waking moment. If she stopped, even for a second, then what would she have left? Who would she be?

She walked, deep in thought, until a familiar face shocked her back to the present. Hugo was standing in the line snaking away from the kebab truck parked along the street, his dark coat collar upturned, his shock of blond hair wayward in the breeze. He looked over and saw her as she drew closer, raising his hand in a hesitant wave.

Cassie paused. She hadn't seen Hugo since that afternoon after the funeral. She remembered the broken, haunted look in his eyes, and the brief moment of comfort she'd found in his arms. "Hi." She drew level with him, awkward.

"Cassie." Hugo looked carefully at her, as if he'd been expecting a different kind of greeting. "I . . . How are you? How have you been?"

Cassie shrugged. "It's your turn," she said, deflecting the question by nodding at the man waiting behind the counter.

Hugo stepped forward and placed his order, then turned. "What do you want?"

"Oh, I didn't—" Cassie began, but he shook his head.

"Let me buy you dinner. It's the least I can do."

She paused. She hadn't eaten since a snatched sandwich at lunch, hours ago. "Thanks. Fries, with cheese and curry," she said.

Hugo relayed the order with a faint smile. "That was Evie's order."

"She introduced me," Cassie explained. "She swore it was delicious, and she was right."

Hugo paid and reached up to accept the polystyrene and brown-paper-wrapped packages. They walked away from the truck, and he passed Cassie her container, which was steaming the air with a pungent smell of spices. "You didn't answer me, before, when I asked how you were."

Cassie busied herself with the wrapper, prising open the lid and digging her plastic fork into the mound of molten cheese and fries. "I'm . . .

fine," she said with another shrug. "I can't change anything, you know? Life goes on."

"That's what everyone says." Hugo's voice was quiet. They walked a little while longer back toward the college, but when the Raleigh gates came into view, he veered instead toward an iron bench, set back by a small café, closed after dark.

Cassie hesitated, then took a seat beside him. "What about you?" she asked. "How are you dealing?"

Hugo looked at her, his dark eyes glittering black in the neon street-light. "You mean, since the last time you saw me? I want to apologize for the way I acted. Olivia was right; I was drunk, and I shouldn't have taken it out on you." He reached out and placed his hand on hers.

"It's fine." Cassie stared at his hand, overlapping hers in the dark. His fingers were pale, but they burned hot against hers. She felt a shiver from the contact and quickly drew her hand away. "It was a hard day, for all of us."

"But especially you." His voice had something in it, a note of careful observation that made Cassie look up again. Hugo was studying her, his gaze unwavering. She remembered her moment of weakness, confessing the truth about her mother's death.

"Forget I said anything." She turned her attention to her food, scald-ing her lips with a quick forkful. "We were all acting out of character." To her relief, Hugo didn't press the issue. They sat in a companionable silence for a moment more, eating in the streetlight. When nothing was left but a congealed mess, Cassie rose to her feet. "I better get back. I have a tutorial in the morning."

"I'd have thought they'd be giving you a free pass." Hugo got up and discarded their wrappers in a trash can nearby.

"They are," Cassie admitted. Her tutors had clearly had some kind of private meeting, because for the past few weeks her lack of essays or class participation had gone without note—even from Tremain. She showed up, sat silently through her classmates' discussions, and left

without a word when the session was up, feeling everyone's eyes on her and the knowing looks of speculation. "But still, I can't let it all slide. I should at least show my face."

"I'll walk you." Hugo fell into step beside her as they crossed the street. Cassie didn't argue. But when they passed into the courtyard, instead of leaving her there, Hugo stayed with her all the way to the lower door.

"I'm fine here," Cassie told him, reaching to unlock the door, but it swung open without resistance. She hesitated, remembering the last time the door was left unlocked.

Hugo saw her expression. "Does anyone else live here?" he asked, moving ahead of her into the stairwell.

Cassie shook her head. "It's just classrooms down here. And then our apartment."

Hugo began climbing the stairs, Cassie following close behind. "I'm sure it's nothing," she protested. "The porter said he'd send someone to pick up Evie's things. They probably just left the door unlocked." Hugo stopped suddenly, and Cassie bumped right into his back. "What is it?" she asked, and Hugo stood aside.

The door to the attic was swinging wide open. Cassie took a breath and stepped into the flat.

It had been ransacked, torn apart. Chairs upended, the table swept clean. The floor was littered with broken china and books, and the taps had been left running in the kitchen, flooding the floor with a sodden gush.

Hugo swiftly moved to turn the faucet off. "Did you keep anything valuable up here?" he asked, grabbing a clump of dish towels to try and mop up the flow.

Cassie, stunned at the mess, picked her way through the debris, trying to process it. "Nothing. I mean, I have my laptop, but it's barely running. There's no jewelry or cash . . ." She looked around, before suddenly realizing. "Evie's things!" She rushed to the bedroom, but it was a disaster zone. The boxes she'd painstakingly packed full of Evie's

clothing and belongings were torn open, the room strewn with the delicate silk dresses and pretty scarves she'd so carefully folded away.

"They left the artwork," Hugo called from down the hall.

"I never even noticed it," Cassie called back. "Is it worth anything?"

"They didn't think so."

She remembered her own valuables and quickly went to her room. It too had been upended, but when she felt her way to the back of the wardrobe, the panel there was in place, untouched. The files on her mother, the photographs and ticket, were untouched, along with her passport, tucked safely away.

"Everything okay?" Hugo's voice came from the doorway. Cassie quickly stuffed the files inside her bag and emerged from the closet.

"I don't understand it," she said, looking again at the mess. "How did they get past the gate? What did they think they'd find?"

"I don't know. Cash, maybe. Laptops, iPhones." Hugo carefully righted the desk chair that had been thrown aside. "We've had a bunch of break-ins since term started. I guess the thieves think all Raleigh students must be hoarding away the crown jewels, and if you left the front door unlocked . . ."

"I didn't," Cassie insisted. "At least, I don't think I did . . ." She tried to think back to the morning, but she'd rushed out so fast, she couldn't picture herself locking up as she left. Every morning was a sprint, to get out of the damn attic before she could pay too close attention to the beam up overhead and the empty silence of the place.

"You can't stay here," Hugo said. "Pack up what you need. You can crash with me."

Cassie opened her mouth, but he fixed her with a steely look. "You're really going to fight me on this?" he demanded. "We can report it in the morning. It's too late now."

She thought the better of protesting. She couldn't imagine sleeping there, not in the midst of such chaos. "I don't need anything." She looked around again and shivered. Who had been here, picking through

her things, disturbing Evie's last possessions? The sooner she was out of the flat, the better. "Let's just go."

Cassie assumed Hugo lived on the college grounds, but he walked them out of the front gates and half a block away, down a winding residential side street set on the edge of the Magdalen fields. He stopped at a sandstone-fronted town house at the end of the row and opened the front gate. Cassie followed him up the path, through an overgrown front yard, to the ornate blue front door.

"This isn't student housing," she realized, stepping inside. Hugo flipped the lights on, illuminating a foyer that stood two stories high. In a stark contrast to the antiques and disheveled elegance of the Raleigh accommodations, Hugo's home was a modern, loft-style home, all white and chrome and glass. Cassie looked around the open-plan living area, spotless save research papers and books strewn around the leather couches.

Hugo gave a wry smile. "How did you guess? They lost patience with me, kicked me out."

She nodded, suddenly overwhelmed with tiredness. "Thanks for letting me stay."

"Of course." Hugo directed her up the wrought-iron spiral staircase to the mezzanine level, where there was a bed and nightstand. "There are fresh linens, extra blankets in the closet over there. Bathroom's just behind that screen. I'll be downstairs if you need anything."

"Oh." Cassie stopped. "I didn't think. I can take the couch—"

"Don't be ridiculous." Hugo softened. "I've fallen asleep there so many times, it's curved quite nicely to my back. Sleep well." He gave her a crooked smile, then returned downstairs.

Cassie sank down on the edge of the bed. Everything was white, a blank slate, not like the rooms back at Raleigh, dancing with shadows and memories, looming in the dark. She barely managed to kick off her boots and crawl into bed before falling into an exhausted sleep.

She ran.

Through the tunnels, her feet bare on the stone floor. Torches blazed along the main pathways so she veered deeper into the labyrinth, tripping down hidden stairs and along the dark, winding corridors until the air became heavy with decay and doors groaned their protest as she heaved them open. Still, she ran.

The chanting was getting closer, a dizzying hum that echoed off every wall, no matter how far she fled. It was all in her mind, she told herself. It had to be. A shadow suddenly reared up in the gloom and she stumbled in fear, falling hard in a bloody scrape of skin on sharp stone. But there was no time for pain, not with the knife gripped, slick in her hand, or the faint clatter of footsteps getting louder. Closer.

She hurled herself around another corner and up another flight of stairs, almost crying out with relief when she saw a familiar carved archway. Beyond, she knew, was a side tunnel, and past that, freedom.

He stepped out of the shadows—

"Cassie!"

She awoke with a scream, still caught in the terrible fear driving her on through the tunnels. He was there, the dark shadow, but there was no escape. He held her, his grip biting into her arms, shaking her, relentless.

"Cassie, look at me. Wake up!" Hugo's voice broke through the blackness. Cassie gasped, jolting back into her skin to find she was in his bed, tangled in his sheets. Daylight flooded through the windows, illuminating the concern on Hugo's face as he gripped her arms tightly.

Cassie caught her breath, shaking. "I'm sorry, it was just . . . I was . . ."

"A nightmare," Hugo finished. "You scared me." He slowly released her.

Cassie swallowed. Slowly, her heart rate slowed, her blood pounding steadily in her ears.

Hugo sat back with a rueful laugh. "Well, that's one way of waking me before ten. What were you dreaming about?"

"I don't remember." Cassie blinked as the threads of the vision dissolved away under the light. Everything around her was smooth and crisp, comforting in its stark modernism. "But it was so real . . ."

"After Evie, I couldn't sleep for a week. Nothing but falling dreams. Falling into an endless dark."

Cassie slowly shook her head. "This was different. It felt like I'd been there before."

"Where?"

She frowned, trying to remember. "I . . . It's gone."

There was a pause, and Cassie realized she was gripping Hugo's hand. She released it quickly.

Hugo rose to his feet. "It's nearly six. I'll go call the porters, tell them about the break-in."

"I can do that," Cassie objected.

"It's fine. You get yourself together," Hugo told her gently. "Take as long as you need."

When Cassie saw her reflection in the gleaming bathroom mirror, she understood why Hugo had looked so concerned. Her skin was pale, with dark shadows blooming under her eyes. She looked thin and

gaunt, her dark hair in tangles. She'd been so distracted and anxious since Evie's death, was it any wonder Thessaly had seemed so worried about her?

She showered under the powerful jets and dressed, taking one of Hugo's shirts to wear with her jeans. He was on the phone out on the back patio when she made her way downstairs, so she turned to the kitchen instead, searching out eggs in the refrigerator and flour and baking supplies in the cupboards that lined the galley.

"I didn't know you cooked." Hugo found her whisking batter in a bowl, a griddle pan already set on the range.

"Barely." Cassie shrugged. The truth was, she'd never had access to a kitchen like this, with its expanse of marble countertops and space-age stove. She still felt on edge from the night and had reached for familiar tools, a comforting routine. "My mother taught me a couple of recipes. Pancakes," she explained, ladling the thick batter onto the griddle. "American style."

Hugo fetched down plates and cutlery, laying the dining table for two. Now that the exhaustion of the night had been washed away, Cassie looked carefully around the apartment, noticing the modern artwork and touches of life around the room: a bronze globe on the mantel, clothbound books on the shelves.

"How old did you say you were, when . . . ?" Hugo asked, then quickly corrected himself. "I'm sorry, you don't have to talk about it."

Cassie paused. "Fourteen," she finally replied, focusing on the food preparation.

"I'm sorry."

She looked up. Hugo was watching her, his dark eyes full of quiet sympathy. Cassie shook it off. "Have you lived here long?" she asked brightly. "Olivia said you'd been at Raleigh for years, right?"

"Seven years." Hugo's reply had a note of self-deprecation in the tone. "Three as an undergraduate, then another four churning through

my master's, and now a Ph.D. I got this place a while back; Livvy helped me find it. She helped decorate too," he added. "As you can probably tell by all those baking implements I've never once used."

Cassie noticed the casualness with which Hugo referred to his purchase of the property; it wasn't a rental, and he didn't mention his parents' support. He probably had a trust fund depositing a monthly stipend in his account every month like clockwork. "Why do you stick around?" Cassie asked as she flipped the pancakes from the pan and brought them to the table. "It can't be the academics. I don't think I've ever heard you even mention your studies. What is your doctorate, anyway?"

"Oh, something about logic and pure mathematics, I won't bore you with the details."

"So why stay?" Cassie took a seat. The china was matching, heavy and white, with orange juice in cut-glass tumblers and silverware like the kind they used in the grand hall at college.

Hugo gave her the ghost of a smile. "You sound like my family. 'Why won't you grow up and take responsibility?' 'You're destined for greater things than an adjunct professorship.'"

"Ah," Cassie breathed, realizing the truth. "You're hiding."

"I'm pursuing higher learning," Hugo argued.

"You're hiding," she corrected him. "Well, Oxford's the best place for it. It's this . . . bubble, away from everything. The normal rules don't apply."

"The world keeps spinning." Hugo gave a slight smile. "But here everything stays exactly the same. Well, most things." He dropped his voice at the end of his sentence, looking down.

Cassie paused, acknowledging Evie's absence. "So what do they want you to do? Out there in the real world."

Hugo shrugged, his hair falling forward over his eyes. "Join the family business."

"Which is?"

"Power." Hugo's expression twisted. "The Mandevilles . . . we run things. Companies, newspapers, countries."

"Olivia's father." Cassie remembered. "He's in the British parliament."

"Uncle Richard. My father passed when I was young, so he's like a father to me too."

"I'm sorry." Cassie felt a pang of empathy. No wonder he seemed so understanding when she talked about her mother. He'd lost someone, too.

Hugo shook his head. "I was too young, I don't even remember him. My mother didn't cope too well, so I spent most of my childhood with that side of the family. Grandfather has a family estate in Sussex; we all just piled in there."

Cassie could picture it, a clatter of children, all together. Would that have been her fate, had she known her real father? Instead of the progression of lonely house, stepfather, and then the angry isolation of one foster home after the next. "And now?" she pressed. "Are you still close?"

"What is close?" Hugo replied lightly. "We're family. That's all that matters. These are good." He changed the subject deftly, taking another helping. "How do you get them so fluffy?"

"Secret ingredient." Cassie smiled, remembering her mother, bright-eyed in the kitchen, humming along to country songs on the radio. For a moment she felt her mother's presence, stronger than ever, not a shameful secret or burden to carry, but comfort.

They ate in peaceful silence for a while longer, until a sound came from the front foyer, the key turning in the door and the clatter of a new arrival. Cassie tensed. "Hugo? When are you going to have that front step fixed? I've told you a hundred times." Olivia breezed into the living room with grocery bags and an armful of newspapers. "Hi, Cassie." She smiled, seemingly unsurprised to find Cassie there. "Who wants fresh bagels? I went by the place on my way here."

Hugo looked irritated. "Liv, I told you I was busy this morning."

"I know, but when I heard about the break-in, I had to come right over." Olivia turned to Cassie. "Are you okay? Did they take anything? I can't believe someone walked right in like that."

Cassie wondered how news had spread so fast. "I'm fine. They were long gone by the time we got there."

"Thank god Hugo was with you," Olivia said. "We should file a complaint against the porters. Security is a joke; they just sit around watching TV all night."

"No, it's fine," Cassie protested. "Like I said, it didn't look like anything was taken."

"Good." Olivia went to the kitchen and put on the radio, unloading her bags and getting extra plates, filling the space with a bustle of noise and activity. "I invited Paige and the rest over for brunch," she called. "Miles is having a tantrum again, but he promised to bring some good champagne."

Hugo turned to Cassie. "I'm sorry," he murmured. "I told her not to come."

"It's fine." Cassie got up. "I have to get back anyway. I'll need to follow up on the report about the break-in, and classes . . ."

"Oh." Hugo looked taken aback for a moment. "I understand."

"But thank you for letting me stay." Cassie felt a strange tug of regret. She would have happily lingered for the rest of the morning, leaving the outside world behind.

Hugo nodded. "Anytime."

*Back at Raleigh, Cassie went through the official report with a bored-*looking police officer and the college porters. She'd wondered briefly if Charlie would be the one to speak with her, but they sent a different man; he barely looked around the trashed room before sighing. "And nothing was taken?"

"I don't think so. There wasn't anything valuable here." Cassie righted an upside-down chair and took in the mess with a fresh stab of regret.

"If you don't know whether you locked the door or not, there's not much I can do." He shrugged. "I'll file the report, let you know if anyone turns up."

The police officer went back downstairs, leaving Cassie alone with Rutledge. "Well, that was a big help," she told him, rolling her eyes.

"You can always count on the local coppers to take the easy way out," Rutledge agreed. He began helping her straighten up: righting a coffee table that had been knocked over and picking up books from the floor.

"You don't have to do that," Cassie objected.

"Don't you worry about me." Rutledge gave her a smile, his weathered face lined deep with wrinkles. "Those kids can wait a while longer to have someone change a lightbulb."

Cassie started in on the boxes of Evie's things, now strewn around the room. "Will you be able to get these sent to her parents soon?" she asked, folding clothing back into the boxes. "I know there's no rush, but . . . I hate having to look at it all."

Rutledge nodded. "I'll take care of it. Did they want anything kept here? Her academic work, maybe? Some folks like to donate it to the libraries."

"I don't know." Cassie frowned, worried. "I didn't ask. Maybe—" She was interrupted as a phone began to ring. She had to pause for a moment to realize it was the ancient landline that had sat dormant for months on the end table. Cassie picked it up. "Hello?"

"And another week passes without access to modern technology." Elliot's voice was impatient.

"How did you get this number?" Cassie smiled. Across the room, Rutledge gestured he had to leave. She mouthed her thanks as he closed the door behind him.

"A little something called the student directory. Believe me, I'm the first person to access the file in years. For once you should be grateful this place is stuck in the Dark Ages."

"Thank you, Elliot," Cassie said lightly. "Now, what did you need?"

"It's what you need, actually," Elliot replied. "I checked the borrower logs to find that title your Rose Smith authored."

It took Cassie a moment to remember. So much had happened since leaving the library the day before, Rose's suicide had been pushed to the edge of her mind. "Of course, thanks," she said. "What was it?"

Elliot paused. "It was an essay on the origins of Raleigh and the School of Night."

Cassie felt a chill. "The School of Night . . ." she repeated. "You mean she was studying it?"

"In a way. Like I said, it was an anniversary archive thing, not official academic work. She probably just threw together some old articles and polished it up for the big celebration." Elliot sounded tense.

"This book, where is it? Can I read it?"

"Not right now." Elliot's voice was reluctant. "It's on loan."

"Who borrowed it?" Cassie demanded, gripping the phone tightly. "Maybe I can track them down. Is it due back soon?"

"No." Elliot paused.

Cassie made a noise of frustration. "What aren't you telling me?"

After another long moment, he replied in a rush. "It was Evie, your roommate. She was the last person to check it out. The only one," he added. "That thing sat in storage for ten years before she requested to see it."

Cassie caught her breath. "Wait right there," she ordered, dropping the phone to the table. She hurried through the apartment to Evie's room, the boxes into which she'd just meticulously repacked all Evie's books and files. Cassie tore through the boxes, looking closely at the contents this time. She checked every title, but it wasn't there. And neither were her notes. The fat notebooks of articles and papers, the binders Cassie remembered seeing around the flat. She'd been so busy thinking about valuables, but when she'd said nothing had been stolen in the break-in, she'd been wrong.

They'd taken Evie's research. All her study into Raleigh and the founding of the college. Sir Walter Raleigh.

CASSIE WALKED SLOWLY ALONG THE RIVERSIDE PATH AND stretched her tired shoulders. It was early morning, and the winding route had plenty of joggers, but there was still no sign of the one she was looking for.

She turned over the fragments that haunted her, broken pieces that didn't seem to fit.

Genevieve DuLongpre. Rose Smith. Two dead girls, over twenty years apart, with nothing to connect them, except the School of Night.

A rumor. A whisper. An ominous phrase scribbled on the back of a photograph that somebody had planted in Cassie's mailbox. Evie's stolen research.

Rose's death, her mother's disappearance, Evie's suicide: they were all connected. And maybe they were only the beginning.

Cassie caught a flash of motion up ahead on the path. A morning jogger wearing a black hooded sweatshirt, covering the hard icy asphalt in long, steady strides. "Charlie." Cassie stepped out onto the path, greeting him as he drew near.

Charlie slowed to a stop, running in place. "Miss Blackwell." He smiled, mock formal, tipping his hood at her.

"I need your help."

Charlie laughed. "No 'how have you been?'" he teased her. "'It's a cold snap in the air.' 'How about that game on the weekend?' Just straight to the favor, is that how we're going to play it?"

Cassie felt a flash of guilt, but she pushed it aside. "You owe me," she pointed out.

His smile dropped at the memory. Charlie pulled out his earbuds and stopped moving. "What can I help you with?"

They went to a café away from the usual student haunts. Even so, Cassie felt anxious, checking over her shoulder, wondering if she was being watched. Somebody had broken into the apartment to steal Evie's notes; maybe they were keeping tabs on her too.

"I need access to police files," Cassie told Charlie, when they were ensconced in a corner booth with two cups of coffee.

"Well, sure," Charlie replied, kicking back in his seat. "Just come on down. We leave the keys out on the table, take a look at whatever you want."

"I'm serious." Cassie pulled a slip of paper from her pocket and slid it across to him. "These two girls, they were students at Raleigh. They both died. Suicide. I need to see the police reports."

Charlie looked wary. "What's this about?"

"I don't know yet," Cassie replied honestly. "But something . . . Something's not right."

He glanced at the slip where she'd scribbled their names and dates of death. "This one died just a few weeks ago?"

She nodded. "Evie. She was my roommate. One minute she was fine, and the next . . ."

"I'm sorry." Charlie frowned. "But if you're looking for answers, I'm not the guy for the job. Try talking to her friends, or parents—"

"It's not like that," Cassie interrupted him. "This isn't just about her. Both those girls were looking into the same thing, a secret society at Raleigh. And I know how that sounds," she added, seeing his expression. "But something's wrong, I feel it in my gut. They both were digging around into this School of Night, and they both ended up dead."

She stopped talking as the waitress slammed down their orders: dry toast for her and a full English breakfast for Charlie, the large plate packed with eggs, sausages, and baked beans. Cassie waited until the waitress was back in the kitchen before leaning over the table and continuing. "I know it might sound crazy to you—"

"Might?" Charlie raised his eyebrows as he dug into the food.

"But too many things don't add up," Cassie insisted. "Evie wasn't suicidal, no matter what people say. And the other night someone broke into our apartment. They trashed the place and stole her research: research that might have pointed to this secret society."

"Again, might," Charlie emphasized.

"That's not all. After Rose died, her best friend left the country: she changed her name, took on a whole new identity. You don't do that unless you're running from something, something bad."

Charlie still didn't appear swayed.

"Look, can you just find the files?" Cassie asked, feeling desperate. "If there's nothing suspicious, then fine. But people are dead. And all of this . . . It feels wrong. I can't just let it go."

Charlie gave her a long look and sighed. "Fine, I'll find the files," he finally said. "But not because I think there's anything crazy about it. Because I owe you. After that, we're square, okay? No coming to me asking to be let off speeding tickets."

"I don't drive."

"You know what I mean." He set down his knife and fork, and Cassie realized he'd cleaned his plate in barely a few minutes. "Is that it?"

She paused. "Well, yes."

"You haven't made all this up as a pretext to see me again?" Charlie grinned. "Because you could have just asked me to go get a beer. You didn't have to spin me a yarn about mysterious deaths and secret societies."

Cassie couldn't find it in herself to laugh along. "Evie's dead," she said quietly. "This isn't a joke to me."

Charlie stopped. "Right. Sorry." He pulled a few notes from his pocket and threw them down on the table. "I'll see what I can find for you. You got a number I can reach you at?"

"It's on the paper."

"So it is." He gave her a nod. "You had any more problems with that Sebastian fellow?"

"No." Cassie flinched at the reminder. "He took the rest of this semester off."

"Good. I'll be in touch." Charlie sauntered out, pausing to exchange a few words with the waitress that made her laugh and swat him with her dish towel.

Cassie stayed a while longer in the corner booth, sipping her coffee and watching the city bustle to life outside the window. It was December now, the skies flint gray, and the streets full of shoppers and students yawning their way to morning lectures. She had one more paper to turn in before the end of the semester, and then there would be four full weeks of vacation break.

She slowly swirled her spoon in the coffee. She was chasing ghosts, in a strange town far from home. But Providence had never been home, not really. She was looking for something to hold on to, and ever since that package had arrived with her mother's name on it, the glittering prospect of the truth had been that one thing, her beacon in the night. But like the horizon, that truth kept retreating, always just out of reach, morphing into a new challenge and more unanswered questions. First her father, then her mother's true identity, then Rose's death, and now Evie's research too.

Now Cassie wondered, looking out at the city. Would she ever find what she was looking for?

*The end of the semester came and went in a loud burst of revelry from stu-*dents outside Cassie's windows. There were final dinners, and cocktail mixers, and a raucous "bop" in the underground college bar, blasting

cheesy pop music late into the night. Cassie ignored it all until finally, blissfully, the rest of college departed and she was alone on the empty quads, the bell tower ringing out the hour to a silent, deserted campus.

She thought she'd welcome the peace, a break from the demands of her academics and the whispers that still trailed her down the hallways, but instead, Cassie felt on edge with the silence, jittery and out of place. Her attic hadn't felt safe since the day she'd discovered Evie's body, and even though the streets outside in the city bustled brightly with Christmas lights and holiday shoppers, inside the Raleigh walls everything was ominous and still. She found herself escaping the college grounds as much as possible: lingering in the library after her shifts and staying in the café at Blackwell's until closing time, nursing a cup of tea and working her way through thick stacks of books from the fiction department. Some days she didn't see another soul around Raleigh aside from the porters and a few professors like Tremain, who scurried around the grounds with distracted expressions on their faces, no doubt buried in research.

A week slipped by, and then two, until Cassie was closing up the library on December twenty-third for the Christmas break. Even the dedicated scholars of Oxford put their studies aside for a few days, although by the look of the reluctance with which they packed up their things and finally filed out of the building, they would have preferred to celebrate among the dusty books.

"I wasn't sure I'd catch you."

Cassie felt a shock of recognition at the voice even before she turned. Hugo was on the steps outside, his hands in his pockets, a chilled flush on his cheeks.

She hadn't spoken to him since spending the night at his house; she'd assumed the imposition was an event not to be mentioned again. "Hi," she replied, awkward. "I didn't know you were still in town."

"I just popped back up for the day. I had an appointment I couldn't miss. And then I remembered you might be working tonight. Walk you back?" he offered. "Unless, of course, you have other plans."

Cassie shook her head. "No plans."

She fell into step beside him, heading back toward Raleigh. The streets were busier than usual, all the high street stores open late for last-minute shoppers. "I often wonder, what's the point?" Hugo noted with a wry grin, watching a woman struggle under the weight of a clutch of paper bags. "Half this stuff is doomed to sit in the back of a cupboard somewhere, gathering dust."

"It's the ritual of it all," Cassie agreed. "Gift exchanges, dinner, the big game. In America, at least," she added.

Hugo smiled. "Here we have the Boxing Day football. Where everyone sits around getting drunk and bickering about old grudges until you all can't wait to get out of the house."

"Is that what it's like at your house?" Cassie asked, curious. For the last decade, her experience of holidays had always been as an observer, seeing flashes of other families as she worked overtime shifts in stores and restaurants.

"Not quite," Hugo replied. "This year, it's all political strategy and planning. The general election's coming up in May, and that's the only thing on the agenda. Uncle Richard has half his advisory team camped out at Gravestone."

"Do you think he'll win?" Cassie asked. It was odd to her, the way Hugo spoke so casually of his uncle's campaign for the most powerful position in the country. A different world, where power was as automatic as breathing, something to be grasped, tangible, not a distant vague dream.

Hugo let out a sharp laugh. "He better. Otherwise family occasions will be a nightmare." He paused, then corrected himself. "No, I don't mean that. Uncle Richard would be a good prime minister. He's been working toward it as long as I can remember. Practically my whole life. And now it's getting closer, do or die—you can understand why everyone's a little on edge down there."

"What about Olivia?"' Cassie asked, remembering the fire in her eyes when they'd talked about politics that night at the Union.

Hugo sighed. "She loves it. She's down there pitching in right now, image consulting, ideas for reaching out to the younger voters. I can't think of anything worse."

"She'd trade places with you in a heartbeat, you know." Cassie didn't know where her words came from, but it was too late to take them back.

Hugo stopped walking. His gaze met Cassie's with a curious look of recognition. "I know," he said slowly. "I've told them all a hundred times, she's the one suited to carrying on the family name. She could run a small country; half the time I think she already does. But they're all so set in their ways, they won't even hear of it. Women have never been the ones to take the stage in our family. They make good marriages, then stay in the background, steering things from behind the scenes."

"It sounds positively Elizabethan," Cassie joked, as they started walking again. The bright lights of Ahmed's kebab truck came into view, and without discussion they moved to take a place in the line.

"I wish I was laughing." Hugo gave a self-deprecating sigh. "Listen to me, complaining. I'm lucky, I know. I just wish . . ." He looked down at Cassie with a moment of sudden intensity. "Do you ever feel like the past has wrapped its chains around you and won't let go? That everyone else's decisions keep dragging you back, until you can't even see which direction to turn?"

"More than you'll ever know," Cassie replied with a ghost of a smile.

Hugo paused. "I just wish I could be left alone to make my own mind up, for once."

"What would you do?" Cassie asked. She turned to the vendor and ordered, remembering Hugo's choice from the last time and waving away his offer to pay. Food in hand, they walked back toward Raleigh. "I mean it," Cassie continued, picking up the question she'd asked before. "If you had no parents, no family making demands. What would you do? Who would you be?"

Hugo was silent for a moment—so long, Cassie wondered if she'd asked the wrong thing. "I'd like to travel," he said quietly. "Not the way

they do it, luxury hotels and tours, but just see the world for a while. What's out there. I'd quit this stupid doctorate. I always thought . . . No, you'll think it's stupid."

"Go on," Cassie urged him, strangely curious now. She wanted to know his answer, who he was hiding underneath the privilege and charm.

"I wanted to be an explorer when I was younger." Hugo looked bashful, more self-conscious than Cassie had ever seen. "There are still parts of the world where people have never stepped foot, can you imagine? Jungles and rain forests and mountain ranges. To go where nobody else has ever been, be the first to ever lay eyes on something." For a moment, his face was lit up in the dark, full of youthful enthusiasm, and Cassie caught a glimpse of the boy he'd been once, wide-eyed and curious, before this sardonic, jaded persona had slowly taken grip of his soul. Then, just as swiftly, the self-deprecating mask slipped back into place. "I suppose it doesn't take Freud to analyze that one," he added. "Wanting to strike out to the ends of the earth, away from family and duty. It's rather clichéd. What about you? Who would you be without family pressures? Or are you not so weak as to buckle under their grip like me?"

They'd reached the Raleigh gates. Cassie stared at him, her mind going blank. He was trapped by the presence of family, but she was controlled by the absence of it. In a way, her mother's legacy was just as stifling as the expectations Hugo was dealing with. Cassie felt she had no choice: from the moment she'd found the package pointing to Oxford, her destiny was set. She would chase down the truth until all was revealed to her; it wasn't a choice so much as a calling.

Again, the questions lingered in her mind: Who would she be when this was over? What would she have to hold on to, when there was no more chasing left to do? "I don't know," she admitted finally. "This is all I've ever been."

"No," Hugo corrected her, reaching out. His palm slid against her cheek, cupping her jaw, and he stared down intently into her eyes. "You're so much more than you even know."

Cassie froze. She felt the shiver of sensation, his hand burning against her skin, but more than that, something in his eyes: dark loneliness she recognized, because she felt it every day. A hunger, drawing her in.

Hugo's eyes darkened, and suddenly he was leaning in, closer, until she could feel the whisper of his breath against her skin. All she had to do was lift her lips to his, but she remained frozen in place, paralyzed, the hesitation strung in the air between them.

What did he want from her? Cassie lurched back. "Good night," she blurted, putting three feet of safe distance between them.

Hugo straightened, blinking. "Uh, right." He swallowed. "You'll be okay—"

"Fine." Cassie said shortly. She clutched the paper bag of takeout and slipped backward inside the gates.

"Wait," Hugo called. "I . . . we're having a New Year's party. Down at Gravestone. A whole crowd. Come."

Cassie swallowed. "I can't," she lied. "I have plans here. But thanks." She didn't wait for his response before she turned and walked swiftly away, as fast as she could manage without breaking into a run. But even as she strode through the dark courtyard, the night air frozen on her skin, she felt the burn of his touch on her cheek, felt the shimmer of something dark and alive twisting in her blood.

She'd forced herself to forget their meeting in the courtyard, the sharp unease she'd felt at his presence. After Evie died, it had seemed to fade into the background, drowned with grief and guilt and the way that Hugo seemed to understand what she was going through. But now that panic flared to life again, a thunder of adrenaline in her veins. Fear, mixed with something even more dangerous.

Desire.

CHARLIE CALLED ON CHRISTMAS DAY MORNING. CASSIE HAD been sitting around with nothing better to do than channel-hop old holiday movies, so she arranged to meet him at a pub on the outskirts of the city. When she arrived, she found him nursing a pint of beer in the cold of the empty garden out back.

"Can't we go inside?" Cassie asked, shivering. She was wrapped in her duffel coat and scarf, but her fingertips were almost numb from the winter cold.

Charlie shook his head, glancing anxiously around. "This, you don't want anyone to hear."

Cassie's heart clenched. She'd almost given up on hearing from Charlie. After two weeks of silence, she wondered if he'd been avoiding her request, or he was just too busy with his regular life to take the time to check into Rose's death.

"It took me long enough to get to the files," he began. "I said you were a researcher doing a story on student suicides, and I didn't think it would be a problem; we get requests like that all the time. So I filled in the paperwork like usual." He paused, his blue eyes searching hers. "The next morning, I get called in to see the inspector. He grills me for half an hour. Wants to know who you are, why those files. He tried to play it off like confidentiality, you know, respect for the families, but he was rattled. So I told him it was no skin off my nose. I dropped it."

Cassie tried to hide her disappointment. "Thanks all the same," she said, already wondering how she could get access to those suicide files.

"Wait a minute," Charlie corrected her. "I'm not done. I told the inspector it was finished, and then I waited. I didn't have a chance to get near the files for a while, everything's kept on-site, you see, in a fancy new storage wing. People all over the place. But this week, it thinned out. Lots of sick days, people phoning it in for the holidays. I was able to get in there and have a good dig around."

"And?" Cassie's hopes rose. The cold was forgotten, and the discomfort of the wooden bench. All that mattered was the sheaf of photocopied pages Charlie ceremoniously withdrew from his inside coat pocket.

"And you're right. Something's off." He fanned the pages out on the table, and Cassie grabbed the nearest one. "There wasn't much on your friend Evie. The coroner's report was straightforward. Asphyxiation by hanging, no foul play. But Rose Smith . . ." He sighed. "I read the investigation report back to front, and it just doesn't add up. They said suicide, right? But nobody even saw her by the river that day. They found her coat on the bridge, and a note back in her room, but that's it. Now, suicide is plausible, don't get me wrong. But they didn't even declare her a missing person. Just announced it, case closed. It was too clean."

"What do you mean?"

"I know how to read a report. The subtext, the stuff between the lines, and this . . . They wanted it tied up with a fucking ribbon, quick too. They dredged the river, found her things, and that was it. Usually an investigation will go on for months if they don't have a body, but they closed this in a couple of days. And that wasn't all." Charlie took a breath. "It got me thinking, the reason they were all so quick to jump to conclusions about the suicide was there had been a whole rash of them that year. Five deaths in the previous couple of months. Stands to reason, right? If all those other kids topped themselves from stress and whatever, this girl must have done the same. So I looked into them, the other deaths." Charlie reached out and pushed the other papers

toward Cassie, a thick wedge. "They were just the beginning. In the years nineteen ninety to ninety-five, there were sixteen suicides reported at the university."

"Is that a lot?" Cassie asked, trying to understand this new direction.

Charlie gave a grim nod. "Double the national average."

"But Oxford is a stressful environment," Cassie said slowly, repeating what Thessaly had told her in their counseling session.

"Sure, but then you'd expect the rates to stay steady," Charlie argued. "Instead, look." He pulled a piece of paper from his coat pocket, neatly folded. It was a rough timeline with Xs marked along the years. "You get clusters. And going back too—I searched the records for all mentions of suicide going back as far as I could. It's the same. The rate is steady, a few people every year, then every twenty-five years or so, a big new cluster. In the midsixties, they had ten bodies show up in the space of five months."

"Why didn't anyone notice?" Cassie asked, her mind racing.

Charlie shrugged. "Who's going to connect the dots?" he asked. "The deaths don't get investigated on our end: once it's a suicide, that pretty much wraps it up. The families are too focused on their own grief. Occasionally, you'd get a researcher or someone talking about the epidemic of tragedy, so the colleges would launch a mental health campaign, or some kind of help line, but that's it. People move on, you see: students, staff—nobody stays in the same place here for long. They leave, a new crop of students arrives, and everyone forgets what happened before."

Cassie stared at the diagram, the tiny crosses marking so many lost lives. "These are all students?"

"Mostly." Charlie nodded. "Some locals too. But they didn't get such a fuss. Not so high profile."

"And you're sure it's not just a coincidence," Cassie tried. This wasn't just two deaths that didn't add up, but dozens, stretching back

half a century at least. This was way over her head. "College attracts brilliant, unstable people. They get fixated on the work; any kind of failure can set them over the edge."

"Look at it," Charlie said, tapping the paper. "Does that look like a coincidence to you?"

The timeline was impossible to ignore. Cassie traced the line, trying to imagine all those unexplained deaths, how anyone could turn his head and look the other way for so long. "What do you think it is?" she asked. "A serial killer? More than one?"

Charlie shook his head slowly. "The timeline is too spread out. Most killers will strike within ten or twenty years. This goes back to the nineteenth century, at least."

"So it's bigger than just one person." She shivered. "What do we do next?"

Charlie pulled his coat closed. "Well, I don't know about you, but I need to get home. My mum's got a Christmas roast in the oven, and if I'm not back to peel the spuds, there'll be hell to pay."

Cassie blinked in disbelief. He'd delivered her proof that there were dozens of unexplained deaths at Oxford, and now he was talking about holiday meals? He must have caught her anxious expression because he sighed. "Look, there's something here. I believe you. We need to figure out what's been going on. But there's nothing we can do today. It's Christmas. Go home, relax, we'll pick this up next week."

"Home," Cassie echoed. As if she could simply put this aside now, when it was so much bigger than she'd ever imagined. "Sure. Right."

She got up to leave, but Charlie paused. "Where are you celebrating, anyway?"

Cassie was still thinking about the cluster of Xs and stumbled out her response. "Um, nowhere. I don't really do the holidays."

"You don't do . . . ? Right, come on." Charlie beckoned. "My mum would string me up if she knew there was a stray wandering around."

"I'm not a stray!" Cassie protested. "And I'm fine, really. I'll get take-out and watch *It's a Wonderful Life*. Fine, see?" She forced a smile, but Charlie just rolled his eyes.

"You'll sit around obsessing over this lot, you mean. Come on," he said again, softer this time. "What's the harm? We're a loud, obnoxious bunch, but it's Christmas. Everyone should be with family, even if it's not your own."

Cassie felt a pang. Her last Christmas with her mother had been a good year, her mom stable enough to remember presents and a tree. She'd baked cinnamon cookies and played Christmas songs while Cassie watched from the kitchen counter and tried desperately to re-member this: the safety, the comfort and joy. She'd known she might not get another Christmas like that; she just hadn't known she would never get another at all.

Something in her twisted with a lonely ache. She found herself nod-ding. "Okay," she told Charlie, self-conscious. "Thank you. I'll come."

*Charlie's family lived on the outskirts of the city, in a residential cul-de-*sac full of redbrick houses and overgrown front yards. Several of the houses were strewn with gaudy Christmas lights, but none were as elab-orate as the plastic Santa and snowmen propped on the roof of Charlie's house, flashing a rainbow of lights even in the bright of midday. "Now, you might want to brace yourself," he warned her, slamming the car door of his beat-up blue Honda. "They were just breaking into the Bai-leys when I left, so it's probably bedlam by now."

Cassie followed him up the walk, curious. Even from here she could hear noise from inside the house, and when he unlocked the front door, it burst out in a chorus of chaos.

"Mum! Kirsty took my new skirt from Topshop and you know she'll stretch it out!" A teenage girl was thundering down the stairs, closely followed by another girl around sixteen dressed in a tight vest and red miniskirt.

"Will not, you're the one who needs to stop eating all my Ferrero Rocher!" They pushed past Charlie and Cassie without slowing for breath, racing to the back of the house.

Charlie gave Cassie a grin. "Welcome to the madness."

Another girl backed out of the living room, juggling a baby on her hip. "Liam! Liam, put that plug down! What have I told you, sockets aren't toys!" She turned, seeing them in the hallway. "Charlie, there you are. Can you keep your nephew from electrocuting the cat? If he blows the fuse, we'll never get dinner cooked."

"Cassie, my sister Rhiannon," Charlie introduced.

Rhiannon gave Cassie a brief look. "Can you take her?" she asked, thrusting the baby at her.

"I, what?" Cassie didn't have time to argue; the infant was already in her arms.

"Just for a sec, I've got to go give her dad a bollocking. Charlie, the plug!" she ordered, before marching outside.

"Duty calls," Charlie grinned, heading into the living room.

Cassie caught her breath, alone for a moment in the hallway with a baby in her arms. When Charlie had said his family was a handful, she hadn't realized what he meant. For a second, she thought about making her excuses and a quick exit, but then Charlie poked his head back around the door with a friendly grin. "Well, don't just stand there."

"Sure. Sorry." Cassie followed him into the living room, crammed with old faded sofas, a big-screen TV, and a huge, gaudily decorated tree. Charlie was on his knees, tickling a toddler who shrieked in delight. He looked up. "Sorry about Rhiannon. These are her brats."

"Oh." Cassie blinked, wondering how old she was. Not more than eighteen, at most.

Charlie caught her look and chuckled. "Yeah, that about sums it up. You should have seen Mum's face when she came home from school and told us she was pregnant with this one." He attacked the toddler again. "Should've known he'd turn out to be a terror. That one's Daisy," he

added, nodding to the baby Cassie was holding awkwardly. "And those two whining girls you saw tearing through here before are my youngest sisters, Kirsty and Laura."

"Wow." Cassie swallowed. "Big family."

"Yup." Charlie swung Liam over his head to sit on his shoulders. "And Uncle Fred and Aunt Trudy are here too. Don't worry," he added. "They're too busy not speaking to each other to pay any attention to you."

Charlie was right. As the various members of the Day clan wandered in and out of the room, Cassie found she could sit unnoticed in the corner, bouncing the placid baby on her lap as the noise continued around her, Charlie and his sisters bickering over half a dozen different things. She found it hard to keep up, but Cassie didn't mind: it was relaxing to simply watch the madness whirl around her, the loud, affectionate hustle of family life. Nobody asked her about her own family or plans, they just set her to work peeling potatoes in the overpacked kitchen, while Charlie's mother kept a watchful eye on five different pans of food and his sisters flipped through gossip magazines and texted their friends.

"So how long have you known our Charlie?" his mother, Maureen, asked when Charlie had been sent up on the roof to adjust the TV aerial. She was a loud, blousy women in her fifties with a feathery cut of dyed blond hair and the kind of sharp gaze that left nothing unnoticed.

"A couple of months," Cassie replied. "But I don't know him all that well."

"So you're not his girlfriend?" one of the sisters, Laura, Cassie thought, piped up.

"No, it's not her," the other teenage girl answered for Cassie. "He dumped her the other week, remember? She was getting too clingy."

"They always get too clingy. He's such a man-whore." Laura rolled her eyes.

"Don't talk like that about your brother," Maureen scolded. "He's just looking for the right girl, that's all." She turned back to Cassie with

a worrying gleam in her eye. "And you're a student at one of the colleges, are you? Clever girl."

"Just for the year," Cassie explained quickly, lest Maureen get the impression that Cassie was that right girl Charlie needed. "Then I go back to America."

"Hmm." Maureen paused. "Well, shame." She turned back to stirring the gravy. "It's hard for him to meet a nice girl; all he does is work."

"And get drunk down at the pub," Kirsty muttered.

"I don't suppose you have any friends . . . ?" Maureen was asking when Charlie came back in.

"What did I miss?" He looked around.

"I was hearing all about your love life," Cassie told him, with a teasing grin.

Charlie groaned. "Mum! What have you been telling her?"

"Nothing bad," Maureen protested. "Just I can't understand why a boy like you can't find a nice girl. You're a real catch, you know."

"I'm too young to settle down." Charlie pretended to act annoyed, but Cassie could tell he didn't mind. "I've got another ten years of bachelor kicks in me, at least." He winked at Cassie.

Maureen beamed at him, clearly adoring. "That's just what your dad said before he met me. You mark my words, when you meet the right girl, you won't know what hit you."

Cassie watched them. She could see they'd had this exchange a hundred times and would probably have it another hundred more. She felt a tightness in her chest, a familiar ache. The love between Charlie and his family was so casual, they probably didn't even realize how lucky they were: the way they dipped into each other's conversations, entering and exiting rooms mid-thought; even the way they all moved through the house was a ballet, an unconscious but constant motion.

"You all right?" Maureen asked, looking over.

"It's just . . . the onions." Cassie pointed to the freshly chopped pile with relief. "I'm going to get some air." She put down her peeler and

headed for the back door. There was a small patio outside the kitchen, and a thin strip of lawn, browned and overgrown in the winter. A children's play slide was set up at the end, and Cassie went to perch on the step, gulping in deep breaths of chilled winter air.

It was the holidays, she told herself, fighting back tears. This time of year brought up memories for everyone, and now all the things Cassie had worked so hard to push down were bubbling to the surface again, brought on by the memories of cinnamon and nutmeg in the steamy kitchen air. It would pass, it always did.

"Hey."

She looked up, quickly wiping her eyes. Charlie was coming down the garden toward her. "Don't tell me they drove you away already. I was thinking you'd make it through lunch, at least."

"No, it's not that." Cassie forced a smile as he reached her. "I'm fine. I just needed—"

"Some air," he finished for her. Charlie studied her carefully, then shrugged off his jacket and draped it over her shoulders. "You'll catch your death out here."

"Thanks." Cassie swallowed, feeling self-conscious.

"Sure you're okay?" he asked again.

She nodded. "It's just the holidays."

"You miss your folks?" Charlie lowered himself onto the step beside her and pulled a pack of cigarettes from his pocket. "Don't tell her indoors," he added. "I'll never hear the end of it."

"Your secret's safe with me," Cassie replied.

Charlie lit a cigarette and inhaled a long breath. "What about yours?" he asked, turning to look at her with a searching stare.

"What?" Cassie blinked.

"Your secrets." Charlie took another drag. "What's all this research really about?"

Cassie paused, her old lie to Elliot sticking in her throat. It shouldn't have been hard to explain, again, about the family friend, and her nat-

ural curiosity. But for some reason the lie wouldn't come. Maybe it was because of the loud chatter and music drifting from the house, the home Charlie had invited her into without a second thought, as if revealing his life to her was the most natural thing in the world.

Cassie reached into the pocket of her jeans and pulled out her slim wallet. She slowly unfolded the picture of her mother and Rose she kept there and passed it to Charlie.

"The dead girl," he said, recognizing her.

"And that's my mother." Cassie pointed to Margaret's face. "After Rose died, she dropped out. Changed her name, moved to America. She's dead now; she killed herself too, ten years ago. But she never once told me she'd even studied at Oxford. That's how I know there's something rotten going on here," she added, meeting Charlie's steady blue eyes. "She ran. She ran from something, and I need to know what it was."

Charlie held her gaze, thoughtful. Then he slowly folded the picture and caught sight of the writing on the back. " 'Black is the badge of hell, the hue of dungeons, and the school of night,' " he read.

"Someone put that in my mail," Cassie explained. "It's a reference to a secret society at Raleigh. At least, I think it is. Rose wrote a paper on the society," she added. "And Evie checked it out just a week before she died."

"Curious and curiouser." Charlie took another long drag on his cigarette, then ground the stub out under his heel and stood up. "We'll figure it out," he said quietly, holding out his hand to help her up. "We'll find the answers you're looking for."

He sounded so certain, Cassie couldn't help but believe him. Then his face crinkled into a familiar grin. "But right now, there's a roast turkey and five kinds of vegetables waiting on that table. Murder and mayhem can wait. First, we eat."

Christmas lunch was a boozy, drawn-out affair with traditional crack- ers and paper crowns. Cassie let herself get swept along in the flow of

conversation and laughter, savoring the brief glimpse of happily dysfunctional family life. After the dishes were finally cleared, Charlie's sisters disappeared to go hang out with their friends, and the remainder of them retired to the living room to watch TV.

"Okay to stay for a bit?" Charlie asked, looking over from where he was sprawled beside Cassie on the couch. "I ate so much I can't move an inch right now. I'll drive you back after the movie."

"Sure," Cassie agreed, glad of an excuse to stay longer, wrapped in the warmth of a woolly throw and his family's friendship.

"Hold on starting the movie," Maureen called from the kitchen. "I'm just making a pot of tea."

Charlie began channel-hopping, until his uncle spoke up. "Pause there. Let me take a look at the news." Charlie turned the volume up. It was a story about the upcoming election, shots of the contending politicians out greeting constituents and posing with Santa Claus. Cassie watched carefully when Richard Mandeville came on-screen, a handsome man in his late forties with salt-and-pepper hair and an engaging smile.

"What do you think of him?" she asked Charlie, nodding at the TV.

He shrugged. "They're all the same. They like to talk tough on law and order, but you can bet whoever gets elected, they'll be slashing our budgets before the year is out."

"I know his family," she said, still watching the news conference on-screen. Mandeville was speaking at some event, looking confident and sincere in front of the crowd. "His daughter's at Raleigh."

"Of course she is." Charlie gave a laugh. "All that lot went to Oxford. The kids you're there with now will be running the country in twenty years' time."

Cassie was about to reply when she caught something on-screen that made her heart stop. It was footage from a previous occasion, Mandeville shaking hands with someone, but the people weren't what caught her attention. It was where they were standing that made her breath catch.

"Charlie," she whispered, pulling the photo back out of her wallet. "Look." She showed him the picture of her mother and Rose, sitting at a table in front of a wall of portraits.

On-screen, Richard Mandeville was shown chatting with some business leader or politician. In front of the same wall of portraits, the very same dining room.

Gravestone Manor. The Mandeville family estate.

Charlie looked back at Cassie, his eyes searching her face. "No," he said, before she had a chance to even say a word. "You can't."

"I have to get in there," she declared.

"You can't just go waltzing in," Charlie said, shaking his head. "He's about to get elected prime minister; there'll be security for miles. And even if you found a way in, they'll throw you out on your ass the minute you start digging around."

"No, they won't." Cassie realized her chance. "I have an invitation."

HUGO INSISTED ON SENDING A CAR FOR HER. GRAVESTONE WAS in the middle of the countryside, he told her; local trains and buses weren't running through the New Year. So Cassie sat nervously in the back of the sleek black BMW, watching the driver in his peaked cap as Oxford melted away in the rearview mirror and the motorways snaked through the clouded green landscape toward her destination.

The phone in her hands buzzed with a text.

All OK?

Fine. Not there yet.

Call me the minute anything happens.

Charlie had balked at the idea of Cassie disappearing into the depths of Sussex without any way to call for help. He'd arranged a meeting before she left and pressed his sister's outdated cell phone into her hand that morning as Cassie prepared to depart.

"Don't do anything stupid," he warned her. "Just get the lay of the land. For all you know, there's nothing linking the Mandevilles to any of this stuff. It could just have been a coincidence about the photo."

"Nothing about any of this is a coincidence," Cassie replied grimly, but she took the phone all the same. Charlie was still looking at her with concerned eyes, so she sighed. "I'm not going to go charging in there making wild accusations," she reassured him. "I just want to see what

that place is all about. Besides, it's a party. Hundreds of people will be there. Nobody will notice if I take a look around."

As the car wound its way through the Sussex countryside, Cassie wondered what it was she was looking for. She'd had nothing but suspicions and instinct driving her on until now, small threads that, once she tugged them, only unraveled another row of neat assumptions. But now that Charlie was involved, everything felt more real, the doubts and whispers that had only circled in her mind now taking shape in the hushed conversations they exchanged in the background of the noisy pubs on the outskirts of the city.

He believed her. Something was going on. And the body count had been rising for years now, decades, a long trail of heartbreak and tragedy.

Would Gravestone be the key, Cassie wondered now, as the car wound its way through the Sussex countryside, or was this just another fool's errand? But as the green patchwork woodland grew denser outside the car windows, taking her farther from the comfort of busy motorways and clustered towns, Cassie's heartbeat sped in her chest in a skitter of nervous anticipation and she felt a growing sense of dread. What secrets was Gravestone hiding? And if some dark conspiracy was lurking there, did that mean Hugo was a part of it, too?

After two hours in the car, Cassie's nerves were stretched to their breaking point. Finally, they turned onto a winding country road that took them through a copse of woodland. Then the trees cleared, and Cassie took a sharp breath as Gravestone came into view for the first time.

It was stunning. Gravestone was a sprawling Elizabethan manor on the hillside below them, built in burnished red brick and slate tiles. The driveway circled around a formal fountain, and as they approached, Cassie could see the neat lines of formal gardens fanning out from the mansion, giving way to lawns and a lake glittering beyond the gardens in a brief burst of sunlight.

The car drew up outside the front steps, wheels crunching on the gravel. It was late in the afternoon, and already two dozen cars were parked outside—a gleaming row of Bentleys and Rolls-Royces—as well as a couple of white vans from which uniformed staff were unloading boxes of flowers and party supplies. Cassie climbed out before the driver had time to come around to open the door for her and gazed up at the three stories of twisting ivy and iron-paned windows.

"I can take your case, ma'am." The driver took from her the battered weekend bag that she had hastily packed.

"Thank you," she started to say, but he'd already disappeared into the house.

Cassie took a deep breath and slowly climbed the front steps. The doors were open, so she entered, her eyes adjusting to the gloom in the wood-paneled and imposing grand foyer, with a wide staircase spiraling upward and a mezzanine level above. There was a faded grandeur to everything: the heavy velvet drapes blocking light at the windows, the damask and brocade upholstery on the furniture, antique tables and coatracks at every turn.

She wandered deeper into the house. One grand room gave way to the next, all decorated with the same heavy wooden furniture and antique fabrics. It was like a museum, perfectly restored, and Cassie could almost imagine the original inhabitants strolling through the same rooms, five hundred years ago.

"Cassie!" She turned just as Olivia enveloped her in a hug. "What are you doing wandering round here? We're over in the East Wing. Come on." Olivia linked her arm through Cassie's and steered her on. "Did you have a fun Christmas?" She was dressed in jeans and a silk shirt, her hair pulled back in a loose braid. "The drive down here is such a drag, I know, but I'm so happy you could make the party. Mother's been planning it all year; it's her crowning achievement." She laughed as they crossed a hallway and turned into what Cassie guessed was the newer portion of the house. Here, the walls were white and airy, and although

antiques abounded, there was an elegant, almost Mediterranean look to the rooms, rustic and faded. "We're rather squeezed for space," Olivia continued, "so I had to put you up in the Hartley suite. It overlooks the stables, so no view, I'm afraid, but at least you're not near the chicken run." She added in a confidential tone, "I saved that for Miles. He always sleeps until noon so I thought the rooster would be a nice wake-up call for him. Here we are!"

She led Cassie into a large kitchen lounge area. Paige, Miles, Hugo, and the rest were sprawled on cozy settees and around a rustic farm table, and French doors flooded the room with light. "Look who made it!" Olivia announced. Cassie gave a wave.

Hugo got to his feet, smiling. "Was the drive okay?" he asked, coming closer. In a flash, Cassie remembered their parting outside the college: the tension, and the almost kiss.

"Yes, fine." She turned her head, accepting his welcome kiss on her cheek. His lips brushed her skin, and she felt a rush of sensation.

"Good." Hugo looked satisfied. "I'm glad you changed your mind."

"Well . . . Oxford is pretty dead right now," she replied, awkwardly. "It sounded like fun."

"The most fun," Paige interrupted, joining them to hug Cassie hello. "The Mandeville New Year's bash is the stuff of legends."

"Literally," Miles piped up. "I believe a certain Booker Prize–winning novelist set a crucial scene here in one of his last tomes."

"That's just rumor," Olivia said, laughing.

"Sure, because how many original fifteenth-century mazes are there in the country?" he countered.

"There's a maze?" Cassie asked, moving to sit with them at the huge farm table.

"Yes, and don't go wandering out there alone," Paige warned her. "It's a bitch to navigate."

Olivia squeezed Paige in a hug. "This one got drunk last year and stumbled around for an hour before she had the good sense to call me."

"It was dark out!" Paige protested.

"Don't worry," Hugo said, meeting Cassie's eyes with a smile. "We learned from our mistakes. This year, there's a guide trail."

"Which takes all the fun out of it," Olivia said, pouting.

Cassie just smiled along. As the afternoon slipped past in a leisurely procession of food and gossip and laughter, she found herself looking around the room, studying her companions with a new scrutiny. Were they part of the mystery of the School of Night? It was hard to believe anything sinister was lurking behind their easy smiles as Cassie watched Olivia and Paige pore over fashion magazines, Miles idly read from his iPad. Their lives were ones of parties and play, through the clubs and exclusive bars of London and Oxford. What use would they have with murder and darkness? And more, could they really be capable of such things?

Hugo caught her eye. "Everything good?" he asked, raising an eyebrow. She nodded, again feeling a flush of awareness from his eyes on her, and she was relieved when Olivia declared it was time for the girls to go get ready for the party.

"At least try to make an effort," she scolded Hugo affectionately as they exited. "A T-shirt is not allowed."

Olivia took Cassie up to the room where she'd be staying. For all Olivia's apologies about the squeeze, it was still a high-ceilinged, palatial room with a four-poster bed and ornate tapestries hung on the walls.

"The dress code tonight . . ." Cassie paused. She'd reluctantly packed the same black silk dress Evie had loaned her for the formal dinner at Merton College they'd attended, after finding it crumpled in a laundry hamper in her room. Now, seeing the flurry of activity downstairs and hearing the group's tales of past excess, she wondered if she'd need something more dressy. "Is it going to be formal?"

"Hugo didn't mention it? God, men can be so oblivious sometimes." Olivia rolled her eyes. "Don't worry, you can borrow something of mine."

Cassie flushed. "You don't have to—" she began to object, but Olivia cut her off.

"Nonsense. I've got tons of dresses; Daddy is always dragging me to some fund-raiser or another. And we're about the same size." She scrutinized Cassie with a practiced eye. "I know just the thing. I'll have Perkins bring it over, don't even think about it."

"Thank you," Cassie said. She seemed to be accepting favors from Olivia and Hugo an awful lot recently, but they offered them so easily, as if it was nothing at all. And, Cassie supposed, as she showered and got ready for the big event, it really wasn't. They'd lived their lives so full of privilege, every need always met. They didn't know the panic of poverty, or how tightly one held on to things when there was so little to hold at all. When she'd first met them, she'd resented them for it. Cassie remembered her prickly detachment when she'd first arrived at Raleigh, and the way she'd viewed everyone with the same jaded, bitter eyes. But if she was truly honest with herself, she'd misjudged them, Hugo and Olivia most of all. They'd welcomed her so readily into their world, she felt almost guilty coming into their home under false pretenses.

After taking a long shower, Cassie emerged from the bathroom to find a dry-cleaning bag on the bed. Inside was a floor-length gown in the palest of blush pink silk. It was unlike anything she'd ever worn before, so flowing and feminine, but when she slid the soft fabric over her head and saw it settle over the slim curves of her body, Cassie had to catch her breath. She looked like somebody else. Someone refined, elegant, innocent.

Somebody who would be able to wander the halls of Gravestone without a whisper of suspicion, just as she'd planned.

Cassie slipped on her heels and fastened her hair back in a simple twisted knot, then headed lightly down the stairs. She could hear the sounds of music and conversation drifting from the other side of the house, but instead of moving toward it, Cassie carefully veered away and headed deeper into the long series of passageways and rooms. There

were libraries and formal lounges, a portrait gallery, and more. In each room, Cassie carefully checked the paintings and furniture, looking for the background she'd memorized from the photo of her mother.

At last, she stepped into a dining room in the far corner of the main house and felt a jolt of recognition. The dark green walls, the ornate picture frames. . . . This was it. Cassie walked slowly to the spot just in front of an imposing portrait. This was where the photographer had stood, and her mother . . . her mother had sat right there, in the throne-like carved wooden chair. Cassie rounded the table and slid into the seat, running her fingertips lightly over the whorls and rosettes carved into the wood. She tried to imagine the scene from the day the photograph was taken: Rose sitting beside her, glasses raised in a toast. Who else had been in the room with them? What had been the event? Another wild party like this one, the house crammed full of strangers? Or something smaller, intimate? A dinner with a purpose. A meeting of like minds and coconspirators . . .

"Comfortable?"

Cassie startled. An older man stood in the doorway watching her, and when he stepped out of the shadows, she realized he was the man she'd met on the very first day of term at Raleigh—the one who'd caught her sneaking into the master's office. This time, he was dressed in an immaculate tuxedo, his shock of white hair smoothed back from his deeply lined face, but his eyes were just as chilling as she remembered: coal black, and staring straight through her.

Cassie jolted to her feet. "I'm sorry," she stuttered, her heart racing. "I didn't—"

"Please, don't get up." The man gestured her to sit. His words were polite, but the tone was an order.

Cassie awkwardly slid back down in the seat again, trying to collect herself. She was an invited guest, she reminded herself. He couldn't possibly know what she was doing there.

The man moved closer, his movements surprisingly lithe for some-

one of his age. He traced the tabletop and regarded her with undisguised curiosity. "Many great men have sat in that chair."

"What about the great women?" Cassie couldn't help but reply.

The man blinked, then his lips creased in a smile. "Women too." He paused, those black eyes still raking across her. Cassie tried to hide her unease. "We haven't been introduced," he said at last. "Henry Mandeville." He didn't hold out a hand to shake.

"Hugo's grandfather?" Cassie asked.

He raised an eyebrow, and in an instant her assumption was confirmed. It was the same wry arch she'd seen so many times on Hugo's face, the same jawline under Henry's cheeks, sagging a little with age.

The same deep unease shivered through her body as when she'd first encountered Hugo that night.

"You know my grandson?" Henry asked.

"I'm at Raleigh," Cassie replied quickly. "With Olivia too."

Henry gave a small nod, but his scrutiny didn't stop. "And you decided to take a look around the place."

Cassie felt herself wilting under his stare. "I'm sorry, I was curious."

"You should be careful with that." Henry's gaze didn't falter. "You know what they say about curiosity . . ."

It struck Cassie how alone they were, how far from the party. This wing of the house was empty and still, and they were the only two people around. "Of course," she apologized again. "I'm sorry. I should get back to the party. They'll be wondering where I am." She scurried from the seat. Henry didn't move as she approached the doorway, his head tilted slightly in thought.

"What did you say your name was?" he asked as she passed him.

Cassie froze. "Cassandra," she managed to reply, thanking her mother for the first time for the new identity. "Cassandra Blackwell."

"Hmm." Henry Mandeville stared at her for another long moment, the seconds ticking past as Cassie's panic fluttered in her chest under those cold black eyes. "A pleasure to meet you, Miss Blackwell."

Cassie nodded quickly and then fled toward the burst of noise and laughter now echoing from the front of the house. Toward safety.

The countdown to midnight spun on in a whirl of champagne and music, glittered jewels and a crush of tuxedos and silk. The grand ballroom at Gravestone lived up to its name: the huge room stretched the length of the house, its polished floors packed with hundreds of drunken revelers. Cassie drank everything in, overwhelmed by the cacophony of colors and sounds. Everywhere there was a mounting sense of anticipation, the hours slipping past too quickly to hold on to, the minutes dissolving in another flute of fine champagne. She tried to stay alert and watchful, but soon Olivia and Paige pulled her into the whirlwind, dancing through the night in the center of the crush, their shoes long since kicked off and forgotten, a parade of dance partners spinning them across the room. Cassie gasped for air, giddy, the brief burst of celebration lifting her out of the heavy numbness she'd been living in for so long.

"Having fun?" Olivia yelled over the music, gripping both of Cassie's hand tightly. She was grinning ear to ear, spinning them in the middle of the crush.

"Yes!" Cassie laughed, her heart racing with the dancing and bubble of champagne fizzling in her blood. And she was, the last threads of guilt and grief chased away under the sparkling chandeliers and glitter of confetti, a kaleidoscope of elation she wished could last forever.

They whirled on until Cassie's head was spinning and her stomach lurched with a dangerous pull. "I'm going to take a break," she called through the din, but Olivia and Paige were already onto new partners, tuxedo-clad men who swirled them off the floor.

Cassie struggled through the crowd, emerging at the edge of the crush. She asked a waiter for directions, then headed down the hallway towards the bathroom. Inside there was a brief moment of peace, the cool white marble steady under her hands, cold water a relief on her flushed cheeks. Cassie caught her breath, gazing at her own reflection in the

ornate gilded mirror. Her eyes were bright, her features alive and joyful. A stab of guilt ricocheted through her chest. She wasn't here for partying and drunken fun. She was here for a purpose, and all this was just a distraction from her true cause. Evie. Rose. Dozens of dead bodies.

The doors flung open, and a crowd of women tumbled into the room, gossiping loudly with drunken shrieks. Feeling sobered, Cassie smoothed her hair and tugged her dress back into place before slipping back toward the party. It was almost midnight, and she could hear the revelry in the ballroom rising to a fever pitch. Couples and partygoers spilled out into the lounge rooms and hallways, clutching bottles of champagne and calling out their celebrations. Cassie ducked aside, narrowly avoiding a knot of red-faced young men in white tails who came charging through the house with a yell.

She was so busy recovering her balance she almost missed Hugo's grandfather weaving determinedly through the knot of people, trailed by another man in a badly fitting suit. Tremain.

Cassie startled with recognition. She hadn't known he moved in these circles, but she supposed it made sense, the way he'd supported Sebastian through their meeting. As she watched, Tremain followed Henry Mandeville into the ballroom, a fearful look on his face. Cassie picked up her skirts and hurried after them.

It was hard to keep up in the crowd, the whirl of color and distraction, but Cassie snaked after them, following them across the room. They didn't stop to take a drink, or even acknowledge the party at all; they just moved with determination out the French doors at the far end of the room.

Cassie slowed, edging closer to the door. She peeked out, not wanting to be seen, but the long stone balcony was empty, save for a couple busily groping in a grab of passion at the far end. She stepped out, confused, and looked around. There was no sign of Henry and Tremain at all, but as she moved closer to the balustrade, she heard voices drift up from the dark garden below.

"You're busy with the party. I shouldn't keep you."

"I called you for an update. Now talk."

Cassie couldn't see the men on the steps below, but she recognized the voices. Tremain sounding uncharacteristically hesitant, and Henry Mandeville, cold and authoritative. Their voices were faint, snatches on the cold night breeze, so she leaned out farther, straining to hear.

"There's nothing new to report. The case is closed; the coroner ruled a suicide."

"What about the officer who was poking around? What was his name?"

"Charles Day," Tremain's voice came.

Cassie's heart stopped. They were talking about Charlie.

"He won't be a problem," Tremain continued. "Our man at the station says he dropped the request; it was just a routine media inquiry. You know, tragic history of the storied college."

"Hmm." Mandeville's response was chillingly low. "Do you know who he was talking to? My source in the data department says someone has been searching the university records too. I don't like it, Matthew," he added grimly. "The Genevieve girl is one thing, but pulling records for Rose too? Somebody's talking."

"I'm sure it's nothing." Tremain sounded desperate.

"I told you at the time, boy, it was badly done." Mandeville's voice was threatening. "I left Rose to you, and I've been regretting that choice ever since. We can't tolerate mistakes, not now. The rising is in a matter of weeks. There's no place for error." He paused. "Perhaps we should have this Charles taken care of."

"That won't be necessary," Tremain replied hurriedly. "Everything's settled down now. No reports, nothing. I promise there's nothing to worry about."

"There better not be." There was a long pause, and then Mandeville spoke up again. "You serve at the school's pleasure. Don't disappoint me again."

The sound of footsteps came, heading back toward her. Cassie lurched away. She quickly crossed the balcony, slipping into a shadowy alcove, and held her breath, hoping she was out of sight.

Henry and Mandeville climbed the stairs. Mandeville disappeared into the ballroom, but Tremain paused a moment, looking out across the gardens. The lights cast a shadow across his face, his expression tense. Then he turned back to the house and headed inside.

Cassie stepped out of the alcove, her mind racing and her heart beating fast in her chest. Evie, Rose . . . The Mandevilles were responsible for the deaths; there was no other explanation for what she'd heard. But how?

Cassie fumbled her phone from her slim clutch purse and quickly tapped out a text.

Don't ask any more questions until I get back. Will explain later.

"Who are you talking to?"

Cassie whirled around with a gasp. Hugo. "You've got to stop doing that!" She quickly hit send and tucked the phone away. "Just a friend," she added. "Wishing her happy new year."

"You're early." Hugo grinned. He made a show of checking his watch. "You've got another sixty seconds by my reckoning."

"In America, I've got another few hours," Cassie told him with a hurried smile. Her heart was still racing in her chest, but something about the way Hugo was looking at her in the dark made it skip even faster. "Where have you been?" she asked. "I haven't seen you all night."

He shrugged. "Parties aren't really my thing."

She made a noise of disbelief. "Please, you guys make it an art. I remember Evie would stumble back at five or six in the morning almost every night."

There was a pause. A shadow slipped across Hugo's face at the name. "I'm sorry," Cassie whispered.

He shook his head. "Don't be." He took a step closer, and then another. "I guess things change, that's all. People change."

Cassie blinked up at him. "You think you're different now?" she asked, her voice a whisper. They were alone in the shadows of the balcony, suspended partway between the loud cheers in the ballroom and the empty black of the garden beyond.

Hugo reached out and brushed a strand of hair from her face. Cassie felt the touch as if she'd been burned. "You look beautiful tonight," Hugo said, not answering her question.

Cassie tried to breathe. She felt unbalanced, standing so close to him. Too close.

Inside, the crowd began to chant the countdown. "Ten, nine, eight!"

"Tell me your resolution," Hugo murmured, dipping his head closer to hers.

Cassie felt a pull, something deep inside keeping her frozen in place, barely breathing. "I . . ." she began, fighting to remember.

"Five, four!"

Hugo slid a hand around the back of her dress, pulling her toward him. Cassie faltered.

"Three, two, one!"

"Happy New Year," Hugo murmured, as his lips closed the distance and finally met hers in a searing kiss.

CASSIE DIDN'T STAY FOR THE REST OF THE PARTY; SHE RETREATED upstairs to her room as soon as the confetti settled. Still, even sitting in the quiet, alone and far from the revelry below, she felt the shadow of Hugo's lips on hers, the quicksilver of adrenaline in her veins.

It had only been a moment, the kiss. As soon as the cheers of New Year had receded, he'd stepped away with a quiet smile. Guests had spilled out onto the balcony around them, and the moment was broken, but Cassie couldn't forget the way she'd felt in his arms.

She'd wanted more.

Shivering, she locked the door behind her and stripped off her dress, pulling an old sweatshirt over her head and sliding between the heavy covers of the bed. But sleep was impossible with her heartbeat still racing in her chest, and the swirl of questions circling her mind. Cassie tossed and turned, trying to fit the pieces together in a way that made sense, but it was all a jumble of half-truths and suspicion. The only thing she knew for sure was that nobody here was to be trusted.

She wasn't sure how long it was until the dark finally claimed her, but sleep offered no rest. She dreamed again of catacombs, of running panicked through the darkness, searching her way out of the stony crypts. He was there, the figure in the darkness, calling to her with a force she didn't understand, until—

Cassie woke to the sound of her own gasps, panting for breath in the dark room. She clutched the bedclothes and waited for the nightmare to recede again, still feeling the dry heat of the stone tunnels, the

sharp taste of blood in her mouth. *It was just a dream,* she told herself, chanting the words in her mind until they blocked out the terror. *It was all just a dream.* Slowly, her pulse evened, and she could breathe normally again. She looked around, her eyes becoming accustomed to the dark.

There was a strip of faint light across the room. The door was ajar.

Cassie's heart stopped. She struggled out from under the blankets and darted across the room. The door swung open under her hand. The hallway outside was empty.

Cassie backed into the bedroom, closing the door with a click. Her mind raced. She'd locked the door behind her when she'd returned to the room, she was sure of it. These were old wooden frames, ornate and heavy; it couldn't have swung open by accident.

Somebody had been there.

Shivering, she felt suddenly vulnerable and exposed, there in a house where nothing was as it seemed.

She heard faint laughter from outside the windows. Tugging her sweatshirt down over bare thighs, Cassie crossed the room and opened the iron-paned glass wider, peering out into the pitch-black night. Security lights were set along the walls, casting a glow over the side of the house. As she watched, a cluster of shadows skirted the building, their voices hushed. Drifts of laughter carried up to her on the night breeze, along with hissed *shhh* sounds.

Cassie ducked back, her heart pounding again, but this time with anticipation, not fear. She pulled on her jeans and sneakers, fumbling in the dark, then quickly left the bedroom, tiptoeing swiftly down the hall and main staircase to the ground floor. It took her a moment to get her bearings, lit by the low light of the lamps along the hall, but then she quickly raced back through the great ballroom, now littered with spent confetti and empty wineglasses. Outside on the balcony, the night air was a shock of cold against her skin; she bound down the flight of stone steps to the garden and hesitated, looking around.

It was a cloudy night, cold and crisp, and the moon was almost hidden. There was no sign of the movement she'd seen from her window. Cassie was alone, the black stretching around her, dark hedgerows looming up in the night.

Then she caught a glimpse of light, flickering across the lawn. A lamp or cell-phone display. Cassie took off across the lawn, jogging slowly, trying to keep to the edge of the gardens where shadows would mask her figure. She skirted around the edge of the walled garden, following the light that danced and bounced ahead of her, heading farther away from the house. As she drew closer, she could hear voices—louder now that they were out of earshot of the main building.

"Why do I always have to be the one to carry everything?"

"Because you're a big strong man, silly."

"Right, cast feminism aside the moment you want a favor."

"Shh, cut it out. Someone will hear!"

"Relax, Liv, it's four in the morning. Nobody's listening."

Cassie crept after them, picking out the voices. Olivia, Paige, Miles . . . there were half a dozen people in the group at least, heading toward the large shadowed hedgerow on the far side of the lawn. She kept her distance, careful not to come too close in case they heard her footsteps, but she needn't have worried, their laughter carried back to her until the flickering light went dark and the voices were swallowed up out of hearing.

Cassie arrived at the hedge and stopped. It was the entrance to the maze, she realized, the square-cut bushes lining a gravel path, snaking into the black. Her heart fell. She could hear Olivia and the rest of the group inside, getting farther away from her, but she could barely make out the shrubs in front of her; would she even be able to find her own way in the dark if she let them get too far ahead?

She'd come too far to turn around and slip quietly back to her room. She stepped onto the pathway, gravel crunching under her feet as she reached to trace her way along the first, leafy wall. Her fingertips felt their way along the wood and scratchy branches, leading her deeper

into the maze, the hedges looming above her, blocking out even the faint light of the moon. The only sound was her own heartbeat, drumming in her chest.

Cassie stumbled on, praying she wouldn't miss the route. Olivia and the rest would know the path by heart, but she had terrible visions of fumbling around in the dark until morning and, worse, having to explain her nighttime wanderings. She was just beginning to wonder if she should have turned back to the house when her fingertips found something soft against the branches. A ribbon pulled taut, tied between the branches. Cassie felt a rush of relief, gripping tight to the guide. No wonder they were moving so fast ahead of her. Someone had tied the ribbon in place to steer people through the twisting paths. Cassie took hold, running the ribbon between her hands and following the path marked along the branches, her footsteps quickening until she could hear voices again.

"Pour me another!"

"Shh."

"You can stop that now. We're miles from the house, nobody will hear."

Cassie silently crept closer. She found a gap in the hedgerow, a narrow sliver of a window, and she crouched down, peering carefully through the gap.

On the other side, the center of the maze was marked with a crumbling stone fountain and several statues. Olivia, Paige, Miles, and several others were setting lanterns around the perimeter, flooding the space with light. There were more people than Cassie had expected: she recognized Olivia's professor friend, Lewis, and a few of the party staff, two waitresses who were still dressed up in their uniforms, their hair falling out of their pinned styles, and a flush-cheeked boy who couldn't have been more than nineteen. They were clutching bottles of champagne, giggly and full of anticipation.

"So what's the big surprise?" one of the girls asked.

Paige smiled at her, moving closer to stroke her hair back from her face. "The after-party is the surprise," she said, laughing. "Were you expecting something more?"

"She means the good stuff," Miles spoke up, languid, from where he was lying on his back on the edge of the fountain. "Who brought the gear?"

"I did." Olivia settled on a blanket and patted the spot beside her. Lewis dropped obediently down. As Cassie watched, Olivia pulled a slim box from her bag, carved and ornate. She opened the lid and offered it to Lewis. He took something from it and lifted it to his lips.

Olivia offered the box to the girls.

"I don't know . . ." One of them hesitated. "I think I'll just stick with the booze."

"Don't be scared." Paige reached into the box and lifted her fingertip to the girl's lips. Cassie caught a glimpse of a tiny white pill on her finger. "It'll be fun," she murmured, slipping the finger into the girl's mouth and following with her lips, leaning in to kiss the other girl until she broke away, giggling and flustered.

The box was passed around until every guest had taken a pill. But only the guests; none of the Raleigh group took one, Cassie noticed.

"Now what?" The blond girl looked around. "I don't feel anything."

"You will." Olivia smiled. Lewis lay down, resting his head in her lap like a pet, and Olivia slowly stroked his head. "You'll feel everything."

Cassie stayed glued to the gap in the hedges, watching with a growing sense of unease as the guests passed champagne and chatted among themselves. Olivia was too calm; she was waiting for something, Cassie could tell. And it was the same with the others. They relaxed, watching the newcomers with such a calm sense of power that it reminded Cassie of lions on the savannah, lazily circling their prey.

Then Lewis let out a whimper.

Cassie startled at the noise. Olivia's eyes drifted closed, her head tilting back, an expression of ecstasy on her face. Lewis's body jerked, shuddering on the ground, and Cassie could have sworn she saw the air shimmer between them, a surge of energy pulsating up from where Olivia's hand rested against his head.

Cassie caught her breath, looking to the rest of them. One of the partygoers lay on the bench beside Paige, moaning softly as Paige cradled her body. The boy was on the ground beside Miles, thrashing as if in the grip of a nightmare. And all the while, the air pulsed around them, a vivid glow emanating from their bodies like an aura, some whirl of energy. Cassie shivered, unable to look away. She couldn't explain what was happening, but somehow, she understood. They were taking something, drawing some kind of power from their victims, delighting in the surge of energy that crested between them, an unholy bond. It was wrong, that much was clear. A violation. The noises the guests were making were faint, animal, whimpers of distress, while Olivia and the others seemed to revel in it, their faces lit up and euphoric, almost orgasmic in the glowing lights. Everything in Cassie's body screamed at her to run, but she bit back the compulsion. She had to find out more.

Slowly, the group came up for air, releasing the guests who lay motionless beside them. All except Olivia. The energy hummed around her, and Lewis thrashed again, his whimpers turning into cries.

"Liv," a warning voice came, and then Hugo stepped out of the shadows. Cassie gasped. He'd been there all along?

"Liv, you need to be careful," Hugo warned again "Liv!" He strode over and pulled her back from Lewis. Olivia's eyes flew open.

"What are you doing?" she demanded, panting and disheveled.

"You're going too far," Hugo exclaimed. "I told you, you've fed too many times. You need a new source."

"But I like this one," Olivia said, her voice pouting. "His mind is so . . . delicious." She stroked Lewis's hair again, possessive.

"And soon there'll be nothing left," Hugo replied grimly. "God, can't you control yourself for once? You know what happened last time."

Olivia caught her breath. Her hair shimmered gold in the lantern light, her skin radiant with exhilaration. "How many times do I have to tell you I'm sorry? I didn't know how unstable she was. Lewis is fine. I know how far to take him." Olivia ran a hand over him, a smile teasing on her lips.

Hugo didn't relent. "And Evie was fine too, until you pushed her over the edge."

Cassie's blood ran cold. She clutched the branches for balance, her mind racing back over what she'd seen. They'd done this to Evie?

"Hugo, enough with the stern father act. You're ruining the fun," Miles spoke up. He stretched lazily, trailing one hand over the boy's comatose body. "Come play with my guy, he's fresh. Brimming over with youthful possibility."

"I'm not in the mood." Hugo's face was set, his jaw clenched.

"Look, I'm sorry." Olivia sighed again. "It was an accident. It wasn't your fault."

"You should never have done it in the first place," Hugo told her, angry. "There are rules. She was one of us."

"If propriety's what's got you all riled up, where's Cassie?" Olivia asked, giving a wicked smile. "You said you'd bring her. It's not like you to miss a feed."

At the mention of her name, every muscle in Cassie's body clenched with fear.

There was a pause. "She's proving . . . resistant," Hugo replied at last.

The others sat up, looking interested. "Resistant, how?" Paige asked.

Hugo looked reluctant. "I don't know, I've never felt anything like it. I can form the connection, but then it's like her mind is closed off to me. Something's pushing back."

Cassie felt sick. He'd done this to her—or, at least, tried to?

But the others weren't surprised by the revelation, only the fact he hadn't succeeded.

"So she's strong . . ." Olivia mused, thoughtful. "Is she a candidate?"

"No," Hugo replied quickly.

"The rising is soon. We need an offering," Olivia pressed him.

"We've got Lewis," Hugo said. "You said he'd volunteer."

"He'd do anything if I asked," Olivia said dismissively. "But if Cassie is stronger . . ."

"I said no," Hugo barked. "You don't touch her, you hear me?"

There was silence. Cassie forced herself to still her breathing. She was crouched, unmoving, but a single motion could reveal her presence. And then what would they do with her?

Olivia stared back at Hugo coolly. "I hear you, cousin. Loud and clear."

"Enough bickering." Miles yawned. "Time to trade. Paige?"

"Be my guest."

The group turned back to their prey, the air shimmering with energy again. Cassie watched, helpless as the bodies twitched and whimpered, drained of something essential, something that should never be taken. She felt a shudder of revulsion. She'd seen enough. But as she eased back from her hiding place, her foot crunched on the gravel.

Hugo's head turned.

Cassie froze. For a terrible moment, it was as if he stared right at her, as if he saw her hiding there in the bushes. Her heart beat wildly in her chest, her muscles screamed in their fixed position. Finally, he looked away without a word.

Cassie exhaled. Paige began talking, something about a party next week, and Cassie took the chance to creep backward, step by excruciating step. She longed to turn and run, flee this terrible scene as fast as her feet would carry her, but she knew the smallest sound would reveal her presence. The hedges stood tall around her, a dense wall of dark, as

she gripped the ribbon with a trembling hand, retreating through the twisting maze until the voices were a hum behind her.

"Cassie." The whisper came from right behind her. Hugo, a shadow looming in the dark.

Cassie let out a scream. She tried to run, her sneakers scrabbling on the loose gravel, but he was faster—clamping a hand over her mouth and pulling her back into the hedges. She fought, panicked, but he held tight, trapping her arms at her sides. "Shh!" he hissed. "They'll hear you!" He forced her face around so she could see him in the dark. His eyes were panicked. "Trust me, Cassie," he ordered. "Relax!"

Cassie fought harder, every sense alive and screaming with fear. Her instincts had been right, that first night they'd met. All along, she'd been a target. A potential victim. The night she'd stayed at his house, the open door here at Gravestone . . . What had he done to her? What would he do now?

"Cassie, please!" He was begging, but she couldn't listen. She wouldn't be fooled again. Cassie lashed out with her elbow, making contact with his ribs. He doubled over, and she lunged for freedom, but he caught her, tumbling them both to the ground. She kicked out, but he pinned her down, rolling on top to straddle her, trapping her arms against her sides.

"No!" she cried out, and then she felt it. His hand on her forehead, a dark pressure building where he touched. Cassie struggled again, but it was no use. Something was invading her mind, slipping inside, a darkness snaking deep into her thoughts.

"Relax," Hugo whispered again. She fought, tried to push it out, blocked it with everything she had, but it wasn't enough. Something in her mind reared up in answer, reached toward the blackness and gripped hold tight.

The shadows came rushing in. Dark and cold, an endless winter's night. Hugo was everywhere, a tidal wave of pure sensation spiraling

through her, burning like black fire in her veins. It felt like home. Cassie fought with everything she had, but her own mind was betraying her. It demanded more, reaching for him, craving release.

"Let go," Hugo whispered. "It's going to be okay." He held her gently, and Cassie was powerless to resist. The shadows rose up to claim her completely, and then there was nothing but black and red, anger and power, an ecstatic whirlwind in her veins.

CASSIE WOKE TO DAYLIGHT FLOODING THROUGH THE HEAVY drapes. She stretched, disoriented for a moment under foreign sheets and blankets, the mattress below her soft instead of the lumpy narrow college bed.

Then it came rushing back to her. The maze. Olivia and the group, caught up in fevered celebration, the whimpers of distress from the bodies on the ground. And Hugo, holding her down, the dark shadow slipping into her mind.

Cassie jolted upright, breathing fast. How had she gotten back to her room? What had happened to her after Hugo caught her? She checked under the covers, but she was dressed in her nightclothes, sweatshirt and boxer shorts. Her jeans were folded over a chair in the corner where she'd left them, before—

Before what?

There was a light tap at the door. It swung open before Cassie had a chance to react. Hugo leaned into the room. "Good morning, sleepyhead," he said, greeting her with a smile.

Cassie tensed, but Hugo just yawned. His hair was in disarray, and he was dressed in jeans and a sweatshirt. "Breakfast is ready downstairs. You might want to get a move on if you want any bacon," he added with a wink. "Miles is determined to devour every rasher in the county."

He closed the door behind him. Cassie sat there, her heart racing, trying to process what had just happened. Hugo was acting as if nothing

was wrong, as if he hadn't discovered her hiding in the maze. As if he hadn't held her down, and . . .

What?

Cassie shivered, trying to fit the fragmented memories into something real, but now, in the light of day, the shadows of the previous night seemed to shift and blur in her mind. Just what had she thought she'd seen? Her memories were fantastical. Impossible. With every moment that passed, the darkness of her mind seemed to mutate even more, until she wondered with a shudder just what had been real, and what a terrible dream.

But as Cassie dressed and packed up her things in her overnight bag, her heart clutched with the same deep instinct she recognized so well. Run. Run now, and far away. Run before it was too late.

Cassie forced herself to calm down. Hugo had acted as if nothing was wrong, so she needed to take her cues from him. Maybe he'd told the others about finding her in the maze, or maybe there was nothing to tell. She just had to keep it together until she was safely away from this place.

Downstairs the hallways were empty, but Cassie found the group in the kitchen, groaning with hangovers. The smell of fried bacon filled the air, and everywhere there were mugs of coffee and plates of food. It was chillingly domestic, as if nothing had changed.

"You're awake!" Olivia bounced out of her seat and greeted Cassie with a hug. "I thought we were going to have to send a search party to drag you up. How are you feeling? You didn't look too hot when you left us last night."

"I'm fine," Cassie answered automatically. She forced a smile as she looked around the room, shocked to notice the guests she'd seen with them last night: the two waitresses and the boy. All three were ravenously eating toast and chatting with Miles and Paige like nothing had happened. "What about you?" Cassie turned back to Olivia, accepting the cup of coffee the other girl thrust in her hand. She looked at her carefully, studying her face for any hint of revelation. "Did you guys party long after I left you?"

"A little." Olivia gave her a sunny grin. She didn't look as if she'd been up all night. Her skin was glowing, her eyes bright with energy. "But these guys couldn't take it. They're getting old, isn't that right, cuz?" She playfully nudged Hugo as he passed her to get more toast.

"Ancient," he replied, laughing. "Decrepit. I'll be needing a walking stick and wheelchair soon enough."

Cassie swallowed back her unease. She took a couple of slices of dry toast and slid into a free seat beside Lewis. Out of everyone, he looked the worst for wear, with dark shadows under his eyes and a slightly vacant look behind his spectacles. "Are you okay?" she murmured, remembering with a shiver the way he'd cried out in pain under Olivia's touch.

"What's that?" Lewis blinked. "Oh, yes. A few too many glasses of champagne." He gave her a rueful smile. "I must remember I'm not as young as I used to be."

"I thought I'd find you here." A cool voice came from the doorway. It was Henry Mandeville, immaculately dressed. Cassie remembered his conversation with Tremain and tensed. Henry's gaze flickered over the group, landing on Hugo with a twist of dissatisfaction. "Remember we have the New Year's Day race at noon. You'll be needed for photos."

Hugo's jaw tensed. "I thought Olivia was doing that instead."

"We need the whole family," Henry said, his tone final. "The car leaves in an hour." He looked around the room again, his eyes landing on Cassie. They seemed to pierce through her.

Black is the badge of hell. . .

Cassie broke the stare, looking away. Henry murmured a few more instructions to Olivia, and then left.

"Big plans?" Cassie asked Hugo.

Hugo gave her a rueful look. "Some local charity tradition. We need to go smile and wave for the campaign cameras." He leaned over to snag some bacon from the plate in the middle of the table. "You should come," he suggested. "I mean, it's a drag for us, but it could be fun for you. A slice of British rural life."

"I don't know," Cassie replied quickly. "I need to get back to Oxford."

"Are you sure?" Hugo's smile turned flirtatious. "We didn't get a chance to talk after last night."

Cassie almost choked on her coffee. "Last night," she repeated, her mind racing.

"Midnight," Hugo replied. He looked at her, his smile fading a little. "You remember? We . . . celebrated. Then you rushed off to bed so fast, I didn't know what happened."

Cassie stared at him. Was this all part of an elaborate lie, or had she really dreamed up the whole thing? Hugo's face seemed guileless and open, but she couldn't forget the darkness in his gaze, the shadows slipping through the edges of her mind.

"I'm sorry," she muttered, looking away. "I wasn't feeling too good."

"Tell me about it," Paige yawned, interrupting. "We all went kind of crazy."

"Speak for yourself." Olivia laughed, slipping one hand through Lewis's hair, a gesture of ownership, Cassie couldn't help but think. Of possession. "I feel just fine."

Olivia invited her to stay another day: they'd be holding a movie marathon that evening, and taking a traditional countryside hike. Cassie did her best to sound regretful as she explained she couldn't stay. "I have to get back to work."

"At the library, right?" Olivia's gaze was inquisitive. "That must be useful. You probably have access to all the old files and archives."

"Not really," Cassie lied. "I just deal with the front desk stuff. You know, returns and shelving. They don't trust us with the really important things."

"Oh. Well, it's been great having you down. We'll have to get together when term starts. Lunch, and cocktails."

"Absolutely." Cassie managed to sound enthusiastic, and when Olivia hugged her good-bye, she did her best not to flinch. "I can't wait."

"I'll walk you out." Hugo picked up her bag before Cassie could

object, heading outside and down the front steps to the drive. "I'll be back in Oxford next week," he told her, setting her bag down by the car.

"Okay." Cassie was trying her best to seem calm, even as her pulse raced with fear. She waited, wishing the driver would arrive.

Hugo took two steps closer and leaned in to whisper in her ear. "It's all right, I didn't tell them."

"Tell them what?" Cassie jerked back from his touch.

"Last night."

Cassie's heart raced. Was this a test? She swallowed back her fear. "You mean, the kiss?" She tried her best to seem confused. "I'm sorry, it's all kind of a blur. I didn't sleep too well. You know me and nightmares." She gave a careless laugh. "I guess it really was too much champagne."

Hugo studied her, searching. "That's all right," he finally said, stepping away. "We can talk back at Oxford. What's your number?"

Cassie didn't want to stay a moment longer so she quickly rattled it off. "Thanks for having me." Cassie's voice sounded high and panicked to her ears, but she forced herself to reach up and land a quick kiss on Hugo's cheek before she got into the car.

Hugo closed the door behind her, but she didn't relax, not until the engines started and they pulled away.

Cassie let out a shaking breath, her whole body trembling.

"I can turn the heat up, if you need?" The driver turned from the front seat.

She hugged herself tight. "I'm fine," she said quickly, counting down until Gravestone disappeared in the rearview mirror, swallowed up by the woodlands and hills. Then she pulled out her phone and tapped a text to Charlie.

I'm coming back. We need to talk.

Cassie had the driver drop her back at Raleigh, but as soon as he drove away, she turned in the opposite direction and made straight for the

place Charlie had texted her, an address past High Street on the other side of town. The whole way, she couldn't help but check over her shoulder, wondering if someone was watching her. She knew Olivia and Hugo were miles away at Gravestone, but she couldn't shake the knowledge that Mandeville and Tremain had known about Charlie—known he'd been asking questions at the police station, known someone had called up the records in the library. What else did they know?

She walked fast, regretting her heavy overnight bag, which dug into her shoulder by the time she reached the address. It was a newly built apartment block, drab concrete and red brick, and when Charlie buzzed her up, the interior was no more uplifting: three flights of concrete stairs, echoing with the sound of TV broadcasts on the other side of the doors.

"It's not exactly Raleigh," he greeted her with an apology as he ushered her inside.

"I don't care, as long as that lock works." As Cassie stepped inside the neat apartment, she let out the breath of tension she'd been holding for two days now. She dropped the bag to the floor and looked around as Charlie drew the dead bolt across. The apartment was small and sparsely furnished, with a large flat-screen TV mounted in pride of place on the wall, and a lone houseplant wilting in a pot in the corner.

Charlie fetched her a glass of water, looking at her with concern. "What happened?" he asked.

She caught her breath, wondering where to begin, but there was no easy way to say any of it, so she opened her mouth and simply told him everything. The conversation she'd overheard between Henry Mandeville and Tremain, the room from the photograph, and what she'd witnessed in the maze that night—everything except Hugo discovering her, and what happened after. She didn't even remember for sure herself, and she knew Charlie would only worry if he learned about the danger she'd been in. "I know it doesn't make any sense," she finished before he could say a word. "But I saw them. What they were doing . . . This isn't normal, Charlie. This is . . . something else."

He watched her for a moment, then got up. "I've been digging too, looking at the deaths."

"Charlie!" Cassie felt a flash of panic. "I told you, they have a source at the station. They'll know you've been looking for something."

"Relax, sweetheart." Charlie gave her a familiar cocky grin. "I used Bradshaw's password and login. They won't know jack." He went to the stack of boxes in the corner and began taking out files. "I was looking for a pattern, something that linked the deaths besides their being students."

"What did you find?" Cassie leaned forward in her seat. Part of her had been scared Charlie would back off, or worse still, not believe her, but he'd taken her account of the New Year's party in stride, as unruffled as ever. Maybe she wasn't crazy, after all.

He spread photos out on the floor, grouping them by date. "They fit a pattern. First of all, they're smart. Not just Oxford clever, but brilliant. Winning prizes, publishing papers—these kids were all at the top of the pile. Not just kids, either; there were grad students, some professors too."

"Like Lewis," Cassie said.

Charlie nodded. "But they weren't rich kids like the Mandevilles; they didn't move in those circles. A lot of these guys were scholarship kids, working class. Except your Evie," he added with a frown. "That one doesn't fit."

"Hugo said so," she replied, remembering. "He was angry at Olivia for pushing her too far. He said, 'She was one of us.'"

"Makes sense; they don't shit where they eat, to put it bluntly," Charlie agreed. "Some kind of twisted class loyalty. The lower classes are disposable, but they protect their own."

"But from what?" Cassie asked, chilled. She looked at the faces, so many tragic deaths. "We know from what Mandeville said they're involved in the deaths somehow. But they weren't killing those people, out at Gravestone. I don't even know what they were doing." The shadows.

The darkness creeping into her mind. Cassie had no words for it, no explanation. She still wasn't sure if that part had been real, or just her fear and panic, her imagination run riot.

"You said they mentioned the Rose death." Charlie rocked back on his heels. "That it was different, somehow."

Cassie thought back. "Badly done, that's what Henry said. It's like he was angry with Tremain, specifically over that one. He was worried," she added. "As if that was a loose thread."

Charlie nodded. "I found the next of kin for Rose. She's local, just a few miles away." He offered a hand to help Cassie up, giving her a wry grin. "Let's go unraveling."

Rose's aunt Doris was in her seventies, a wiry gray-haired woman who shuffled around the house using a metal walker. She insisted on settling them in her floral-papered living room with tea and biscuits before they could even get around to asking any questions. "Such a shame," she said, sighing as she settled awkwardly in a rocking chair in the corner. She nodded at a photo on the mantel, showing Rose beaming in her matriculation robes on what must have been her first day at Raleigh. "It's been close to twenty-five years now. She would be married, have wee ones of her own."

"I'm so sorry," Cassie murmured. She felt a strange sense of affinity with this Doris woman. Rose had mattered enough to Cassie's mother for her to give Cassie her name; that meant she was more of a family to her than anyone else had been. "I hope you don't mind our talking to you."

"No, it's fine." Doris gave them a smile. "Is that tea all right?" she asked.

Cassie turned to find Charlie slurping down the last of his cup, nothing but crumbs left on his plate. "Lovely, thanks." He grinned. "Nothing like a nice cuppa."

"Let me get more of those biscuits." Doris rose to her feet.

Cassie leaped up. "I can go."

"Oh no." Doris waved her away. "Going back and forth to the kitchen is the only exercise I get these days. Arthritis in my knees," she explained. "I won't be a moment. I know I've got some shortbread stashed away."

"You're spoiling me, Doris," Charlie teased, as Doris shuffled out of the room.

Cassie jabbed her elbow into his ribs. "Charlie!" she hissed. "We're here to get information."

"And she'll be more likely to remember things if she's relaxed," Charlie retorted in a low voice. "You want to just roll right up and ask, 'Hey, about your dead niece, you think she was killed by unnatural demonic forces?' instead?"

"I didn't say demonic." Cassie shivered.

Charlie fixed her with a look. "Well, whatever happened, we're about to go digging up a whole lot of ghosts for this nice old lady. The least you can do is eat some bloody biscuits."

Cassie obediently reached for a digestive as Doris returned with a fresh tray. "There, you're just like my brother." She laughed, pouring more tea for Charlie. "He'll put away the whole pack before his supper."

"Is that Rose's father?" Cassie asked.

"No, she was my sister's girl." Doris settled back into her seat. "They live down in Eastbourne now, moved not long after she died. They couldn't stand passing the river every day, wondering if she was still out there." She shook her head slowly. "Such a shame. She was such a bright girl. We used to joke that we didn't know where it came from. Her father was a postie, and our June worked as a teller at the bank. They didn't go to university, none of them, and there Rose was, bright as a button. Even as a girl, you couldn't get her nose out of a book. All the rest of the family would be sitting round for tea, and she'd be off in a corner somewhere reading. We were all so proud when she got into Raleigh. Lord, you should have heard the commotion when that letter came. We never thought one of our girls would be at a school like that."

Cassie felt a pang. She'd been so focused on the Mandevilles and her mother, it had been easy to forget that the names on the list of dead were real people, with real families all suffering from the loss. "How did she like it?" Cassie asked gently. "Some people can find it hard to adjust. It's a pretty intense environment."

"Oh, she loved it," Doris said emphatically. "She was having a ball. Parties all the time; she loved her professors too. That's why we couldn't understand when it happened." Her voice faded, eyes filling with tears. "If she'd just reached out, told us how she was feeling, then maybe . . ."

Cassie felt a surge of guilt, but she pressed ahead all the same. "Did you meet any of her friends at the time?" she asked. "Remember any of their names, perhaps?"

"Well, there was Maggie of course, Margaret." Doris smiled affectionately. "They bunked together in the same building at college. Those girls were inseparable."

Cassie swallowed back a lump in her throat. "Did you meet her?" she asked in a quiet voice.

"Oh yes." Doris smiled. "Our Rose brought her around a couple of times, for Christmas, like, and at the weekends. She was American, like you," she added. "So it was too far for her to go back just for the holidays. Lovely girl, smart too, like Rose. Those girls would chatter for hours, we couldn't keep up."

Cassie nodded. This was another piece of her mother's life, right here in this house. Moments that were gone, faded, as much a memory as Rose now.

Charlie placed a reassuring hand on her knee as he leaned forward. "The thing is, Doris—I can call you Doris, right?"

"Of course you can."

"Well, the thing is, we'd love to chat to more of Rose's friends. Find out more about her time at Raleigh."

"I'm sorry, love." Doris shook her head. "It's so long ago. And Margaret was the only one she brought round. I guess she was worried what

they'd think. That lot are all so fancy," she added. "But they were just wonderful after it happened. They gave her a beautiful service in that chapel of theirs. The whole college came out."

"I know," Cassie breathed, remembering Evie's service, still a raw wound in her chest. "When it happened . . ." Cassie paused. "Had you any warning at all? Some people can find the pressure a lot, the workload, the new environment."

Doris shook her head. "It was a shock to all of us, poor Margaret especially. She was just inconsolable after. She couldn't go on there; she ended up going back to America. But Rose never said a word. Some people, maybe you can see the signs, but nothing seemed wrong. She was a little quieter, maybe," she added, thoughtful. "I remember she came home for the weekend, just before. . . . She had a lot to think about, she said. They had exams coming up, and I think she'd had some kind of offer for a summer job she wasn't sure about taking."

Cassie sat up, alert. "Did she say what kind of job?"

Doris frowned. "I'm sorry, it was all so long ago. Maybe it wasn't even a job, but an opportunity? Yes, that's what she said. A life-changing opportunity, with important people."

Charlie scribbled in his notebook. "Is there anything else you can think of, anything she might have mentioned, any detail at all?"

Doris let out a sigh. "I'm sorry, love, it was such a difficult time. I think we all tried just to forget. I'll talk to our Pete, see if he remembers anything."

"Thank you," Cassie told her, even as she felt a wave of disappointment. There was nothing new here, nothing that could steer them closer to any answers. She rose to her feet, and Charlie followed suit, grabbing the last few biscuits and stuffing them in his mouth. "You've been really helpful. I'm sorry to bring it all back."

Doris sighed. "It's all right. I hope I can help with your research. Tragedy like this is just senseless. To lose a girl like that. . . . She had her whole life ahead of her."

She showed them into the entry hallway. Charlie passed her a slip of paper with his number. "If anything comes to mind," he said.

There was the sound of a key turning in the door. Doris turned, brightening. "That'll be my brother now. Rose's uncle. Maybe he can help."

The door swung open, and an older man ducked inside. "I can't stay long," he said, shaking out an umbrella, "They need me to cover the lodge tonight." Then he looked up, and Cassie felt a shock.

It was Rutledge, the porter from Raleigh College.

RUTLEDGE FROZE IN THE DOORWAY.

"These nice people were just asking about Rose," Doris explained, oblivious to his shock.

"Is that right?" Rutledge cleared his throat. "Well, shame I can't stay. Like I said, I have to be getting back." He took a package of books from under his arm and gave it to Doris, avoiding Cassie's gaze. "There you go, should keep you busy for the week."

"Thanks, love." Doris leaned heavily on her walker. "Are you sure you can't sit down a minute to talk? Your memory's always been better than mine." She turned to Cassie with a smile. "Practically photographic, this one. I swear, he can remember what we ate for tea in nineteen eighty-five."

Cassie's head spun, but Rutledge didn't linger to reply. "I'll pop by tomorrow," he said quickly, squeezing Doris's hand. "Nice to meet you both." He tipped his cap and then was gone, back into the rainy evening.

"Thanks so much," Cassie said quickly, lunging for the door. She could hear Charlie make his apologies behind her, but she didn't pause for Doris to see them out. It had fallen dark while they'd been talking and now the streets were cold and damp, but up ahead, she made out the swiftly moving figure hurrying away. "Wait!" she called, her feet pounding after him on the pavement. "Please, wait!"

Rutledge didn't slow. She chased him to the end of the street, grabbing his arm and pulling him back around to face her. "You knew Rose?" she demanded, panting.

He tried to pull away, looking around fearfully. "Lower your voice, girl. I don't want any trouble."

"Then what's going on?" Cassie cried in frustration. "Why won't you talk to me? What do you know?"

"Let it be, love." Rutledge gave her a desperate look. "You don't want to see where this leads."

Cassie struggled to keep her temper down. "Just tell me!"

Footsteps sounded on the pavement behind them, and then Charlie drew level, looking back and forth between them.

"He knows," Cassie told Charlie, desperate. "He works at Raleigh. He's Rose's uncle. He knows something."

Rutledge made to leave, but Charlie blocked him. "You're not going anywhere," he said, a warning note in his voice. "We've been chasing shadows around this bloody town for too long."

A car's headlights cut through the dark, slowly driving down the street. Rutledge flinched, turning his body away from the car and hiding low under his umbrella until it had passed. "I don't want any trouble. You shouldn't have gotten Doris mixed up in this." He watched the car disappear, clearly shaken. "She doesn't know anything."

"But you do." Charlie stepped in closer, looming above Rutledge. "Angie's Caff, on Wiltmore Street," he murmured, so quiet only the three of them could hear. "Be there in half an hour, or I'll come knocking on Doris's door every day this week. If the people you're so worried about haven't noticed her yet, they will soon. Come on," he added, turning back to Cassie.

"But—" she protested. "We can't just—"

"He'll be there," Charlie promised. "Won't you?"

Rutledge looked between them and finally gave a nod. "I wondered when you'd come looking," he said to Cassie with a resigned look. "But then, you're your mother's daughter, aren't you? Too clever for your own good."

♦ ♦ ♦

His words haunted her as they walked back into town. "He won't come," she said, pulling her coat around her to protect from the cold. The streets were eerily empty of tourists and pedestrians, the city still half bare and sleepily recovering from New Year's revelry.

Charlie was walking fast, his head down. "We know where to find him. He'll come."

Angie's had one of the only Open signs on the street. It was the place Cassie had met Charlie before: steamy windows and fried food, and a bored-looking waitress who waved them to the back corner booth with barely a second glance. Cassie slid into a seat as Charlie checked around them. Save for an elderly couple drinking tea and a couple of middle-aged men reading the sports pages, they were alone.

"I can't believe he knows who I am." She reached up to touch the cracked pendant at her throat, the lone memento from her mother. "All this time, he was right there. He could tell us everything."

"Are you sure you want to know?" Charlie asked in a careful voice.

Cassie looked at him. "What are you talking about?"

"You saw the guy," he continued, looking uneasy. He glanced around them. "He was scared out of his mind. Jumping at the smallest sound. What you saw at Gravestone . . ."

"I don't know what I saw," she protested.

"You know it wasn't good. Look, Cassie." He reached across the table, catching her hand. "I've been looking into this for weeks now, and you know what I've found? Bodies." His voice dropped. "Dozens of them. Hundreds, even. Maybe more we don't even know about. Whoever they are, whatever they're doing, they're not fucking around."

"No, they're not."

They broke apart. Rutledge was standing by their table, his expression set in a cautious grimace. He took a seat, falling silent until the

waitress had taken their orders for tea. "Well then," he said after she had departed, meeting Cassie's eyes, "here I am."

She took a breath, not sure where to begin. "You know who I am. Who my mother was?"

Rutledge gave a sharp nod. "Not at first, but, aye, I put the pieces together. You weren't too careful, running around like that. Only one person I know would be interested in Margaret Madison's files."

Cassie sat back, her mind racing. "The photo of them in my pigeonhole," she whispered, "the School of Night quote on the back . . ."

"We thought it was time you started looking in the right direction," Rutledge said. "Knew who your friends really were."

"We?" Charlie picked up on the word. "Who else is a part of this?"

Rutledge paused, giving Charlie a wary look. "Who's this?" he asked.

"He's with me," Cassie replied.

Rutledge sized him up. "You trust him?"

"You can say whatever you need, mate," Charlie answered for her, scowling. "I'm not the one hiding anything here."

"You don't know what you're getting into," Rutledge said calmly. His gaze flicked back to Cassie. "You too. You need to think about what you're digging up here. Old bones, bad blood. Some things are better left buried."

"It's too late to say that," Cassie exclaimed, frustrated. "You're the one who's been sending me in circles for months now!"

Rutledge frowned. "It wasn't supposed to be you. It was Maggie we needed. They wanted her back here to end it all."

"Who are they?" Cassie demanded. "What are you talking about? Please," she added, exhaling in a rush. "I need to know what's happening. About the Mandevilles, and the society. Everything. You don't know what this means to me. I've been looking for the answers for so long. I need to know the truth."

Rutledge searched Cassie's expression, and he finally gave a nod. "They've always been here," he began, leaning in so only they could

hear. "Before my time, before any of us. It's in the foundations, see. When they founded the college, they built it on something dark, some power, blacker than anything. They wanted knowledge, Raleigh and the rest, and they struck an unholy bargain to get it. I don't know how it works," he added, before Cassie could ask the question. "And I don't want to. It's safer that way."

"Safer?" she repeated. "People are dead!"

"Aye, and my Rose is gone too." Rutledge scowled at her. "So don't you go judging me. I've paid the price for their wickedness, more than anyone."

Cassie fought to control her temper. "You said they wanted my mom to come back. Who did? And how did you even find her? She changed her name when she left, she never said anything."

"Who do you think helped her leave?" Rutledge gave her a sad smile. "But you're getting ahead now. If you want to know the whole story, you need to hear everything." He waited for the waitress to deliver their tea before he began. "I've been working at Raleigh since I was a lad. My father, he worked there before me, and his father too. It's the same with a lot of the staff, we go back just as far as they do. You don't notice us, the staff," he added, with a twisted smile. "You all just take it for granted we'll be there. Cleaners, groundskeepers, mailmen. We disappear into the background, but mark my words, we notice you. We see everything. Well, it wasn't long after I started that I heard the stories. A society, hidden at the college. The School of Night. Taking things that weren't theirs to take, doing things that went against man and God. Nobody said anything, not right out, but we all knew something wasn't right. All those deaths. Suicides, they said. I found one of them myself. A boy what hung himself, took a belt to the back of the door frame." He shook his head, pausing before he continued. "There was a rhythm to it, I saw it after a while. A few years would pass, and we'd wonder if this time it was over. But then, just when things got settled, the darkness would come again."

"Why didn't you say something?" Cassie couldn't help but interrupt. "If you saw . . . If you knew . . ."

"And tell who?" Rutledge gave her a bitter look. "They've got the police in their pockets; everything gets swept under the rug. Besides, what is there to say? It's open and shut, no evidence, nothing. And that's our livelihood on the line." He sighed, a scowl of self-loathing on his face. "It's a devil's bargain, it is. I watched, and I didn't say a word. Until Rose."

Rutledge took a long gulp of tea. The cup shook as he placed it back on the saucer. "Aye, I knew things weren't right. I begged that girl to apply somewhere else, anywhere but Raleigh. But she didn't listen. She'd visited me there, see. She'd been picturing it since she was a kid, wouldn't hear it any other way." He sighed. "Even so, I thought maybe . . . It had been a quiet few years. Normal, like. But all that changed. There was a crowd of kids that year, there always is one: the top families, the ones who go way back. Your lot, it's those Mandeville kids. Back then, it was their father and his crowd. Aristocracy, they used to be, and some of them still are. Rose got mixed up with them, your mum too. Parties, late nights, trips away—" Rutledge broke off to take a ragged breath. His eyes were watery. "By the time we realized, it was already too late. Rose was in deep, worshipped the ground they walked on. They had her thinking like she could be one of them, move in those circles. Your mom was the sharp one," he added, giving Cassie an approving nod. "She worked out something wasn't right with them, came to me to help. But still, Rose was too stubborn. She wouldn't listen, not until . . . Not until it was too late."

"What do they do?" Charlie leaned in. "To make people kill themselves like that. I checked all the files; they're clean. It's suicide, every time. Nothing suspicious about it, nothing to raise any red flags."

Rutledge sighed. "I've seen a lot of things over the years. Had a lot of time to wonder. How someone can just lose her mind like that. Lose track of who she is, why she needs to stay alive. But maybe they didn't

lose their minds." He paused, looking at them carefully. "Maybe some-one took them."

Cassie caught her breath, remembering the group in the maze. The way the air shimmered around them, the energy that seemed to pulse. Away from their victims, toward Olivia and the rest. It was beyond sci-ence and logic, beyond anything she'd believed could exist.

"They're feeding off their minds, somehow?" Charlie creased his forehead in a frown.

Rutledge shrugged. "These kids . . . It's like someone takes some-thing away from them and sends them spinning off the edge."

"Evie wasn't herself," Cassie said slowly. "Before . . . before she did it. She crashed so hard; one minute she was fine, the next it was like she was falling apart at the seams."

Rutledge nodded. "Rose too. They took something from her, she's never been the same. Never was the same," he corrected. "That's why I helped your mum. Got her away from them before they could ruin her too. She knew too much; they would have never just let her go, not with you coming too. Running was her only hope."

If he'd known her mother then, helped her, she might have confided in him. Cassie's heart sped up. "And my father?" she asked hopefully.

Rutledge sighed. "I never asked, and she never said."

Charlie fixed Rutledge with a stare. "So what do you want with Cassie? If you wanted to protect her all those years ago, why not just tell her the truth now?"

"I didn't want you here." Rutledge looked to Cassie. "Let sleeping dogs lie, I say. But the others . . . The staff, they've had enough. It's here again, the deaths. The cycle. They're building to something big."

"The rising," Cassie whispered.

Rutledge looked at her sharply. "Where did you hear that?"

"At the party. Olivia said 'the rising is soon.'" Cassie shivered.

Rutledge nodded. "From what we've figured out, that's what it's about, every twenty-five years or so. Some kind of ceremony or ritual, a time

they come together and renew whatever unholy business they're a part of. Seal the bond for the new generation, so they can go out into the world, and do . . . God knows what else."

His words sank through Cassie like a rock. She'd been so focused on this city, these few names, she hadn't even begun to think about the bigger picture. "You mean, it's not just Oxford?" she asked, her heart sinking.

"They're everywhere." Rutledge gave her a sharp look, like she should have known better. "What do you think these people do once they graduate? Mandeville's just the beginning. These people, they run companies, governments, all the world over. And this rising . . . it's what gives them the power. We noticed that's when the deaths start, around this rising ritual, like they're building their strength, taking more than they should."

Cassie remembered what else Olivia had said. They needed an offering. Someone who would do anything for them.

Rutledge cleared his throat. "The rising's coming. That's why we wanted your mom. She was one of the only people strong enough to get away from them. She resisted them, I don't know how. That's why we sent her that package, to make her come back and finish this for good. We'd almost given up hope when you arrived, asking questions, making a mess of things. Why didn't she come?"

"She's dead," Cassie said softly.

There was silence. Rutledge's face fell. "So it's just you now."

"Us," Charlie corrected him. "And you still haven't explained what you wanted Cassie's mum to do. These are powerful people. Christ, one of them's about to get elected the bloody prime minister. How are we supposed to stop them? What can the two of us possibly do?"

Rutledge looked at them sadly. "Without Margaret, there's nothing anyone can do. They take what they want, and we clean up the mess they leave behind. And this . . . it's only the beginning. They're out there, all over the world. Taking more than their fair share: starting wars

and profiting off the carnage." He bolted to his feet. "Your mother was the smart one," he told Cassie, desperation and weakness in his eyes. "She got out while she still could. Don't make it all in vain. Run, before they leave you with nothing left at all." He quickly turned and wove his way through the café tables, disappearing out into the night again.

Cassie sat back, reeling from his story. She met Charlie's gaze across the table.

"You believe any of that?" he asked, searching.

She slowly nodded. What Olivia and Hugo were doing was real; she'd seen it with her own eyes. The dead bodies and broken lives they left in their wake were real. It wasn't just Oxford: their wickedness was spreading, unchecked, across the whole world. And nobody was going to stop them.

Unless she did.

"SOMETHING'S NOT RIGHT," CASSIE TOLD CHARLIE OVER THE phone, pacing in her attic. It was the last night of vacation; tomorrow the rest of the students would return, and with it her schedule of tutorials and lectures. It seemed almost absurd that she would have to turn in essays and debate the merits of coalition governments after everything that had happened the past few weeks, but Cassie knew she would have to keep up the appearance of her academic activities, at least if she wanted to remain at Raleigh long enough to figure out the final pieces of the School of Night.

"You want to narrow it down for me, darlin'?"

She had to smile. "Rutledge," she clarified. "He's keeping something from me, I can tell."

"What that man isn't sharing could fill a bloody book." Charlie sighed. She could hear the TV on low in the background, and for a moment she pictured him in the bright and comforting warmth of his flat across town. "But short of holding him down and giving him an enhanced interrogation, I don't know what more he's going to tell."

Cassie bit her lip. "It's been bugging me, the way he talked about Rose. He said she's never been the same. Present tense."

"He's an old guy," Charlie pointed out. "They get things jumbled all the time."

"But they never found her body," Cassie pointed out. "If he was able to get my mother away from them, give her a new identity, a fresh start, why couldn't he have done the same for Rose?"

"You think she's still alive?" Charlie asked slowly.

"I don't know what I think anymore!" Cassie sank down on a chair. "I feel like those philosophers I've been studying. One day someone comes along and says, 'By the way, everything you think you know about the world is wrong.' All this is so crazy, and yet I've seen it with my own eyes."

Charlie sighed. "I suppose I could run a check on property records," he said reluctantly. "See if Rutledge has anything stashed away."

"It would be remote," Cassie said eagerly. "Maybe not even in this country. You heard him; he would have wanted to get her as far away as possible. Can you track his passport too? See if he's made any foreign trips?"

"I'll see what I can do," Charlie agreed. "But what about you? They're coming back soon, aren't they?" He didn't need to say who.

"Tomorrow. I'll just have to pretend everything's normal," Cassie said with a shiver of unease. She still hadn't told Charlie about what happened with Hugo. She wondered if she would be able to keep pretending with Hugo too, or if he'd see through her act. "I'll be fine, Charlie, don't worry. Term's starting tomorrow; I can just be busy with school. They'll understand."

But as she hung up and lowered the phone from her ear, it lit up with a text.

Back at Raleigh. Grab a drink?

Hugo. Cassie stared at the handset, her heart in her throat. She quickly tapped out a response.

Working. Sorry. Another time!

She went to the windows and pulled the drapes, checking the bolt on the door. She shivered, feeling the chill of the dark outside, and the shadows that waited, lurking. Watching.

She'd told Charlie she could pretend everything was normal. But how was she supposed to fake idle chitchat with these people, having seen the things she'd seen? How could she pretend that everything was all right, when her mind was really racing to explain the terrible truths she'd discovered?

And if they realized she knew what was going on . . . Cassie's eyes lifted to the beam across the living room, picturing Evie's limp body.

They'd killed Evie. They may not have fixed the noose around her neck, or looped it across the wood, but they'd driven her to it, drained what self-preservation she had left until her mind was broken and empty.

Cassie felt a fresh determination. She would find a way to stop them, somehow. She had to, before they put an end to her themselves.

*Hugo texted twice more over the following days, but each time Cassie re-*plied with a casual excuse. She threw herself into her schedule of lectures and essays, exiting Raleigh by the back gates and hiding in the modern library across town to avoid any run-ins with Olivia and the rest. She felt like a thief and a spy, creeping around the college, her heart galloping as she wondered if one of the group would be lurking around the next corner. Charlie checked with her twice, sometimes three times a day, clearly worried. "You can crash with me," he told her, in another hurried phone call as she walked to meet Elliot at his studio. "That room isn't safe, they already broke in once."

"And how would that look?" Cassie challenged him, striding fast through the lunchtime pedestrian rush. "They know you're digging into Rose's files. If they haven't put the pieces together and connected me yet, they will soon." She checked the address Elliot had sent as she approached a narrow row of town houses tucked down a side street. This was the place. "And speaking of digging, have you been able to do that search on Rutledge yet?"

"Not yet." Charlie sounded frustrated. "My chief inspector's been breathing down my neck. But he's out this afternoon, I'll do it then."

"Call me after. And Charlie? Don't worry so much."

"Don't get into so much trouble," Charlie replied gruffly, before hanging up.

Cassie tucked her phone away. The front door to Elliot's building was open when she tested it, and she could hear laughter and music coming from upstairs. She climbed the narrow staircase to the top and found a party in progress, spilling out of Elliot's tiny flat.

"Cassandra!" Elliot emerged from the din, with a bottle of champagne in each hand and his hair in a mess. "A happy new year to you! Don't you look . . . ? Well, I was going to say well rested, but you look like you've been sitting in a dark corner binge-watching old *West Wing* episodes all break. No, wait, that was me." He kissed her exuberantly on both cheeks, clearly a little drunk.

Cassie jolted back, surprised. "What's the party?" she asked as Elliot nudged her inside. "It's a little early for champagne, isn't it?"

"Darling," a man interrupted from beside them, "it's never too early for champagne!"

Cassie laughed, still confused. The tiny flat was crammed with people and paintings, Elliot's canvases and art materials propped against every wall.

"We're celebrating. My bon voyage, in fact," Elliot beamed.

Cassie's spirits fell. "You're leaving?"

"Au revoir to you all!" he declared grandly. "Hitching my bag over my shoulder and setting out into the great wide world. Well, London," he corrected. "I got an exhibition!"

"You mean, a patron," that same strange man interrupted again, a jealous edge to his voice.

"Now, now," Elliot grinned. "I'll be sure to spread the wealth and introduce all you starving artists to my new rich friends."

"No thanks," the other man replied. "Being a kept man, funded by some millionaire to create, is the antithesis of artistic freedom." He stalked off.

"Congratulations." Cassie tried to sound enthusiastic, even as disappointment swelled in her chest. Elliot was one of her only friends in town—and her ally researching in the library archives. Without him . . . She tried to recover. "So tell me everything. Who's this patron?"

Elliot cleared his throat. "The Mandeville family trust."

"Mandeville?" Cassie repeated, shocked.

"Oh, right, you know the kids, don't you?" Elliot said. "Anyway, it's just a grant to do whatever I want for a year, but who knows where it could lead? They're connected with all kinds of private buyers and galleries. It's my chance to get out of here," he added, looking at her anxiously. "I can't stay stuck behind that desk forever."

"Right, of course!" Cassie forced a smile. "It sounds great." But she felt a chill, knowing Elliot was getting in deeper with the Mandevilles. Was this about her, she wondered? A way of removing an ally, her source of research? Elliot had tracked down all that information about the School of Night; perhaps they'd noticed and decided to get him out of the picture. It wasn't just her own safety she was risking with all her investigations. She'd put Elliot in harm's way too without even thinking about it. She could only be grateful they'd chosen this grant scheme and not some other, more permanent solution. "I'm sorry." Cassie quickly pulled him into a hug.

"What for?" Elliot extricated himself, frowning at her. "I should be sorry. For leaving you holding the fort at the library," he added.

"Nothing, just . . . Congratulations on the job." Cassie swiftly changed the subject, peppering him with questions to cover the brief outburst. "When do you start? Will you have a studio at least as luxurious as this one?"

Elliot's departure gave Cassie new concern about her investigations, and the stakes that were rising for everyone involved. She hadn't realized the risk she was placing on the people around her: Elliot, Rutledge, and Charlie too. The deeper she dug into the School of Night, the greater the

danger had become, until she found herself flinching at shadows as she walked home and startling at the sound of voices outside her window, wondering if Hugo had finally told the others about finding her in the maze, if they knew she was her mother's daughter, *if, if, if . . .*

It was almost a relief when it came time for her first tutorial back after the vacation. Cassie set aside her research into Margaret, Rose, and what few articles she could find on the School of Night and turned her attention back to the weighty philosophy tomes she'd been studying, preparing her essay in plenty of time. But as she crossed the college grounds the next morning to Tremain's office, she couldn't help but wonder how deeply he was entrenched in the dark goings-on of the group. From the brief conversation she'd overheard between him and Henry Mandeville, it sounded as if Tremain had been involved in their lies for years, all the way back to Rose and her mother. Tremain had been fearful of the older man, that much was clear, but that fear only made Cassie resent him even more. He was to blame for Evie too. They all were.

Cassie climbed the staircase to his office and caught her breath, forcing her emotions back under control. She had to pretend everything was normal, she couldn't let him see the truth. She braced herself and pushed the door open.

"Ah, Miss Blackwell, you're still gracing us with your presence then." Tremain turned from his stance by the bookcase. His gaze flicked over her with an icy edge. "I wondered if we would be seeing you again. Please, join your classmates." He nodded to the seating area, where Julia and Sebastian were waiting.

Cassie's heart caught in her throat. She felt a rush of blood pounding in her ears. She hadn't seen Sebastian since that terrible night he'd attacked her; she'd almost forced herself to forget about him. Cassie could make out a scar running above his right eye to his hairline. Sebastian glared at her, his hatred seething and clear to see.

Cassie shrank back, remembering the feel of the wall scraping against

her back, the rough grip of his hand on her throat. "No . . ." she murmured. She looked to Tremain, stunned. "You can't be serious."

"About what?" Tremain stared back, impassive. "Are you able to join us for your tutorial today or not?"

Cassie gulped for air. She couldn't believe she was expected to sit in the same room as her attacker, debate philosophy as if nothing had happened. How could Tremain do this to her? What was he trying to prove?

"We don't have time for your dawdling, Miss Blackwell. I've told you before, if you have a problem with your classes, you can always withdraw from your studies and leave Raleigh." Tremain stared at her as if he was just willing her to go.

Cassie took another deep breath and walked over to the nearest chair. "I'm fine," she bit out determinedly, taking a seat. She met Sebastian's glare, forcing herself not to look away first. "We can get started whenever you want."

Cassie wasn't sure how she made it through the hour. All she could focus on was Sebastian's presence, just inches away from her. She couldn't help but let her gaze drift to the scar on his forehead. She could barely remember inflicting the blow that caused it; that part of the night was still nothing but a haze to her: anger and desperation and violent force. She should have felt guilty, she knew, but instead she felt a twisted sense of pride that at least he wouldn't forget his sins so easily—they were there in the mirror, every time he looked.

She hated him. She hated him, and Tremain, for forcing her back here again—remembering in flashes the detail of that night, reliving it in a dozen tiny ways as the conversation continued around her until finally the chimes of the Raleigh bells pierced through the room and Cassie could leap to her feet again.

"A moment, Miss Blackwell." Tremain stopped her before she could bolt from the room.

Cassie clenched her jaw and waited, her anxiety turning to anger as Tremain flipped through some papers on his table and made her stand there awkwardly as Sebastian and Julia left. Finally, she couldn't take it anymore. "Is this some kind of game to you?" she demanded, angry.

Tremain's head snapped up. "Excuse me?"

"Putting me in the same room as that . . . that animal." Cassie gripped her files to her chest to keep from shaking.

"As I recall, he was the one left in a hospital bed," the professor pointed out. "He's already missed several weeks of tutorials because of your actions. It would hardly be fair to make him sacrifice any more."

Cassie's fury beat hard in her chest. "Do you really hate me that much?" she whispered.

Tremain's face slipped for a moment, and she thought she caught a flash of guilt, but then his expression smoothed again, superior and sneering.

"You flatter yourself, Miss Blackwell. I'm merely trying to educate here. And as such, you've proven more of an obstacle than an ally in my goals."

Cassie gave a sharp nod. This was useless, even she could see. "Is there any reading you'd suggest for next week's essay?"

Tremain stared at her, clearly thrown by the question.

"On the list, you mention several articles," Cassie elaborated, pulling out her printed sheet of the semester's reading list. "Is there any in particular you'd recommend for the next class?"

"I . . . uh, the ones with the asterisks should suffice," Tremain recovered, and Cassie felt a curious pride for having unbalanced him. If he thought she would turn and run, he was mistaken.

"Then I'll see you next week." She tucked away her notes and strode from the room, her heartbeat still racing as she descended the staircase and emerged in the cloisters.

Sebastian was there, waiting for her.

He took two steps toward her, his expression set in a scowl. "Do you know what you did to me?" he demanded, pushing back his hair. "Fifteen stitches. I was lucky you didn't take my eye out, you crazy bitch."

Cassie held up her hand before he could say another word, her anger blossoming into pure rage, red hot and familiar. "Don't," she ground out. "Don't talk to me, don't look at me. If you so much as lay a hand on me again, I swear to God, I will fucking end you."

Sebastian must have seen the look in her eyes, because he faltered. Cassie pressed her advantage.

"You think I hurt you last time?" she continued, stepping in close enough to see the flexing of nerves in his jaw. "You think you know pain? That was nothing. You deserve to be dead, and next time I won't be so stupid as to let you live." She spun on her heel and walked away. Her hands were shaking and she felt dizzy and weak. It was stupid to threaten him, after everything the college had put her through, but she didn't care.

She hurried fast across the campus path until she was finally alone in her attic and could sink to the floor inside the door and let the tears fall, hot and wretched on her cheeks. Crying wouldn't solve anything, she told herself, over and over until the tears finally stopped. She would just have to live with the knowledge that Sebastian was out there on campus. Another person she would have to avoid.

Cassie let out a hollow laugh. The list was growing every day. Hugo, Olivia, now Sebastian too. They were all the same in the end, taking what they wanted, leaving nothing but devastation in their path. Preying on the weak, letting their privilege and connections clean up the mess they left.

Darkness had fallen by the time Cassie pulled herself off the floor and ran a bath, exhausted from the morning's ordeal. She was neck deep in the scalding water when her cell phone sounded in the next room. She

pulled herself out of the tub and wrapped herself in a robe, reaching her phone just before it went to voice mail.

"Cassie? What the hell? I've been calling all day!" Charlie's voice was frantic with worry.

"I'm sorry." Cassie swallowed, her mouth dry. "I guess I didn't hear."

"You can't ignore my calls," Charlie told her. "I was about to come over there and knock down the bloody door."

"I'm fine," she told him, tired. "I just had a rough day. What's going on?"

"You might be right, about Rutledge," Charlie replied. "I checked property records and nothing showed up. But there was an incident report from a town out in Wales, ten years ago. Police were called to an address there, and Rutledge is listed as a witness on the scene."

"What was the place?" Cassie asked, alert now.

"A care facility," he replied. "Long-term mental and elderly support."

"A psych ward?" Cassie breathed.

"Near enough." Charlie let out a sigh.

Cassie looked around the room, trying to collect her thoughts. "How soon can we leave?"

"I can't get away. The chief's put me on paperwork duty, and I'll be snowed under all weekend," Charlie replied. "If you can wait until next week, I'll make some more calls, maybe we could find someone there who—"

Cassie cut him off. "I'm going. Not next week, now. Tonight. There's no time to wait. Whatever this rising they're planning is, we need to know more. Rose is the only one with the answers now."

"But what if she's in no state to give you any?"

Cassie caught her breath. She didn't know what the School of Night had done, but this was her chance to finally learn more about the society—and her mother. "Send me the address," she told Charlie. "I'll leave first thing in the morning."

CASSIE MADE HER WAY TO THE OXFORD RAIL STATION WHEN IT
was still dark out the next morning. The streets were empty except for
the garbage collectors and early deliverymen; still, she couldn't help but
check over her shoulder at every turn, wondering if the footsteps she
heard behind her were real, or just the product of her nervous imagi-
nation. Ever since she'd heard about Elliot's new job, it had struck her
just how far the School of Night's power extended. They knew enough
to have the police cover up the suicides and press Charlie to stop his
digging, but this was different: smaller, specific, and too close to her.
Did she know about her own research yet? Who knew where else their
power reached?

When finally she spotted the station, brightly lit and just bustling to
life, she let out a sigh of relief. She purchased her ticket, and a greasy
morning sandwich from the stall just inside, but even when she was set-
tled in a seat in a half-empty carriage, she couldn't quite relax. As the
train pulled away, and the houses and looming spires of Oxford gave
way to the rolling green hills and fields of the countryside, Cassie rested
her cheek against the cool glass and tried to pull herself together.

Evil was lurking at Raleigh, the kind she'd never allowed herself to
believe in before now. All her life, Cassie had known the terrible deeds
humans could inflict upon each other, out of rage and lust and selfish
desires. She'd always accepted with a numb resignation the sins that
could reside in a man's heart as a part of his nature. But this, this was a

darker evil than she'd ever before imagined. This was unnatural. And if her theories were right, this had been happening for years. Decades.

Centuries.

And the darkness wasn't just at Oxford, but spreading across the world, Rutledge had told them. Each new generation's members of the society going their own way: feeding and using that power to fuel their own ambitions. Cassie shivered to imagine the power a group like this could wield for its own ends. Power that could form governments and start wars, power that could reshape the world in the society's own selfish, cruel image.

Could a group like that be stopped, with such a dark legacy running through it? Cassie watched the countryside bleed and blur into a mess of gray outside the windows, and she hoped with everything she had that Rose would have the answers. She was in too deep now to turn back.

The train was almost empty by the time it deposited Cassie at a tiny, rural station, hours later. She stepped off the train alone to find the skies were dark and drizzling, and the countryside extended around her in a sea of murky green, one lone road twisting into the hills. The local stationmaster was the only sign of life, dozing on his stool behind the ticket counter.

Cassie tapped on the window, her trepidation growing. "Excuse me?"

He slowly blinked. "What's that? Ah, yes. Can I help you?"

"I'm looking to get to . . . Edgeley Falls Home." Cassie checked her scribbled address. "I didn't realize it was so far from everything." She'd been imagining a town, at the very least, somewhere with taxis and streetlights and a place to stay for the night before the long trip back tomorrow.

"Don't worry, there'll be a bus along soon." The man checked the clock on the wall. "It'll take you to Edgeley Village, about ten miles thataway." He nodded vaguely.

"Is that where the home is?"

"No, for that you'll need a car. Ask at the local pub for Arthur, and he'll drive you out."

Cassie remembered Charlie's insistence that she text regular updates. He'd been anxious enough about her going on this trip alone, she didn't want him to worry more. She pulled out her phone to text him, but the stationmaster chortled.

"No signal out here, love."

He was right. The bars marking her cell reception were completely flat.

"It's just the valley, you should have better luck in the village."

"Thanks." Cassie picked up her bag and headed down the steps, waiting with a shiver at the bus stop on the corner. She looked around at the swath of nature and found herself wishing for the busy traffic of Oxford.

The minutes ticked past until eventually a bus rolled into view from around the hill. Cassie bought a ticket to the village and climbed aboard, taking a seat behind a couple of women clutching grocery bags and gossiping loudly about their various family goings-on. By the time the bus pulled into a small village several miles later, Cassie knew the intimate details of their wayward sons' lives and was almost reluctant to disembark and leave their friendly chatter behind.

Edgeley Village itself was a touch more comforting than the wide open wilderness beyond: old houses clustered around an overgrown square, with a small church, general store, and wood-beamed pub on the corner. Cassie quickly texted Charlie to say she'd arrived, then headed for the pub and Arthur the taximan.

"The home, eh?" The plump, brassy barmaid gave Cassie an inquisitive look. "What do you want up there?"

"Just visiting," Cassie said vaguely, casting a sideways glance at the other patrons, a cluster of old men in the corner and two boys who couldn't have been more than sixteen, drinking pints of beer with feigned nonchalance. "The stationmaster said Arthur would take me up?"

The barmaid clucked. "If you'd called ahead . . . Our Arthur just went out on a job to Withyham; he won't be back until tonight."

Cassie's heart fell.

"You could always walk it," the woman suggested.

"Is it far?" Cassie asked, brightening.

"Two miles, maybe, but the road takes you right up. You can't miss it."

"Thanks." Cassie cast another look outside the windows. She'd be back later than planned. "Is there any place to stay around here for the night?"

"We have a room upstairs," the barmaid replied. "Small enough, but it's only twenty quid a night."

"I'll take it. Thanks."

The weather didn't seem to be clearing any time soon, but faced with a wasted day, Cassie resigned herself to the damp and set out, following the barmaid's directions along the one country road. The wind whistled around her, sending chills down the edge of her coat and up under her cuffs, but Cassie put her head down and pressed on, and before too long, Edgeley House loomed into view.

Cassie stopped. Edgeley House was perched on the top of a hill, silhouetted against the cloudy sky: a square-fronted stone mansion, eerie and dark. She made her way through the heavy gates and up the drive, climbing the stairs to ring the front bell.

After a moment, the door swung open. A girl about her own age looked out, wearing a navy nurse's uniform, her hair caught in a bun. "Can I help you?" She had an Australian accent, friendly and warm.

Cassie felt a wave of relief. "Hi, I'm so sorry I didn't call ahead, but I'm here to see one of your . . ." She searched for the correct word, finally settling on, "Residents."

"Come on in before you catch your death." The girl held the door wide, ushering Cassie indoors. "Christ, it's awful out there. Nothing but rain, every day for a month now. I don't know how they stand it, I'd be slitting my wrists by now. Shit." She caught herself, looking guiltily around. "I probably shouldn't say that here."

"It's okay." Cassie smiled, immediately warming to her. "I'm Cassie, by the way."

"Trish." She shook Cassie's hand. "I'm new. Nurse Janice is out for the morning."

She headed deeper into the warm, simply decorated reception area. Cassie looked around. It had the feel of a doctor's office: old magazines on a coffee table, framed sailboat pictures on the wall, a faint smell of antiseptic lingering in the air. "It's nice in here," she remarked, surprised.

"Bet you were expecting a real spooky haunted house." Trish gave her a grin. "Me too. Man, when the taxi dropped me off on my first day, I was pissing myself. But it's not so bad, really. We've got about twenty patients, lounges, a games room, even gardens for when the weather clears up." She checked her computer screen behind the desk. "Who are you here to see?"

"Rose," Cassie replied, hoping Rutledge hadn't changed her name completely.

Trish brightened. "Rose Anderson? That's great. She doesn't ever get visitors. She'll be so pleased." She tapped at the computer, then paused. "I don't have anything down here. . . . Are you family?"

"She's my godmother," Cassie lied. "I'm only visiting England for a few weeks, so I thought I'd come by and see her."

"Well . . . I'm not supposed to let just anyone in without clearing the paperwork." Trish looked around, before giving Cassie a wink. "But I'm sure it can't do any harm." She rounded the desk again and beckoned Cassie to follow as she headed down a hallway.

"How is she?" Cassie asked. "I mean, is she . . . ?"

Trish gave her a sympathetic look. "She has her good days and her bad. The medication helps, when she'll take it, anyway. Most of the time she just keeps to herself. She likes to draw, landscapes, some still life too. She's in the craft lounge now, I think."

Trish turned a corner, toward the back of the house, and then they arrived at a large, light-filled atrium. Several patients were sitting around

the room, watching TV, reading, or simply sitting alone. Their expressions were blank or sleepy-eyed, and many of them were dressed in pajamas and thick fluffy dressing gowns. Trish led Cassie to the corner, where a dark-haired woman in her forties was standing in front of an easel. She wore a pair of loose slacks and a knitted sweater in splashes of blue and violet. A paintbrush was poised in her hand, the canvas empty in front of her.

"Rose?" Trish approached gently. "Rose, dear, you have someone here to see you."

Rose turned, blinking at them with vacant eyes. "Janice?"

"No, dear, I'm Trish, remember?" Trish took the paintbrush from Rose's hand and steered her to a nearby armchair. "Your goddaughter Cassie is here to visit, isn't that nice?"

Rose stared blankly at Cassie. She looked like a different person from the girl in the photograph with her mother, emptied out somehow, a faded recollection of what once had been.

"How about I get you both some tea?" Trish offered. "And you can have a nice chat."

Thank you, Cassie mouthed gratefully, taking a seat beside Rose. Trish retreated, and they were left alone in the corner, looking out across the wet, windy valley.

"Hi," Cassie said softly to Rose.

Rose crumpled her forehead in a frown. "I don't have a goddaughter. Do I?" Her voice wavered, her eyes watery and distant.

"No," Cassie reassured her quickly. "But you knew my mom. I'm Margaret's daughter. Do you remember her?" She reached into her pocket and unfolded the photograph, showing it to Rose. "Margaret," she pressed again. "You were at school with her, remember? At Raleigh College."

At the mention of the school, Rose's expression became fearful. She half bolted up from her seat. "I'm not supposed to, not supposed to say. My uncle—"

"It's all right." Cassie calmed her. "Your uncle says it's okay. Pete, right? I know him and Doris. Everything's okay."

Rose stared at her, trembling, then slowly sank back into the chair. "It was a dream," she whispered, twisting her bracelets around her thin wrist. "It was all just a dream."

"What was?" Cassie asked, leaning forward. "What do you remember? Do you know what happened, before you came here?"

Rose's eyes flicked away. "Maggie?" Her voice rose. "Did Maggie come back? She was only supposed to be gone an hour, she told me, she was coming right back."

"No, it's just me. Cassandra, her daughter." Cassie forced herself to stay patient. "I need you to think carefully, Rose. I need to know what happened. Is there anything you remember from back then? Anything at all. You were studying English," she reminded her. "You lived above Granville quad, do you remember that?"

Rose looked at her again, and her eyes seemed to shift into focus. "The roses bloomed in summer. They were everywhere, white pillows, like clouds."

"That's right." Cassie's hopes rose. "They're all along the pathways, they're still there in the late summer. And you roomed with Margaret. With Maggie."

Rose smiled. "We were a pair, all right. The times we had . . . Where is Maggie? Why hasn't she come?"

"She wants to," Cassie lied again, feeling a pang. "She'll come as soon as she can."

"She was a good friend." Rose's eyes became watery. "The best."

"I know." Cassie reached across and patted her hand. "I'm sorry she can't be here."

Rose absently patted back. "You look just like her, you know. I can see it, right here." She cupped Cassie's jaw and turned it from side to side.

Cassie's heart clenched in her chest. "Really?" she whispered.

"Clear as day." Rose nodded. "You're a good girl to come see me. Nobody comes anymore. It's been so long."

"I'm sorry." Cassie took Rose's hand from her face and squeezed it. "What about your friends from back then? The others, not Maggie. Do you remember them?"

Rose smiled. "Oh yes. The parties . . ." She sighed wistfully. "I wore blue to the winter ball. Maggie found the dress first, but we tossed for it, and I won. She was fine though; she looked good in anything. Richard was so dashing in his suit. We danced so long, my feet bled. The blisters!"

"Richard?" Cassie asked with a jolt. "Not Richard Mandeville?"

"We all called him Dicky." Rose giggled as if she was a teenager. "He hated it, especially when his daddy came around. You should have seen his face."

"What happened with Richard?" Cassie dropped her voice, watching Rose intently. "What did they offer you, Rose? Your aunt said there was a job, do you remember? An opportunity you couldn't pass up."

Rose stared at her. Slowly her smile faded. "It was supposed to be beautiful," she whispered, her eyes turning bleak. "They told me the centuries would open and the truth would rise. Rising, the rising, it was all so beautiful."

Cassie swallowed, feeling a chill whisper down her spine. "What happens, Rose? What happens at the rising?"

Rose took a shaking breath. "There's no way out," she said, her voice hoarse. "Once you go down there, there's no way back. The tunnels will eat you alive."

"Tunnels. What tunnels? Where does it take place? How can I stop them?"

"You can't." Rose stared at her. "*In fine est principium quoddam ad cognoscendum verum*. In the end there is a beginning, for the knowledge and the truth."

"What does that mean?" Cassie asked, trying to hide her urgency. "Is that from the ritual? Were you there?"

"To become, you must end. It all ends, everything dies!" Her voice rose.

"It's okay." Cassie tried to hush her, but Rose looked at her wildly, her eyes suddenly fevered and bright.

"Where did you get that?" she demanded, suddenly grabbing hold of Cassie's necklace. "You can't take it, it's mine! They told me I was special, that I would rise, rise. The darkness is inside of you. You can't get it out!"

Cassie pulled away in vain, choking, until suddenly Trish was there, tearing Rose back. "What did you say to her?" Trish demanded, as another woman rushed over. Around them, the other patients took up Rose's wail, some of them crying and babbling in confusion.

"There, there," the other woman said briskly. She carefully pinned Rose down against her chair, pulling a syringe from her uniform. She pushed back Rose's sleeve and punctured inside her elbow with a swift, well-practiced movement. The plunger went down; Rose flailed a moment more, then stilled, whispering, "You can't get it out. You can't get it out."

Cassie, shaken, rubbed at her throat, trying to breathe normally. The woman spun to face her, her face drawn in a thin-lipped scowl. "What did you do?" she demanded. "She hasn't had an episode in months."

"I'm sorry," Cassie stuttered, her throat raw. "I didn't mean to, we were just talking . . ."

"Who are you?" The woman turned to Trish. "What's she doing here? There are no visitors scheduled. Rose can't deal with outside guests."

"I'm sorry, Janice." Trish gulped. "I didn't think, she said—"

"It's not her fault." Cassie rose to her feet, interrupting. "I'm sorry I upset her. I didn't mean any harm."

Janice glared. "Who did you say you were?"

Cassie backed away. "I'll go," she promised. "Really, I didn't mean to cause a scene."

Another patient began crying. Janice looked past Cassie, distracted. "You've done enough," she said. "You can see yourself out."

Nodding, Cassie sent a last look at Rose. Her mother's friend was lolling in the chair, her eyes unfocused, her lips mouthing words that nobody would hear. The girl she'd used to be was gone.

Cassie held back tears as she turned and walked away, back down the hallway and out through the reception area into the cold, damp gloom outside. It was pouring down now in sheets of icy rain, the hills looming dark in the dim twilight, but Cassie didn't flinch against the cold. She kept walking, her head down against the wind, rain mingling with the tears that finally streamed down her cheeks.

Rose. Evie. So many more besides. Bright sparks burned out, brittle shells of memory, heavy caskets in the grave. They were supposed to do great things, lead important lives, and instead they'd been left with nothing while their abusers strolled on into their own bright futures, unaffected. Unremorseful. Even Cassie's mother had had her life stolen: fleeing a promising education, forced to spend years on the run, fearful of who might be in pursuit. Cassie twisted with guilt when she remembered how much she'd resented their nomadic lifestyle, the way her mother would uproot her without warning every few years, driving them on further from any stability or normal life. Cassie had blamed her depression, blamed her for everything, as if they were selfish choices and not the desperate acts of a mother trying to save her child. Margaret had done her best for Cassie, and Cassie had never even known. Never thanked her for the sacrifices that had saved her life.

Cassie was so consumed by the bitter ache in her chest that she didn't notice the car approaching from the outskirts of the village until its headlights cut through the downpour, dazzling her for a moment in their glare. She leaped back out of the road just in time as it sped past with a dull roar, splashing her with muddy water from the ditch.

Cassie swore under her breath as she stumbled back into the road, drenched, but the car was already disappearing into the distance. There was nothing to do but continue on toward the village, her soaked sneakers squelching with every step. Luckily, she was close, the steeple of the local church lit up just around the bend. Cassie thought gratefully of the room waiting for her at the pub, and the cozy fire of the wood-beamed lounge room.

The sound of a car engine came again behind her. Cassie made sure she was walking on the side of the road, leaving plenty of room to pass, but instead of driving ahead, the car idled slowly behind her, headlights bright.

Cassie shivered. She glanced back. The lights were too bright to make out the driver, but she was almost certain it was the same car. Why had it turned around?

Fear clenched in her chest. She walked faster, breaking into a run as the walls of the church came into view through the pouring rain. The car sped up, keeping pace behind her, the engine growling on the empty street.

Cassie sprinted down the road and turned off through a side gate into the churchyard. She ducked behind a wall and waited, her heart pounding, willing the car to continue past.

The sound of the engine cut. A door opened, then slammed shut. Footsteps crunched heavily on the gravel.

Cassie turned and took off through the churchyard, sprinting blindly through the rain. Lights from the church cut through the yard in places, and she veered through the shadows of tombstones and statues. She could hear her pursuer now, his footfalls getting closer as she skirted the main church walls and clattered down the front steps that led out into the village square.

She caught her breath, looking around for help, but the village was deserted in the rain, empty streets in all directions. The pub was across the square, lit up like a beacon of safety, so she took off toward it, fear

screaming in her mind as she heard the footfalls behind her again and the pant of angry breath, closer, closer—

Cassie was almost across the street when she felt a grip on her arm, and then she was yanked violently back. She screamed as her assailant struck her hard across the face, sending her tumbling to the ground. She gasped for air, reeling from the blow, but there was no time to recover, not when he was grabbing her leg, dragging her into the shadows of a nearby alleyway. Cassie opened her mouth to scream again, but her cry was cut short by the sharp blow of a boot against her stomach. Another blow came, and then another, pain exploding through her ribs with every cruel kick. She curled into a ball, whimpering. The boot came again, aimed for her head, but she rolled out from under the blow and grabbed the foot, yanking hard to bring her assailant crashing to the ground. She scrambled to her hands and knees, but he was on her in an instant, throwing her back down so hard her head cracked against the stones. Pain splintered through her.

Her attacker crawled up, straddling her as his hands closed around her throat. In the dark of the alleyway, she could only see the shadows of his face, a man she didn't recognize, totally blank and determined as he choked the life from her body. She struggled, clawing desperately at his face as her lungs burned and vision blurred. But he was too strong, unmovable, and gradually her strength drained away. The darkness rose up to meet her. *This can't be the end,* Cassie thought frantically, hopelessly. *Not here, not like this.*

Suddenly, there was a sound, the sickening crunch of metal making contact with bone. The pressure on Cassie's throat eased, and her assailant crumpled down on top of her with a guttural moan. She shoved him aside as something dropped to the ground with a metallic ring. A wrench, bloodstained now.

"Come on," her rescuer ordered, extending a hand. He stepped out of the shadows, and Cassie froze as she made out his face for the first time. Her professor, Tremain.

Her attacker let out another groan, moving on the ground beside her. Cassie broke free from her daze and grabbed Tremain's hand, struggling to her feet. "Who is he?" she gasped. "What's going on?"

"There's no time," Tremain ordered, pulling her toward the street. "You have to trust me."

But Cassie yanked away. "Why?" she cried. Her heart was racing, and her head still rang with dull pain. "Why should I trust you, after everything you've done?"

Tremain turned back, his face drawn in the streetlight. "I'm trying to protect you, Cassie." He paused, some unreadable sadness in his eyes. "I'm your father."

CASSIE'S HEAD SPUN. IT COULDN'T BE TRUE.

"I don't believe you—" she protested, but Tremain cut her off.

"There's no time." He dragged her across the square to where an old blue Fiat sat parked on the corner and shoved her into the passenger seat before crossing to the driver's side.

Cassie clutched the seat, reeling. Tremain piled inside and started the engine, taking off with a squeal of tires on the wet street. He careened through the square, glancing anxiously in the rearview mirror. "Put your belt on," he ordered. Cassie numbly did as instructed as they turned onto the main road and sped out of the village, winding into the hills.

Tremain's jaw set with determination as he peered through the dark rain. Cassie shuddered. This man, who had done nothing but belittle and criticize her, who was bound deeply in the School of Night, he couldn't be her father.

"How badly are you hurt?" Tremain glanced over at her. "Are you bleeding?"

Cassie slowly raised a hand to her head. It came away sticky and wet. "Just a little," she whispered. "My ribs . . . I think something's broken."

"You'll have to make it back to Oxford," Tremain said, not unkindly. "We can't stop. I don't know who else they sent."

"Who was he?" Cassie's voice grew stronger. "What the hell just happened to me?"

"What happened is you couldn't just leave things be." Tremain kept his eyes fixed on the road ahead. They were speeding far above the

limit, driving almost blind through the dark. "What were you doing? They've been following you since Gravestone, damnit. In the city I can protect you, but out here there's nothing to save you. You were lucky I intercepted Henry's orders."

"Orders for what?" Cassie gulped. "Who was that man? Why did he hurt me?"

"Because you're dangerous!" Tremain exploded. "Digging into old files, asking questions. I covered for you as long as I could, but once he knew you were visiting Rose, there was no stopping him."

Cassie inhaled in a gasp. "You know about Rose?"

Tremain shot her a scornful look. "We know everything, Cassie. Richard had a soft spot for Rose, and he made a bargain that she'd be left in peace. She's too far gone to be a threat, rambling about things that nobody can make sense of. Except someone like you." He wrenched on the wheel again, flying around a narrow bend.

Cassie grabbed hold of the window rail. "Stop," she protested, grabbing his arm.

Tremain shook her off. "There's no time."

"I don't care," she yelled. "I need you to stop the car right now!"

Tremain scowled, but he hit the brakes, pulling off into a low ditch at the side of the road.

There was silence for a moment while Cassie caught her breath. Then she turned to him. "You said you're my father." His face was dark in the shadows, but she searched it regardless for any sign of recognition or resemblance. "I don't believe you. It can't be true."

Tremain let out a sigh, refusing to meet her gaze. "I didn't want you to know. It's safer for you this way."

"I don't understand." Cassie swallowed. "You've been . . . Ever since I started, you've done nothing but be a complete asshole to me. Trying to make me drop out, forcing me to be in a room with Sebastian. How could you? If you say you're trying to protect me—"

"Raleigh isn't safe, damnit!" Tremain turned with a scowl. "You think I wanted this? When I realized who you were, who your mother was . . . I've been trying to get you away from there. To get you out while you still can."

Cassie shook her head, still clinging to the possibility that this was a trick, some kind of game to fool her into trusting him. "Why not just tell me?"

"If anyone knew, it would all be over. Don't you see?" Tremain demanded harshly. "It's about family. The society, it's in the bloodlines. Passed from generation to generation. If they knew you were mine, they'd never let you go." He inhaled a ragged breath. "It may not have seemed like it, but I was trying to protect you. And now it's too late. They think you're a threat. They sent him to deal with you, and he won't be the last." He slammed his hand against the steering wheel in frustration.

But Cassie didn't care about her attacker. She was too focused on the other thing he'd said. His words sank in with a slow wave of understanding. "I'm one of them?" she asked, feeling the truth snake through her system, a black poison in her veins. "This thing, this darkness, it's in me too?"

"I'm sorry," Tremain replied, his voice gruff. "That's why you can't stay. Right now you're dormant; it's all just potential. But if you go through with the rising and they make you a member . . . There's no going back." He turned to her, his eyes bleak with an empty resignation. "The things you'll do, the choices you'll make . . . You can never take it back. Never."

They drove the rest of the way to Oxford in silence. Cassie slumped, numb, her mind whirling with questions she couldn't ask Tremain. She didn't want to know what his answers would be.

She was one of them. The knowledge echoed through her with a terrible finality. Like Hugo and Olivia. She had that in her, in her blood. And

Tremain . . . He was part of her too. The father she'd always wondered about was nothing but a weak, corrupted man, bound in service to an ancient evil.

Cassie hadn't realized until then the secret dreams she'd been clinging to: that finding her father would somehow provide the family she'd been missing all those years. That knowing him would fill the emptiness, quiet the aching place in her heart that had been broken ever since her mother died. That somewhere was a normal, loving family who would open up their arms and welcome her into their fold, and she would leave her broken, restless life behind. She knew it was naive of her, the hopeful fairy tales of a woman without a home, but now, faced with the stark reality for the first time, Cassie felt those dreams finally die.

She must have fallen asleep with the mantra of disappointment in her mind, because when Cassie blinked her eyes open, she found the sky pale with dawn. They were turning off the motorway, on the outskirts of Oxford, suburban subdivisions passing by outside the windows.

"How do you feel?" Tremain's voice was more impatient than concerned.

Cassie shifted, feeling the pain in her stomach and ribs. "Okay, I think," she lied.

"I'll drop you at the college. Collect your passport and anything you need. I'll take you to the airport. We'll figure out where you'll go from here."

Leave? Cassie shook her head. "I'm not going anywhere."

"Don't be a fool," Tremain told her harshly. "Didn't you listen to a single word I said? They know you're after them. That man they sent is only the beginning."

"No, you're not listening to me," Cassie insisted. "I'm not running. Somebody has to stop them."

Tremain let out a bark of laughter. "Stop them?" he turned to her, his forehead creased in disbelief. "What the hell are you thinking? Do

you know who they are, what they've done? You can't end this, nobody can."

"Have you even tried?" Cassie challenged. "Or do you just bow and scrape to the Mandevilles, doing their dirty work?" Something struck her for the first time, and she gaped at him, her fear rising. "Do you feed too? Do you hurt people like they do?"

"No!" Tremain ground out. Then he paused. "Not for a long time," he admitted. "Not since I was a student too. I saw the damage we do. I swore I would never do it again."

Cassie thought back, the pieces finally clicking into place. "My mother," she breathed. "You fed on her."

Tremain stared straight out of the windshield, gripping the steering wheel, his knuckles white. "I made mistakes," he said, low. "I've regretted them my whole life."

Cassie felt bile rise in her throat. Of course, why hadn't she seen? Her mother's depression, the mood swings, the suicide . . . She'd noticed the similarity with Evie's behavior, but she hadn't considered for a moment that Margaret's instability might have been from the same wicked cause. The School of Night. Tremain. It was all because of him. Margaret may not have shown the signs of it at Raleigh, but she hadn't escaped without damage.

"You know she's dead." Cassie's voice rang with bitter loathing. "She opened her wrists when I was fourteen. I found her body."

Tremain flinched. "I didn't know then. I didn't know anything until you arrived here. The missing files, the break-in . . . I put it all together." He turned, pausing at a red light. "I promise you, Cassie, everything I've done since then has been to protect you." He looked at her urgently, pleading with his gaze. "That's why you can't stay. Don't you see? Either they discover you're mine, or they kill you first. Either way, you'll never be safe, not at Raleigh. And I couldn't live with myself if . . ." He broke off, his voice ragged.

"If I became another of your guilty secrets." Cassie clenched her fists. "Another victim of your selfish crimes."

"It's not like that," Tremain tried to protest, but Cassie could see the spires of the college up ahead. She couldn't take another moment in close proximity to this man, not after everything he'd done.

"I can't talk about this anymore, not right now." She grabbed the door handle, pulling it open. "I need time to think."

"Wait," Tremain cried, but Cassie scrambled out of the car. She slammed the door behind her and started down the street, wincing at every step as she wove through the students and tourists who filled the sidewalks. Her stomach throbbed, and she felt dizzy and nauseated. Her mother was dead, her own life was at risk, and worst of all, she was part of it now. The School of Night, the darkness, the conspiracies. It was in her blood, tying her down. Tremain was wrong when he said she should run. She couldn't escape this, not even if she tried.

Cassie turned through the Raleigh gates, her mind still spinning. She'd barely been away a single day, but her brain was flooded with too much new information: Rose, Tremain, the rising—it all blurred together in a terrible tangle, until all she could think of was collapsing in her bed and sleeping for days.

Her cell phone sounded, sharp through her haze. When she checked the screen, she saw Charlie's name—and a dozen missed calls.

"I'm fine," she answered before he could demand an explanation. "I'm back in Oxford. We'll talk tomorrow, okay?"

"That's not why I called." Charlie's voice was heavy.

Cassie felt a tremor of fear. "What is it?"

"Rutledge died last night."

Cassie froze in the middle of the damp courtyard. "What happened?"

"They're saying it was a mugging. He got beaten in the street, and his wallet went missing." Charlie sounded grim. "He died of a heart attack in the end."

"Oh God," Cassie breathed. Guilt crashed around her. This was her

fault. She'd gone looking for Rose; she'd forced Rutledge to talk. He'd been scared, he'd known they'd find out, but she'd wanted answers all the same.

No, a voice reminded her. *This was the society. Their blood, their crimes.* And, like Tremain had said, they wouldn't stop until everyone was silenced. Cassie felt a flash of fear. "Are you okay?" she asked Charlie. "You need to be careful now, more than ever. If they know about him, they have to know you—"

"Never mind me. What did you find out there?"

"Nothing," Cassie lied, glancing around. She was alone on the path, the nearest people students in the distance, heading to the library. She turned away, dropping her voice as she continued. "Rose was too far gone. She didn't make any sense."

"Damnit," Charlie cursed. "Look, you lie low. Be careful. We'll find a way to meet tomorrow."

"No," Cassie objected quickly. "They'll be watching you. Let's just leave it for now. I'll call you when I can get away."

Charlie sighed. "It's on us, you know."

"I know," she said quietly. "Stay safe." She hung up, sick with guilt. Rutledge had saved her mother, done his best to keep her safe. And now he was gone, and she was the one to blame.

She looked around anxiously, then hurried down the path to her rooms.

Alone in the apartment, she could finally catch her breath. Exhaustion hit her, heavy in every aching limb. Cassie went to her room, stripping off her damp clothes and pulling on a sweatshirt and pajamas. She crawled under the covers, but sleep didn't come. All she could think about were the people she'd endangered, the lives she'd risked.

Elliot had made a narrow escape, but Charlie could be next. Cassie shivered, picturing Rose's vacant stare and the way she'd gazed out, unseeing, at the Welsh hills. Death wasn't the worst the School of Night could inflict on a person. She snuggled deeper under the covers. Maybe

Tremain was right. Maybe she should leave Oxford—if not for her sake, then for Charlie's. But then he'd be left here alone. He couldn't just up and disappear like her, he had family here, a home. She'd dragged him into this, too deep, and now be would be left to pay the price.

Rose. Evie. Margaret. Rutledge. The names blurred, but one face stayed steady in her mind as Cassie finally fell into oblivion. Matthew Tremain. Her father.

Cassie woke with a hand clasped over her mouth. "Don't scream." Hugo's voice came from just inches away.

She panicked, going rigid.

"I mean it; I'm not here to hurt you," Hugo insisted, his voice soothing. She blinked, making out his silhouette looming above her in the dark. "I'll let you go, you just have to promise not to scream. Do you agree?"

Shaking, Cassie gave a jerking nod. Slowly, Hugo let her go. In an instant, she brought her elbow hard across his face, making contact with his cheekbone in a crack. He swore, stumbling backward. She lunged for the lamp by the bed, flooding the room in a low golden light.

"I told you, I won't hurt you!" Hugo struggled upright, breathing hard.

"And I don't believe a word you say." Cassie pulled her legs up against her chest, looking frantically around for a weapon or escape. Hugo was blocking the way to the door, rubbing his cheek, his hair disheveled and his shirt askew. "What do you want? How did you get in here?"

"I told you, we need to talk. You've been avoiding me." Hugo stepped closer, his face suddenly creasing with concern. "Christ, what happened to you? Are you hurt?"

Cassie stared at him in disbelief. "What happened . . . ?" she echoed. "You know what happened. Your grandfather sent someone after me, to shut me up for good. Have you decided to do your own dirty work for a change?"

Hugo blinked. "No, I swear, I had no idea . . ." He moved toward her, but Cassie jerked back again. "I promise," Hugo said again, spreading his hands in front of him. "I'm not going to hurt you. I'm here to help!"

"I've heard that too many times today," Cassie said sharply, but she faltered, seeing the sincerity in his eyes.

"Then let me show you." Hugo swallowed, looking anxious. "Let me show you what this is all about. I swear I won't hurt you."

Cassie slowly exhaled. She didn't trust him, she couldn't, but she wanted answers. "Okay," she said weakly. "We'll talk." She ignored his hand and pulled herself onto her feet, but a wave of dizziness washed over her and she stumbled hard.

In an instant, Hugo was at her side, holding her up. "God, Cassie, what did they do?"

"I was lucky." Cassie met his eyes. "The porter, Rutledge, they killed him."

Hugo frowned. "I heard that was a heart attack."

"Sure," Cassie said, tired. "And Evie committed suicide. Don't tell me you don't know how this goes."

Hugo swallowed. Up close, she could see his skin was pale, shadows under his eyes. "I was so worried about you," he murmured, guiding her out of the room. She felt his body pressed against hers and forgot for a moment the angry accusations whirling in her mind. Was this the reason she felt such a connection to him, because deep down, they were the same? Cassie tried to push the discomforting thought aside.

Hugo helped her into the living room and turned on the lights. Sebastian was sprawled on the couch, unconscious.

"What . . . ?" Cassie's whole body tensed. She turned to Hugo. "Why did you—?"

"You want to know what this is about," he said, his dark eyes silently pleading with her. "There are things I can't explain. But I can show you, if you'll let me."

Cassie took a breath, and then another. She looked from Sebastian's slumped body to Hugo and back. This was it, the moment she'd been waiting for. Ever since that night in the maze. She sank into a seat opposite the couch. "Explain."

Hugo took a short breath. "We've always been this way," he began. He didn't sit, but instead started pacing, slowly. Uncertain. "At least, I have. They told me it's in the family. When Raleigh founded the college, he and his friends made a pact. A bargain. They wanted knowledge, more than anything else. Pursuit of a higher purpose. It wasn't meant to be—" He broke off. "It wasn't meant to be like this. But they called up something, some dark power. It gave them that knowledge, but at a price. Power, it isn't created, you see, it can only be taken." Hugo met her gaze, conflicted. "Taken from somebody else."

Cassie swallowed. "Go on," she told him quietly, glancing at Sebastian.

"The School of Night kept their secret hidden," Hugo continued, raking one hand through his hair. Cassie wondered if he'd been rehearsing this speech. "They passed it down through the ages. There's a ritual, a ceremony of sorts that happens every generation, reconnecting with the original darkness. A way for each new member to pledge his loyalty and renew his gift." Hugo's voice twisted on the last word, and he paused before continuing, "If you don't take part, your powers fade, you become a shadow of yourself. So to prepare, you have to build your strength. You have to feed."

"And give an offering," Cassie said, quiet.

Hugo looked up. "How did you . . . ?" He stopped. "Yes," he admitted. "An offering. Each member has to bring someone, a willing sacrifice. The darkness uses them as a vessel, for the new member to feed. The power comes from the consent, the risk the chosen take to become one of us."

"You can create new members?" Cassie struggled to follow. "I thought this was hereditary."

"It is." Hugo nodded. "But there's a promise that if you're strong

enough you can become a member, even if you weren't born into it. But nobody . . . Nobody has ever survived the ceremony."

"That's what they offered Rose," Cassie realized. "They told her she could become one of them."

Hugo hung his head. "The stronger the offering, the more power granted to the family." He paused. "The more power we have to take."

Cassie felt a twist of sick fascination. All those willing sacrifices, blinded to the danger, hoping they would be the lucky souls to ascend to the privileged few. Hoping they would be the one exception.

"How does it work when you feed?" she found herself asking, looking to Hugo again. "That's what you were trying to do to me, wasn't it? When I had those nightmares, when I was sleeping at your house. Did you plan it from the start?" She paused, thinking. "The break-in, that was you too, wasn't it—stealing Evie's research?"

Hugo looked ashamed. "Olivia said we had to make sure there were no loose ends. But it wasn't part of the plan when I ran into you. I just wanted to make sure you were safe."

"So you took me back to your house, and tried to . . . tried . . ." Cassie couldn't even find the words.

"I'm sorry." Hugo met her stare head-on. "I never meant to hurt you. I just needed to know why I felt this way. The connection between us, you feel it too."

Cassie looked away.

"I didn't feed from you, if that's worth anything at all," Hugo added, sounding remorseful. "I couldn't. Your mind is too strong. I've never felt anything like it before. It's like you're one of us."

Cassie didn't speak. She wasn't about to tell him what she'd learned about Tremain; she'd barely begun to accept it for herself. She nodded to Sebastian's unconscious body. "Why did you bring him here?"

Hugo turned. "I want to show you. How we feed." Hugo raised his eyes to Cassie's with a new intensity. "You won't understand until I show you. Will you let me, please?"

Cassie gaped at him. She wished she could deny him, tell him to leave and take his twisted games with him, but the truth was, she wanted to know. She needed to see it for herself.

She swallowed, watching Sebastian's chest rise and fall. "How does it work?" Her voice was surprisingly steady.

Hugo blinked, as if he wasn't sure what she was saying, but then he crossed to Sebastian's figure and sat beside him on the couch. "I need contact," he began, reaching to place his fingertips lightly against Sebastian's temple. They came to rest on his scar, the thin line of red Cassie had already marked. "And then . . . It's hard to describe, but I feel the power, reaching out into his mind." Hugo met Cassie's eyes across the table. He inhaled a sharp breath and then exhaled. Cassie watched, transfixed, as the air around Sebastian's head began to shimmer and shift. Just like before, in the maze.

Hugo licked his lips and relaxed back against the couch cushions. The pulsing became stronger, until Cassie could see the energy flowing from Sebastian, up through Hugo's hand. Hugo's face changed, his skin glowing with health again, the shadows melting away. His eyes snapped open, holding Cassie's gaze—their darkness gleaming with power, with possibility. "It feels . . ." he breathed. "It feels like nothing else. I can taste it, the power. All his mind's potential, everything. It's inside of me now."

Cassie felt something pull in her chest. A hunger. A need she'd felt before, and never known why. She slowly rose to her feet and approached them, settling on the other side of Sebastian. Tentatively, she placed her hand on his head, her fingertips overlapping Hugo's.

Hugo stared at her. "You can't . . . You're not like us."

"Try me," Cassie said, and closed her eyes.

Up close, she could feel the energy pulsing out of Sebastian. The air was thick with it, a shimmering, seething force. Taking a long breath, she tried to relax. She didn't know what she was doing, only that some instinct drove her on, reaching, dismantling her body piece by piece

until she was nothing but power and thought and dark intent. She felt Sebastian resist, but she pushed on, slipping deeper past his defenses until she was everywhere, surrounding him, invading him. Sebastian's mind split wide open, and it all came rushing out to her. Raw power, glittering in her veins.

Cassie gasped, her eyes flying open. Hugo was staring back at her, his own gaze steady in the dim light. He twisted his fingers through hers, both of them clasping to Sebastian.

The darkness consumed Cassie, blossomed within her, the blaze of hunger sharp and wild. She felt it pulse, loud enough to drown her dizzy heartbeat. An anger. A wretched need she knew by heart. She'd been hiding it for so long, even from herself, but there was no avoiding the truth anymore.

This was right. This was her purpose.

Nobody would ever hurt her again.

"I'll do it," she told Hugo, snapping back into focus. He stared at her, not understanding. She dove deeper into the rush, shuddering as the energy coursed through her system. "I'll be your offering at the rising," she clarified. "I want to be one of you."

CASSIE STEPPED OUT OF THE COLLEGE GATES AND WALKED quickly down High Street in the direction of the main lecture theater. Pausing at the lights, she cast a sweeping glance behind her. There. The slim young man in a dark jacket and baseball cap. She recognized him from the previous morning: trailing her to the sandwich shop and back, keeping a casual twenty feet between them but never letting her out of his sight. He'd been outside the Radcliffe library too, leaning against the wall smoking a cigarette when she emerged after her shift, and she'd caught a glimpse of him behind her as she returned to Raleigh that night. Now, as she crossed the street in a tide of students, he picked up the pace, carefully stalking her through the morning traffic, following her every move.

Cassie felt her stomach skip with nerves as she kept walking, careful not to let her unease show. She wore a bright red winter cap, making her easy to spot in the crowd. She clutched a set of notebooks to her chest, just a regular student on the way to her morning lectures. At least, that's what she needed him to believe.

It had been three days since she'd arrived back in Oxford from her trip to Wales. Three days since that night with Hugo and Sebastian. She hadn't been able to get away to figure out her next move. The School of Night may have figured out that Charlie was her contact in the police force, but she couldn't risk revealing her connection to Tremain.

Not if her plan was going to work.

Cassie paused outside the lecture halls and pretended to check her phone, making sure her tail got a good long look at her. Then she headed inside, but instead of following the other students up to the lecture auditorium for the morning program, she ducked down the hallway, weaving her way through the building until she emerged through the back doors. There, the gates opened on a narrow cobbled alleyway that ran from Merton College all the way to the back entrance of Christ Church. She glanced around, but her tail was nowhere to be seen. Clasping her books to her chest, she pulled off her hat and quickly walked away, keeping her head down.

She ducked through the gates of Christ Church College and traversed the grid of lush green quads and grand old buildings. It was considerably larger than Raleigh, and it took her five minutes of wrong turns before she managed to find her way to a back stairway and climb to the room on the third floor. She tapped lightly on the door. It swung open, and Charlie ushered her inside. "Did you lose him?" he asked, looking past her, out the window to the quad below.

"I think so," Cassie said, stepping inside. Tremain was pacing by the fireplace of the old study, the office of a colleague, he'd said, someone who was out of town for the semester. "I've got an hour before the lecture is finished."

"We won't need that long." Tremain's face was set in a scowl. He glared at her from behind his wire-rimmed spectacles. "We shouldn't be meeting at all. I told you, you need to leave Oxford, for your own safety."

"And I said I'm not going anywhere."

Charlie came behind her, touching a gentle hand on her arm. "What's this about, Cassie?" he asked, glancing back at Tremain. She'd spoken with him over the phone to fill him in on what had happened in Wales, but he still didn't trust Tremain—and had been vocal about it. "This cloak-and-dagger shit, he's right, it's not safe."

"I needed to see you to tell you what I've decided." Cassie took a breath. "The rising is in five days. It's the one time where the connection to the darkness will be open. It's the only time they'll be vulnerable, open to attack. So I'm going to be at the ceremony. I'm going as Hugo's offering. I'm going to end this for good."

There was silence as her words sank in. Cassie braced for their reactions.

"You stupid, foolish child." Tremain got to his feet. "You've lost your mind."

"He's right." Charlie scowled, crossing his arms. "You said yourself, nobody survives that ritual."

"But it's possible," Cassie objected. "That's the promise, isn't it? That if you're strong enough, worthy, then you'll be accepted. It's my chance: if I can destroy that connection—"

"In five hundred years, not a single soul has made it out intact." Tremain looked at her, clearly aghast.

"But I'm different," Cassie pointed out, a note of bitterness in her voice. "It's in my blood, the power. Your blood. They don't know that you're my father, and that gives me the advantage. They've never tried this with one of their own as an offering. And Hugo promised to protect me."

Charlie made a snorting noise of derision. "You believe him?"

"I don't know." Cassie glanced down. "But he says he wants me to make it through. He tried to talk me out of it at first, but I insisted." She looked back up at the two of them. "This is my chance. Our only chance to stop them. I'm right, aren't I?" she asked Tremain. "The connection to the original darkness, that's their weakness."

Tremain looked ill. "I won't have any part of this. I warned you!"

"So what am I supposed to do?" Cassie demanded, her anger rising. "Run for my life, sit idly by, like you have? How many times have you looked the other way?" she said scornfully. "How many bodies have you ignored?"

Tremain looked away. "I've made my choices," he said quietly. "I know my limits."

"Fuck your limits!" Cassie yelled. "Year after year they've been destroying lives. Not just here, but all over the world. Mandeville will be prime minister; he'll run the whole country. You might be able to ignore that, but I can't. Tell me what happens in the ritual, how we can defeat this . . . this power. There has to be a way to—"

"No! It's a suicide mission." Tremain cut her off, his face pale. "They can't be stopped." He shook his head, then grabbed his coat and made for the door. "It's madness, all of this." His eyes moved past Cassie to Charlie, his face softening in a twisted plea. "Talk some sense into her, please." Then he left, closing the door behind him.

Cassie fought to stay calm. She didn't know why she'd expected more from him. For years, Tremain had done nothing but take the easy way out, cowering in the shadows while Henry Mandeville and his ilk ran rampant across the city, leaving a trail of devastation in their wake. She turned to Charlie. "You understand, don't you?"

Charlie unfolded his arms and walked toward her, his expression grim. "I understand that you want to go blazing in there, but that doesn't mean you have a hope in hell of pulling it off!" He reached her, staring down into her eyes. "Cassie, think about this, please. You don't know anything about this ceremony. How many there'll be, or what—"

"Two dozen for the ritual at least, I'm guessing," Cassie interrupted. "Plus the offerings. This is a big deal, renewing their power, so there'll be representatives from every family, and the new members they want to induct. I don't know where it'll be held, but it has to be somewhere on Raleigh lands. Somewhere they can hide. Underground, maybe, in the catacombs. Rose talked about the tunnels."

"And how will this go down?" Charlie demanded. "How can you even be sure what to expect? You can't go in there unprotected."

"Hugo will be there—"

"Hugo's one of them. He won't have your back."

"It's the only way," Cassie said quietly. She looked at him, pleading. "Can't you see? There's no way to stop them if they just keep renewing their power. Tremain was right; there are too many of them, the blood-lines don't just fade away. But if I interrupt that power somehow, find some way to sever the connection to the original darkness—"

"If," Charlie spat. "Why don't you just admit you don't know what the hell you're playing at. You've seen what they've done!"

"I've seen it, and I've felt it too." Cassie swallowed, not wanting to admit what she'd done with Hugo. "I know how their power works. I know I can beat it." She'd felt the hunger, knew what it took to invade someone's mind. She could turn that ability back on them when they'd least expect it.

Charlie walked to the window and took a ragged breath. "You won't back down," he said, sounding resigned.

"I can't." Cassie took his hand, pulling him back around to face her. "Don't you see? It's already too late. They know I've seen too much. I can run, but we both know they'll find me. Some day my body will show up: here, or in America. My mom had to change her name, take on a whole new identity just to get away. They won't let that happen twice. I would spend my life running, Charlie, but . . ." Cassie took a breath. "But it's not too late for you."

He looked up sharply. "What are you talking about?"

"You can't help me anymore," she said simply. "This is my battle now."

"No, Cassie—"

She squeezed his hand. "I have the invitation. They think I want to try and achieve power and glory like the rest of them. They'll never see it coming."

"It's too dangerous," Charlie argued.

"Since when did that ever stop me?" Cassie smiled weakly.

His brow knitted. "If you find out where the ritual is taking place, I can find a way in. We could—"

"No, Charlie," Cassie said firmly. "You have too much to lose. If they know you're in this with me . . . Think about your family. Are you going to put them at risk too? Laura and Kirsty and little Daisy and Liam too?"

Charlie stared at her. "That's a low fucking blow."

"The School of Night doesn't care about morals. I'm only saying what you already know. You've done so much for me already," she added, softer. "I couldn't have gotten this far without you. But this was always my fight. I have to see it through alone now."

"Don't bullshit me." Charlie tried to pull away, but she held tight.

"I mean it. You've had my back, and nobody . . ." Cassie felt a lump in her throat, a wave of emotion she fought to keep back. "Nobody has ever done that for me before. Thank you, okay? You always do the right thing." She dropped his hand and turned away. It was true. Charlie was the first person she'd trusted in years, perhaps her whole life. He'd put himself in harm's way simply because it was right, risking everything to help her, no matter the cost.

"I didn't do it because it's right. I did it for you." Cassie felt his hand on her shoulder, and then Charlie yanked her around, lowering his mouth to capture hers in a kiss. She froze against him in surprise, feeling his lips hard on hers, and the ragged desperation in his tense body. His mouth searched hers, searing, before abruptly pulling away, cool air where his lips had been. "Don't go getting yourself killed," he said gruffly. And then he was gone, leaving her alone in the study with the sound of his footsteps on the stairs and the burning imprint of his lips on hers.

Cassie's sneakers pounded on the frostbitten dirt the next morning. She ran hard, her lungs burning, her body not yet recovered from the attack in Wales, but she pushed it on regardless. She needed the space to clear her head, the action to distract her from the itch in her veins.

She was hungry. Not for food, or sleep, or anything else she could so easily satiate. This was a darker craving, one that clawed in her system,

demanding and sharp. She wanted to feed again. To taste the power. It had been building ever since that night with Hugo, blossoming in her a little more with every passing day. She was trying to ignore it, drown it out with her determined plans for the ritual, but after four days, it was loud enough to taste. She'd woken with it screaming in her veins.

Cassie ran on, sprinting hard. The route was busy, students out for a stroll, and some tourists too, idling at the lookout points to snap photographs of the meadow view, the Raleigh tower looming above the quiet sandstone walls.

She wondered how their minds would taste.

She'd only had a moment with Sebastian, only begun to explore the depths of his mind before Hugo pulled her out of the daze. But it had been enough to awaken that wild hunger. If this was driving the School of Night, they would never be stopped. It had been unlike anything else she'd ever felt before. Except . . .

Cassie stumbled on the hard earth, coming to a sudden stop. Her breath steamed the frosty air, and memories she'd fought to keep back invaded her mind. A dark night. The sound of her bedroom door. Her stepfather, drunk, the way he'd been every night since before her mother died. But this time, he didn't just pass out on the couch like usual. This time, he wanted something more.

He didn't get it.

She'd told the local sheriff he'd been unconscious when the fire started, and that much was true. They said he'd probably left the gas on, knocked a candle over. A drunken shame. But she still could hear the rough grate of the match striking, bright in her rage, and feel the victory that had pulsed wild in her chest as she watched it all burn to the ground.

She'd always been this way.

At least she had a reason now. The things that had made her different, made her wrong, they were because of this. She couldn't have fought them if she'd tried.

Cassie forced herself to breathe deeply, turning to begin her run back in the direction of Raleigh. It may have been in her nature—this hunger, this ruthless violence—but that didn't mean she couldn't make a choice. She'd been fighting the legacy of her mother's undoing her whole life; now, it was a new inheritance she had to resist.

She would stop them all, before it was too late. It was the only chance she'd have. Tomorrow would be the end, one way or another.

She ran on—and prayed her hunger would fade.

Cassie was still aching from the run when she let herself in the apartment and went to the kitchen to run a glass of water.

"Good morning, Miss Blackwell."

Cassie startled, whirling around so fast water splashed to the floor. Henry Mandeville was lounging in a chair by the window, watching her with an amused icy stare.

She forced herself to act calm. "Your family has a way with locked doors," she commented. She turned back to the sink and refilled the glass before taking a few steps toward him. "To what do I owe the visit?"

Henry raised an eyebrow. He was dressed immaculately in a three-piece suit, a pocket square peeking from the breast of his jacket, his white hair combed neatly back. "I understand you're to be our offering," he said.

Cassie met his gaze. "That's correct."

Henry narrowed his eyes. "It's a great honor to be chosen to represent us," he said slowly. "To have the opportunity to ascend to our ranks."

Cassie remained cool. "I understand."

"And you know what the ritual will demand of you?" Henry rose to his feet, slowly crossing the room to her.

Cassie nodded, her heart beating fast. Henry came to a stop in front of her. "You're a hard girl to find, Miss Blackwell." He emphasized her name, as if he knew it was a falsehood. "Few records, even fewer friends. We are some of the greatest families in the land. Our lineage stretches

back for generations, unimpeachable. What makes you think you deserve to walk among us?"

Cassie swallowed. "I thought I had to prove I deserved my place. Isn't that what the ritual is all about?"

Henry didn't seem impressed. "My grandson is very important to me. It's time he left this . . . nursery behind and took his rightful place at the head of the family. This ceremony will cement his fate." His hand shot out to clasp Cassie's jaw. She flinched back in shock, but he gripped her tight with bony fingers. "Let's see, shall we?" he murmured, running his thumb across her cheek.

Cassie shivered. She could feel the coldness of his stare, the black depths of those eyes, but somehow, she couldn't look away.

She felt the darkness, creeping on the edges of her mind.

Cassie gulped. This was a test, to see if she was worthy of being their sacrifice. She couldn't resist him, not unless she wanted to reveal her strength.

Closing her eyes, Cassie let him in. It took everything she had not to fight it, the coldness slipping into the recesses of her mind, the shadows that blotted out her thoughts, her memories, but Cassie forced herself to hold back. To stand, silent, compliant, and let him explore with chilling leisure. She wanted to run screaming, she longed to fight. *Not now,* she told herself, clenching her nails deep into her palms, feeling tears sting the corners of her eyes. *Not yet.*

Henry released her, stepping back. Cassie surfaced, shaking.

"Interesting . . ." Henry paused, watching her, as if savoring a fine wine. Cassie's breath came fast. She wondered if he could tell she was different, if, somehow, her mind had revealed her secret.

Finally, he nodded. "You'll do." His business completed, he turned to leave.

"Wait," Cassie found herself calling after him. "What happens after the ceremony? When— *If* I pass the test?"

Henry gave her a cool smile. "Then, my dear, your real life begins. As one of us, you will achieve anything you desire." He tilted his head. "What is it you want from life? Fame, fortune, riches?" There was a note of derision in his voice.

Cassie blinked. She couldn't think of a lie, so she told him the truth instead. "I want to be so powerful that nobody can ever hurt me again. I want to be untouchable."

Henry's face was almost approving as he surveyed her again. "A noble aim. Good luck to you, Miss Blackwell." He nodded, and then he was gone, a dark shadow on the stairwell, a black smudge beneath her window as she went to watch him walk away.

SHE DREAMED THE SAME AS BEFORE: OF DUSTY CATACOMBS AND flaring torches, of running and panic and fear. She dreamed of darkness, and when she woke, the hunger was thick in her veins.

Cassie lay awake, and she counted the minutes. This was her last night. Her only night.

This was the end.

AFTER ALL HER RESEARCH, ALL THAT TUGGING AT THREADS AND loose ends, Cassie still didn't know the true danger she was walking into that night. That was the real secret of the School of Night; let people whisper about privilege and power, but in all the centuries of rumor, there was not one hint of the darkness lurking beneath their aristocratic surface. She had nothing to guide her through this mysterious ritual, nothing but instinct and a desperate hope that whatever she was facing, she would have the strength to match it. Destroy it.

Tremain wasn't sharing their secrets, perhaps out of a misguided hope she would still call off her plan, and Hugo remained frustratingly vague. All he would tell her is that the night would begin with dinner, a formal meal for the whole society in one of Raleigh College's private dining rooms. He picked her up at nine P.M., dressed in a suit, his expression nervous.

"You look beautiful," he said, taking in her appearance. Cassie had chosen Evie's black dress to wear. An honor, and a reminder.

"Thanks," she said, self-conscious. "I just need to get my purse." She went back to her bedroom, slipping on a pair of heels and fastening her mother's necklace at her throat. Her expression in the mirror was anxious and full of secrets. Cassie forced herself to take a breath, fighting back the nerves that were twisting in her stomach.

This was it. There was no time for fear, not anymore.

Back in the living room, Hugo helped her into her coat. "You packed," he said, looking around the sparse room.

Cassie shrugged. "Just in case." Packing her things, she'd methodically stripped the apartment, wanting to save some poor porter the task of collecting her belongings the way she'd done for Evie. It was easy to dismantle her life in Oxford: to pack away her notes and return library books, file her last essay and lay her robes out on the bed to be returned. As usual, she wouldn't leave a mark on this town; she would disappear as quickly as she'd arrived. Aside from Charlie, there would be no one to remember her. It would be as if she'd never existed at all.

Charlie had tried to call her in the days since their last meeting, but Cassie had forced herself not to answer the phone. It was futile talking to him again: he would only try to dissuade her, and now she was more determined than ever.

"Shall we?" she asked, holding out her arm, but Hugo suddenly moved to block the door.

"It's not too late," he said urgently, his dark eyes meeting hers. "You don't have to do this."

Cassie blinked, startled. He couldn't be wavering now. "You said it would be okay, that you'd protect me."

"I know, but . . ." Hugo trailed off. He looked conflicted, and Cassie couldn't help but feel a bitter irony. Now, of all times, he was having a crisis of conscience. He thought she was going into this blind, another willing sacrifice, and Cassie had to play that part right up until the end.

"What's wrong?" she asked carefully. "Have you changed your mind?"

Hugo swallowed. "No, I just . . ." He looked away. "You know the risk. Nobody has ever survived," he admitted quietly.

"Nobody is like me." Cassie replied, before realizing she might have given away too much. She knew she had the society blood running through her veins, but that secret was her only advantage going into this ritual. She tried to play it off as brashness. "I mean, you said it yourself, it felt different, when you tried to connect with me. I can do this."

"But even so . . ." Hugo paused. "This life, the cost . . ." His ex-

pression hinted at an inner anguish. "It traps you, Cassie. It's a gilded prison, and once you're inside there's no way out."

She watched him, wondering how deep this indecision ran. Could she use it for her plan? "Would you take it back, if you could?" she asked. "End it all—the power, the pain?"

Hugo frowned. "What do you mean?"

Cassie knew she had to tread carefully. "I mean, be your own man for a change, instead of following the family line." He'd complained to her before of the frustrations of living up to his name—the expectations that came with being a Mandeville, all the weight that entailed. If he would help her, during the ritual, if he could turn his back on everything . . . "Imagine if you could just be free," she urged him. "To do whatever you wanted. No pressure, no rules."

Hugo gave her a resigned smile. "There's no use imagining. My destiny was decided a long time ago."

"But wouldn't you want the chance to choose?" Cassie pressed. Having him as a true ally could make all the difference. "Tonight—"

But they were interrupted by a clatter of footsteps on the stairs. "You're going to be late!" Olivia cried, bustling into the room. She moved between them, linking her arm through Cassie's. "I can't tell you how happy I am that you'll be joining us," she said, offering a brittle smile. "I know you'll do just great." Her dark eyes were guileless, her expression bright and sincere. Cassie would have believed her, had she not seen the truth hiding behind Olivia's perfect smile that night in the maze.

"I think I will, too." Cassie faked a smile, following her to the door. She shot a glance back at Hugo, but he was looking away. "I'm so excited about the ritual," she continued, to Olivia. "Do you know what will happen?"

Olivia shook her head. "It's my first time too. But everything will be fine; it's just a formality," she reassured as they crossed the quad, their silk dresses whispering in the night breeze. "A lot of funny old role-play. Don't even worry about it."

Cassie couldn't even feel surprised by the lies. "What a relief," she said, playing along. "I'm sure it'll be fun."

As they walked along the pathways, Hugo following behind, Cassie couldn't help but notice the other students heading in noisy groups to the bar for a drink, or walking back from the library, weighed down with books. They were in a world of their own, oblivious to the ancient rituals about to play out inside the walls of their beloved college, the darkness corrupting the very foundations beneath their feet. Could that have been her life, Cassie wondered, if she hadn't stumbled onto the School of Night? What if she'd let her quest for the truth about her mother drop at the first hurdle and turned her attention instead to her essays—joined clubs and teams, thrown her determination toward a different goal?

"What are you thinking about?" Olivia demanded brightly as they entered the far building.

"Oh, nothing," Cassie said easily. "Just an essay I have due next week."

Olivia laughed. "Believe me, after tonight essays will be the last thing on your mind. You'll have far more important things to think about."

She was right. It was hopeless for Cassie to imagine some other life. She would never have quit her pursuit of the truth; it wasn't in her nature. These were her choices. There was no escaping the person she was. And tonight, she would make the School of Night pay for their crimes—or die in the process.

*Olivia led the way up to the second floor of the cloisters, where a stern-*faced man stood guard at the door. His gaze swept over them, and then he stood aside with a silent nod.

Cassie stepped inside with Hugo, her nerves growing. People were milling around the grand room, drinking glasses of wine and creating a pleasant hum of laughter and conversation. It looked like any ornate dinner party. She scanned the crowd, recognizing with a shock several of the faces lit up with excitement and expectation: politicians, titans of

business, and the media. Rutledge was right; this stretched to the highest echelons of society. Cassie stifled a tremor. If she didn't stop them, their power would only grow, unchecked. The death and destruction would be visited upon a new generation.

"Let's get some drinks in," Olivia declared excitedly. Hugo glowered at her, but Olivia just shrugged. "What? It's supposed to be a party." She flagged down a passing waiter carrying a tray of glasses of champagne, took one for herself, and handed one to Cassie. "To our newest member." She raised a glass to Cassie, and Cassie mirrored the gesture, chilled by her carefree demeanor. Did Olivia realize the fate that lay in store for Cassie, or was she simply being naive?

Cassie saw Lewis enter, looking pale and nervous. He lit up, however, when he saw Olivia and wove through the crowd to meet them. "Don't you look smart?" Olivia cooed, brushing down his lapels. "Are you excited? I can't wait."

Lewis managed a grin. "Of course, darling."

Olivia glanced across the room. "They're calling for us, Hugo." She nodded to where Henry was beckoning. "Better go pay our respects."

Hugo placed a hand on Cassie's shoulder. "All right?" he asked.

She nodded. "Just fine." She watched as the pair made their way across to their family. Henry was glowering watchfully; Richard, the future prime minister, smiled vaguely with that sense of warmth and comfort that had won him the hearts of the voters. Cassie wondered where their wives were, if they were welcome at events like this or if they kept to their place at home and let the men of the family handle the dark business at hand.

Cassie turned back to Lewis. He was visibly sweating in his smart dinner jacket, tugging at his tie. "Look at everyone," he murmured awkwardly. "It's half the bloody cabinet in here tonight."

"Did Olivia tell you much about the ceremony?" she asked carefully.

"Not much to tell, is there?" Lewis looked at her with a weak smile. "Just a few old incantations, right? Nothing to worry about."

Cassie felt a flash of guilt. She knew the truth, but he was going in completely unprepared. "But did she explain how it all works?" she pressed, wishing she could warn him somehow, give him one last chance to back out.

Lewis swallowed, then gave a brief, reluctant nod.

"And you're okay with it?" Cassie said, shocked.

Lewis looked past her, across the room. "Liv says I'm strong enough." He swallowed again, as if he was trying to convince himself. "She says there's never been anyone like me before. She'll protect me. She'll make sure I make it through."

A chill spread through Cassie's body. That was what Hugo had told her: that she was different, that he'd protect her. Was it all part of the same lie? Had he fooled her into believing she'd make it out alive?

A gong sounded before she could reply, and they were called to take their seats at the long, ornate dining table. Cassie was shown to a chair beside Hugo, and Lewis, next to Olivia. Across the table, Miles sat, drinking happily, his hand on the shoulder of a boy Cassie recognized from the Radcliffe library. He was blush-cheeked and clearly nervous, no more than nineteen years old. Paige was farther down too, beside a blond girl whose eyes darted around the room. She met Cassie's curious stare and gave a tentative smile.

Henry Mandeville stood at the head of the table and tapped his glass for silence. "It's a great pleasure to gather you all here tonight," he began, his voice ringing out across the room. "To see old friends, and share in ancient customs. For society is surely founded on tradition: the passing down of our rituals and history from one generation to the next. Tonight, we share that history, that noble tradition, with a new generation. The sons and daughters we've watched so proudly grow will now take their place as adults among us, part of our legacy to this world."

Cassie glanced around. The guests were all nodding, smiling. She saw fathers and sons share a shy smile, looks of pride and achievement.

"But it's not just those who have inherited our customs who we cele-

brate tonight," Henry continued, his voice thick with pride. "As history marches on, it is our newest members who will fuel us in the coming years. These brave souls are taking the ultimate risk to join us, a risk that will be rewarded to the lucky few. Their fresh blood will give us power, expand our horizons, and set this noble group on our course in the coming years."

Cassie hid a shudder. *Fresh blood* . . . It was no lyrical turn of phrase he was using. All around the room, the older members raised their glasses in a gruesome toast.

"So, as our ancestors before us, let us dine and be merry before the trials to come." Henry looked around. "We may know—"

The main doors swung open, cutting him off. As all heads turned toward the interruption, Cassie had to stifle a gasp of surprise. Tremain, dressed in an impeccable suit, strode into the room.

Whispers filled the air, hushed gossip of surprise and scandal.

"What's going on?" Cassie asked, not taking her eyes from Tremain. Her heart began to race. She hadn't seen or spoken to him since that day in the study. What was he doing here?

"I don't know," Hugo murmured. "He's not one of us, not anymore."

Cassie watched as Henry moved to intercept him. The pair met nearby, close enough for her to hear. "I'm surprised to see you here, Matthew," Henry murmured, icy and threatening.

Tremain stared back, unmoved. "I've come to make amends," he said. "You were right, all along. I can't deny my true self."

"You want to join us again?" Henry seemed surprised.

"I've fought it long enough. Rejecting my heritage was a foolish mistake." Tremain inclined his head in a gesture of compliance. "It's time I accepted my place again and celebrated the rising with you all, as I should have done years ago. Family first."

Henry paused, then finally broke into a chilling smile. "Welcome home, friend." He shook Tremain's hand. "Join us for dinner. I'm pleased to welcome you back."

Cassie watched them take their seats, her heart in her throat. It didn't make any sense—until Tremain caught her eye across the table. His face was impassive, but he gave her the smallest flicker of expression as their eyes met. She realized at last what this was all for.

He was here to help her.

Cassie felt a surge of gratitude for this man who was a stranger to her, but her father nonetheless. It may not have made up for what he'd done to her mother, but it was something: a gesture, a final attempt to make amends.

It was all she had.

Dinner crawled by. Around her, the society members happily tore into the fine food and wines, laughing and chatting with one another. It was a reunion of sorts, Cassie supposed, seeing old friends greet each other and reminisce about times gone by. She was sickened and fascinated all at once, that such a terrible ritual could be made an occasion of joy, that they were so inured to their crimes they didn't hesitate over their rich slices of venison and game.

Cassie was struck with the enormity of her task. She'd been so focused she hadn't allowed herself a thought of failure, but now, looking around the room, she felt the chill of uncertain fear. There were dozens of people here: powerful, ruthless souls with years of dark deeds to protect. Even Henry Mandeville alone would be a formidable opponent, but the rest of them too . . . ? Cassie swallowed, overcome with a nauseating wave of insecurity. Maybe Tremain was right, and this was a foolish flash of hubris, thinking for a moment that she could be the one to dismantle such an ancient, sprawling evil.

Her thoughts were interrupted by the clatter of chairs being pushed back. People were rising to their feet. Hugo touched her hand. "It's time."

Cassie's pulse quickened. He had been silent for much of dinner, picking at his food beside her. Now, she wondered what was running

through his mind. Were his promises of protection nothing but lies, to lull her into security? "Where are we going?" she asked, following him as they filed out of the room.

"The catacombs beneath the college," Hugo replied quietly. "We have chambers there, the same rooms that Raleigh and his group used in the beginning."

"And nobody notices?" she asked, glancing at the procession. They were quite the group, walking through the cloisters in their formal finest.

"It's a private dinner, they happen all the time." Hugo shrugged. "The entrance is well hidden and protected. We'll be safe. This is our college." And it was, Cassie realized. Raleigh, the great institution, belonged to the School of Night completely. Behind these sandstone walls, the society's members ran a private fiefdom where the rule of law or morals didn't reach.

Cassie saw Tremain step into an alcove up ahead. She waited until Hugo turned to speak to another member, then she stopped beside Tremain, pretending to fix her shoe strap. "You changed your mind?" she whispered.

Tremain looked ill. "It's still not too late for you," he murmured. "If you went now, you could be out of the country before dawn. Please, Cassie . . ."

"No." Cassie straightened, meeting his eyes. "I'm seeing this through. And either I can count on you, or you're no use to me."

Tremain's jaw clenched. "I'll be there," he said sharply. He glanced around, then leaned in. "Once it starts, they'll lock the doors to keep you inside. If you need a way out, there's a back staircase from the crypt. Take a right from the hallway, keep going until you reach the surface. Charlie will be waiting by the north gate."

"Charlie?" Cassie felt a pang of fear. "No, he can't. I told him—"

"He wouldn't listen. Don't worry about him, there's no time. Listen to me. You'll need to wait until the connection is open. That's when all

the society will be joined with the darkness. Henry is the key; he'll be the one you need to take down. The rest will fall."

Cassie nodded, thinking fast. "Is there anything I can use as a weapon?"

"Whatever you can find. I'll do what I can for you," Tremain whispered. "But I'm weak. It's been too long since I fed. I'm no match for any of them. I'm sorry."

"Cassie?"

Cassie turned. Olivia had turned back and was frowning at her. "Thank you," Cassie murmured, not looking at Tremain, then straightened, going to catch up with Hugo and Olivia.

"Something wrong?" Olivia demanded.

"Just these shoes," Cassie replied. She could feel Hugo's eyes on hers, assessing, but she turned away. There was no time to falter now. She pulled her coat around her and followed them into the shadows of the courtyard, to the base of the North Tower.

She tried to reassure herself. She had a plan, allies to help her. Tremain would be in the ceremony, and Charlie was waiting outside. Together, they could bring down the society. They wouldn't see it coming.

Then she saw a familiar face at the back of the crowd. Her heart stopped.

Elliot.

He was speaking with Henry Mandeville, their heads bent together in hushed conversation. He passed Henry something, some old book, and Henry nodded approvingly.

Elliot was tangled up in the society too? Cassie didn't understand. He was supposed to be in London, miles away. Betrayal sliced through her as she watched the man she thought had been her friend. He and Henry Mandeville spoke a moment longer, and then Elliot slipped away, toward the college exit.

Henry glanced over and saw Cassie watching them. A smug smile splintered cruelly across his face—a smile that told her he knew exactly what she was feeling.

Cassie felt sick. Her mind raced back over everything she thought she'd discovered: her mother's name, Rose, the existence of the School of Night at all. Elliot had been helping her every step of the way. It was his research that had guided her down this path, his information that led her to this moment.

It had been him, all along.

She realized with sickening powerlessness that Henry had set this up. He wanted her to discover them; he'd been pulling the strings since the moment she stepped foot in Oxford. Every discovery had been laid out for her to find; each piece of the puzzle had been delivered to her like a poisoned gift. He must know about Tremain being her father, that she was one of them. He was testing her, to see if she'd live or die by their ritual.

She'd been played from the very beginning.

Cassie wanted to run. The odds were against her now; there was surely no escape. But the group was filing into the tower, and Hugo was by her side, guiding her inside. She'd been here before, during her first official tour: tourists often traipsed through, climbing the twisting staircase up to admire the view from the top of the tower. But now, instead of heading up the stairs, the group had pushed aside a heavy tapestry, revealing a door in the base of the stairs. The tunnel beyond was dark, and full of shadows.

Cassie paused, and she felt Hugo against her back. "Trust me," he whispered, urging her on.

She had no choice. It had all come to this. Cassie gathered her courage and stepped into the dark.

THE STAIRCASE TWISTED DOWN BENEATH THE COLLEGE, THE narrow path lit by torches bolted to the walls. The lights flickered, leading them on, until Cassie reckoned they must be beneath the great chapel. It was a twisted thought: that deep below the surface, generations had been worshipping a different power, hidden from sight and the world.

She expected the air to turn damp, but the air remained cool and dry no matter how far down they went. Eventually, the tunnel opened into a series of anterooms, each with heavy barred doors. Finally, they emerged into a large, cavernous space, the walls hung with intricate old tapestries and oil paintings, perfectly preserved. The floor was sunk in a series of shallow circular shapes around a small pool of water, and at the head of the room a stone platform set with candles and a silver bowl served as an altar. Presiding over them all was the great man himself: a portrait of Sir Walter Raleigh, his expression aloof and determined.

Hugo guided Cassie to the sunken area in front of the pool. The other offerings were arranged around it until they formed a circle; the members of the society took up positions behind them: a second ring, enclosing them.

Cassie looked around the room, her heart beating rapidly, as the last member stepped inside and the doors swung shut behind them with a low boom. Every instinct was screaming at her to bolt. But it was too late. She forced herself to take a long breath and looked to Hugo, but his gaze was fixed on the ground, avoiding her eyes. Across the room,

Tremain did meet her eyes, and gave a jerky nod, but the uncertain expression on his face did nothing to soothe her racing nerves.

Henry moved to stand in front of the altar. "Here, in the place our legacy began, we come together to renew our sacred bonds," he began. Other members started chanting along with him, a low hum that chilled Cassie to her core. How many times had they all spoken these words? Made their sacrifices? "To build greatness, to pursue the highest virtues of all. We make our offerings to you in the darkness, that we may be made strong and know the purity of your great gift." Henry took a knife from the altar and held it aloft. Cassie could see the strangely curved blade, and an ornate jeweled hilt. "From blood, to blood," Henry intoned, slowly drawing the blade across his palm. He stepped down to the middle of the arena and let the drops fall, dark into the pool. "This is my claim."

He held out the knife and Hugo moved past Cassie, repeating the words in a hurried voice. He didn't cut deeply enough with the first stroke and had to draw the knife across his skin a second time, wincing as the blood welled to the surface.

"From blood, to blood." One by one, the rest of the society members descended to the pool. Their blood dripped into the water, until it was a swirl of dark red in the dim light. Cassie's heart beat faster with every passing moment. Their voices blended, echoing in the room until she couldn't tell where one ended and the next began, an ominous chorus humming deep in the background.

"And now, we make our offerings to you," Henry announced. "They give themselves willingly, for the sake of our legacy and the true power. As it had been from the first and will be until the last."

Cassie felt hands on her shoulders and startled. Hugo had stepped closer, holding her as the rest of the members all moved to hold their offerings in some way: a hand on the crown of the head, a touch to the back. She could feel the heat of his body, just inches behind her, and the tremor in his hand. "Shh, it'll be all right," he reassured her, as Henry began a

Latin incantation. The words drifted over her, foreign and weighty in the dim light. Lewis was beside her, shaking like a leaf, and on her other side, Paige was stroking her girl's hair, soothing, whispering in her ear as if to keep her from bolting.

The hum grew louder, whispers rising in the dark, snaking all around them. The torches flickered on the walls, plunging them into dark as Cassie fought to stay calm. Her instincts were screaming at her, every muscle vibrating with panicked need. She shouldn't be here. This was all wrong.

And then she felt it, a deep shiver of sickness that rolled through her entire body. An awareness of something cold. Something ancient. Something evil.

The torches wavered again, and in the dark, Cassie saw something twist, churning in the pool in the center of the room. As she watched in horror, something dark began to rise.

Hugo tensed behind her, but Cassie couldn't tear her eyes away from the apparition in front of her. It was blackened, formless, darkness in its purest form. This was it, the hunger made manifest. And even through the fear, Cassie felt it call to her, awakening something deep in her chest.

The group fell silent as the darkness twisted, a shadow above the pool.

"We make these offerings to you," Henry called. "Take them, and grant us our knowledge."

The darkness spread. Cassie stayed frozen in place, watching as it shifted and divided. It spanned out from the pool, like spokes on a wheel, snaking across the floor toward her, toward Lewis, to all the offerings. She recoiled, but Hugo's grip tightened on her shoulders. He held her in place, his fingers digging into her skin as the shadow rose from the floor in front of her, a dark column that swayed and hissed.

And then it took her.

Cassie felt the invasion, the darkness creeping into the edges of her mind. She'd thought she'd felt power when Henry had visited her that

night, but his was just a faint echo of this obliterating force. It was a hundred times stronger, wilder. Ravenous with age and neglect. She felt it, a cold, dreadful thing, and she fought it with everything she had. She struggled, sending a desperate look to Tremain, but he shook his head and mouthed, *Not yet*.

Cassie gasped for air. She couldn't hold it back, not even for a second. It was too much, too dark; it slipped through her mind, wrapping around her very soul. She shuddered, feeling the blackness seep through every part of her, a sharp pain blooming behind her forehead.

And then she felt a second force, slipping through the gaps the darkness had forced wide open. Hugo, reaching, feeding on that power through her, as if she was nothing but a vessel for the darkness. Cassie felt him splintering through her and dropped to her knees with a cry, overwhelmed. All around her, she could see the other offerings falling to the ground, their masters shimmering with black energy beside them. She felt her mind overlap with every other in the waves of darkness. Hugo, Olivia, Henry, feeding, frenzied and dark. The offerings, panicked and in pain . . . They were one. They were it. It passed through them, and around them, taking everything they had.

Cassie fought to stay conscious. This was the moment she'd been waiting for, the moment they were all linked. Taking all her courage, Cassie forced her panicked mind to still. She ignored the cries of pain around her and took a shaking breath, focusing on the darkness, tracing its contours with her mind, feeling for its shape. It shifted under her focus, ephemeral, but she clung tight, searching for some sure point in all the chaos: a root to its form.

There.

Beneath the whirl of hunger, she felt a seam in the form: a jagged edge, the split in reality that was letting the darkness through. Cassie grasped the shape, holding tight even as she felt her strength draining, forcing herself to keep hold of that one point, the beginning of everything. And the end.

Ripping herself from Hugo, she shut her mind against him and fought the darkness with everything she had. She felt its surprise, rearing up to turn on her, hissing and seething in the dark. The very ground beneath her rumbled and shook as the darkness released the others, severing their connection. There were shouts of confusion and pain as they were ripped free from the power. Out of the corner of her eye, Cassie saw everyone fall to the ground. Tremain, Hugo, Olivia, sprawling in the dirt alongside the wasted bodies of their sacrifices.

She was the only one left. Except . . . Henry. Still standing, rigid at the altar. But he wasn't standing. Cassie gasped, seeing him rise, inches from the ground. The darkness was channeling through him now, fighting her, invading deep within her mind. The pain was unbearable, splitting her brain apart, so thick she could taste the blood in her mouth, hear her own screams as it carved deeper, taking everything she had.

The walls shook again, rocks and debris crumbling from the cavern ceiling. The torches fell, one catching a corner of a tapestry, blazing up in the dark cavern. Some members were recovering now; Olivia dashed past her, racing for the door, but still, Cassie didn't dare drag her eyes away from her target. She dropped to her knees and crawled toward the altar, fighting for balance as the room shook.

Henry was all blackness and shadow, a terrifying specter as he turned to her, his eyes the darkest she'd ever seen. Cassie grabbed the knife from the altar and lunged. The knife slid into his stomach, and he let out a chilling scream, reeling back. Inhuman. Unsatiated.

The blackness recoiled, the dark shadow hissing and flickering as it snaked out of him and into the pool. But Henry's power didn't fade. His hand thrust out, grabbing at her neck, choking the breath from her lungs. Cassie flailed against him, but his grip was too strong. "Hugo," she heard him call, blood pounding in her ears. "You must complete the ritual. You can't let it go!"

Cassie gasped uselessly, her lungs burning as she dangled over the ground. Above her, the cavern boomed and crumbled, the floor beneath

Henry shaking as if the earth itself was giving way. Hugo pulled himself up and crawled toward them, scrambling over bodies of the offerings that lay groaning, motionless on the floor.

"No," Cassie gasped. "Please!"

But Hugo's eyes were dark as the night. He reached out and grasped Cassie's hand, and Cassie shrieked as the force drove through her again. Hugo drove inside her head, latching on to the dark power that Henry was supplying, drawing it through her until Cassie was nothing but a vessel. She struggled to hold on, but it was too much. "Hugo," she whispered weakly, feeling the life slip from her body. But his face was a mask of ecstasy, a stranger in the dark. She didn't know this man, or his earlier promises; all was lost in the surge of heat and power.

Lanterns fell to the ground; paintings slipped from the walls, crumbling around them; but still, Hugo held tight. The darkness streamed through Cassie, ravaging, until she could barely feel herself at all. She was no person, no mind, nothing but a portal, feeling the power fill her up and empty out, over and over as Hugo grew stronger, clambering to his feet, holding her tighter. "Please," she gasped again with her last breaths. She looked to him, her vision blurring. His face was alight with rapture, eyes wild and black.

Cassie sagged in Henry and Hugo's cruel embrace, darkness filling her, blotting out the last flickers of light. The ceiling crumbled, rock raining down as the few survivors cried out and crawled for cover. She would have wept, if she'd had the strength to muster tears. This was what she'd come here for, to die an ignoble death on a dusty cavern floor? She'd let them down. Her mother. Evie. Rose. She'd failed them.

As if from far away, she heard a desperate, guttural cry, and then someone dragged Hugo from her body. The connection weakened, and she surfaced in time to see Tremain charging back to knock Henry to the ground. He released her, stumbling back. Through her daze, she saw Tremain, scrambling wildly to hold him down. "Go!" Tremain yelled hoarsely, his hands at Henry's throat. The body beneath him

twisted and hissed, screaming an unnatural cry. "You have to destroy the portal!"

"But—" Cassie gasped for air. Another chunk of rock fell from the ceiling, crashing to the ground between them. She quickly turned to the pool, the dark shadows seething within. She grabbed a torch from the ground and thrust it in the water.

The flames flared high, an unnatural blaze in the dim cavern. She stumbled back from the heat as an inferno roared, mingling with screams that echoed from the pool, a century of darkness boiling in the depths. Cassie stared, transfixed by the flames. The portal was burning up, the connection severed at last.

Suddenly, another chunk of rock fell from the ceiling. The flames spilled from the pool, rearing higher to block Tremain and Henry from view on the other side of the room. "Go!" she heard Tremain cry. "You have to get out of here!"

"What about you?" she screamed back.

Another section of the ceiling toppled down. She leaped back, watching with horror through the flames as Tremain and Henry were buried under the rubble.

"Tremain?" she cried, as the room shook and trembled. "Where are you?"

But there was only the sound of screams and fire burning out of control. She was all alone.

THE EARTH LET OUT ANOTHER VIOLENT RUMBLE. CASSIE REELED back, shielding her head from the storm of debris raining down around her. She grabbed the bloody knife from the floor and stumbled across the room, skirting the flames just as another quake gripped the cavern. She clutched onto the door frame as the world shook, watching in horror as the tunnel caved in ahead of her.

Wheeling around, she tried to remember what Tremain had said. There was another exit, right from the main doors. She felt along the wall until she found the ridge of a hidden door. She wrenched it open and raced into the tunnel just as the ceiling gave way behind her. Stumbling and gasping, she ran, grabbing a torch from the wall to send shadows bouncing along the wall as she plunged deeper into the dark.

Cassie felt a black fear grip her heart as she ran. This was the place of her dreams. The tunnels, the torchlight. Her feet were bare on the dusty ground and she gripped the knife tightly in one hand. She heard echoes of the ritual chanting humming off every wall, and she told herself it was all in her mind. It had to be. A shadow suddenly reared up in the gloom, and she stumbled in fear, falling hard on her hands. But there was no time for pain, not with the knife gripped, slick in her hand, or the faint clatter of footsteps getting louder. Closer.

Scrambling to her feet, Cassie plunged on, climbing higher up the twisting staircase until she stepped through an open door and emerged with a gasp in a dungeonlike room. There was light through a slim window ahead, the surface at last, but Cassie's relief only lasted for a split second.

Inside the room, Olivia stood over Charlie's crumpled body, her eyes black, her smile a mask of cruel delight. "You're too late," she told Cassie, breathing heavily. "He was delicious. Like Evie," she added with a smirk.

Cassie had no time to think. With a cry of rage, she launched herself at Olivia, sending them both crashing to the ground. Olivia clawed at her, nails scratching at Cassie's skin, but Cassie still held the knife. With all the force she could muster, she thrust the knife into Olivia's stomach.

Olivia let out a cry, going rigid against her. Cassie pulled the knife out, and Olivia flinched back, whimpering in pain as she clutched at the wound.

Cassie scrambled away from her, her hands wet with blood. "Charlie?" she cried, panic freezing her blood to ice. "Oh God, Charlie?" She crawled over to him, reaching out, cradling his head in her hands. "Please," she whispered. "Oh God, please, Charlie. Please wake up!" Terror and guilt crashed over her. He was the one good man, the one good soul in all this.

He let out a low moan. Her heart surged. "Wake up," she whispered. "It's okay, I've got you now."

Slowly, his eyes fluttered open. Cassie let out a sob of relief. "Are you hurt?" she asked, brushing his hair back from his forehead. "What did she do to you?"

Charlie stared back blankly, his blue eyes empty and expressionless. Cassie felt her blood turn to ice. "No," she gulped. "No, you're going to be okay. You have to be!" She tried to reach out with her mind, to smooth and mend the damage Olivia had left behind, but she was too weak. She could barely touch the edges of his broken mind. She shook him, desperate, but he just lolled back, a rag doll, unseeing. Unthinking.

"Charlie!" Her sob broke. She felt the earth quake again, but Cassie didn't care. She clutched his body, sobbing, as grief shattered around her. He shouldn't have been there, shouldn't have paid the price for her fight. She was the one who deserved this, not him.

There was another violent shudder, and the door from the tunnels burst open. Hugo stumbled into the room. His eyes landed on her, frantic. "We have to go!" he ground out. "The foundations gave way. The whole place is caving in!" He moved past her, toward the last steps to the surface. "Cassie, come on!" Hugo grabbed her hand, trying to drag her to her feet.

Cassie resisted, blind with tears. "I can't leave him!"

"It's too late," Hugo exclaimed. "Cassie, we have to go!" He pulled at her, but she clung to Charlie, refusing to let him go. She was suspended between them, strung taut.

And then she realized.

Cassie sucked in a breath, and before she could think twice, she reached out with her mind again—not to Charlie this time, but to Hugo. She latched on tight to his mind, clawing deep in a savage sweep that made him cry out in pain. Cassie gripped deeper, pulling at all that darkness, that ancient force, so fresh and ripe in his mind. She drank it in, dizzy with the sudden rush of power, filling her up to the brim.

Then she cast it out. Into Charlie, into his empty mind. She poured everything she had into Charlie and then more besides. She reached with her mind, smoothing over the broken, jagged edges, filling him with power and potential again.

"Cassie," Hugo gasped, falling to his knees beside her. But Cassie didn't stop, didn't pause for a second as the life rushed out of him, flowing through her in a thick rush. It glittered in her veins, channeled into Charlie, making him whole and new until his eyes flew open and he lurched forward with a gasp.

"What . . . ?" he panted, clawing at the air. His gaze met hers, widening with blessed recognition this time. "Cassie? What are you doing to me?"

It beat around her, a crescendo in her ears. She felt it flow, calling to her, demanding.

"Cassie?" Charlie's voice seemed distant and weak. "Cassie, let me go!"

She jolted awake, wrenching free from the darkness with a gasp. Charlie gripped both her hands, searching her gaze, alert. "Can you hear me, Cassie? What did you do?"

She gulped, her heart racing. "I brought you back." She turned. Hugo lay motionless on the ground beside his cousin, Olivia's blood pooling around them both.

The earth gave another shake. "Come on." Charlie pulled her to her feet and dragged her to the stairs. She stumbled upward behind him, her limbs like a deadweight. "Almost there," he urged her on, half carrying her up the stairs.

They stumbled through the doorway into the shock of freezing night air. Cassie looked around, blinking. They had emerged on the far side of the college, through an opening in the very walls of Raleigh itself, the thick stone hiding their tunnel escape. Across the meadow, she could see the sandstone of the college lit up. The North Tower was engulfed in flames, blazing against the dark night. Sirens sounded, noise and commotion filtering through the dark. Cassie sank to the wet grass.

"It's over." Charlie gripped her tightly. "You did it. You're okay."

Cassie didn't reply. She held him in the darkness and listened to the sirens scream.

⤜ AFTER ⤛

MATTHEW TREMAIN WAS BURIED ON A BRIGHT SPRING MORNING, in the churchyard overlooking the river. Cassie stood at his graveside and watched the casket lower into the earth. They'd found his body in the rubble, along with the rest of the School of Night. A cave-in, the official report had said. Unsound foundations. A private supper club gone terribly wrong.

Nobody objected to the official investigation verdict, Charlie had made sure of that. The TV news networks ran glowing obituaries to Richard Mandeville, a promising politician whose great career had been cruelly cut short. There were murmurs about what exactly had led to his demise, but nobody wanted to raise any more questions about the goings-on at Raleigh College. Soon, attention turned to the next scandal: another government minister in a compromising position, a new celebrity feud to fill the column inches. The deaths faded to memories; they would not be mourned for long.

Except by her.

Cassie listened to the priest read and felt the sting of tears in her eyes. She'd barely known him, but in his final moments, her father had proven his worth. He'd sacrificed himself to save her, just as her mother had done so many years before.

She hoped she had made their selflessness worthwhile.

The ceremony was small, just a collection of professors and students from the college come to pay their respects. There was to be a reception

too, at a tutor's house, but Cassie ducked away after the service, walking to meet Charlie on the edge of the graveyard.

"So what now?" he asked, as they strolled slowly toward the street.

"I could use a drink." Cassie gave a rueful smile. "And wasn't your mother promising to cook me Sunday roast?"

"I meant, after that." Charlie stopped. "You're all wrapped up here, aren't you? I mean, the society is destroyed, isn't it?"

She nodded slowly. "The hunger to feed, it's fading every day. The members out there who weren't at the ceremony should be weaker already. Eventually, their power will be gone."

"They won't be able to feed off anyone else?"

"I don't think so. The connection is gone; it changed. I just hope it's over for good."

"So are you heading back home now, or what?" Charlie looked away, casually, but Cassie could see through his façade.

"I don't think so," she replied. "Not just yet. I have another semester of study on my scholarship. I figured I could stick around."

Charlie grinned. "Admit it, babe. You can't bear the thought of leaving me."

She laughed. "Please. No, I just was thinking . . . I don't know what I'm going to do next. I've spent so long focused on my mom, on this, that I never really considered my future."

"And now?"

"Now I guess I'll find out." Cassie squeezed his hand. They stepped onto the sidewalk, and into the flow of people passing by. Tourists, pedestrians, and the surge of students. The bells rang out above them, and the spires loomed bright in the sky.

It was springtime in Oxford, and everything was in bloom.

AUTHOR'S NOTE

This books contains a mix of historical fact and fiction, and locations both real and imagined in Oxford, inspired by my time spent studying at the university. Although Sir Walter Raleigh attended the University briefly, Raleigh College does not exist, but I picture it situated in much the same location as Magdalen College, on the banks of the river Cherwell. While Raleigh was a contemporary of Shakespeare and known to have associated with other prominent thinkers of the era, the existence of a "School of Night" has never been proven. The famed quote from *Love's Labour's Lost* is open to many interpretations, and has been debated by scholars and historians with far more knowledge of the era than I.

ACKNOWLEDGMENTS

A huge thanks to everyone who made this book possible, it really was a team effort. To Richard Abate for all his guidance and tireless enthusiasm; Gary Ungar, and Rebecca Friedman. Thanks to the amazing team at William Morrow: Katherine Nintzel, Marguerite Weisman, Jessie Edwards, Molly Waxman, and Stephanie Vallejo.

A big thanks to my former Magdalen classmates, who donated their old essays to jog my memory of our syllabus. Thanks also to the staff, and my professors, Dr. Christopher Brooke, Dr. Lizzie Fricker, and Dr. Krister Bykvist among them, who made my time at Oxford so memorable—and inspiring.

Finally, thanks to the friends and family who offered me such support and enthusiasm: to Elisabeth Donnelly, Brandy Colbert, Lane Shadgett, and Elizabeth Little. To my mother, Ann, thank you as always for everything.